Too Late to Pray

A Novel

T.W. Lofgren

CONTENTS

Dedicated to Kilgore Trout.
Don't laugh at others if you can't laugh at yourself.

THE FUTURE IS NOW

"What can I say? I tried my best. We all did. The task was too great, and so, we failed."

— A BUTTERFLY IN FLIGHT: THE BIOGRAPHY OF
THOMAS SPEAKER BY JAMIE LIVINGSTON

"Awooooo! Hellooo, my fellow Americans." A shredding guitar riff blasted out of the radio. Thomas Speaker jumped at the noise. "I am Reverend Richard Richman, and you're listening to Rowdy Reverend Ricky's broadcast ministry. Awooooo!"

Thomas Speaker cringed as he jumped to the radio, turning the volume down in one swift motion.

How could anyone listen to such nonsense?

He sat back down and picked up the new briar pipe, a gift from one of his listeners celebrating his move back to his home-town in southeast Ohio.

Still, it was important to hear what others were saying. It helped him to better direct his own ministry.

"Coming up is your chance to enter our newest contest. Yes

indeedy! You could win fifty thousand big ones." Rowdy Ricky only had one volume—loud.

"We're talking about smackeroonies, baby. Good ol' American greenbacks." The reverend let that sink in.

"You may ask how we could afford such a magnificent prize. Let's just say the good Lord has directed the money our way from an anonymous donor."

Thomas pictured Ricky giving a wink at this point. *Anonymous indeed! It's probably coming from that Texas charlatan, Heggy.* Thomas looked around his own office, fighting down the guilty feeling. He had lobbied the government to set him up with the latest equipment and 50,000 watts of broadcast power. He argued it would be a part of the Emergency Broadcast System. Friends in high places prevailed, and they pulled funding from a Defense Department appropriations bill.

Reverend Rick finished extolling the virtues of his donor. "But first, I have a special guest. Congressman Troy Trublu is here to talk about America's commitment to our friends in the Middle East. Congressman ..."

"Thank you, Reverend. It's a pleasure to be on your show. And, might I say, an extreme honor to be serving the people of the great state of West Virginia."

Thomas recalled briefly meeting the congressman in one of his many visits to the capital. Trublu was a brash thirtysomething who wore his blond hair slicked back like the greasers from Thomas's childhood. He pegged the congressman as a glad-handing, fast-talking wheeler-dealer and took an immediate dislike to the man. He wondered what would cause the congressman to visit the reverend's facility, just across the Ohio River from Thomas's location.

"It's certainly good to have you here, sir." Rick shuffled some papers. "I understand you just returned from a trip to Israel, visiting our troops stationed there."

"Yes, yes. And I had the opportunity to see the wonderful work being done by the volunteers from God's Official Orators for

Israel. They are doing such a magnificent job of logistical support for the troops."

"The Reverend Heggy's group? They are truly on a Christian mission over there. Why, I believe—"

The radio went silent, and the desk lamp went out. Thomas stared at it a moment, then looked at the wall clock. The second hand continued its sweep around the dial. *Battery-powered. Of course!* He hit the on/off button for the lamp. Nothing. He stood to go to the radio as footsteps pounded on the front porch. Doc Livingston burst through the office door.

Doc was breathless. "It's happened. Messages are coming over the short wave." He stared, wild-eyed. "I ... we ..."

"We expected this." Thomas motioned for Doc to sit down and took his seat back. "We've prepared as best as can be, Doc." He pulled open the bottom desk drawer and pulled out a red file folder. "THE END" was written on it in big block letters. "Do we have any details?"

Tears welled in Doc's eyes. "Yeah. From the shortwave. New York and DC are nuked. There was some sort of EM pulse weapon used also. It looks like the electrical grid for all metro areas is down. What's next?"

Thomas opened the folder. "We stay with the plan." The desk light came back on as the backup generator kicked in. The radio came on with a loud hiss of static. "Let me know when I can make my first broadcast. After that, I'll join you all at the town council chambers."

Doc took a deep breath and stood. "Yes, of course. But ... our work—"

"Our work will continue." Thomas's voice was firm. "We knew this would likely happen. Now we work to bring hope to those who would listen."

"And for those who won't?" Doc's lips trembled at the thought of an answer.

"Chaos."

THE COLLAPSE

"It was appalling. For the life of me, I never expected so many of us to turn on each other. We were lucky to escape the worst of it, hidden away in our corner of Ohio."

— A BUTTERFLY IN FLIGHT: THE BIOGRAPHY OF THOMAS SPEAKER BY JAMIE LIVINGSTON

The radio died. Not that it mattered. John Darby was tired of listening to the noonday blathering of the preacher. What caught his attention was the sudden quietness of the Roundhouse. The architects who designed this particular unit of the Stateville Correctional Center were unconcerned about such creature comforts as peace and quiet. If anything, the four floors of cells surrounding the central courtyard amplified the smallest whisper, each joining the constant din.

Darby sat up. The momentary silence gave way to a noisy click as electronic locks unlatched and cell doors slid open.

Jumping to the doorway, he peered out cautiously, not sure what was happening. All around the cellblock, the image repeated itself. Two floors below, the prisoners leaped from their cages and darted across the floor, heading to the guard tower. The four guards stepped from the safety of the bulletproof glass. Two stood at the top of the stairway and fired into the crowd surging up. The others took up position on opposite sides of the tower, shooting randomly into the crowd.

Darby looked down, a maniacal grin slashing across his face.

"Remember what my ol' man would say—'When caught in a kill-or-be-killed situation, make sure you're not the one killed.'"

He shook his head and laughed.

"That was good advice, Daddy, 'cept you forgot your first rule —don't trust nobody, not even your son."

He shook the bars, remembering the look on the ol' man's face when Darby put the gun against his forehead.

"There's only ten thousand here, Pops. That's not enough to share."

He barely heard the gunshot as a small hole appeared in his father's head, belying the damage a .22-caliber slug could do as it tumbled out the other side.

His memory faded—a blur of cops surrounding him, his surrender, and the trial. His attorney argued that he wasn't guilty of bank robbery since he did not succeed at it; that is, he did not actually rob the bank. He succeeded in getting the charge reduced to an *attempted* bank robbery. He also claimed to be innocent of murder, arguing that he acted to stop the bank robbery. It didn't work. There were too many witnesses.

The life sentence bestowed upon the twenty-year-old seemed silly to him. The world was falling apart outside the prison walls. There was talk of nuclear war. Then what? Darby surveyed the carnage below. *This is what.*

No, John Darby was not a religious man, but he praised the devil this day.

Pandemonium reigned below. The guards were quickly over-whelmed, their bodies mutilated as the human dregs took their vengeance. Prisoners who held grudges with their fellow inmates took the opportunity to settle old scores. The young murderer stepped out to the guardrail and surveyed the damage.

"Darby!" John turned to see his neighbor hanging back at his cell door. Bill Bradshaw was no fool, either. The two had struck up a sort of friendship when John arrived.

You have no friends here. Darby gave a curt nod as the other man slipped from his cell.

"What's going on here? How'd the doors open?"

Darby's eyes gleamed as he sneered. "End of the world is all."

He stepped back into his cell. "Git yer shank. We're getting out of here."

Darby dug along the side of his mattress, found the small hole, and dug out the toothbrush. Holding it up, he tested the pointed end made by rubbing the hard plastic on the concrete floor. Grunting in satisfaction, he stepped back out.

Bill was waiting with his own shiv gripped between his teeth. He grasped a homemade rope in both hands—a confirmation of the rumor about an inmate found garroted the week before.

Darby nodded his approval. "This way." He headed toward the stairs. "I've got a plan."

Bill nodded his assent and fell in behind Darby.

"Whatever you want, boss. I got your back."

Darby glanced over his shoulder and smirked. "That's what I like about you, Bill. You follow orders—for a price."

"I got a half dozen cigarettes for offing that dude. 'Sides, he deserved it, killing his mother. A boy shouldn't be killing his mom."

"The way I heard it, it was his mother-in-law." Darby shook his head.

They made it down to the main floor. The Roundhouse held over three hundred prisoners at capacity. About one hundred orange-clad felons were milling around the floor, the others lying along with the guards, bleeding out.

One of the men brandished a shotgun as he strode toward John Darby. Darby came face-to-face with him, looked him in the eye, and with a sudden downward thrust, jammed his toothbrush into the man's jugular.

Bill's expression matched the dead man's. "What the fu—"

"They say he raped a little boy." Darby picked up the weapon, noting it was a Kel-Tek KSG-25 with a full magazine. He laughed in appreciation.

The commotion drew the others' attention, and they began ringing around these two new arrivals. Darby turned and shoved his way past them, making for the guard tower. Bill followed closely, eyeing each of the other inmates, looking for any sign of trouble.

They got to the stairs and took them two at a time until they reached the first platform and turned to face the growing crowd.

"The way I sees it"—John Darby yelled out, so everyone could hear—"we're in charge now!"

A shout went up from the gang. Bill laughed, shaking his head in agreement, a demonic light in his eyes. Darby squinted at him.

"Wait for it!"

Soon the hall was quiet. The Roundhouse at Stateville prison had housed the worst of the worst criminals. During the war, the military even recruited among these, promising freedom in exchange for their service. Those that remained were too deadly and deemed not safe enough to trust even in the limited capacity of "cannon fodder."

Darby surveyed the gathering group. A dozen drew in closer while the others held back, waiting to see how things played out.

"What now?" Bill asked the question on everyone's mind.

John looked around.

"Now?"

It occurred to him that they were choosing a leader. He pointed his gun at the group as his thoughts raced. There would be only one person for that job; he would make sure of that.

"Now, I have a plan."

The inmates looked at him expectantly as he glared down at the group.

"Here's what we do."

One stepped forward.

"Who made you the boss anyway?"

Darby let the shotgun reply.

"Anyone else have any questions?"

The crowd took two steps back, ignoring their comrade's body.

"Good."

Darby handed his weapon to Bill and descended the steps, walking into the crowd. Grabbing at the first two men he came upon, he pulled them aside, then seized two more.

"You fellers go to the mess hall and collect all the food you can. We're gonna need to eat when we move out of here."

The four stared at him. Darby glared back. "Are you stupid or what?"

"I ain't taking orders from some punk!" The inmate snarled and looked away.

A gunshot rang out from behind Darby, sending the man reeling. Darby spun around to see Bill brandishing the shotgun. "I've got your back, *boss.*"

"You crazy mother!"

Bill let out a whoop.

"That's me! I'm a wild man. Call me *Wild Bill Bradshaw!*" He let out another whoop. "An-and boss. Yo ... you're like a mean ol' bear."

Bill looked out at the crowd. "Boys. We got us a ol' grizzly bear for a leader."

Darby sneered and turned back to face the rest. He grabbed the nearest escapee by his shoulders. "Any objections?"

The man shook his head, trying to squirm out of his grasp.

Darby spun him around and gave him a swift kick in the ass. "Go get us food!" he bellowed. The other two stepped back, but Darby seized the closest, repeating the order. "Go!" he barked and grabbed the next, shoving him along.

Spinning around, he pointed to a group of six others.

"You men! I want you to get in there and go to the armory.

Grab all the weapons and ammo you can find." They nodded quickly and were off.

"And a map. I need a map." One gave a thumbs-up sign.

More orders followed, and raiding parties went out. Darby now had Bill and three others standing alone on the floor.

Bill let out a whoop. "Yessir. You sure do know how to boss!"

"You got a problem with that?" he snarled, looking from man to man.

"Not at all, boss." Bill nearly spat out that last word. "Not as long as you do right by us."

Darby glared from man to man until each looked away. "What I figure"—his voice went quiet—"is that anything right for me will be right for you. Right?"

"Right," they all mumbled.

"Right?" the Grizzly bellowed.

"Right, yeah, right." They nodded their acceptance.

SANCTUARY

Not all of the subjects of the stem-cell experiments survived. Those that did, like Speaker, moved away from the large cities and their research complexes.

— A BUTTERFLY IN FLIGHT: THE BIOGRAPHY OF THOMAS SPEAKER BY JAMIE LIVINGSTON

"Now do you girls understand why I brought you here?" The old scientist slammed his fist on the table. "I *knew* it would come to this."

Judith cringed. Her father was always right, at least in *his* view. One would think that after more than twenty years it wouldn't matter to her. But it did. For starters, she hated being called a girl. For Chrissakes, didn't he realize that she and Sarah were grown? And now he seemed to take joy in the now silent broadcast—pleased to be proven correct again. The great prognosticator! She ticked off his most recent accomplishments in her head: leaving the clinic in Cleveland behind for this rural setting, insisting on using his daughters as control subjects in the genetic research, his pioneering work in stem-cell research, and on and on. *Probably deserved a Nobel Prize for that—if they ever gave them out again.*

Her twin, Sarah, never put up with it. "Okay, Dad. You called it. It's the end of the world. So what do we do about it?" She stood, ready to go head-to-head with him.

Judith jumped between them, holding Sarah back. "Don't you start in. This is serious."

Their father squared his shoulders. "Serious? Yes. The end of the world? No." He turned to look out the window. The little village they called Sanctuary stretched down the valley. "It *is* the end of civilization, however."

Judith stepped next to him, placing a hand on his shoulder. "So what comes next? The newscast talked about nuclear war, cities destroyed ..."

Sarah stood back, arms crossed and fuming. "The end, Dad. Death and destruction. Like you said, the end of civilization. Now what?"

Their father turned to his fiery-haired daughter. "Now?" He smiled. "Now we rebuild it all. That's why we created Sanctuary. Nearly a hundred scientists and their families are here, far away from what will happen in the cities. We'll be safe. We'll survive— and thrive. After all, we're the best of humankind."

Judith touched his shoulder. "Is that possible? I know you built the village to be self-sustaining, but what about the people living here? Can *we* do it?"

"The Council of Elders have the plans made up. We ran the algorithms, played out the likely scenarios and built our little town with those results in mind." He pointed out the window. "We chose this remote spot of Michigan, tucked away in this valley, as the best hideaway."

"And we're self-sustaining." Judith directed her remark at her sister. "But won't the windmill give us away? It's too big to ignore."

The geneticist glanced up the hill. "It feeds the neighboring town also. These next few weeks will be rough. We'll have to defend ourselves from marauders, maybe take in some refugees, but we're so far off the beaten path, I suspect there won't be many of those." He smiled at Sarah. "And we have guns. Now do you understand why I insisted you become a marksman?"

His daughter grimaced. "And used cutouts of people, not deer, for target practice? Yeah, I get it." Sarah joined them at the window, studying her father's face. "Why did we really come here?"

"Ah! We never did talk about that, did we?" The scientist reached out and pulled his daughters together. "You two were part of a control group—healthy, young, able to receive the treatment with no complications. We needed to keep an eye on you. Make certain you weren't, um, contaminated. We have to be careful when you breed."

"Breed?" Sarah pulled away. "What? Are we some sort of lab rats to you? Unbelievable!"

"Now, dear, don't take it that way." Her father grew stern. "We have the best of intentions for you. The cellular treatment allows you to heal quickly, that's all. We need to see if you can pass it on genetically. Simple as that."

Sarah's eyes widened. "What? You want to choose our husbands? Oh, I'm sorry, our *mates?* We left the city so we wouldn't meet other guys? Why? Were you afraid some stranger might *contaminate* us?"

"Precisely!" the geneticist enthused. "That's how a controlled experiment works."

Judith joined her sister. "That's going too far. Even for our father. We are no longer part of an experiment." Her green eyes flashed. "I'll bet you don't have an algorithm for mutiny."

The man stiffened. "Judy, Judy, Judy! I'm your father. I've always looked after you, had your best interests in mind. Besides, if you weren't part of the experiment you would have faced the draft—shipped off to who knows what war zone."

Judith poked her finger at him. "We are NOT girls. I am not a Judy. We are capable of thinking for ourselves, thank you."

Sarah got in her father's face. "If you weren't our father, I'd be tearing your eyes out."

"No more experiments, Dad." Judith pushed her father and sister apart. "Furthermore, with all that's happening, we'd be better suited to forget your damn experiment and concentrate our efforts on surviving."

Their father clapped his hands and laughed. "Finally! I knew you could do it. You just needed a little push."

Judith looked at Sarah, trying to understand.

Their father continued. "It's about time you women took control. I was very concerned you might not have it in you. But now I see the fire in your eyes. Perfect!" He rubbed his hands together.

"Sarah, you have your mother's temper, that's for sure. I wish you could have known her. What an Irishwoman." He clapped her shoulders.

"And my dear Judith." He beamed at the dark-haired woman. "You've been schooled in organizational management. Your talents will come in handy."

Judith looked at him, mouth agape. "Are you saying you've been *programming* us also?"

"We never thought of it as programming, per se, but I guess it is. As the saying goes, teach your children well. That's what parents do. You'll see."

Sarah pulled away and joined her sister. "That's not right. You can't just take someone, your own daughters even, and make them into who you want them to be."

"True. Not if they have an independent streak like you two have demonstrated." He scratched his chin. "No matter. We make do with what we've got. Speaking of that, I think it's time you gir — er, women became members of the council."

Judith looked at Sarah and frowned. "Okay. We join the town council."

"But—" Sarah blurted.

"But within the year, *we* will be making the rules."

JUST ANOTHER DAY

There are few written records of those dark days. Those survivors who made it to Speaker's town in Belmont County, Ohio, told of battling illness, famine, and the wrath of raiding parties.

— *A BUTTERFLY IN FLIGHT: THE BIOGRAPHY OF THOMAS SPEAKER* BY JAMIE LIVINGSTON

John Darby abandoned his birth name early on, preferring his new nickname, Grizzly. It fit the disposition of an angry young man. It didn't take long for him to look the part, either, as he allowed his dark beard and hair to grow wildly.

Grizzly's instincts were those of a wild animal also. The escape from his maximum-security prison at the south end of Lake Michigan gave him few options. Chicago and Milwaukee lay to the north. *Too many people. Who knows what the hell they'll do now?* Due south was a similar problem with large cities like Louisville, Kentucky, and St. Louis, Missouri. But going west was nothing but farms and small farm towns. They should be easy pickings for his miserable little troop.

His initial band grew into a horde of several hundred, and

Grizzly came to regard himself as a match for Ghengis Khan, the great Mongol leader of old. There was one material difference. Grizzly had no horses. Those animals proved more useful as a food source, and his warriors—both men and women—were as good at being pack animals as they were at fighting.

Winter was his worst enemy, forcing them to shelter in place for months. It was a different sort of prison in the minds of a murderous person. The craving for action ate at them so that when spring arrived, they were always prepared to move on, to find a new victim, to taste battle.

Seasons progressed from one to the other. Years passed by, and the remnants of civilization entered a new reality. Grizzly's reputation spread throughout the Midwest and beyond. He made sure that his raiding party always allowed a few survivors to escape. He wanted the word to spread. Grizzly was on the prowl. And then ...

"Bradshaw! BRADSHAW!" Grizzly strode among his men as they staggered into the field. He shoved each one, pushing them to move along.

"Sorry, Grizzly," one muttered, evading the bear's swift boot. Others looked down, avoiding his glare.

"BRADSHAW!" the bear roared.

"I'm here, boss." Bill came limping up, drenched in sweat and blood. His sweat, but somebody else's blood.

Grizzly held a rag to his own cheek, dabbing at the slash above his left eye and down his cheek. The boy who delivered that blow tasted the bear's blade.

Grabbing Bill's shoulder, Grizzly shook him. "What the hell happened back there?" He indicated the small town now a quarter-mile away. "Who scouted it?"

"Honest, boss. We did!" Bill stared in bewilderment, knowing where Grizzly's anger could lead. "Pete and that new feller checked it out real good. There weren't nobody in it. Not yesterday." He continued to babble. "Pete's a good man, been with us since the start. You know that."

"Where's Pete?" Grizzly growled, his face in Bill's.

Bradshaw leaned away. "He—he didn't make it." Bill looked back toward the town. "An—and the new feller—he's gone too."

Grizzly pushed him away. "It was a setup. I had a feeling about that guy."

They found him living alone on the open prairie a week earlier. He said his name was Smythe. "With a 'Y' as in why not?" The guy smirked. Grizzly thought he was too young and healthy-looking to have lived there alone. Still, he was willing to join the horde, and he claimed knowledge of the area.

Smythe described the small town ahead, said there might still be stuff in the farm supply store. Always on the lookout for useful provisions, Grizzly took the bait and marched his men down the main street. They had grown overconfident through the years, lost their discipline, and now strode massed together past empty two-story buildings.

Two blocks in, Grizzly stopped and sniffed the air. *Something's not right. It's too quiet.* He looked up as a concrete block came hurtling toward him. "Trap!" He barely got the word out as he stepped aside. More large chunks of concrete rained down, crashing onto the troop.

"Turn around! Get the hell out of here!" His men's screams drowned out the words as a barrage of arrows turned them into pincushions. Grizzly pushed through, turning them around. Coming out the rear, he stared down the street in disbelief. A line of men in military fatigues blocked their exit. They knelt in a single line, rifles at the ready. *Where the hell did they get those?* He heard the order to fire, and the guns erupted. His men fell.

Grizzly pushed back through his men. "This way!" He led them forward and turned down an alleyway. Another band awaited, brandishing spears, knives, and clubs. He fought down his panic. "Attack!" With a bellow, he rallied his men. They were familiar with this sort of fight. He strode ahead, brandishing his Bowie knife.

A defender slashed out with his sword. Grizzly took a quick

sidestep. Still, the blade grazed him, leaving a deep gash above his left eye and into his cheek. A practiced thrust of the Bowie knife gutted his attacker. *That's more like it!*

Grizzly looked at the soldier and laughed. *Kids. These are just kids!* He snorted. "Kill! Kill them all! We're getting the hell out of here." A shout went up. His men now outnumbered the small group of soldiers. They showed no mercy.

Now he stood in the open field outside of town. Bradshaw stood beside him, silently counting the stragglers as they staggered past. "A hunnard and twenty, counting us, boss."

"Jeezus K. Rist!" Grizzly kicked at the ground. "More 'n half gone. How?"

Bill stepped back, not wanting to deliver any further bad news. "That Smythe feller … he said those folks got themselves organized on the other side of town. He said they were trying to live peaceable lives, not bother anyone." He glanced around, wondering if he should run. "Said he wanted adventure. That's why he was out on his own."

Grizzly pulled his knife, held it to Bill's face. "Peaceable, my ass. The man was a spy. We shoulda knowed it." He waved the blade, still wet from his last victim. "YOU shoulda figgered it."

"Boss!" Grizzly spun around, growling at the interruption. Two men approached, supporting a third between them. "Charlie here. I think he broke his leg." One of them nodded toward their comrade.

Grizzly marched up to them and got in Charlie's face. "Well, I guess that makes you a liability, don't it, Charlie?" The man whimpered.

"WE don't need no more liabilities." Grizzly held his blade high. "WE don't need no more mistakes." He turned slowly around, noting he had his men's attention. "An' MOST of ALL, we don't need no Charlies!" He plunged the knife into the wounded man's gut, wiggling it.

The two dropped their dead weight and stepped back, looking for an escape.

Grizzly took a deep breath, then another, calming down. "Never again. Grizzly won't ever get fooled again!"

ANNIVERSARY BROADCAST

"My calling? How do I explain it? At first it came as a feeling deep inside me. One I didn't understand. I turned to meditation and prayer—a lot of prayer."

— A BUTTERFLY IN FLIGHT: THE BIOGRAPHY OF
THOMAS SPEAKER BY JAMIE LIVINGSTON

"Hello, hello, hello." Thomas Speaker began the broadcast, speaking slowly and distinctly. "My name is Thomas Speaker. Welcome to today's broadcast. It is twelve noon, eastern solar time." He chuckled. "That is, according to the sundial in our courtyard, here in sunny southeast Ohio."

He looked around his office space as Carlos provided the Spanish translation. Decades ago, the authorities for the Emergency Broadcast System set up the facility in Thomas's hometown. He insisted on taking over the old Victorian mansion on Main Street, converting the library into his office and broadcast booths.

Here we go again! Thomas took a deep breath.

"Thank you, Carlos. I appreciate your service." Thomas waved to the young man on the other side of the glass. Carlos gave a thumbs-up and smiled in return.

The pastor leaned in toward his microphone. It was an antique, found at a radio station to the west. The station's call letters fanned out above the mic in broken disarray—WK_P.

"To all those listening out there, welcome to our daily broadcast. Today is September 4, the thirty-third year of the New Era. It's a special day for me, for it marks the anniversary of my ministry."

He hesitated, considering what would come next. "I began preaching thirty-seven years ago as the Forever Wars were coming to a head. Back then, I volunteered for a human challenge study. Science advanced to the point of developing a method to convert the appendix into a stem-cell generator. The researchers needed to conduct clinical trials to prove its efficacy.

"As for me, I had hit the lowest of lows, bottomed out, if you will. I abused drugs and alcohol and probably flirted with a mental illness or two. The doctors selected me for the trial because of this. I guess they figured if the treatment failed, I would not be a significant loss to society."

Thomas shifted his weight and placed his elbows on the table, clasping his hands under his chin. "But the treatment worked. My body became rejuvenated as the stem cells replaced the worn-out ones. I lost my addictions."

Carlos stopped his translation and looked at the pastor, his mouth open in surprise. Thomas winked at him.

"And now you would find it hard to believe that I am one hundred years old. Imagine that!"

Carlos finished the translation and leaned out of his booth. "But Pastor Thomas, you don't even look half that age. At least from what I know of older men."

"I'll take that as a compliment." Thomas chuckled. "Truth is, the military funded the research in the hopes of finding a way to reduce battlefield injuries. Imagine a soldier self-healing in the middle of a firefight. Maga!"

The pastor stopped abruptly, looked around the studio and laughed. "You know, there was a time when a radio station wasn't allowed to broadcast a four-letter word like that." He shrugged.

"Anyway, I had plenty of time on my hands while undergoing the treatment. I studied philosophy and religion. A lot." He leaned back in his chair and brought the mic closer. "Call it my 'Come to Jesus' moment. Actually, it was more like come to God, what with all those frauds piggybacking onto Jesus for their personal gain. I had my epiphany and decided to begin a ministry that reflected on God's teachings—no matter what religion represented him."

"My folks say your teachings saved them." A teenage girl stood at the doorway.

Thomas waved her in. "Ah, my assistant, Alice B., has arrived."

The girl stepped forward and sat in the chair next to Thomas. "They say it wasn't just your sermons but your practical advice that got them through those end times. I mean, they were just kids like me back then."

"That's kind of them." A wan smile crossed his face. "I think the world was ready to hear my message. People were tired of being lied to and taken advantage of, especially by their spiritual leaders. There were those folks like the Reverand I.T. Heggy and his God's Official Orators for Israel. I couldn't believe people would fall for a group named GOOFI! Maga!"

Alice was startled. "Pastor! Children are listening. Mind your language."

"I'm sorry, and you are right, my young friend. I get so angry, remembering what all we lost and the cost of it all. Ma—"

Alice scowled. "Mom and Dad told me about the war—the nuclear bombs, cities destroyed, even whole countries laid waste. Israel—"

"Three nukes on Jerusalem alone. Yes. Most of the Middle East became a wasteland. We were lucky, if you want to call it that. We only lost New York, DC, a couple of major cities out west. I suppose they ran out of nuclear bombs." He paused, thinking.

"Then the EM pulse weapons hit. The electromagnetic bursts took out the electric grid across the country."

"And afterward." Alice gripped the desk edge. "Dad says that's when you helped most. When everything went crazy."

"Yes?" He shook his head. "The government fell apart. People rioted. Murder and mayhem ruled. Then the diseases hit. There was no medical care. With our green energy power supply, we kept up daily broadcasts centered on survival techniques. And we never neglected the love component. Love thy neighbor. Work together, and we could get through it."

"And they did." Alice leaned back. "Maybe not many, but enough. Look at how your town has grown. At least from what they tell me."

"It's true." Carlos poked his head out. "When my wife and I found our way here, maybe one thousand people were living here. Now look. At least twice as many."

Thomas smiled. "It was always a small town. I remember growing up here. But when Doc and Maggie Livingston, myself, and a few others came, it was nearly a ghost town. That was before the bombs fell." His eyes focused on a spot in the distant past. "The government wanted us as a backup to the Emergency Broadcast System. It turned out to be quite a blessing, actually. We were state-of-the-art with solar and wind energy for electricity, a new tower, and enough broadcast power to cover over one hundred miles. My message of peace, love, and understanding resonated with many throughout the country. Through their generous donations, I was able to maintain my broadcast ministry without government help."

Thomas squirmed in his chair. "What was it good for? No one thought we'd turn on each other the way our society did. Not even me."

Sadness tinged his voice as the room grew dead silent. Carlos caught the pastor's eye, nodding toward the microphone.

"I …I …" Thomas's voice cracked, and he coughed. "I tried,

dear listener. I tried. Somehow, we were spared the worst of civilization's collapse. But we watched and bore witness to it."

Alice turned aside, blinking away a tear. Thomas took a deep, ragged breath.

"I believe we are still doing useful work. People continue to arrive in our small town. Like Carlos said, we now have a population of over twenty-five hundred. We do hear from other outposts such as Mama Ruth Lyon's down in Mississippi. Then there are farming communities in Nebraska and Michigan. We've even received short-wave communications from Europe, Australia, and Brazil.

"So, if nothing else, we are extending hope to what we all once believed was a lost species. Humankind is rebuilding. I trust that we shall be better stewards this time around." He paused as Carlos completed the translation and looked his way. They nodded together in approval.

"With that, and as always, I extend an invitation to all who are listening to come and join us. We can use your help in any form. I'll turn the mic over to my assistant. She'll provide general directions and landmarks to guide you."

Thomas smiled at the teen sitting next to him and turned the microphone her way.

"Thank you, Pastor Thomas." She beamed. Her voice tinkled like a small silver bell. "This is Alice B. For those who may be coming from the north …"

Thomas pushed back his chair and studied the young girl. *Such enthusiasm! Ah, the spirit of youth.*

He picked up his old briar pipe from the desk and rubbed his thumb around the charred bowl, thinking of the different uses it provided. He didn't need to consider the ill effects of tobacco. But weed? The stem-cell healing did not counteract the effects of psychoactive medications. *Maybe it's because the drugs activate the body's natural chemicals.*

Alice coughed loudly. Thomas looked up as she nodded urgently toward the microphone.

"My apologies. It seems you caught me napping." He smiled at the girl. She just rolled her eyes.

"No problem, Pastor. Here's the mic back." She shoved the instrument across the table.

"Thank you, Alice." He pulled the microphone toward him and scooted his chair closer.

"That should wrap it up for today. Our invitation stands to all who are listening. Please come and join our community. Or, like some of the other groups, let's open up our hearts and communicate. We can build a better world. This is Thomas Speaker at AM 800 kHz, 91.5 MHz, and shortwave, signing off for now."

A CHANCE MEETING

"There are times, especially when I meditate, that I feel a special connectedness with all things … all people. That's what I want to share with others. How we're all interconnected."

— A BUTTERFLY IN FLIGHT: THE BIOGRAPHY OF THOMAS SPEAKER BY JAMIE LIVINGSTON

James Robert Hendricks turned off his radio and unplugged the solar cell. Stuffing the items into a faded purple and gold cloth bag, he began mumbling.

"Well, happy anniversary to you, Pastor. Too bad the whiskey's all gone. Elsewise, I'd propose a toast. Here's to Pastor Thomas Speaker, our fearless leader for these past thirty-five or more years." He held up his hand, pretending there was a glass in it.

"And you would say, 'Thank you. Thank you very much.' And we would each take a sip and smile, and all would be right with the world."

James stepped to the edge of the porch and looked at the sky. To the east, a small white dot reflected the sunlight—a communication satellite from those days long ago. To the west, yellow-gray clouds were roiling, a sign of worse things to come.

"I'm sorry to report that not all is right with the world, Pastor." He spat out his distaste. The saliva quickly soaked into the weathered porch floor. "Not even after thirty-seven years of your ministry. Maybe all is well and good in your part of the world, but look at what I've got."

In the farmyard, high summer had dried the grass into a parched prairie. Corn in the garden patch yielded skimpy ears, now withered on the stalks. It had been a bad year for his part of Kansas.

"Maybe it's time to go." He looked at the barn. "I can't do much more with the truck. The only other folks left around here are no good, and—"

He scanned the horizon; a dust cloud rose in the west. "Riders!" He pulled binoculars from a hip pouch. "I wonder if it's the same two from the last visit." He shook his head. "Same as it ever was."

He had lived alone at Watchtower Farm for nearly thirty years. The world was falling apart when he returned from college to take refuge there with his folks. Like their neighbors, they decided to hunker down and ride it out. But things got worse. The memory still burned of how he was out in the pasture, checking on the horses, when gunshots alerted him. Racing to the homestead, he saw his father crumpled on the porch, shotgun in hand. A stranger lay wounded on the ground. As James approached, the man raised a pistol. James showed no mercy and slashed the wounded man's throat.

Rushing up the steps, he bent over his father. Dead. Shot in the chest. James grabbed the gun, confirmed that one barrel was loaded, and kicked in the door. Two more marauders perched over his mother's lifeless form. The blast from the shotgun kicked one across the room. James stepped forward and brought the butt end up under the other's chin, sending him reeling. Two quick strides and James stood over him, pummeling the raider's head until gray matter oozed out of his face.

"I never had to kill anyone else since then." James raised the binoculars and thought a moment. These two Riders had been rummaging around his farm several days back, digging through the old farmhouse and finding nothing. James had made sure of that.

He bowed his head, remembering how he had buried his parents in proper graves and stripped everything of value from the marauders' corpses. Their bodies became meals for scavenging animals.

That's when James left the house's comfort behind, taking up residence in the storm cellar some thirty yards away. The entrance faced away from the home. He allowed scattered farm equipment to conceal it further. A makeshift periscope cobbled together from PVC pipe and bits of mirror, and looking like an air vent, allowed him to keep an eye on things from inside.

That day his visitors hadn't spent more than ten minutes in the house. They stood on his porch. Then one, a woman, pointed to the sky. The clouds gathered and turned gray. The other had nodded, and they got on their horses and rode off.

Now, watching their approach, it occurred to him—*I bet they took up residence in town.*

"Those poor horses." His voice was raspy, dry. "Looks like they barely feed 'em. Lucky for me, they didn't try to get to the barn the other day." The horses kicked up dust as the Riders turned away from Watchtower and rode off. The wind began to howl.

James secured the binoculars in their case and hurried across the yard to the barn. He made sure nothing was lying loose around his project. *Wouldn't want anything tossed and wrecked by the wind.*

Reassured that he had protected the old Ford Ranger, James pulled the double doors together and slid the two-by-four securely in place.

"Best a body can do."

The wind was picking up force, howling past the old building. Debris flew across the dusty yard. Looking up, he saw it. "Maga! This one's too close."

A funnel cloud was rapidly forming, its rat tail descending to the earth not more than a quarter-mile away.

Fighting his initial panic, James started toward the storm cellar. One hand raised to protect his face; he kept an eye on the dancing cloud as dirt and trash pelted him. He doubled over as he reached the door. The noise was deafening.

As he pulled on the door, it was torn from his hand and beat back and forth on its hinges like a loose sheet of paper. A high-pitched feral growl cut through the roar of the wind. Quickly scanning the area, he saw a black animal flying toward him, legs extended and claws out, eyes wide with terror. The tornado had thrown it directly at him like a football. Instinctively, James braced himself and snatched it into the crook of his arm. The force threw him backward, and he tumbled down the cellar stairs. There was a brief tussle as the two struggled to disengage themselves. Then James ran back up the short flight, grabbed the flapping door and, with a desperate effort, heaved it shut.

His back to the door, he allowed himself to slide down to a sitting position. He was breathing hard from the effort. Crashing, snapping noises cut through the roar outside like a guitar riff as the storm rapidly dissipated.

"Bang your head!" He quoted a favorite song from long ago and laughed.

"What's so funny, Jim Bob?"

"I think the farmhouse bit the dust," he replied, squinting out a crack in the door. Late-afternoon sun poked through, piercing to the bottom of the steps.

It dawned on him then. That first voice was different, not the talk-to-himself low, mocking voice that came in his head. This one was grandfatherly-like. Somehow smooth and gruff at the same time. And it wasn't in his head. This voice came from downstairs.

James turned and peered into the gloom of the cellar. Dust motes floated in a shaft of light. There, at the bottom of the steps, sat a jet-black cat staring up at him, his golden eyes almost mocking.

"Looks like living alone all this time has finally caught up with me. Did you just say something to me?" The cat stared back at him. "Well, I swear I heard a voice come from down there." James's voice grew louder. "And you're the only other one in the cellar. So if anyone was talking to me, it would have to be you, cat. But cats don't talk. They can't talk. So I am going crazy. I must be in-ins—"

The cat shook his head. "Humans. When are you going to figure out that it's not all about you?"

James stood and slowly descended the steps, his back to the wall while trying to keep some distance from the cat. "How can you talk?" He still wasn't entirely sure the cat had actually spoken.

"Why, by moving my lips and tongue, just like you." The cat slowly enunciated the words. James saw that, indeed, the cat's lips were moving. "What's surprising is that you're finally listening to me. We animals have been talking for eons. It's you humans who haven't been listening. Well, except for maybe that Dr. Dolittle. By the way, thanks for catching me. I thought I was heading to the next life." The cat stretched.

James kept the distance between them as he made his way to a cot at the back of the cellar and sat down.

"No problem. Glad I could accommodate you. Well, hell's bells. I can't believe I'm talking to a cat." He pulled his knees to his chest and rocked back and forth. "Not crazy, not crazy," he mumbled over and over.

"Snap out of it, Jimbo!" The cat jumped onto the nightstand next to the cot. "Here, light the lamp, and I'll try to enlighten you."

James gathered his wits. It helped to have something concrete to do, some goal to achieve. He fumbled for matches, raised the mantle, and lit the lantern. A soft, warm glow filled the room. He turned to face the cat, the match still flickering between his fingers. The fire crept down until it singed him. "Maga!" he yelped and shook his hand.

The cat laughed. "I was going to tell you to pinch yourself to prove you weren't dreaming, but that works even better." He chuckled and settled next to the lantern. "This is quite astonishing, actually; I found a human who can listen. It's amazing!"

"Wha-what do you mean?"

"Oh, most people hear us, but they only hear the sounds of our voices," the cat continued. "You know, like 'meow' or 'mew' or 'purr.' But you, you listen to my words. So now we can communicate."

James's brow furrowed. "Y-you mean cats have always been talking to us?" He was incredulous.

"Not just us cats," he replied. "Horses, whales, and dolphins—you name it. Oh, and dogs, of course. Those poor saps! They would do everything in their power to get you to listen. But did you? No."

The cat dropped down from the stand and started to pace, agitated. "You humans are so wrapped up in your little world, thinking you're the masters of the universe, ignoring the bigger world around you. What has that gotten you? This." He huffed as he looked around the cellar. "Humans messed things up big this time, what with that Middle East war and nuking each other and all. Now you're stuck in a hole like rats. No offense to rats, mind you. At least they know what they're about."

"B-bu-but the—"

"But, but, but!" The cat jumped back on the stand and got in his face. "Your entire species is nothing but a bunch of imbeciles. You stopped trying to talk with each other, to work out your problems. You allowed selfishness to rule. You wanted everything for yourselves. You couldn't even share with other humans."

The cat sat down. "Well, no use crying over spilled milk. It's time to pick up the pieces. Check the scope, will you? See if it's safe outside."

James rose. He didn't like taking orders, having spent over thirty years living alone. His only help came in the form of the faint voice occasionally heard on the radio. Questions bubbled up, but before he could speak, the cat stood.

"Come on, come on," he urged. "We've got a lot to do. Up periscope!"

James gave in. Pulling himself together, he went to the angled PVC and peered in. "So what's your name?"

The cat sat down again, tail sweeping back and forth. "Thomas Henry Edward Cat, but most people just call me 'the cat.'"

James panned the periscope, taking in the view. "Why so many names?"

"Well, you know that we cats have nine lives. So we take a new name for each life. The newest name gets tacked on the front of the list."

James took his eyes from the scope. "So I could call you Tomcat, eh?" He smirked.

"Don't go there!" The cat stood. "That was a long time ago, back when I was Edward. They called me 'Fast Eddie.' I was young and made mistakes, yes. And no, I'm not proud of it. I named myself after one of the Christian saints for this lifespan. It helps to remind me to be a better creature."

"So you picked the doubting apostle? Fascinating!" James peered back into the scope. "Well, the farmhouse is gone."

"What about the barn?" Thomas vaulted to James's shoulder.

"Ow! Mind the claws, will ya?" He flinched under the cat's weight. "It's still there."

Turning to the new arrival, he jutted out his jaw. "What's it to you, anyway?"

The cat leaped to the floor, wary. "You mean your project? You've got two marauders taking a keen interest in your place. Couple that with the fact that you have the only means of a quick escape, and you ask what's it to me?"

James faced the cat and leaned down. "Just what do you know about me?'

"Oh, for pity's sake, Jimbo." Thomas shook his tail and began to pace. "I know about the truck. I know about your plan to head east. I know you want to join Speaker's enclave. Why do you think I've been hanging out around here? It's certainly not for the food. I want to hitch a ride."

"How do you know …? You've been spying on me!" He bent closer, scrutinizing the cat's face. "You're that cat!" he exclaimed. "The one with the star on his ear. I've been calling you Lucky. What kind of luck is this?"

Thomas took a deep breath and sat down. "Look, Jim, you don't think we just happened to get thrown together by a storm, do you? Everything—and I mean *everything*—happens for a reason. Yeah, I've been hanging around here. I was trying to get up the courage to approach you, you know, do the cat thing, rubbing against your leg, letting you scratch my head till I purred —the sort of thing you assume all cats do. It's very degrading for us cats, by the way. I didn't plan to get caught in a tornado. But it happened. Why? Probably to get us talking and working together.

"Oh, and about that name, Lucky. I'm genuinely not into nick-names, so please, call me Thomas."

"No problem, hombre." James shook his head.

Thunder boomed outside as heavy rain began to fall. James went back to the periscope. Just then, lightning crackled, and a beam of light pulsed from the scope.

"That was close. Another second, and it would have blinded me."

Thomas dropped his head. "As I said, there are bigger things afoot here. Whatever the reason, I feel compelled to get to Speaker's town. Something drew me to this place, so I checked it out. I found you working on the truck a few days ago. That's why I was hanging around." He looked earnestly at James. "I was hoping to catch a ride with you whenever you got it together to leave. Now I can see why. You are more than a ride. You understand my words. I believe I'm called to start a language class, to teach humans and animals to communicate. You're my proof to humans that we can do it. Our souls are intertwined, linked if you will. We have a mission."

James nodded. "Well, we're not going anywhere with weather like that out there. No one can go out in that."

They fell silent. Years ago (so many years ago!), James as an engineering student, studied alternative fuel sources for vehicles. Back then, the push was on to wean America off of gas and oil, to become energy-independent. His project was to convert a Ford truck over to an alternate source, whether propane, biodiesel, solar electric, or some other fuel. James's idea was to hybridize these alternative sources to get them to work together.

He was able to avoid the draft because his proposal caught the military's eye. His design was showing much promise when the Middle East war took a turn for the worse. Abandoning school, he managed to haul the rig to Watchtower Farm, where he had continued his work.

Sheltering with his parents, James was able to pick up a government broadcast on an old AM radio. He listened to Thomas Speaker, the preacher who had called the government to task regarding the war and now was sending out the only ray of hope for rebuilding humanity. The pastor's daily broadcasts were full of survival tips—everything from proper food preservation to safe scavenging of building materials. More important was his daily spiritual message. It gave him hope. James was determined to join this preacher.

He considered the cat and huffed. "Well, I was hoping for a partner. Guess you'll have to do. Besides, you can see pretty well in the dark. That'll be helpful."

"Whoa, big guy." Thomas's tail twitched. "We can't drive in the dark. Too many hazards. Bridges are down, and flash floods and earthquakes have cut the roads. It'll be slow going even in broad daylight."

"Yeah, I guess you're right." James sat back at the periscope and peered into it. It was weird how he had come to feel close to Thomas. It was as if they had known each other all along. They fit.

"Well, the farmhouse is definitely totaled," he reported. "The barn looks to be untouched, so the truck should be okay, too. I guess we got lucky, eh, Luck—er, Thomas?" He tried to crack a smile.

Thomas got serious. "I'm telling you, luck has nothing to do with it. Something guided us to this moment."

"What? Like the hand of God pushing us along?" James choked back a laugh.

"Humans!" Thomas used the word like a curse. "Why do you bother having a Bible if you don't pay attention to what it says?" He was pacing again, agitated. "Look, get this. Beyond the physical body, we are made up of mind and spirit too. Our mind tries to bridge or make sense of the connection between spiritual and physical. You and I have connected through the spirit. It's just that your physical self doesn't want to accept it."

James tried to shrug off his distress. "Oh, I understand about body, mind, and soul," he offered. "It's just that they're separate. You know, body, mind, soul." He pointed to himself, his head, and made a circle with his arms as he spoke.

"Not separate." Thomas sounded exasperated. "Three in one, just like your god. You're made up of godstuff."

"What do you mean, godstuff?"

"Most people call it soul or spirit. It's the part of God within all things. It's what connects us all. You know—'use the Force, Luke.'"

"*Star Wars* psychobabble." James was disappointed. "Look, it's getting late. This is all too much for me to take." He got up, went to a shelf, and grabbed a couple of jars. "We'll eat and get some sleep. Maybe take this up in the morning."

"Call it what you will, but that is how it is." Thomas bounded to the shelf and sniffed at a jar. "So, what's for dinner?"

"That's green beans, and this"—James pulled a sack from a cupboard—"is smoked rabbit."

"*Smoked* rabbit? Yummy!" Thomas exclaimed as he padded across the shelf. "Tonight, we dine in style."

ESCAPE PLAN

"One can only imagine the plight of those left on their own. The challenge would be to survive sickness, the weather, and others."

— A BUTTERFLY IN FLIGHT: THE BIOGRAPHY OF THOMAS SPEAKER BY JAMIE LIVINGSTON

James awoke to a faint light flickering in his eyes. Holding up his hand to ward off the annoying beam, he squinted into the dim cellar. Thomas was on the floor, nudging a small hand mirror. He caught the solitary ray of sunlight that had passed through a crack in the door and was now reflecting it up into James's face.

"Rise and shine, Jimbo! We've much to do," he announced.

James groaned as he got up and stumbled to the shelf where he had prepared dinner the night before. He pulled a plastic jug of water off a shelf and poured some into a large bowl. Then, taking a deep breath and sticking his face into it, he blew bubbles. He grabbed for a towel and wiped his face. "Probably won't have time for a shave, eh."

"Eh, no. Harley and Honda will be coming, if not today, then certainly by tomorrow."

"Who?" James began to place canned goods in a battered plastic tote.

Thomas jumped up and peered into the box. "The Riders. That's what they call themselves, anyway. I think they stole the names from the bikes they used to ride. You know, Harley Davidson and Honda? Anyway, I've been keeping an eye on that pair. About the time they ran out of gas, they came across the horses grazing in a field. Fortunately for the horses, those two couldn't use their bikes. I hear horseflesh is pretty tasty."

James grimaced. He had a fondness for horses going back to the farm's early days, where they proved so useful. He remembered the palomino he used to ride out to the fields, checking the fence lines and cattle.

"Say, Thomas, do you suppose my horse was trying to talk to me?"

"Most likely. Horses and dogs, in particular, tried for generations to get people to listen. What thanks did you give them? More work, or else you would prissy them up for show and tell. And when one would finally break through to you and save your rear end in a house fire or some other disaster, you get all goofy calling it a miracle or something. Geez! You humans are just so out of touch." He was getting agitated again.

"Okay, okay, I'm sorry the human race screwed everything up." James feigned remorse, falling on his knees, raising his arms as if in prayer. "Please forgive me, Lord."

"Right, right." Thomas took a deep breath. Calming down, he jumped to the floor. "Let's get packed."

Once outside, the two surveyed the damage. The house's roof lay in a crumpled pile fifty yards away while the walls were a jumbled heap. The barn was intact; the only damage was a cornstalk embedded in its side.

James let out a low whistle. "One has to wonder."

"One does." Thomas drew silent.

The moment passed, and they both hurried to the barn.

Inside, the old Ford Ranger seemed to glow softly in the

warm, dusty sunlight. Stacked in its bed was an odd assortment of tanks and apparatus, the hybrid fuel sources.

Thomas leaped to a fender. "Nice work! The flywheel to store energy is a nice touch. That can keep us moving when the gas runs out."

"Yeah," James agreed. "The big problem was getting enough methane to fill the tanks. The original plan was to convert animal waste from the farm, but, well, no farm animals and …" His voice trailed off as he recalled those dark days after civilization collapsed.

"Well, the sun did come out again." Thomas tried to sound lighthearted. "And when the sun shines, the photovoltaic cells will work just fine. You did good, Jimbo."

"Yeah, well, as I said, there's not enough methane to run it for long." James fiddled under the hood, slammed it shut. "So I'll have to get it out into the daylight and get it charged up. Probably take the better part of the morning."

"It's gonna be a bright, sunshiny day," Thomas quipped.

James smiled, remembering a familiar tune. "Bum, da bum. Bum. Ba, bum." He held his fist to his mouth, beginning the rap.

"It's clear to me that the rain is gone." Thomas, caught up in the rhythm, barked out the words.

"Bum, da bum. Bum. Ba, bum." James did a little jig as he pushed the shed doors wide open.

Thomas sprang to the hood. "All our troubles are just a con."

"Bum, da bum. Bum. Ba, bum." James danced, swaying his arms above his head.

"The sun shines bright on this wonderful day."

"Bum, da bum. Bum. Ba, bum."

"Take a moment to stop and pr— Maga!"

James cut off the beat and followed Thomas's gaze. "It's them." His shoulders slumped. Who else could it be in this desolate land? On the distant hilltop, sunlight glinted off the Riders' binoculars. They would have seen movement, zeroed in, and now would be heading toward them at full gallop.

James made sure the truck was in neutral and went to the rear. Pushing with all his might, he groaned with the effort. "It would've helped if you'd been a horse rather than a cat," he grunted.

Thomas ignored him. He had been sniffing around the bed of the truck. "I think you have enough methane to get this thing running, Jim." He dove to the ground. "Maybe by the time it runs out, we'll have enough juice stored to run on electricity or even the flywheel. We don't have to run long or fast to beat out the horses, maybe an hour at best. Given the shape they're in, they'll have to give up by then."

"Yeah." James looked into the distance, saw tiny puffs of dust rising as the horses sped toward them. "I figure we get thirty-five, maybe forty miles an hour on the methane. The batteries will drop us down to thirty, tops. But we've gotta get moving. Now!"

"The horses won't be able to catch us, and if we get three or four hours of driving in, the Riders will need days on foot." Thomas sounded hopeful as he jumped into the cab. "And that's if we stop, which we won't do till we can hide. Let's go!"

James heaved himself into the driver's seat. With a twist of the key, the engine sputtered, coughed, and choked. James muttered a prayer, then tried again. Another sputter and the engine coughed into life. "Hallelujah!" he shouted, kicking the truck into gear. It crawled forward slowly as the rising sun beamed promises of a better day.

As they picked up speed, Thomas looked back and saw that the Riders were falling behind. He chuckled, balancing on the back of the seat. "Well, it's not exactly a high-speed getaway, but it works."

TWO SISTERS

"Those of us who completed the stem-cell trials successfully fled the clinic. No one wanted to be in a large city when civilization failed. I often wonder what happened to the others."

— A BUTTERFLY IN FLIGHT: THE BIOGRAPHY OF THOMAS SPEAKER BY JAMIE LIVINGSTON

Judith placed the walnut container on the kitchen table. It was about the size of a shoebox, handcrafted by the village's carpenter. The dovetailed joinery and fitted lid spoke of her years of experience. A brass plate was the sole decoration. It was engraved with Judith and Sarah's father's name, his date of birth, and his date of death.

Sarah appraised the cremains of their father. This was an annual ritual—exchanging Father's ashes. "My turn already? We should have dumped them in the Cuyahoga River like he wanted."

"We have no idea how dangerous the journey back home may be—even after all these years. Besides, I like our annual memorial service. It's good to reflect back on where we've been." Judith sat across from her sister, waiting for the expected response.

"Even though Dad was such a cold-hearted SOB till the end? There's some things I'll never understand about you, sis."

Judith smirked. "That was ten years ago. You can't hold on to the past forever. Let it go, Sarah."

"Easy for you to say. You were his favorite—hand-picked for town council, a natural-born leader, he'd say. A politician always and oh, so smart."

"For pity's sake! Be honest with yourself. You couldn't stand to be confined to administrative duties. Besides, you've done all right with yourself, keeping the town's security intact."

"Ha! Four aging techs who can barely walk their rounds hardly makes for a security unit." Sarah shrugged.

Judith began to laugh. "Still … which one of them came up with the sign idea? Remember?"

"That was Herb. 'Put signs up on the roads running past our little commune,' he said. 'Big letters—PLAGUE TOWN AHEAD —that'll keep 'em out.' Well, it worked." Sarah chuckled.

Judith stared off in the distance, reflecting. Over three decades had passed since they established Sanctuary. She spent the time next to their father, learning the politics of running their small commuity and taking on some of his traits. She, too, became calculating, playing townspeople off each other as she helped shape their destinies.

"It's for their own good," Dad would tell her. "You must have everyone working toward the same goal. You can't allow differing opinions."

A wan smile crossed Judith's lips. She and Dad made a good pair. He was cold, curt, insistent. She was warm, smiling, soothing. He would stir the pot angering the other council members with his demands. She would step up, with a calming voice and smile, and smooth the ruffled feathers. In the end, it was her cajoling that resulted in decisions being made per her father's wishes. Some called her manipulative. Whatever. It got the job done.

"Hello in there." Sarah waved a hand in front of Judith, breaking her revierie.

Judith blinked. "Sorry. I was just remembering … thinking about Dad."

"A trip down memory lane? That's a lonesome journey."

Judith stood and went to the stove. "What do you mean? Water's hot. Want some tea?"

"Certainly, but make it something mellow. The boys will be home soon." Sarah leaned back in her chair. "As for memories, you know how they can be selective, reflect only your perspective. Other people would've seen the same events from a different viewpoint."

"Yes, yes. But it's the overall picture I think about. The collective memory, if you will."

Sarah appraised her sister. "Okay, so the collective memory is what we call history. Everyone sort of agrees on the highlights—names, places, dates. That stuff. But it's the personal stuff that really matters. That's what motivates people."

"Says the amateur psychologist." Judith placed two mugs on the table and returned to her seat. "Besides, does anyone even care about history anymore? It's all we can do to survive."

"Give yourself some credit, sis. You and Big Ben have been our guiding light for more than ten years. Folks are having babies—our two are growing so quickly—the farms are sustainable. We've got a growing community. Not bad, I'd say."

Judith leaned over her mug, allowing the steam to envelop her face. Memories flashed by. Their father arranged the marriage between her and his fellow researcher's son, just as he had for Sarah. Good breeding stock was his analysis of the men. And he was right, of course. Their sons were mature for their age, able to be trusted on their own. There was no time for childhood nowadays.

"Yes, not bad." Judith pushed her mug aside. "Just like Daddy planned. I guess what I regret most is that our boys can't be kids. Know what I mean?"

Sarah ran her fingers through her hair, a sign she was growing impatient. "What? You want to spend the day at Cedar Point, ride the roller coasters? Those days are long gone. Fading memories, if anyone remembers them at all."

"It seems our generation was the last one to have a fun childhood."

"Not true. Remember when the boys let all the chickens out of the coop?" Sarah laughed.

"Remember? It took the guys hours to round them all up. Meanwhile, that old rooster started chasing Brandon around and ..."

"Yes! His daddy made sure we had chicken for dinner the next night." Sarah fell silent, memories of her deceased husband flooding back. Judith respected the moment.

The silence was broken as their two boys barged into the room lugging a five-gallon bucket.

"Hey, Mom!" Ben and Brandon spoke together, laughed, and tried again. "Fresh trout—" Ben began. Brandon completed the sentence. "For dinner."

"You two are like two peas in a pod." Sarah reached up to tousle Brandon's hair.

Judith received a quick peck on the cheek. "Where's your dad?"

"Heading to the council hall. Said he wanted to see if he could catch some of the elders." Ben kicked at the pail, confirming the fish were still alive.

Brandon elbowed him. "We came across old man Jenkins from town. He seemed upset. Said he was coming to tell us about some nomads or something."

Sarah looked to her sister. "What do you suppose that's all about?"

Judith stood. "Looks like we better find out."

LEAVING KANSAS

"This connection, how do I describe it? Sometimes it feels like I'm attached to a golden thread that spirals out and is attached to others. Other times there's a feeling of someone in my mind, sharing my thoughts."

— *A BUTTERFLY IN FLIGHT: THE BIOGRAPHY OF THOMAS SPEAKER* BY JAMIE LIVINGSTON

James Robert Hendricks Sr. was proud that his land, Watchtower Farm, was just south of Lebanon, Kansas. "We are smack dab in the exact center of the United States of America," he told his kids as they gathered for dinner. He referred to a map of the United States to make his point. "There!" And his finger poked at the map. "That's the land your grandfather chose for us. Here we are exactly between the Atlantic and Pacific oceans. Equal distance both ways. Makes you think, don't it?"

"Whatever." His daughter, Margaret, slumped into her chair, toying with her dinner. For her, farm life was boring. Every day played out the same—school, chores, and homework. Now her sixteenth birthday was fast approaching—draft age. That thought frightened her. She had few choices.

As devout Christians, their parents had instilled a firm conviction for peace and love in the two children. Now open warfare raged around the world, testing those beliefs. She tried to reconcile her love of family, farm, and country with the need to fight in the war. It didn't work. So now what?

His son, however, did think about it. Surrounded by miles and miles of fertile farmland, James Junior loved the land. He had taken a quick liking to working on the farm equipment, helping his dad with the big combine and tractor's maintenance and repairs. It was natural for his talents to gravitate toward his chosen major in mechanical engineering. An oil crisis and the soaring cost of fuel set him to work on developing alternative fuel vehicles.

James's thoughts returned to the present. *All gone now.* His sister, Margaret—Maggie, he corrected himself—had escaped to Canada with their parents' blessings. He wondered if she was still alive. *She would be, what? Forty-seven or -eight, I think.* As for James, in the years after the collapse, while working on the old truck, he had considered the route to Ohio and Thomas Speaker's settlement. Now, bouncing along the potholed highway, his thoughts turned back to their present dilemma.

"Which way?" Thomas broke his reverie.

James glanced over his shoulder. "So you read minds, too." It was a statement of fact, not a question.

Thomas chuckled. "You don't have to be an Einstein to figure out what you're thinking."

"Well, the original plan called for me to head south on 281 and then take I-70 east through KC and St. Louis just like in the past when I headed off to college. Now—"

"That's a terrible idea," Thomas objected. "The freeway system is in chaos what with overpasses and bridges down. Besides, anybody using it is probably looking for an easy way to be up to no good. Likely to be Riders or worse, and they'll be desperate. That's not to mention the big cities like Kansas City, St. Louis, or wherever. If anyone has survived there, they will be dangerous. We wouldn't survive."

"Good thing we turned north then, huh?" James smiled broadly.

"More than likely, it was your gut doing what your head knew it had to do." Thomas stretched. "Still, we need to head east."

"No problem, my man! We'll catch 136 just north of here, and then it's a straight shot to Indianapolis. We'll bypass all the big cities till we get there. Maybe we can catch up to some other decent folks, you know, survivors like us."

Thomas swallowed hard. "Maybe."

James glanced in the mirror, keeping an eye on the road. Nobody was following close enough that he could see. He shot a glance in Thomas's direction. "Your tail is doing that thing again. What's bugging you?"

The cat jumped to the dash. "Sometimes, I think all humans are idiots."

"What do you mean by that?" James scowled.

"Do you have any idea what is out there?" Thomas tilted his chin to the windshield. "There be monsters!" His voice dropped low. "Not just lions and tigers and bears, but human monsters. Worse than those two back there."

"Okay, okay, I know." James grimaced. "I know about monsters. Men like that"—he cocked his head to the rear window —"they killed my folks. And I saw what one did to Mom. My mom! Believe me; it was easy to kill him. Easy."

Tears came to his eyes. "And I can take on those two back there, too. I've got a gun now and plenty of ammo. I was even thinking of setting up a trap. We've got a big enough jump on 'em. I could find a place to hide the truck and bushwhack 'em— two quick shots, bam, bam, it's over; we won't have to deal with them anymore. And—and ..." He swallowed hard and pounded the steering wheel.

"Whoa, take it easy, big guy." Thomas's voice turned soothing as he stretched a paw to touch James's hand. "Think it through. Those two have survived these past years by hunting and killing, especially killing other people. You're a farmer. You don't even think as they do. You can be sure that they're not just following us. When they spot us, they'll plan the kill and execute it. I've watched them in action before. They are natural-born killers." The cat pulled back. "Look. I know your anger. I understand your grief, but now we have to keep our wits if we're to survive." He paused and stared into James's eyes. A thought came. "That rabbit we ate last night."

"What about it?" James wiped a fist across each eye.

"How'd you feel when you killed it?" Thomas continued to look deeply into his eyes.

"Well, I ...I ..."

"You cried. You cried because you hated taking a life, any life. You're a farmer, Jimbo. You don't have the killer instinct. The best you can do is to get us to Ohio. That's where you can best use your talents. We're at the beginning of a new era. Think about it. Humans working side by side with other species. Communicating with them better than they ever communicated with each other. We've got much more important things to do than bushwhack a couple of rabid dogs."

James slumped back, one hand on the wheel. "You're right," he conceded with a sigh. "It's just that ... that ..."

"I know." Thomas jumped back to the seat. "We all want to do more. Those who are aware of their godstuff, anyway."

James sat up and drove on. At some point, Kansas's farm fields and woods turned into Nebraska's farm fields and woods. They were fortunate in that the few bridges they encountered were intact. Now, off to the west, buildings began to crop up. They were approaching what was once the thriving town of Red Cloud, Nebraska. Thomas jumped up on the rear of the seat, and the two kept a wary eye as they entered. U.S. 281 became Webster Street, or what was once Webster Street. The town was devastated. Burned-out buildings gave way to trees and weeds. They weaved past rusting hulks of cars, their fiberglass body parts stripped away, likely to be used for makeshift shelters away from the dangers a town would now have. Just past the Willa Cather Pioneer Memorial, James made a right turn onto Fourth Avenue. He picked up speed as it became U.S. 136, an arrow-straight two-lane highway that stretched eastward, toward the horizon.

As James eased the steering wheel back and forth, the sleeve of his shirt fell away from his wrist. Thomas looked over.

"What's that?" He nodded toward James's inside left wrist. A small red blemish was showing.

"It's only a birthmark." James shrugged. "I've had it all my life. So they say." He held up his arm and looked closer. "Hey! It kinda looks like the star on your ear. How about that? Maybe that's how we're connected."

"Or it may just be a birthmark. Then again, maybe it is a sign. Sometimes, I get a feeling that there are others like us out there, somewhere. God knows."

They drove in silence for several miles as they pondered this. Suddenly, James pulled over and shut the truck off.

"What's happening, Jim?" Thomas stretched and dug his claws into the seat cover.

"We've got the batteries fully charged now," James hopped down and headed to the back of the truck. He tinkered a bit, then flipped a switch. Electric motors began to hum, one for each wheel. James jumped back in the cab, threw a lever, and the duo were off again.

Thomas caught James's scowl. "What's up, bub?" the cat asked, jumping up to the seatback.

"I'm thinking." His scowl grew darker. "I'm not used to going this slow. Methane's down a quarter already. I'm not sure how long the batteries will last. Never did a road test, you know. On the bright side, the flywheel's humming along, storing up energy. I just don't know how far we can go, and I don't like not know-ing." He pounded his fist on the steering wheel.

"I know what you mean." Thomas relaxed a bit. "It's like when I first came across you. I didn't know if I could trust you, but there you were, appearing to be trustworthy. I didn't like not knowing if I could put my faith in you or not. I finally had to give in to the godstuff connection." He sighed. "You know, my gut feeling."

"There you go with that godstuff BS again!" James snorted. "I mean, get serious."

The cat pushed up on his haunches. "Oh, I am quite serious. Christians call it 'soul' but then ignore it till they're about to die. Buddhists have a better understanding. They'll even try to guide it when the physical body passes."

"Guide it where?" James was staring into the mirror to catch Thomas's reflection. "OK, I get the soul connection thing, but you can't tell me people can tell it where to go."

Thomas laughed. "Well, yeah, you do it all the time! How often did you ever tell someone to go to hell?"

James slapped at the wheel. "That's different! That's, well, that's, what, metaphorical? I guess that's what you'd call it."

"But the point is the symbolic explains the real. Understand this. Godstuff—the soul, if you will—is an active part of each living being. It's our connection to the Divine, to God. People used to claim to be on a spiritual journey, but they'd never act like they were. Posers!" Thomas jumped down to the seat. "It's simple enough to recognize God in each other. Your Bible even tells you that. He made you in His image. It's hard to believe you can't accept that fact." He took a deep breath, catching himself. "Sorry." He sighed, settling down. "One of my shortcomings is impatience with you humans."

"Okay, okay! Yeah, I believe in the soul and all that. Of course. That's what they taught, so that's what I believe. As you said, we believe we have a soul but don't get concerned until the end, until we're dying. Then it's all regret and sorrow. Please forgive me, God. And, oh, don't send me to hell, God." James laughed. "Like the minister said. It's a matter of—"

"Faith," Thomas finished. "Faith. Belief. Those words can't describe it because those words have nothing concrete to base it on. I guess that's why most people don't take it seriously. They need a physical thing. Something they can touch and see."

The conversation continued as the truck rolled down the highway, slowly making its way past the endless fields. The sun passed overhead and fell behind them. The truck's shadow grew longer.

Finally, James pulled to the side of the road. "I guess it's best to stop. It's getting dark, too dark even in the moonlight to be certain the road is clear."

"Just as well," Thomas acknowledged, jumping through the open window. "I was getting hungry." He headed off into the scrub.

James slid out and rummaged through a box in the truck bed, pulling out some jerky, a jar of beans, and a bottle of water. He unscrewed the retaining ring from the container and fetched the bottle opener, a relic from his previous life. He squinted at the barely discernable logo, nearly illegible after the years of use.

"Heineken," he muttered. "Boy, I can't remember what a cold beer tastes like." He chewed on the jerky while working the opener around the jar lid till it popped. Dipping his fingers into the jar, he settled to the ground.

A rustling from the undergrowth caught his attention. He grabbed for his knife, then relaxed as Thomas emerged, a sizable field mouse dangling from his mouth.

"Look what I found," he announced, dropping the creature. "Want to share? I can go back and get another. The poor fellow was too old to put up much of a fight."

James grimaced. "No, thanks. I never did acquire a taste for mice."

"Suit yourself." Thomas placed a paw on the creature and bowed his head. After a moment, he muttered "Amen" and bit into the neck.

James had watched the cat warily. "What was that about?"

"What was what about?" Thomas looked up from his meal.

"You know, that bowed head and 'amen' thing." He pointed his chin Thomas's way.

"Thanksgiving. You gave thanks for your meal, didn't you?"

"Well, yeah, sorta." James's face reddened.

"You should be very specific about it," Thomas lectured. "Don't just 'sorta' say thanks. Be thankful. A living creature gave of itself to feed and sustain you. Even if it's just jerky, you should be grateful indeed."

"I am grateful," James shot back. "I just don't make a big deal of it, you know, all holy and all."

"That's my point exactly!" Thomas stopped gnawing at the mouse. "If everything has godstuff, has a soul, then everything is holy. Prayer is our way of connecting the physical to the spiritual, recognizing the holy. So we must be thankful when one physical being gives itself up for another." He bent down for another bite.

"Yeah, but that's just a mouse." James popped a long bean into his mouth.

"And that's just a bean," Thomas asserted. "And that in the field is a grain of wheat and—and you are James Robert Hendricks. All are living things. They are all connected through the spirit. How can I make it any plainer?" He tore at the mouse, paused, and shook his head. "I thought you were getting it."

James stood. "I do get it. I'm talking to you now so I can see that I have a connection to animals like you. I understand that. But now you want me to believe that I've got that same connection to mice? Come on now."

"And beans and wheat," Thomas said softly. "It connects you to all things, James, *all* things." He picked up the mouse and walked off a short distance, where he dug a hole and placed the body in it. Then, covering it back up, he bowed his head again.

"Ah, geez." James kicked at the dirt and stomped back to the truck. He climbed in and slammed the door shut. Glancing up, he noted the ever-present star glowing in the east. He shrugged.

Thomas jumped in through the passenger window and settled

down. "Let's get some sleep," he said. "Close the window, please."

James reached over and hand-cranked the window shut. "Look, I'm sorry. Okay? I don't mean to upset you, Tom."

"Not to worry. You are aware of it now. You will come to understand soon enough." He curled up and closed his eyes, cutting off the conversation.

"Well, maybe." James leaned against the door and closed his eyes. "Maybe."

UNEXPECTED ALLIES

"We found our safety in numbers, as did most other communities.
It's always best to have a friend or two."

— *A BUTTERFLY IN FLIGHT: THE BIOGRAPHY OF
THOMAS SPEAKER* BY JAMIE LIVINGSTON

The sun pierced through low clouds far to the east, laser beams stabbing down at the revitalized earth. James sat up, stretched his neck from side to side, and yawned. Thomas stirred on the floorboard, forced there earlier when his friend tried to curl up on the seat. It had been a fitful night's rest for both.

James scanned the sky, then squinted into the sunlight. "Looks like some weather in the west."

"Yeah, whatever." Thomas was surly, trying to shake the sleep from his eyes. He sprung up to the seat. "Let me out, will ya? I've gotta take a leak."

James obliged, rolling himself out as he opened the door. The cat darted past and went into the brush to the north. James stepped to the front of the truck to relieve himself. Pulling up his zipper, he turned and caught sight of an undulating gray-brown mass roiling through the scrub to the south like an oily wave.

Small bushes quivered as the mass engulfed them. He thought of floodwaters, but this was different, not shiny like water.

James peered intensely. "What the ..."

The surge halted about a foot from the roadway but continued to swell. A severe-looking creature stepped from the mass. James strained to make out its features. A large field mouse, at least eight inches, approached and stood on its hind legs.

"Hey, mister!" it shouted. "Are you with the cat?"

"H-h-huh?"

"C'mon. C'mon." The mouse pointed up at James, his tattered left ear trembling. "Are you with the cat, and is the cat with you?"

"L-l-look, what's this about?" James stepped back, stopped by the truck.

"Last night!" the mouse snapped. "Last night, a terrible, vicious creature attacked one of ours and carried him off. A cat! That's what my cousins here tell me. A cat! If you brought a cat among us, mister, why, by the great god of us all, I'll eat your eyeballs out, or my name isn't Scrapper." The mouse flicked his frayed ear to make his point.

"Well, now look," James said, but the mouse dropped to all fours and took three steps toward him. James hesitated. "T-Thomas! We have company." He paused and thought a moment. "And they want to know about how all things are holy like you were telling me last night."

"Holy?" Thomas's voice had a lilt to it as he strode out of the scrub. "Last night? Holy? Oh, yeah, holy. Wholly satisfy—" His voice trailed off as he caught sight of Scrapper and his host.

"Oh, hello," he said weakly.

"Hello, kitty." Scrapper's voice was low and mean as he walked up to Thomas, sizing him up. "Let me get to the point. Did you kill our Uncle Walter?"

"Who? What?" Thomas glanced from Scrapper to James and back again. Realization dawned on him. "You mean that brave fellow of yours. Last night, yes, I did, but no, I did not." He returned Scrapper's gaze.

"Just what do you mean?" Scrapper was incensed. "You admit to killing one of our own but say you didn't! How can opposites be true?" He strutted in front of the cat.

"This is how." Thomas crouched to be level with Scrapper. "Walter gave his life to me."

Scrapper stopped pacing and sat in front of the cat. "Explain."

Thomas's voice was soft, almost apologetic. "When we made camp last night, I did go off hunting. I hoped to find some crickets or other night insects. They would have sustained me. Instead, I stumbled across a nest of your younglings. They barely had their eyes open. Their mama wasn't near. Maybe she was foraging for food; after all, it was that time of day. I was famished, and they were such an easy target for me. I was ready to eat my fill when suddenly this old geezer mouse jumped in front of me. Walter, you call him. He could barely walk, let alone put up a fight. And he was hardly a meal in and of himself. I could have killed him on the spot with one swipe." Thomas lifted a paw, claws extended.

"But 'Cat!' he shouted. 'Leave the younglings. They have their whole lives to live. I see that you are hungry. Take me instead and leave these innocents.'"

A tear came to the cat's eye. "By the great god of us all, that elder mouse was right. He had lived long and was ready to pass on. It was right that he sacrifice himself." He paused, allowing the message to sink in. "He walked with me some distance from the younglings. I killed him swiftly and then said the prayer of passing and thanksgiving before he sustained me."

Scrapper sat motionless for a long moment, then got up and walked to the edge of his group. They spoke for a minute in hushed tones. Returning to Thomas, he bowed his head. "The mother of the younglings says your story is true. At least as best as she can get from the younglings." He stood quietly for a moment. "By the god of us all, thank you for showing respect for our kind."

James studied the pair. "So now what, you two?"

A shriek pierced the air. The mice shrank back as one. They all instinctively looked up to see a hawk gliding past. It spotted the crowd and was turning around to descend. He must have thought it was the luckiest day of his life. There were so many potential meals gathered in one place. He folded his wings in and dropped rapidly, barely controlling the plunge. Then, with only a few feet between him and the earth, he spread his wings, gathered wind under them, and headed straight for the mass.

Thomas crouched instinctively. The bird's path took him over the cat and Scrapper. Thomas leaped. His claws raked across the hawk's stomach, and feathers fell away. The startled bird screeched and beat the air, gaining height. He looked around and spotted Thomas. Turning, he shrieked and plummeted down, talons extended.

A gunshot exploded, and the hawk lost several tail feathers. Recovering, it spun around, making a hasty retreat.

"I winged him!" James shouted as he threw another shell into the single-barrel gun. He aimed, but the bird was too far off. "Maga!"

"You idiot!" Thomas cried out. "What were you thinking? Nothing, that's what."

James looked down. "What do you mean? I got him good. He won't be back to bother us. I thought you'd be thanking me." He gripped the gun tightly.

"In so doing, you gave our whereabouts away to the Riders." Thomas shook his head. "Any gain we had is gone."

Scrapper stepped up. "Are you two running from the horse riders?" He didn't wait for an answer. "They're no friends of ours either. They think we're a snack food." He spat in the dirt. "Look, you've proven that you don't mean harm to us. That's for sure, putting your life out there to save us from that hawk. It's sad about Uncle Walt, but it's like you say. He chose the sacrifice. Lord knows what all we do for our kids."

They sat in silence for a moment.

Scrapper broke the quiet. "OK. Here's what we'll do."

. ✳ .

THE SUN WAS STILL LOW ON THE HORIZON. THE CONFRONTATION seemed to have lasted an eternity. In reality, it was less than fifteen minutes. Even so, it appeared the western clouds loomed, trying to push the sun back down.

Scrapper looked at the travelers. "You guys need to get out of here and fast. I'll get our squads together and fan out. If we can delay the Riders in any way, then that's what we'll do. There's a storm brewing, and it could hit at any time."

James nodded. Thomas held out his paw. "Thank you, my friend." Scrapper reached out, and they tapped paws. With a quick nod, they each turned to their task.

James was in the cab of the truck. Wishing to conserve the methane, he had already started the electric motors that would move them down the road. Thomas jumped in and looked out the window. "How much juice?" he asked.

James shook his head. "Not looking good, my friend. It's not looking good. I was counting on the sun to keep the batteries charged, but those clouds moving in…" He glanced toward the west. The rising sun struggled to push back the dark cumulus clouds rolling toward them, threatening heavy rains. "Best bet is to get as much distance as we can before that hits. Then look to hunker down somewhere. That's a nasty one coming."

"Red sky in morning …" Thomas hunched down.

"… sailors take warning. My gramps used to say that all the time. That was back even before the weather got all wonky." He glanced at Thomas. "Pastor Speaker claims we had a nuclear winter. That's what the scientists used to call it. They got it right about the winter. I guess they figured no one would be around to need a weather report after that. But we still have the old wisdom. Red skies in the morning, sailors—and everyone else—take warning."

Thomas looked up. "Yeah. The stories I heard tell of massive destruction. Then there was the die-off. We were lucky to survive."

"I sometimes wonder about that." James put the truck into gear. "I'm beginning to understand your opinion of people."

"Not people, humans. I like people. People like you who listen and are concerned, compassionate." Thomas shook his head. "Humans forgot their humanity, their connection to the universe."

The truck rolled steadily ahead as low-lying clouds hid the threat of a tornado. The mice dispersed and were nowhere in sight. Lightning flashed across the sky behind them.

"It's gonna be a rough one!" Thomas cowered.

"Not to worry, my friend." James's eyes gleamed. "The Riders are worse off. They gotta be sheltering already. We're gonna make it!"

A PASSING

"Physical death allows for the release of the spirit. One must die physically for the spirit to move on to its next incarnation. That opens the spirit to its next lesson."

— A BUTTERFLY IN FLIGHT: THE BIOGRAPHY OF THOMAS SPEAKER BY JAMIE LIVINGSTON

US Route 136 stretched out across the plain in front of them. Engineers of the previous century designed it to be straight as an arrow, running east and west, with occasional jogs to the north or south to connect a small town to the rest of civilization. Now those towns lay deserted. Or so it seemed.

Survivors of the Forever Wars eventually divided into two distinct camps, one good and one evil. There was no longer any room for gray areas of the law. They gave no consideration for the degree of murder, no first, second, or third degree. Not that it mattered to the dead.

James continued to guide the truck due east at a reasonable pace, swerving when a pothole or other obstacle threatened to slow them. The rhythm of the motors and the shush of the tires on the pavement had a calming effect. Clouds gathered rapidly behind them. The sun, rising into the morning sky, fought back against the darkness.

"Nice metaphor." Thomas sat on the dashboard, looking back and forth.

"What do you mean?" James glanced at his friend.

"The sun and clouds are clashing." The cat looked up through the windshield and back out the rear window. "It's a nice metaphor for good and evil, what we're experiencing. You know, dark and light, male/female, positive/negative, that whole yin-yang thing."

"What are you talking about?"

"Life is about balance. Our universe was badly out of balance. Now it's trying to repair itself."

"But … but all the destruction. And so much death. How many millions died?"

"Billions," Thomas corrected. "Billions of souls died. Probably hundreds of billions when you look beyond humans. But they all went on to the next life. That's the way of things."

James snorted. "What next life?"

Thomas grew pensive. "Call it the next life—heaven, hell, Nirvana, the Great Beyond, or whatever. People have a hard time coping with the fact that you do go on beyond this physical life. When you die, that is. Why do you have such a hard time dealing with it? Your religions all teach this truth."

James's knuckles turned white. Thunder rumbled from behind, and he glanced over his shoulder nervously. "Hell if I know!" he nearly cried. "Maybe it's because there's so much to hold on to here. Maybe it's because we're just too scared of what's on the other side. You know what I mean?"

"Yes," Thomas purred. "Oh, yes. I've made death's journey twice now, that I can remember. The first time was frightening, but I made it back to life on this earth. The second time was less so because I learned a few things. I made it back again, and here we are."

"No, no, no!" James pounded the wheel. "I was brought up to believe you go to heaven or hell. You don't come back. You can't come back."

"Ah! That's the ticket. You see, you believe what they taught you to believe. You never had reason to question if it was true or not, till now. Other religions teach differently, and their followers believe just as passionately about their faith as you do about yours." Thomas stared out the window. "What is faith? It's trust. What do you base it on? Experience is all. In the case of your religion, you have no direct experience of God in your life. So you have to take the word of those you trust. What happens when someone breaks that trust? You lose your faith."

The low hum of the electric motors was the only sound for a long while. James sighed heavily. "Now wait. Some people say they know God in their lives. What about them?"

"Do you trust those people? Why or why not?"

"I … I guess I just don't know what to believe anymore." James's voice became a whisper. "It's just that—that—" His eyes darted as he searched for words. "I mean, Mom and Dad were so convinced they'd be going to heaven when they died. They thought my one uncle would go to hell, too." He laughed. "What is heaven, anyway? Or what is hell, for that matter? It never seems to be relevant until you're about to die."

"We are stardust." Thomas looked at his friend. "You, the real you, is spirit. You inhabit this mortal body only for a short time. When you 'pass on,' as they say, it's your spirit that passes on. It goes to another experience. Is that one heaven or hell? Some religions teach that it is you who decides. You decide by the path you walk in this existence. So in that belief system, you lead a righteous life, then you go to heaven. An evil one sends you to hell." He looked out the window a moment. "Those who believe in reincarnation say that a good life leads to a better one next time around. A lousy one leads to a lower form. The life I live now is my third journey." He fell silent, waiting for his words to sink in. "As a cat, that is."

"You told me that before." James looked at Thomas. "Exactly what do you mean? Do you remember your past lives?"

"Somewhat, yes. It's more like a knowing or maybe an intuition or feeling. Déjà vu? It could be that, or rather that's the expression we use to describe it. For me, the best word is 'knowing.' That's because it is so real to me. That's what it's like to be in touch with your soul, your spirit."

"Yeah, but your soul is what goes to heaven or hell." James glanced back at the road. "It's separate from the body."

Thomas chuckled and shook his head. "That's where your human religions have failed you." He laughed again. "They talk about saving your soul in the afterlife but don't want to talk about it or even recognize it in this life." Thomas jumped to the floor and then back on the seat. "Look. It's a part of you. It *is* you! Your soul is your godstuff. It's what ties you to the universe, to God, to the *ALL*."

"I know what they taught me. And you think that we've just been ignoring it all these y-y-years, hell, all these centuries!?" James's eyes blazed. "Why would we do that? Why would we not teach our children how to connect with God? It doesn't make any sense."

"It's all about control." Thomas was firm. "It's always about control and who rules whom. With animals, it's the strongest in the group that leads and controls. You humans have thousands of examples where you allow someone to control you. Sometimes it's with money or the lack of it. Sometimes it's by ideology." He shook his head. "But your soul, that's different. You let others convince you that their beliefs are correct without even looking into it yourselves. I mean, it's about something as important as your soul, your direct connection to God. Why do you entrust that belief to anyone but yourself?"

"I ... I guess we do what our folks tell us to do." James stared at the cat. "I mean, it worked for them. They were happy, so it should've worked for me, too. Right?"

"Not quite. It's all about *your* beliefs. When your parents taught you, there was nothing to force you to question their beliefs. That's all changed now." Thomas reached out, touching James's arm. "At one time, you believed heaven was somewhere in the clouds. Humanity didn't find God waiting there once they learned to fly beyond those clouds. Then you began to understand how the universe worked, at least physically worked, and you didn't find God in that. You were looking in the wrong place all along. So you know what? It's not that God is not there; it's just that God is here." He pointed to his heart. "You are a part of God. You are God's manifestation, if you will. You are godstuff."

"I'm beginning to understand." James looked hard at Thomas. He was silent for a moment as the truck began its way up a slow rise. His eyes widened. "Yes. Of course. If we're connected on the spiritual level and truly a part of it all, how can we harm each other? Harming others harms ourselves because we are connected." His eyes lit up.

"Exactly!"

"But how do we know it's true?"

"Truth is a touchable thing. You will feel it. Then build your belief on the truth you perceive. You must decide what you believe." Thomas's claws dug into James's sleeve.

Suddenly, the truck heaved forward and down. Their stomachs lurched as the world fell away. James turned to the windshield and saw only daylight. "What the—!"

The cat instinctively leaped up, caught at the door, and jumped. His body twisted in midair as he sensed the direction of gravity. Spreading his legs, he took a position for landing and looked down. The ground was still far below. The world had gone into slow motion as he frantically searched around. He spotted the truck plummeting headfirst, took in the giant sinkhole they were falling into, saw James grasping the wheel. All this in deathly silence as the ground rushed up. Then the crash of the truck as it hit the ground. The weight in the bed caused it to pitch forward. Thomas landed and sprang up, racing for James.

"No, no, no!" It was all he could cry, tears welling in his eyes.

The truck rested upside down, steam pouring from the radiator. The dead engine pushed into the driver's compartment. James hung suspended, held in place by the steering wheel.

"James! Jimbo! Jimmy Boy!" Thomas jumped into the cab.

A low groan rattled out of James. "C-c-cat? Thomas? Thomas!" His eyes flickered open, then dimmed.

"I'm here." Thomas reached up from the roof, touching James's cheek. "So how's it going?" He tried sounding positive but knew the answer.

"N-not good. Not good." The reply wheezed out of James. There was a long pause. "What's next?"

Thomas looked straight into his face. James's eyes were barely cracked open, and his breath came in slow rasps. "Next." Thomas remained calm, holding back his tears. "Next, I pray. I pray for your safe journey. I pray to help guide your soul. I pray to meet you again." With that, he lowered his head and began his whispered prayers.

Believers passed the prayers down through the centuries, from the ancients to the present. Thomas's godstuff reached out, touched James's, calmed the fears and reassured him. They felt the connection. Thomas knew it as real, felt the fear melt away. He continued to pray, giving direction for the journey ahead, sensing the acknowledgment.

Hours passed. The threatening storm never materialized. As the sun pushed its way across the sky, the clouds began to break. A single beam broke through and pierced the truck cabin, falling on James's silent body. The warmth stirred him.

"Thomas!" he gasped.

"I'm here." The soft voice came reassuringly as he touched James's face.

"I'm leaving, Thomas."

"Yes," was the simple response. He paused. "Go peacefully, my friend."

James's breath was shallow. "Thomas." His voice was barely

audible. "I see a tunnel and … and light. Go east." The words came slowly. "We'll meet again." He exhaled. He did not inhale again.

Thomas bowed his head and continued his prayers.

THOMAS'S RESPONSE

"I cannot condone killing. How is that possible for someone whose message is to love thy neighbor? Yet, there are times, in defense of ourselves, that another's life must be taken."

— A BUTTERFLY IN FLIGHT: THE BIOGRAPHY OF
THOMAS SPEAKER BY JAMIE LIVINGSTON

T he sound of rocks falling around the truck broke Thomas's meditation. He had sat in silent vigil all night. Now the sky above was turning to gray dawn. The light had yet to reach the bottom of the sinkhole, but voices filtered down. Thomas touched James's now-cold hand. Looking into the frozen face of his friend, he said a silent goodbye and turned his attention to the voices.

"It's hard to see. I dunno, it sure looks like the truck." A male's voice penetrated the gloom.

"If that's what it is, it's gonna be useless to us, Harley." The woman sounded apprehensive.

Thomas sniffed the air, catching the scent of horse sweat. He crouched low, muscles tensed.

"Well, babe, ya never know. There might be some supplies we can use. Those damn mice carried off most of what we had."

"I can't figure out why they attacked us like that. Nearly scared the horses to death."

"An' they ruined the harnesses and saddles. Chewed right through all the straps." The man was irritated. "It's like they was possessed or somethin'." There was a pause; more dirt and stones tumbled down. "Anyway, it looks like we can get down over there. That gully seems to open up. Maybe it'll lead to the bottom."

Thomas widened his eyes to accommodate the dim light. It was the first chance he had to assess his surroundings. The sinkhole seemed to be about thirty feet around and the same deep—a perfect cylinder. It looked as if it had been there for years as, to the south, erosion had eaten away the wall and created a narrow canyon. James's truck had fallen headlong and flipped over on its roof when it struck. It now stretched halfway across the floor of the hole.

More dirt and rocks trickled down. The two shadowy figures peered from the rim and into the darkness. The sound of hooves stomping came from behind them. *The horses smell death.*

"Over there. It looks like a ramp or something is goin' into it. It might be big enough to ride the horses down."

"It's worth a try." Honda hooted. "Let's wait till the sun comes up a bit, though. We don't want to be tripping over our own feet."

"It'll be fine. I'm tired and my butt's sore from ridin' bareback. We shouldn't have ridden all night."

"Well, hell's bells. I wasn't going to stay in that place." Honda looked over her shoulder, suppressing a shudder. "Attacked by mice! That's the devil at work there."

"Damnedest thing I ever saw, that's for sure." Harley rubbed his rear. "Thousands of 'em! It was like they planned it all out or something."

"I'm just glad we could chase them all off, dirty, filthy critters." Honda clutched at her throat.

"Well, that's, er, behind us now." Harley squirmed on the horse's bareback. "Besides, I'm hungry."

"You're always hungry."

"That's because I haven't had much to eat lately. I sure hope that boy packed a lot of grub." They turned away from the edge.

Thomas stared after them, his thoughts returning to the events of the past few days. With a low growl, he determined to avenge James's death.

"Humans!" he spat as his anger grew. He forced it back. More thoughts of humans and their stupidity filled his brain. The resentment grew. He fed the feeling, giving way to it, allowing the anger to build. He fought it down a little but just a bit. The fury burned inside him, threatening to burst forth. He worked to control it.

Slowly clambering out of the truck, he kept an eye on the lip of the hole. Seeing that the Riders had stepped back, he dashed to the opening in the wall. A long, narrow corridor just wide enough for a horse and rider rose to the ground above. The walls were perfectly smooth.

This is human-made. But why? What's down here that would cause them to build a ramp into the hole?

The first light started to crawl down the walls. Thomas continued up the ramp. As he approached the entrance, he caught sight of a clue. At the top was a crude cross planted to one side. It looked like there may have been some other markers as well, but he dared not go all the way out. He trotted back down, a plan beginning to form. The walk gave him time to think. At the bottom, enough light entered the hole to allow him to see some of the detail.

Four rows of white squares dotted the far side of the wall. Thomas cautiously padded around the adjacent perimeter, glancing up to see if the Riders were back. Reaching his goal, he stopped and stared. The panels looked like small doors made of wood about three feet square with crosses or angels carved into them. Each had a name and two dates.

"It's a mausoleum! Who would turn a sinkhole into a mausoleum?" He paced along the circumference, reading as he went. It appeared each row was a different family. "Tragic, so tragic." Thomas shook his head. The date of death on each square was the same.

Thomas thought aloud. "What could have happened? Disease? That's not likely for so many on the same day. Hmm-m-m. Curious. That was about a year ago."

A horse whinnied from across the chasm. Thomas turned quickly and hissed. *The Riders! Of course. Too many died here that day. It must have been some other marauding gang. Still ...* The rage welled up in him. He hissed again. With fangs bared, he ran toward the ramp entrance.

The clomping of the horses' hooves echoed off the walls as Thomas peered up the ramp. The two Riders were slowly making their way down in a single file. Harley led and was talking excitedly.

"Jeez! Look at this, Honda. It's like an open invitation. Come on down and help yourselves, it says. How can it get any sweeter?"

"You be careful down there, Harl. It might be some kinda trap."

"Nah, it can't be." He turned toward her. "You saw yourself; there's only the truck down here. Worst it gets, we'll probably have to pull that farm boy out of it. Or not!" He laughed.

Thomas scrutinized the entrance. The ramp bottomed out a few feet in, so it was flat before it spilled into the sinkhole bottom. The ground was hard. The sun had yet to reach its apex, and the ramp was still gloomy dark while sunlight bathed the sides of the hole. The light would temporarily blind anyone coming out of the passage. Thomas crouched, tensing his muscles. He heard Harley's horse snort, felt the tension between the two of them. "Don't blow it," he whispered to himself.

"Git on now, you dumb lump of dog food!" Harley dug a heel into the side of the horse. The horse snorted again and reluctantly plodded ahead.

Thomas connected to his primitive instinct as he pushed all other thoughts from his mind.

Harley reached the end of the passage and squinted into the light. The cat leaped, screeching as loud as possible, and dug his claws into the horse's neck, raking them down. The horse reared and backed into the passage. Harley pulled on the reins, desperately trying to stay saddled. He failed as the horse rose again, blood streaming from his neck. Harley tumbled off, landing face down.

Thomas let out another loud screech that echoed up the ramp.

Honda's horse got caught up in the panic, kicked out and down. Harley turned his head to see gravity take hold of the horse, hooves pointing toward the Rider's head. It was the last thing he saw.

"Oh, my God!" Honda shouted, jumping from her horse. "Harley!"

The passage proved too tight. There was barely enough room to stand beside the horse. Honda shoved at its flank, trying to get past. Thomas screeched again, and the narrow walls bounced the howl back at the pair. In sheer panic, the animal attempted to turn. Honda, pushed against the wall, felt the full weight of the horse. The sound of cracking ribs pierced the air as she collapsed. The horse heaved herself up, hooves pawing at the wall as she turned and bolted back up the passage.

Thomas, breathing heavily, slowly regained control, the anger subsiding.

"What have you done, cat?" Harley's horse made his way into the passage and stood over him. A trickle of blood ran from the creature's neck, but it was already congealing, a mere flesh wound.

Thomas ignored the question as he surveyed the scene. Harley's lifeless body lay just inside the entrance, his skull crushed. Just beyond, Honda had collapsed. A low moan came from her. Thomas crouched low and slowly approached. He peered into her face. Blood trickled out of her mouth. Her eyes fluttered open, and she tried to focus.

"I know you, cat," she gasped.

Thomas stepped back and hunkered down. "Yes!" His voice was a low growl as his tail writhed back and forth in confidence. "You should recognize me. You've now killed more than one of my friends. Who knows how many others?"

But Honda lacked the gift, and Thomas's words were mere growls and hisses to her. It didn't matter to Thomas if she understood or not. He watched her eyes dim. She coughed blood in a final fit that racked her body. With a low moan, the Rider expired.

"What have you done, cat?" The horse, now standing over the bodies, repeated.

"Assisting Karma," Thomas snapped. "These were evil humans, and their evil has returned to them."

"What have you done, cat?" the horse repeated.

Thomas breathed in, exasperated. "Look, you two were with them all the way. You saw what they did to others—the stealing, the killing, and worse."

"What have you done, cat?" The question echoed off the walls.

The sound pushed Thomas back. "I did not kill them! I was angry. I attacked, but I did not kill them."

"What have you done, cat?"

The question now lodged in his thoughts. *What have you done? What have you done? What have you done?*

"ALL RIGHT! Yes, I took two lives. They were hunting for me. I'm a predator, so I defended myself. It's what living creatures do. They try to stay alive. You, horse, you run away. Is that protecting yourself? No! Running away is all it is. I took a stand. I defended myself. And who knows how many others were saved by my actions? Does that make me guilty of something? I don't think so." Thomas was panting from his outburst.

"It is what it is." The horse lowered his head and sniffed the bodies. "Their spirits have fled. It's too late to pray for them."

"It's too late to pray?" Thomas laughed. "Would you have prayed for them?"

The horse remained silent.

The barking of a dog interrupted the silence. Thomas and the horse turned toward the sound. A golden Labrador was up at the edge of the sinkhole.

"Hey! Over here!" the dog shouted. The sound of human voices echoed down the walls, and several figures appeared at the edge. They gestured as they took in the scene, noting the wreck. From their vantage point, they were unable to see inside the ramp entrance.

The dog ran to the top of the ramp. Honda's horse stood there, quaking with fright.

"What happened here?" The dog peered into the darkness of the corridor.

"The horror, the horror!" the horse wailed. "I don't know. Down there. Look. Look!"

The dog gave up trying to make sense of what she was saying and ran down the ramp. Coming upon Honda's body, he stopped abruptly and sniffed. "What the …! What's going on here?" He looked around and saw Harley's body. Running over to it and snuffling, he let out a howl. "By God!"

Spotting Harley's horse, he called out, "Hey, you there. Tell me what happened. Who are these humans? Speak up!"

The horse shook his head sadly. "Death and destruction." Then, thinking a bit, he added morosely, "Death and destruction again."

"Again!" The dog choked. "Still is more like it. Humans keep killing each other off. What's the point? Can you tell me?" He strode in front of the horse.

"No, but he can." The horse nodded at Thomas.

The dog jumped in surprise. The smell of death had filled his head so that he was unable even to identify the horse odor, let alone recognize this cat who now sat calmly in front of him.

"Good morning, sir." Thomas had regained his composure and now spoke quietly. "My name is Thomas. You are?"

"My name is Michael." The dog planted his four feet firmly as he faced the cat. The hair on his back bristled. "Call me Mike. Everyone does. Be honest. What do you know about all this?"

Mike came face-to-face with Thomas, but the cat was unfazed. He nodded toward the truck. "My companion and I were running from these two." He tilted his head toward the bodies. "They wanted the truck. They're Riders, pillagers, raiders. Call them what you want. It doesn't matter, not anymore. They are gone, and so is my companion."

Michael ran over to the truck where James's body hung pinned behind the steering wheel. He sniffed all around the pickup. "Seems you're telling the truth. There's no scent of those two over here. They took the easy way down, and it was hours after this truck fell in." He glanced up to the edge of the hole. "I tried to tell my people they needed a fence around this place. But they don't understand our language."

"Not one of them?" Thomas was disappointed.

"Not a one," he snorted. "Oh, sometimes one or another will be able to read my eyes but to listen to what I tell them? No, they don't have the gift."

"James did." Thomas choked back a cry.

"What?" Michael's eyes grew wide. "How? When? I mean, you knew him, right? How could he be gifted? Looks like a farm boy to me."

Thomas patted Michael's paw.

"Easy!" he commanded. "Does it matter now? He's gone. I'm not sure I'll be able to meet him again. But I have to try. We were trying to join up with Thomas Speaker."

"Ah! The prophet." Michael stood. "I've heard him on the radio. The people of our commune have been following him. In a way, he saved my life."

"How so?"

"Last year, we were attacked by a group of raiders. Their

leader is a character who calls himself Grizzly." He turned toward the graves. "This is where my people buried their comrades." His voice lowered. "I caught an arrow in my leg. Our nurse was able to save me. She said she learned everything she did by listening to Thomas Speaker. So, in a way, he saved me."

"They passed the knowledge on. That's how it works."

"But what of the killing? Are we no better than humans?" It was the horse. He had come from the entrance and gone unnoticed. Now he looked back. "Your humans are coming."

Thomas was ashamed. "Friend horse …"

"My name is Chadsworth, but my friends call me Chad."

"Er, sorry." Thomas lowered his head. "Chadsworth, may I call you Chad?"

"Knowing what I know now, I would be honored to be your friend, Thomas. Or should I call you Mr. Thomas? How about Mr. T?" Chad began to rattle on. "My mate's name is Melissa. She's also called Mel or Melly. Sometimes I call her Smelly Melly when we're funnin' with each other. She'll call me—"

"Chad!" Michael barked. "My people are coming."

"My apologies, sir." Chad composed himself. "It's been a long, hard life. I get carried away when I have friends to talk with. And now I have friends. I understand. You needed to do what you did. There was no other way. You have freed my Mel and me from those two horrible humans. Thank you!"

Michael sniffed at Chad. "That's a nasty scratch you have there, friend."

"Yes." Chad flinched as a fly landed. "Mr. T had to do it. It was part of the plan to kill these evil humans. I'll be okay."

"You are probably right." The dog sat back on his haunches. "We learned a lot about evil when Grizzly attacked us. As for you, not to worry, my people will fix you up. Look how well my leg healed. The lady has the hands of an angel. Let me tell …"

"Gentlemen, please!" Thomas interrupted. "I need to leave, but first, I must be sure that they'll take care of James's body. I have prayed for his soul's journey. Michael, will your people show respect?"

"I'm certain of it." Michael turned toward the truck. "They call our place a commune, even though they can't communicate with us. I'll do my best to see to it."

"My thanks. I'm afraid they would try to make me a pet or some other silliness. I hope you understand."

"Oh, I do, I do. In all honesty, being a pet to this group isn't half bad. They'd let you sleep inside during the winter, give you plenty to eat. You might want to rethink your plan."

"Thank you, but no. I must go. I believe I have a mission that will benefit all of us if I succeed. Now that I've found James once, I pray I can find him again or at least others like him."

"Godspeed then," said Michael.

"Godspeed," Chadsworth chimed in.

Thomas ducked under the truck just as three human males came from the ramp. They were leading Melissa. The discovery of the two Riders had delayed them. Spotting the wreck, they made a beeline toward it.

Michael ran over to greet them, jumping up on the leader. The distraction allowed Thomas enough time to run to the wall and hide in a small depression. The humans, absorbed in their new find, immediately began figuring out the best way to remove James's body. Thomas skirted the edge and made his way up the ramp. Pausing momentarily, he stepped to the lip. There, perched on the rim, he peered down, confirming their treatment of his friend.

The men worked quickly. Pushing on the seat, they gingerly removed James's body and, within minutes, had it laid on the ground. One found a blanket in the cab and gently placed it over the corpse. Thomas picked up on pieces of the conversation. Two men went back to the ramp, pulled the Riders' bodies out, and laid them to the side. They used blankets from the horses to cover the pair.

More conversation followed. One of the men gathered Chad

and Mel together and headed to the top of the ramp. The humans did not burden them with the corpses.

Thomas ran back to the entrance. As the horses plodded by, he caught Chad's eye. "We're going to their commune. This man is going for help while the other two try to piece together what happened. Silly people! If they would listen, I could explain it. Anyway, they're talking about burying your friend and the others at a different cemetery. This place is sacred ground for them. I don't know what they're going to do with your truck. It's too big to fit the ramp. Maybe they'll make the ramp bigger. Who knows?"

The human heard Chad's talk as whinnies and snorts. "There, there. Easy does it." He calmed the horse. "I'm taking you to Ms. Jessica. She'll take care of that nasty scratch. Then we'll get you two a decent meal. You'll see. Maybe even a bath before the day's through."

Thomas watched as the horses exited the ramp and turned north. He returned to his perch and watched as the other two men went through the truck's contents. One reached in and clicked the key back and forth, then tried the radio. It crackled to life, and a familiar voice flowed out.

"People used to talk about their rights all the time but never about their responsibilities. We are each individually responsible for ourselves as well as our neighbors," Pastor Speaker began his teaching.

Thomas remembered the task at hand. Satisfied that James's body was in good hands, he said a final goodbye and turned toward the east.

THE PASTOR SPEAKS

"As I pursued my spiritual studies, I came to realize that all of our existing religions had a common root. Each one speaks of love as their basis. Not one will command their followers to hate. So why were we fighting among ourselves?"

— A BUTTERFLY IN FLIGHT: THE BIOGRAPHY OF THOMAS SPEAKER BY JAMIE LIVINGSTON

The pastor's voice was calm, reassuring, as it crackled from the nearly dead Ford Ranger.

"Turn it up!" the one villager commanded. "It's Pastor Speaker."

"Just what I was thinking, Brother Andrew. I feared we would miss his broadcast this day."

"Yea, Brother Mark. The pastor always has some timely advice. I'm amazed at how his words strike home."

"Amen to that." Andrew twisted the dial so that they could both hear.

Back at his studio, the pastor read from prepared notes. "The question is asked early on in the Holy Bible, am I my brother's keeper?

"It seems like a silly question, nowadays, don't you think?" He let the question sink in for a moment. "Our very lives depend on each of us watching out for the other. But it was not always so. Before society's collapse, people would question who their brother was. They assumed they needed some sort of familial connection to another to deserve the title 'brother.'

"Hmph. Even within each religion's membership, there was division. Instead of celebrating the diversity of the human family, we looked upon each other with mistrust." He turned the page.

"Rather than discussing and understanding our differences, we used them to divide us. In place of embracing each other as brothers and sisters in the great human family, we shoved each other away, using those beautiful differences as reasons to break us apart." He took on a sterner tone.

"Our religions became compromised. They no longer guided their flocks along a spiritual path. Religious leaders sought only power and wealth for themselves. And they used us, their followers, to gain and retain it. Is it any wonder then that we came to judgment? It was not a punishment by God, but more of a coming to terms with how we lived our values.

"It doesn't take a PhD to understand God's teachings." The pastor slammed his fist down. "God said, 'Love me and love one another.' It seems simple enough to me. Our political leaders ignored our shared moral values. Greed and envy took control. Even our religious leaders fell under this influence. We allowed them to control us. We lacked the courage to stand for what we knew was right, what we felt in our very souls."

He took a deep, calming breath. "I remember receiving my calling to be your guide only after much soul-searching and prayer. I studied the teachings of our spiritual authorities and their disciples. My only hope is that I can pass their wisdom along to you."

"Life is a journey. I don't mean that it is simply a physical one. No. Most importantly, it is a spiritual journey. Consider it a pilgrimage to enlightenment. You each, individually, must make your own journey. Along the way, you will meet others, also on their separate journeys. It is what makes us all brothers and sisters —knowing that our different paths lead to the same destination." He pointed upward. "This is why we embrace each other, why we celebrate our differences. We learn and grow with each person we touch. Each of us is responsible for passing this knowledge on to others. Teach your children. And your children's children. Let God's true teaching prevail. We are all brothers."

Thomas paused. "Well, that's enough of my thoughts for today. I hope that you share them and remember to love the ones you're with.

"Now I believe my assistant, Alice, has some good news for you. Alice?"

"Oh, indeed I do, Pastor Thomas." The girl's excitement radiated from her voice. "Several weeks ago, one of our scavenging teams came across an abandoned radio station. I had no idea what it was they brought me until I did some research. It was surprising to find that music was once stored on these large black discs. They're called 'vinyls,' and they're played on this box with a circular plate on top." She shrugged. "Think of them as big CDs, I guess, and you only need this arm and needle doohickey on a spinning table to play them.

"Anyway, my friend Austin is studying engineering, and he was able to hook the player box up so we can listen to this music and play it for our listeners. I'm so excited! There are thousands of these vinyls, and the music is incredible. I could play it all day!"

Thomas's voice warmed. "Well, such enthusiasm can't go unrewarded. I'm old enough to remember vinyl records, and I've listened to some of them already. They really do bring back memories. Perhaps we can extend the broadcast a bit longer. What's up first?"

"Well, you know how I'm all about the music?" Alice couldn't hide her eagerness. "This song here says it all. It's fun. It has a great beat. And wait till it gets to the horns. The band is called The O'Jays—"

"HA!" They're from a town just north of here. Ohio proud, I must say!"

"Yeah?" Alice giggled. "I thought you might like that fact. And you, my listeners, I hope you enjoy this. It's called 'I Love Music.' Here are The O'Jays."

There was a click as Alice flipped a switch, and the turntable began to spin around. A smooth drumbeat rolled and voices sang out in harmony.

Hundreds of miles away, Brother Andrew stood and began to sway to the tune. Stomping his feet in time to the beat, he turned in a circle.

Brother Mark stood and began a sort of jig as he moved toward the truck.

Andrew laughed at the sight. "It's true what Papa said about you white folks."

"What's that, brother?" Mark swung his arms back and forth, snapping his fingers.

"You don't have much rhythm in your soul, man."

"Oh? Well, I can still enjoy it, can't I?"

"That you can, brother. That you can."

"Speaking of soul—" Mark reached into the truck and turned the radio down. "We've got work to do." He nodded toward the three covered bodies.

"You're right, brother. There will be more help coming from the mission soon. Maybe we can keep the radio on? After all, music makes for light work. Even if it is a grim task."

"This is true. I wonder what they'll play next."

CHRISTIAN CHANCE

"I love animals. If I do say so myself, I think they love me. Sometimes I feel, yes, that's the correct word, I *feel* a connection with them. It's kind of symbiotic, really."

— *A BUTTERFLY IN FLIGHT: THE BIOGRAPHY OF THOMAS SPEAKER* BY JAMIE LIVINGSTON

"No!" he cried. "No! No! No! I can't leave Mama. I can't. I can't! Don't you see?" Christian tossed the ragged blankets off and lay still, listening. Late-afternoon light filtered through the crates, boxes, and other debris that made up his hidey-hole. The voice from his dream had stopped. He felt along the floor, found his marking stick against the wall, and squatted.

The night terror about Mama still held him captive. Wiping the sweat from his brow, he sighed and looked at the wall. He had it covered with markings, groups of six small, vertical lines with a diagonal through them. Mama taught him to count the days this way. She called each group a bundle or week. When he had collected fifty-two of these bundles, Mama drew a box around the group and numbered it.

Christian looked down the wall at his thirty-four boxes, then put a diagonal stroke through his current bundle. He gripped the marking stick and stared at the fourth box from the beginning. It was extra-big, a thick, black mark separating it from the rest. *So many years without you, Mama.* Dropping the marker, he collapsed on the floor. "Mama!" The sob tore from his throat.

He was thirteen years old when Mama brought him here, away from their beautiful home where they hid out the first year of the troubles. This warehouse, built for a bygone era, lay next to a series of railroad tracks. "There ain't nobody going to use those anymore," she declared, staring down the stretch of steel ribbons.

The relic consisted of solid brick and mortar with thick concrete floors and ceilings. Aging pockmarks on the walls attested to recent extreme violence. People tried to use it as their fortress, fought their battles, and moved on. *Or maybe died. That's what Mama said.*

When the troubles started, Mama stopped smiling and got all serious. She kept a tiny radio tuned in to some preacher man who warned about the difficulties to come. And he was dead-on right about everything. Folks had turned on each other, fought for silly things like cars and gas, and even killed each other. Finally, they just up and left town. That's when Mama began collecting stuff. He didn't understand, but she said they would be useful— like batteries, an old wind-up alarm clock, cans of soup, toilet paper, and on and on.

Initially, she made a game of it with Christian. She called it "Exploring," and they went out into the neighborhood and into other people's homes without asking.

It was odd. Mama brought him up to respect other people's things, and now she was sneaking in at night and creeping around and just taking things. "Ain't nobody round to use them no more," she explained.

They found the warehouse on one of the exploring trips. It was raining that night. It started as the kind of rain Christian loved to play in, dancing in the yard and splashing in puddles of muddy water. But soon, the rain turned hard, and lightning flashed. He could tell Mama was scared then. Her eyes got big, and he could see the whites as the sky lit up. She grabbed his hand and began to run. Just run. Other nights she had a plan of where to go, which places she would stop in. Now, she just ran, and it was all Christian could do to keep pace.

Breathing hard, they stumbled through the open bay door of the warehouse. It was the first shelter they came upon, and Mama rushed into it, not even stopping to listen for others like she always did. They went to the back, and she turned as another flash from the storm lit up the area ever so briefly. She put her back against the wall and slid down in a heap. Then she began to cry. Not just the upset kind of crying but the body-shaking, deep sobbing sort like he used to have when other kids had picked on him and picked on him and wouldn't stop till the teacher made them.

Christian still held her hand, sitting beside her. He reached out and patted her head. "It's OK, Mama," he muttered. "It's just a storm."

She looked gravely at him. He couldn't tell if it was rain or tears coming from her eyes, but he could see a deep sadness. "Oh, baby, you know Mama hates the thunder and lightning." She tried to smile, but Christian saw through it. He wrapped his arms around her neck, just like she would do to him. "It'll be all right, Mama. I promise." He tried to sound reassuring. Another sob caught in her throat, and her body shuddered. "Oh, Christian, you are so very special to me," she murmured.

Christian now lay curled up, chewing on his fist. The voice had finally stopped. It spoke to him for three nights now, inside his head. Ever so softly, urging him to leave. Instinctively, he reached inside his shirt, rubbing the mark on his breast. "What to do, Mama?" he whimpered. "What do I do?"

"It's time, Christian. You've stayed here long enough." The voice again! This time it was real, not just in his head. It came from outside, like a soft purr.

"Mama?" He looked toward the entrance of his hidey-hole.

Was it her talking? After all this time, how could she be there? Was it really Mama?

"Now, Christian!" the voice insisted—just like Mama would when she lost patience. Would this one smile at him like Mama did? He remembered how, as a child, he would grin mischievously, then go to her and hug her leg. She would look down, and there would be that smile lighting up her face.

"OK, Mama." He sat up, nodded curtly, and crawled into the entranceway. When Mama built their den, she had stacked empty boxes and trash bags filled with old papers to form a kind of igloo. The entrance was a short tunnel, just high enough for him to crawl through on his hands and knees.

Christian stopped halfway through and shook his head, trying to pull out of his reverie. *Special, always special.* Everyone had called him that—teachers, relatives, classmates. He would beam at them with his toothy grin and wide-eyed innocence. He was so special that they had him attend special education classes where he met other special kids.

It made no sense to him. Mama's Good Book, the one she read to him on quiet afternoons, said everyone was special. When he had asked her about it, she agreed. "The Good Book says we are all special in God's eyes, Christian."

Christian looked up at her. "If we're so special in God's eyes, then why aren't we so special in people's eyes?" Mama just stared down at him, wondering. With a big hug, she said, "That's the whole point, honey. That's the whole point. We're supposed to take these lessons from the Good Book and live them. I guess most folks forgot about that."

The voice outside harrumphed. "Are you coming out or not?" Christian crawled to the end of the tunnel and peered into the gloom. The sun had set, and the moon was beginning its journey across the sky. This was Christian's waking world, away from the sun and the bad people who prowled under it.

"Who?" His voice trembled. Squinting intently, he saw no one.

"A friend." The voice came from the darkness.

Christian crouched, ready to spring. He felt for his knife tucked at his side, found it, and gripped the handle tightly. His eyes darted around the dim warehouse. There was no one to be seen. Then he caught the briefest movement. It was down low to the ground and moving slowly, deliberately. The moon finally showed itself, and a small beam of light fell about five feet from Christian. The creature stepped into it and sat.

"Hello, Mr. Chance. My name is Thomas."

Christian sat back and stared incredulously. "Wha? I ... you ... you're a kitty cat!"

The cat chuckled. "I get that a lot on first meeting."

Kitties don't laugh. Thoughts whirled around Christian's head. *They don't laugh, and they don't talk either. What is this? How could I be talking to a kitty?* He crawled a bit out from the tunnel, curiosity getting the better of him.

Thomas sat on his haunches, tail poised over his head. The tip would twitch occasionally. The minutes passed as they stared at each other.

"You know," Thomas broke the silence, "when it comes to staring contests, we cats win nine times out of ten."

Christian jerked to attention. "H-h-how ...?"

"It's a Zen thing," Thomas joked. "I simply go into my meditation posture. The opponent thinks I'm staring, so he tries to stare back. He blinks first because he's trying not to. I am simply meditating."

"No." Christian shook his head. "That's not what I meant." *How could I be talking to a kitty? Kitties don't talk. That was a matter of fact.*

"It's what we were discussing." Thomas stood and stretched lazily. "I said cats win staring contests, and you asked how. If you wanted to know something else, then ask a different question."

Christian relaxed a little and sat cross-legged in front of Thomas, warming to this new creature. He peered into the semi-darkness, trying to make out the cat. Occasionally light would glint off an eye, and a white star appeared on the cat's left ear.

Christian rubbed the mark on his chest, wondering as he took this all in. He realized he had seen this kitty before.

"You're the one in my dreams. I saw you there. You were talking to me, telling me something. What? I can't remember."

"Yes," Thomas purred, "that's how we first met. It's how I usually first meet people, in my dreams, that is. I dreamt of you and followed that dream here."

His tail flicked back and forth as he rose. "But enough talk. Are you up for walking at night? We must be on our journey."

"What?" Christian sat bolt upright. "I can't leave my mama!" Tears came to his eyes. "Not leaving Mama." His voice trembled.

"Ah!" Thomas sat back down. "We must deal with that, Christian." His voice was calming.

"Deal with what? Mama said … Mama will … Mama is … Mama is—"

"Mama is dead." Fixing on Christian's eyes, Thomas drew a deep breath. "Remember your dream, Christian? Remember the one about Mama? Think hard. Remember."

Christian burst into tears.

"No! Mama, no! The dogs. They were bad dogs!" The tears flowed down his cheeks. He didn't try to wipe them. A sob welled up.

"There's more." Thomas wiped at his eye and choked back his own tears, knowing this was necessary. "Remember, Christian; there's more to remember."

"The bad men!" Christian rolled into a ball, biting his fist. "They came with the dogs. They weren't there before. Where'd they come from? Mama was always careful. Always. But they caught her. She had to pee. That's all, just went to pee, and they caught her. Where'd they come from? I heard her yell. I watched it from here. I was so scared!" He rolled back and forth.

"Remember!" Thomas commanded.

"No!" Christian cried. "No. I don't want to remember. Bad men do bad things. No! Not to Mama. I was so scared. I didn't help. I was so scared."

"You couldn't do anything, Christian," Thomas consoled him. "You know that. You were too young. They would have hurt you too, just like they hurt Mama. And you would be—"

"Dead!" Christian sat straight up. "They hurt her dead. They did everything that bear man said to do. Ugly, dirty, bad man!"

"His name is Grizzly," Thomas spoke flatly. "He is the evilest person this world has known for quite some time. The other men, the bad men, they're scared of him too. That's why they do what he tells them to do."

"No!" Christian was on his feet, pacing. "No. Mama says that the Good Book tells us to be different, to make choices, to choose to be good. Even bad men can choose to be good. Those men wanted to be bad. They wanted to!" He pounded his fist into his palm.

Crouching down, he looked Thomas square in the eye. "You are wrong, kitty. Bad men choose to be bad. Those men—they took Mama. They—they did bad things to her. They did bad, horrible things. I … I saw her, and I could tell. They brought her back to the bear-man, her clothes all ripped apart. Her face, they beat her, then they gave her to him. Do you know what he did? I saw it. My two eyes saw it. I saw what he did. And you know what Mama did? After he finished with her? She looked him square on like I'm looking at you, and she spitted in his ugly face. That's what she did. That's what my Mama did." The anger turned to tears, his voice a whisper now. "That's what my Mama did."

Thomas blinked and backed off. "I saw it in your dream, Christian. It's hard knowing and not being able to do anything. To dream of what you should have done, maybe could have done, yet were unable to do so."

Christian ignored Thomas. "He killed her. He just stuck a knife in her, wiped it off, and walked away. Just like that. Like it was something he did all the time."

He stared into the distance, seeing it all play out again. "Then they dragged her outside. Said the dogs would enjoy a warm meal. I never saw Mama again." He collapsed, whimpering. Thomas approached and nuzzled his cheek. Christian reached out and stroked his head till Thomas began to purr.

"Oh, kitty …" He pulled Thomas close. "My head hurts. An- and my heart —"

"Is broken. I understand. It's okay, kiddo. It's okay. It's been rough on you, and you're exhausted. Let's go in and rest awhile." They retreated to Christian's hidey-hole, and the man lay down, wiping at his tears.

Thomas climbed onto Chris's chest and stretched out. "Sleep now. Sleep softly now." Two heartbeats became one as a warm glow enveloped the pair. Chris lay his hand on Thomas and slept.

WHAT WENT WRONG

"There is an old folk tune that talks about how we justify our actions, any actions, by claiming that God is on our side. Imagine that!"

— A BUTTERFLY IN FLIGHT: THE BIOGRAPHY OF
THOMAS SPEAKER BY JAMIE LIVINGSTON

"Hello, hello, hello." The pastor began his daily broadcast. "My name is Thomas Speaker." He nodded to Alice B., who took up the introduction, advising all listeners of their broadcast frequencies. The pastor only half listened, imagining a distant listener fine-tuning their radio. *Station call letters went away along with most everything else. Still, it's good to let people know how to find us.*

Alice handed the mic back over to Thomas. "I want to talk about the past in today's lecture." He shuffled through the notes in front of him. "I've been discussing contemporary history with some of our younger residents here in the village. Many of them were too young to understand the Forever Wars or even the final days. They or their parents were lucky enough to have survived those times. We all were. Although"— he smiled, looking across to Alice—"some may question that appraisal. What's fortunate about being among the only humans left on the planet? It may be cliché, but all I can say to that is we're alive, and where there's life, there's hope. So we press on.

"A wise person once said something to the effect of 'those who forget history are bound to repeat it.'" Thomas shifted in his chair, found a comfortable spot, and reflected a moment.

"I got to thinking about this because recently, some of our people rehabbed the old courthouse building here in town and are opening our very own library. Fortunately for us, our town is close to several colleges and universities. Since they're, um, unoccupied, we're transferring the library collections found there and installing them here, where most people can access them. The history section alone takes up a full room.

"I found that, unfortunately, the historical reference material only covers up to the beginning of the twenty-first century. After that, most news of the day was in electronic format, stored in massive databases, now all gone." He paused, contemplating where he was heading.

"I want to applaud the efforts of several of our young pioneers who are interviewing and recording the elders of our community, obtaining an oral history." He checked his notes, ticking off an item. "I'm afraid that history will be a bit limited. Most of us elders were in no position to be direct witnesses to those events that led to the nuclear annihilation. You see, the bombs never reached us here in the heartland. However, we can make some educated guesses.

"Here's what happened: The Forever Wars followed directly after the Second World War. That one ended in 1945 of the past era and saw the destruction of most of the industrialized world. The United States of America, God rest her soul, found itself the next great empire-builder.

"Back then, one did not simply decide to build an empire and then go off and do it. You would need a Ghengis Khan for that. Ha!" Thomas's eyes gleamed as he picked up the pace. "Even so, the last two world wars were fought by colonial powers trying to extend their own empires. And those poor folks they colonized had just about had enough of the nonsense.

"You see, the United States of America needed to develop a new method of conquest. One that gave them economic control while allowing the people to believe they were free. No matter where you lived, you would need to trust that your decisions were based solely on your own free will." The pastor became animated, poking at the air.

"Enter God. Or rather, the political leaders in the US of A, God rest her soul, introduced God into their plans. They figured that when their citizens truly believed that God was by their side, they would be ready for a little empire-building. So the campaign began.

"There was a declaration that God would keep a watchful eye on their great nation. They said it in a pledge every child and adult had to take." Feeling the passion build, he jumped to his feet. "Once stated, of course, it HAD to be true.

"Reminders were printed on every piece of currency, too. As a side note, by the beginning of the twenty-first century, people referred to the paper dollar as 'God's Greenback.' Such was the trust put into it.

"Needless to say, none of this could have happened without the religious leaders giving their okay. I mean, secular governments couldn't just abscond with God without His permission." Thomas held the microphone tightly, recalling the days when he preached to a live congregation. He imagined the crowd before him.

Calming a bit, he sat down. "Actually, this part was pretty easy. Heh, they applied the Golden Rule. 'He who has the gold, rules,' that is. The government had the gold, so churches were made tax-exempt. And so were their leaders. They could make as much money as they wanted and not have to pay taxes on it. Judas Iscariot would have wept. He sold Jesus out for a measly thirty pieces of silver. He should have held out for more."

Thomas hung his head and paused, allowing his words to sink in.

"Now, you can't try to control the world without someone taking notice. Russia got a little irked when their empire fell apart during the Cold War with the United States, God rest her soul. That's a whole other story, but basically, a Cold War is one where you don't shoot at anyone. You just build up your weapons pile taller than the other guys' so that each of you is afraid to start a fight. Russia went broke building theirs. America did too, but they put their trust in God. Remember? It said so right on their money. So they just printed more money, trusting in God to cover the tab." The pastor shook his head ruefully.

"Here's where black gold comes in. Some called it Texas Tea. Oil, that is. Back in those days, every industrialized nation depended on the stuff to run everything. And every country on God's green Earth wanted to be in on the action. The best place to get crude oil was from the Middle East. They had so much of it, it seemed to ooze from the ground. The only problem was the Middle East countries didn't want to give the stuff away. No, they wanted a fair deal and respect. Since they didn't get either, they played Russia and the US for suckers, traded oil for weapons, then pointed those weapons on their exploiters."

The pastor drew in his breath. "I know, I know. I'm rambling. Maybe you don't care about any of this. But you need to understand this. It took years, no, decades for all of this to happen. There were many small wars sponsored by the major powers. That's why we called it The Forever Wars; they went on and on and on. Truth be told, these regional wars' sponsors set them up for weapons testing, proving grounds, if you will. We went decades like this until someone got trigger-happy with a nuclear bomb." Thomas's shoulders sagged.

"There are no records left from those final days of the destruction. Suffice to say, once one bomb went off, many others followed. It was afterward, when society fell apart, that took me by surprise. I believed we could rebuild, even after a nuclear war.

No one predicted that utter chaos would follow—riots in the streets, the cities' infrastructure failing, disease—all hope abandoned."

The pastor choked back a tear. "Well, never mind that. We are the survivors of those times. Maybe your parents and other loved ones have since passed on. Here we are now. My hope is that we can rebuild human society. This time we have to do it right. We must learn to get along with our fellow humans."

Another more hopeful smile crossed his face as he looked over at his assistant. "I think that's enough on that subject for now. I'll have other thoughts to share in the future. We do have some good news. Our town council has voted to power the station for an extra hour. That is so Alice B. here can play more music for all of us. What's up, Alice?"

"Thank you, Pastor Thomas." Alice's voice had a way of brightening the darkest thoughts. "I got to thinking about your lesson, and I'd like to follow up with some old folk music. It seems appropriate, especially because this song is about how times change. This musician was famous over seventy years ago. His name is Bob Dylan."

THE JOURNEY CONTINUES

"It's a unique feeling, the sensation of being in touch with another. It's almost like your two souls are interacting, becoming one. It is pure bliss!"

— *A BUTTERFLY IN FLIGHT: THE BIOGRAPHY OF THOMAS SPEAKER* BY JAMIE LIVINGSTON

The morning sunlight filtered into the burned-out basement where the two friends sought shelter the night before. Christian blinked awake and looked at Thomas. *How did this cat find me?*

Their first meeting had left Christian emotionally drained. The memories of growing up in the abandoned city with his mama were vivid. Being forced to relive her terrible death caused something to snap in him. His head had ached worse than anything he had ever experienced. The cat had grown alarmed and allowed him to sleep it off.

When he awoke the following morning, he felt refreshed and somehow different. Things seemed clearer. Like a fog lifted or, maybe, a curtain pulled back. Thomas had shrugged and said something about godstuff, then hurried Christian to packing.

They left Tecumseh, Nebraska, behind the previous day, heading due east. Thomas insisted they stay away from the highway, so they kept to the old farmland, now overgrown with small trees and shrubs. Along the way, Thomas tried to describe how he came upon Christian. The cat noted that Christian should think of it as if Thomas was a magnet being pulled toward steel, with Christian being the steel. He simply had to feel the pull and follow it.

It was beyond Christian. *What about hearing him in my dreams?* That puzzled the man.

Thomas explained that it was their godstuff talking to each other. That made no sense to Christian, so Thomas went on to tell how it was like being soul brothers. That was something Christian understood. Mama had always explained that even if they were apart, she would hold Christian in her heart and soul as only a mama could do. *So this cat is a lot like Mama. 'Cause sometimes I can feel her with me, and I talk to her then. I know she listens.*

Now Christian sighed contentedly. Thomas, who had been sleeping beside him, rolled over and stretched. "Time to be up and on our way," the cat announced. "It looks to be a pleasant day out there."

A nearby stream provided fresh water. Pulling off his shirt, Christian went to it and splashed water under his arms and in his face. Walking back, he toweled himself off with his shirt.

"Say, Mr. Thomas, do you suppose we can follow this stream? Next time we stop for the night, I'd like to wash out my clothes."

"Of course, Christian. My apologies. I forgot people need to do that sort of thing."

Thomas looked closely at Christian. "What's that mark on your chest?"

"This?" Christian sat down and rubbed at the spot over his heart. "Mama called it a birthmark."

"Fascinating."

Christian rubbed at the spot. "Hey, Mr. Thomas. It looks just like the one on your ear. How about that?"

"It is interesting. I wonder if it means anything." The cat gazed at the mark.

Christian beamed. "You know, it feels a little warm. It started to do that when we met. Maybe it's that godstuff you were talking about. It's just a way of it showing itself."

Thomas walked over and sniffed at it. "Yes, perhaps it is."

A quick breakfast followed. Christian had a large backpack full of supplies gathered in his many forays into town. He pulled out a can of beans and wieners and popped the lid. Finding a spoon, he dug in.

"Mama always told me to get the cans with the pop tops." He yanked the tab and offered the can to Thomas.

Thomas peered inside, smelling the contents. "Is that stuff still good after all these years?" He sniffed again and began to drool. "Hmph. It seems to be okay. Well, maybe a wiener or two. And, by the way, my friends call me 'Thomas.' No need for any of that 'Mister' stuff."

Christian pulled the spoon from his mouth and swallowed. "Does that mean we're friends, Mr. Thomas?"

"Why, yes, it most certainly does, Mr. Chance."

"Well, you can call me Chris if you want." Christian grinned. "All my real friends do. But, with all due respect, I should still call you 'Mister.' It shows respect, and Mama always said to respect my elders."

"So be it! Mr. Thomas and Chris. Chris and Mr. Thomas. We're just a couple of caballeros!" the cat declared.

After finishing off the can, they cleaned up, hiding any trace that they had been there. "Better to be safe than sorry," Thomas commented.

"Mama always used to say that," Christian remembered sadly. "Never mind that," he said with finality, more to himself than the cat. "No more living in the past. Let's go." He shouldered the backpack.

Not wishing to push the issue, Thomas jumped up. "Right you are, my friend."

As they headed into the rising sun, the two companions scavenged for food, keeping in sight of each other. They did not stray too far from the road, as it always led to a house or farm. Usually, the home's shelves were empty.

Mother Nature, however, could not be deterred, even by such a cataclysmic event as the end of human civilization. They found that many of the homes still had gardens of sorts. Some vegetables reseeded and persisted. These ripened and continued to provide nourishment to the remaining wildlife.

The days passed, and the two travelers fell into a routine of sorts. Always heading east, guided by the sun in the morning and the eastern star at night. Slowly working their way toward the preacher's settlement.

One evening, they found shelter in a grove of trees, and Christian stretched a length of rope between two. He began cutting branches off a fir to lay over it, creating a lean-to. "How will we know when we find it?" Christian asked.

Thomas looked up to the darkening sky in the east. "There. See that bright star? We keep following it." They had grown close over the days. So much so that each knew what the other was talking about, almost before they spoke a word. "First, there's likely to be more people around as we get near. If not, then trust in your godstuff. It will tell you."

"Like you in my dreams?" Christian asked.

"Yes." Thomas paused a moment, then approached the man.

"Chris, if we ever get separated, promise me you'll keep on this journey. No matter what happens." Thomas looked earnestly up at him.

Christian stooped down. "Of course, Mr. Thomas. Nothing can come between us. After all, we're best buddies. Two caba— caba — what's the word?"

"Caballeros!" Thomas smiled.

"Caballeros," Christian repeated. "That's us. Everything will be OK. You wait and see."

"You're probably right," Thomas agreed. "Still, there are some challenges ahead. If I remember correctly, we should be getting near a river or two. No telling what can happen there."

"Funny you should talk about rivers." Christian scooted under the cut boughs. "Mama always said not to get too close to water. You never know how deep it might be. Besides that, I've had a dream about water." He lay down. "And a boat."

Thomas walked over and cuddled next to him. "Me too," he purred.

THE MAN ON THE HILL

"Evil comes in many forms. Why does God allow it to exist? For one thing, how would we know of good if we didn't know evil? One helps define the other. We may harbor evil within us. Perhaps we need to tap into it, make use of it ourselves."

— A BUTTERFLY IN FLIGHT: THE BIOGRAPHY OF THOMAS SPEAKER BY JAMIE LIVINGSTON

Thomas tossed in his sleep. The image of a boat on the water was back. It had been serene during the past dreams, as if the craft floated on a calm expanse, adrift and empty. Now the water was a raging torrent, and it was unmistakable that he was a passenger. Chris, too, was there, holding on for dear life. *Holding on to what?*

"No. No, ow!" Chris woke with a start, shoving Thomas away. He looked around, bewildered. "Where ... What's happening?"

"Just a dream." Thomas approached, his voice reassuring. "Nothing to worry about. It was just a dream."

"But it was so real." Chris pulled his knees up to his chin and wrapped his arms around them. He began to rock back and forth.

"There, there," Thomas consoled. "Just a dream. No reason to get excited."

Chris stared ahead. Still, he heard a faint hint of worry in the cat's voice.

Sitting quietly, they both heard the sound together. The low gong of a church bell rolled across the distant hills. It tolled a second time, then again. The two friends looked wide-eyed at each other.

"It came from there." Chris pointed to the north.

Thomas stood and went to the edge of the small wood. His ears perked up.

"Oh, yay! Oh, yay! Oy vey!" a human voice sang out.

"What the …" Chris came up beside Thomas.

"I'm not certain. But it's definitely human and male." The bell began tolling again. Thomas looked at Christian. "Let's go have a look, shall we?"

The pair walked north, following the sounds. The bell tolled three times; then the chant was repeated as if it was a call to prayer.

"Oh, yay! Oh, yay! Oy vey! Oh, yay! Oh, yay! Oy vey!"

They crested a hillock and looked down upon a small valley where a creek flowed from the north, bordered by woods. A building stood on the hill opposite them. A bell tower was attached, all clad in white-painted clapboard. Sunlight bathed the scene as the golden orb peeked over the horizon—sunrise and the promise of a beautiful day ahead.

The bell tolled again. From this distance, they barely made out the tiny figure standing in the bell tower until his voice sang out. "The sun is coming! Dootin doo doo, here comes the sun!"

Thomas suppressed a laugh.

Chris looked quizzically at him. "What's so funny?"

"It's nothing." The cat snickered. "It just reminded me of an old, old song."

"Who would write a song about doing doody in the sun?" Chris giggled.

"Maybe the band was called the Dung Beetles!" They both laughed at the idea.

Again the bell rang out, and the man called,

> *Well, great god Ra, here you are.*
> *Shining like the star you are.*
> *Ra, Ra, Ram, Ram.*
> *Rama-lama-ding-dong. Ding-dong!*

"Oh, I can see he's just a fool." Thomas shook his head sadly.

"So what?" Chris was smiling eagerly. "At least he's a people. We can talk to people again! Come on. Let's go meet him."

"You are so right, my friend," Thomas agreed. "But let's be careful. You never know about humans."

"Still, maybe we can find out some news."

"Yes, maybe."

The duo hiked down the hill, staying hidden by the trees. The tolling bell kept up its pace with lines to the song following it.

> *Mohammed, don't be sad.*
> *His coming makes us glad.*
> *Armageddon was a blast.*
> *Too bad it didn't last.*
> *Now here comes the sun.*
> *Dootin doo doo!*
> *Rama-lama-ding-dong. Ding-dong!*

They gingerly slogged across the creek and up the next hill. The trees gave way to a clearing about ten yards from the crest of the hilltop. It held a flourishing garden. A well-worn path wound through this and on up the knoll. Without a word, the travelers stepped out onto it. The song continued.

> *Hallelujah, what a Savior,*
> *We sing at the start of the day.*

> *If you should think about it*
> *Is it too late to pray?*
> *Dootin doo doo!*
> *Rama-lama-ding-dong. Ding-dong!*

The tolling stopped along with the rambling song. It was quiet except for the call of a lone bird. They continued up the garden path to the top of the hill, where a small church stood before them. It looked freshly painted and had a bright red double door, now closed.

The doors burst open. Thomas and Chris jumped back as a tall, lean figure emerged, holding a staff and clothed in a shabby robe held at the waist by a knotted rope. His eyes flashed.

"Visitors!" he cried, throwing down the staff. "I have visitors!"

He danced about as he ran up to them, stopping just a foot away, staring wild-eyed. Chris and Thomas froze in place.

"I don't think he can understand me," Thomas muttered, pacing at Chris's feet.

"What will I do?" Chris whispered, getting nervous. Throughout the journey, Mr. Thomas made all the decisions. When to walk, when to stop. When to eat, when to sleep. Chris assumed that Mr. Thomas was the leader like Mama had been.

"I'll guide you." The cat rubbed against Chris's leg. "Pretend I'm your pet and pick me up. We'll play dumb."

Chris did as he was told, holding Thomas firmly to his chest.

"H-he-hello." Chris gave a weak smile.

"HELLO, my visitor," shouted the man. "I see you brought food." He eyed Thomas.

"He's not food!" Chris was horrified. "We're together. We're ca — cab—"

"Caballeros," Thomas whispered.

"Yeah, caballeros." Chris squared his shoulders.

"No harm meant." The man wrung his hands. "No, no indeedy, no harm meant."

He stepped forward, extending his hand to pet the cat. Thomas met him with a quick swipe of his paw, claws extended.

"No, no harm at all. Besides, Samuel is vegan now, right, Samuel?" The man looked over his shoulder as if talking with someone else. "Right we are!" he exclaimed. "No meat. No meat anywhere, so we have to be vegan. Only plants. Only plants to eat. That's it. That's all." His eyes appraised Thomas again.

"My name is Chris ... Christian." He extended his hand.

The stranger's eyes grew wide, ignoring the greeting. "Chris Christian. What a wonderful Christian, er, church name. That's it. A real good church name. Your parents must think highly of you, bestowing such a name. You are most welcome in our humble church. I am Samuel, Samuel Schietzengiggles. It's a fine German name, don't you know. Yes, we are!" His head bobbed. "Samuel, that's me. Right, right. I have many questions for you."

"Let's move this along." Thomas scowled.

Chris picked up on the clue. "Okay, but first, we are hungry. I can do some chores in trade for a meal or two."

Samuel perked up. "Of course. Where are my manners? Even in these difficult times, one must not forget one's manners." He smiled broadly, still eyeing Thomas. "But no meat! Sad, sad. Carrot stew. We have carrot stew. Yes indeed! Or we can make onion soup. Very tasty, but no b-b-be-beef broth." His head twitched to one side at the mention of beef. "No, no b-be-eef. No c-c-cow. No h-h-horse. No ch-ch-chicken. No d-d-dog. No c-c-cat." A nervous tick caused him to twitch his head at the mention of each of the animals.

Chris tried to calm him. "That's okay. Veggies is about all I eat anyway. Sometimes I have Beanee Weenees, still got a couple of cans. Would you like some?" He dug into his backpack and produced an old can.

"Weenies? Did you say weenies?" Samuel grew excited. "Oh, yes, please. Gimme, gimme, gimme!" He stretched out both hands, fingers wiggling.

Chris handed over the can, and Samuel hurriedly popped it

open. "Ahh-h!" he sighed, taking a long whiff. "Okay, okay, come on in now. I'll make some stew of, er, for you."

Chris put Thomas down. The ragged man gathered up his staff, and the three walked up to the building. A large wooden plaque hung to the right of the door. It had broken letters scratched into it. Thomas read it aloud:

> *Welcome to the Church of the Almighty Dog, er, God.*
> *Known as God, the Almighty, the Creator,*
> *Yahweh, Supreme Being, Jehovah, Allah, Krishna,*
> *Oden, Zeus, etc., and so forth ad infinitum.*
> *(Please wipe your feet)*

"That's a big name for such a small church," Chris marveled.

Samuel turned to him and whispered, "I tried to cover all the bases. You can't be sure which one will come back into power." He threw out his arms. "Anyway, all are welcome here. No pretenses, no preconditions, no prejudgments, no nothing. You can't find a better place to worship your god, whoever he or she may be."

Thomas padded ahead and looked around. Multicolored light streamed through the stained-glass windows and onto the two aisles of pews. Male and female mannequins, dressed in tattered suits and dresses, sat scattered about the first couple of rows. The windows depicted scenes from the Bible. A small table below Noah and the flood held a small porcelain figure of a four-armed man, painted blue. Spent sticks of incense stood in a holder, and dried flower petals littered the tabletop.

Christian pointed at the figurine. "What is that?"

"If I ever get a Hindu visitor, I'll be ready." Samuel winked. "I've got Buddha over here."

Two windows down, Adam and Eve walked out of the garden. Leaves covered their private parts. They were weeping as a bearded old man pointed at the path. Another table stood below the window displaying a bronze statue of a chubby man smiling happily.

Samuel guided them past rows of pews. "I want to be ready for any contingency. You never know who's going to be top dog anymore."

The aisle ended at a raised platform. An altar fashioned from stacked cement blocks and a door slab occupied the center of the stage. A small clock radio sat in the middle of it. Thomas jumped up to check it out.

"Blasphemer!" Samuel rushed forward, his staff raised. "Blasphemer! Get off the holy altar, cat. Get off!"

Chris hurried behind him and caught the staff. "Stop! You don't hurt Mr. Thomas!"

Samuel pulled back. "Mr. Thomas? Who's Mr. Thomas? Are you talking about the great prophet?"

Chris wrenched the staff from the man. "Who? Prophet? I'm talking about Mr. Thomas, the cat there. He's my friend."

Thomas jumped down. "No offense meant."

"He didn't mean nothing." Chris softened his tone. "He's just curious."

"Curiosity killed the kitty cat," Samuel muttered. "Never mind. I feared he would disturb the Voice of the Prophet."

"The what?" Chris and Thomas spoke together.

Samuel pointed to the radio. "There. On the altar. It's the Voice of the Prophet, Thomas Speaker. Every day, when the sun is highest, his voice comes through. He has guided us these many years." His arm swept out, indicating the mannequins. "We listen and follow his instructions. We have survived. The others have gone on a pilgrimage to seek out the prophet. I elected to stay behind with these brethren to welcome any others, such as yourself."

Chris and Thomas were silent for a minute as they watched the old man. Samuel stood quietly, staring ahead.

Chris spoke up. "Yeah, well, look. We didn't mean any harm or disrespect or anything. It's just we haven't seen too many people lately and then to find you and all this—" He pointed to the crowded pews.

Samuel beamed. "It is something. I did it all myself. Well, I had some help from others, but they all left. Now it's just my little flock and me." He smiled at the mannequins. "But I nearly forgot. You're hungry. Why don't you go back to the garden and pick us some fresh vegetables? I'll get a pot going back here in the kitchen." He pointed to a door at the back of the church and immediately strode off.

Soon the sound of rattling pots burst from the small room. Samuel sang out, "Shake, rattle, and roll; God bless my soul!"

Chris grinned. "That's one of Mama's songs." He sighed.

Thomas nodded at the exit. "Looks like it's time for chores." Lowering his voice, he gestured toward Samuel. "Best keep an eye on that weird bird."

MEAL TIME

"I was surprised how far our broadcasts reached. Of course, the shortwave reached out to those who had similar equipment. But most folks depended on how far the AM broadcasts carried. It was always heartening to hear from those who traveled so far."

— A BUTTERFLY IN FLIGHT: THE BIOGRAPHY OF THOMAS SPEAKER BY JAMIE LIVINGSTON

Chris found a reed basket just inside the doorway. Picking it up, they made their way to the garden. The garden area was large, far too big for a solitary person. The vegetables were in neat, well-tended rows. No weeds grew between the plants or in the paths dividing the rows.

Christian let out a low whistle. "I remember Mama talking about community gardens. I had no idea they could be so big."

"I'll bet they had a hundred members, at least," Thomas observed after studying the patch for several minutes. "You're on your own here. I don't know nothin' 'bout pickin' no veggies." He skipped off to explore the church grounds.

"Well, this doesn't look too hard. I betcha Mama would have loved this garden." A sob caught in Chris's throat as he set to work. *I gotta stop letting that bother me. Let the past be back there where it belongs. I gotta be a man now.*

The soil was rich and loamy; the vegetables pulled out effortlessly. He soon had several onions, carrots, and a small head of cabbage.

He inspected the basket's contents. "That ought to be enough for the two of us."

Thomas came padding up. "Better pick some more, my boy," he said cheerily. "Looks like I'm going to be a vegan too. There are no signs of any other creatures around. No rabbits. No squirrels. Not even a mouse. It's kind of weird."

Chris gathered several more carrots and some tomatoes before heading back to the church. Samuel was coming out.

"Ah, my new friend, er, friends!" He stretched out his arms regarding Thomas as he corrected himself. The cat let out a low growl.

"Now you be nice, Mr. Thomas," Chris commanded. "This man is just trying to be neighborly. He probably hasn't been around decent folks like us in a long time. Right, Mr. Samuel?" He looked hopefully at the old man.

"Wh-what?" Samuel had been staring at the cat again. "Oh, yes, that's right. Nobody here for a long, long time." He shook his head as if shaking off after a shower. "Ah! I see you have our food. Come. Come, and we'll make a nice soup."

Samuel escorted them into the small back room. He had converted it into a kitchen with a small wood-burning cookstove, an old table, and four chairs. A makeshift countertop sat against one wall with a sink and a single spigot installed on it.

"Artesian well." He nodded toward the tap. "It's outside. The church used to allow its members to help themselves, especially when the end came. It was the only source of clean water around here. Then everybody left. Poof. Gone. So I ran the plumbing inside. And look!" He pulled aside an old blanket hanging on a line in one corner to reveal a toilet. "I even have an indoor toilet."

A large kettle on the wood-burner was beginning to simmer. Samuel set to work washing and slicing the vegetables.

"I miss having salt and pepper." He shook his head as he placed the ingredients in the pot and put a lid over it. "A-an-and me-me-meat." His head twitched as he pulled out a chair and sat down, motioning to Chris to do the same. "But keep that cat off the table. It's unsanitary."

Thomas jumped into Chris's lap and stared at their host. "There's something about him I don't like," he hissed.

Samuel, not understanding the language, ignored him. "So tell me, traveler, what's your story?"

Chris hesitated. "Well …"

Thomas nuzzled up against Chris's neck. "Be careful not to tell him too much. I have a bad feeling about this guy."

So Chris spoke of his life with Mama and what had happened after the end times. Samuel got up to stir the pot several times, listening attentively.

"And so when I found this cat, I just decided it was time to move on," Chris finished up.

"Just like that?" Samuel looked surprised, handing over a bowl of vegetable soup to Chris. He placed a smaller one on the floor for Thomas and sat down with his own.

"This is degrading," Thomas grumbled as he leaped down. Still, hunger got the better of him. After a silent prayer, he fished out a carrot and gnawed at it.

Samuel picked up a large spoon, dipped it into his bowl, and blew on the contents. "I would think it's pretty dangerous traveling alone these days."

"Well, so far, so good. But you know, I wouldn't have tried it before I met Mr. Thomas."

"Why's that?" He looked to Thomas, wondering.

Chris rubbed his birthmark absentmindedly. "It's hard to explain. Before meeting him, my thoughts were … were foggy. It's like I couldn't think straight. My mama said I was special, and maybe that's why she thought so. She had her hands full taking care of me, that's for sure. But now, everything seems so much clearer. Why, sometimes—"

Thomas hissed loudly. "Don't go there. I don't trust this guy."

Chris picked up on the warning, bent down, and petted the cat's head. "You're right, Mr. Thomas. Food's getting cold." Chris bowed his head in silent prayer.

Samuel stared for a moment. "Oh, yeah, of course." He laid down his spoon and also lowered his head, grumbling.

Chris dipped a spoonful of the stew and sipped at it. He nibbled at a piece of carrot, decided it was good, and dug in. "What about you, sir? If you don't mind my asking."

"Not much more to tell, really." Samuel grew thoughtful. "From what I've heard, the end times seem to be about the same wherever you go. Our civilization fell apart, but the folks around here came together at this church. We vowed to our God to keep together and help each other. But the weather changed—what with those terrible cold spells and all. It stayed so cold one summer, we couldn't grow food. Sometimes it would be weeks before the sun would come out, so we took to eating anything we could find. Anything." His gaze went to Thomas. The cat took a step back and growled.

"We ran out of meat last year." He looked around the room, noting the canned goods lining shelves. "It changes a fella—not having meat."

A squawking, rattling noise broke out in the main church. They all jumped. Samuel headed out quickly, followed by the others.

The source of the noise was the small radio with its volume turned up. Samuel rushed up to the altar. "I keep it turned up so I know when it's time. It's the prophet, Thomas Speaker."

"Hello, hello, hello." The disembodied voice of Pastor Speaker was low and calm, speaking slowly and distinctly. "My name is Thomas Speaker. Welcome to my daily broadcast."

There was a pause; then, a girl's voice recited the broadcast information.

Samuel adjusted the sound and took a seat in the front pew. Their meal forgotten, Chris and Thomas sat across the aisle, just opposite of him.

The preacher/prophet continued. "For those who may have just discovered us, we broadcast at the same time every day. We go by solar time; that is, we use a sundial set up in our square. We begin our broadcasts when it shows noon, for us, that is. Anyone west of Ohio will be behind us. You'll have to wait for the sun to catch up with you. At the end of this broadcast, we'll provide instructions on how to set up your own sundial. Just bear in mind, your noon hour will be later than ours."

The signal faded and disappeared. Samuel got up and turned a dial slightly until the pastor's voice returned.

"We are all in this together, and we all must work together to rebuild human civilization. I have spoken of other human enclaves that exist. We've been in touch via shortwave radio and wireless telegraph. I want to give you an update on that."

Samuel leaned in. "Others? How many others?"

"Glory be!" Chris shouted. "Turn it up."

Samuel returned to the radio and did so.

The preacher continued, sounding more fatherly. "From out east, we have word from President Shirley C. Bancroft, acting president of the former United States of America. Their enclave at the Greenbrier in West Virginia is also receiving refugees from the north, south, and east and growing in number. The Appalachian mountains present some problems, as many of the highways and roads through them are impassible. She reports that an expedition is going back east to assess the situation out along the Atlantic coast. They've only been out for two weeks, and we don't expect them to report back for at least a month. We wish them Godspeed."

The trio hardly breathed as they heard the news.

"Meanwhile," the pastor continued, "we have sent a team down her way. They should be arriving in the next day or so.

We're reestablishing communication and travel routes since they're not that far from us.

"And we have news coming out of the South." His voice took on a happier note. "Mama Ruth Lyon sends word that she is personally making the journey up the Mississippi and Ohio Rivers to visit us. It seems they were able to recommission an old stern-wheeler and hope to make contact with other survivors along the way. Perhaps she'll find some small river towns redeveloping. It's so fascinating to hear of all the progress we are making.

"Speaking of making contact, I have a guest here. She's a recent arrival from the Midwest, from Auburn, Nebraska, I believe."

"That's right, dear." The voice of a soft-spoken older woman came over the air. Samuel stood upright—shocked. He turned the volume as loud as possible.

"My name is Muriel, Muriel Cummings, from the great state of Nebraska. Well, at least it once was a great state. My heavens. It's a wonder anyone is still alive with all that has happened, let alone being pretty well-off. What a wonderful place you have here, Pastor Speaker."

"Please call me Thomas." One could feel the warmth in his voice. "Now I understand you have some important information to pass on to any other travelers."

"Oh, indeed I do!" Muriel exclaimed. "I need to warn folks about where I come from and a man we left behind. His name is Samuel. Samuel Schietzengiggles. It's a fine German name, don't you know? Not that *he* lives up to it."

Chris and Thomas perked up and looked over at their host. For his part, Samuel bent closer, fingering the volume dial.

Thomas jumped to the floor. "Something's not right, Chris." His words sounded like a low growl to Samuel, who glanced their way.

Muriel went on. "Oh, he was a fine man, at first. Very helpful in his little church on the hill, where we would all gather and pray. That's where we first heard of you, Pastor, er, Thomas. On the little radio that he kept on the altar. But something happened to him. I saw his aura change. It was always red, you know. But then it got darker and darker."

"Wait a minute, Muriel. Are you saying that you see people's auras?"

"Oh, yes, indeed I do. Yours is a beautiful turquoise, by the way. But I expected that." Muriel returned to the subject. "Anyway, we were just a bunch of folks who survived the storms and the cold. Sometimes, I think that maybe it was too much for Samuel to bear. You know, the way he is and everything. But then again, he was so nice at first. What makes a person change like that, Thomas?"

"If we knew the why of that, Muriel, we could prevent a lot of suffering in the world. Even now." There was sadness in the pastor's voice. "How did Samuel change?"

"Well." Muriel sounded agitated. "When the food got scarce was when it happened—especially meat. We hunted the area until the deer disappeared, then the rabbits. We all had to pull our belts in a notch last year as winter came on. We made it by rationing what we had. But Samuel—it got to him somehow. He —he turned ... evil."

"How so? What did he do?"

"He became a cannibal. He started eating us!" Her voice grew shrill. "It started with those that had passed on. He didn't kill them, bu-but he cut off fingers at first. We found them in a stew he made. Then there was Mr. Johnson. We caught Samuel trying to cut off the poor man's leg after the fueral service. Stay away from there! Stay away from Auburn, Nebraska! He's a canni—"

"No!" Samuel snatched the radio and shut it off. "Don't listen to that. It's lies, all lies. Samuel's not a canni—"

"Bull!" Chris rose to his feet. "You are a cannibal. Aren't you?"

Thomas was on his feet. "We need to run," he hissed.

"OK!" Samuel roared. "So I like meat. M-E-A-T, meat! I crave it. I must have it!" He fumbled under his robe. "Forget your carrots and your onions and potatoes. I need meat. And you two can stay for dinner!" He pulled out a large carving knife and lunged at Chris.

"Oh no you don't!" Chris dodged to the left and kicked out his right foot. He caught Samuel on the kneecap, and the old man fell, hitting his head on the pew. He lay silent.

Thomas sniffed at the prone figure. "He's still breathing. We may not have much time to get out of here."

"I could kill him." Chris looked down at the limp figure. "I could just take that knife and stick it in him."

"No!" Thomas held out his paw. "That's not our way. I'm responsible for those two Riders. I want no more killing on me. Besides, do you think Muriel and her friends didn't think of that? No. This Samuel is a crazy fool, and we best let him be."

"But what if other folks come this way? We need to warn them."

"You can carve a message into the sign on the church. Something like 'BEWARE—CRAZY MAN!!!'"

"Okay, and I've got another idea, then." Chris looked around. He pulled the rope from Samuel's robe.

Pulling the old man's hands and feet together, he began tying a knot. "This will buy us some time." He pulled on the knot, making sure it wouldn't come undone. "We'll leave the knife, and he can cut himself free. But first, I'll carve that message and grab some more veggies. He may be a crazy fool, but he sure can grow some tasty veggies."

"OK. That's good thinking. I should have thought of it. You're something else."

Chris smiled. "Mama always said I was special."

THE INNOCENTS

"We welcomed all who came our way. Sometimes we'd hear stories of other small enclaves, those that wished to rebuild where they were. It heartened me to learn they listened to my daily broadcasts."

— A BUTTERFLY IN FLIGHT: THE BIOGRAPHY OF THOMAS SPEAKER BY JAMIE LIVINGSTON

"Ben, no! Are you crazy?" A pang of fear gripped Judith Banner. "These might be the raiders those pilgrims told us about." Concern etched her face as she reached out to her husband. The other council members leaned forward, waiting for the chair's response.

Ben squeezed his wife's hand, then let go. "That was nearly two years ago, hon." He looked around the circled tables. "And the pilgrims were out of Kansas or Nebraska—I don't know—too far away for this to be the raiding party they fought off. Maybe they're just nomads."

Charlie MacDuff looked back and forth at the couple. "Maybe. Maybe not." He stroked his white beard, an old habit, as he considered what to say next. "We've never had a problem in the thirty-plus years we've been here. Your father, Bruce, along with Judith's, chose our location well. *Easy Valley*—they finally agreed on a name. A nice, quiet suburb. A real neat place to live." He chuckled. "Ben, you were just a kid, but we did well to keep away from the troubles in those early days. Why, I remember—"

"Oh, be quiet, you old coot." His wife, Marian, shook an arthritic finger at Charlie. "I agree, Dr. Banner and the other leaders did well by bringing us up here away from Cleveland, away from the lab and all the troubles." A sadness came over her. "But the only reason was they wanted to study us, that's all. We were their lab rats." She looked at Ben and lowered her eyes. "Sorry, Ben, Judith, but that's the way it was. Your fathers were more concerned about the effects of those stem-cell treatments than they were about anything else. Not that it did Charlie and me any good."

Ben pounded the gavel. "Okay, okay. Stay on topic, please."

Judith stood. "May I?" She eyed each council member, receiving a quick nod. "Maybe, just maybe, that troop west of here are nomads—friendly folk passing through, that sort of thing." She hesitated.

"But what if they are the horde of raiders the pilgrims told us about? Their people got lucky—had one of their scouts infiltrate the group, found out their true intentions, and were able to ambush them." She shook her head. "We were fortunate to have our scouts stumble upon their camp without being seen. I think that *if* those campers were nomads, they would have more women ... and children ... with them."

Several council members nodded, following her reasoning. Marian spoke up. "We don't have any fighters among us. How are we going to defend ourselves?"

"That's right." Charlie pounded his fist. "We're scientists, technicians, and, by all accounts, that rabble coming our way outnumber us two to one."

"Which is why"—Ben stood, squeezed Judith's shoulder—"we need to make peace with them. Maybe pay them a tribute, you know, part of our harvest, and let them pass through." He dropped his hand and turned back to the council. "We're peaceable folks. I'm certain we can make a deal."

"A deal with the devil? Seems to me we don't have much choice," MacDuff growled.

· ✳ ·

Two days later, Ben stood at the entrance to their gated community. A white cloth drooped from the pole he carried. Judith stood some hundred yards back with the other council members, watching the proceedings.

Grizzly grunted at the offer and made his counterproposal. Surrender or die.

"We're a peaceful community. We mean no harm to anybody. Look, make it two-thirds of our harvest. We'll barely survive the winter with what's left. Just go on your way."

"Maybe you don't understand who *I* am. My army takes whatever it needs. You can join us or not. If not … then die."

"You must understand." Ben stood tall, defiant. "We've survived a lot, built all of this from nothing. Nothing! We won't give it up."

Grizzly stared at the man and sighed. There was no time to argue or bargain with them. He pulled out his Bowie knife and ended the conversation with a quick thrust to Ben's gut.

Judith winced as she suppressed a cry and turned to the others. Her twin, Sarah, grabbed her close. "We will revenge him," she whispered. "We go with Plan B."

Judith pulled back, wiped away the tears, and nodded her agreement. The women squeezed each other's hands and ran off to their homes. The rest of the council members scattered, calling out to the villagers to hide and lock their doors.

Judith covered the two blocks to their home within a minute. As she rushed in, her son jumped to his feet, clutching a backpack.

"Dad?" The boy's voice faltered.

Judith shook her head. "Dead." She walked up to him and put her hands on his young shoulders. "Ben, this is what we thought would happen. We prepared for it."

The boy looked her in the eye, trying not to let the tears fall. Not yet. He sucked in his breath. "I'm ready."

Judith gave him a quick, firm hug. "I know. Dad is proud of you. Now go! Sarah will have Brandon meet up with you out by the cow barn. Head south as fast as you can. When you get there, if anyone is at the outpost, tell them to go with you. We'll do our best to stop these … these …"

"These bastards!" the boy cursed. "Mom, I may be ten years old, but I'm a man now. "We'll make it to Speaker's town before the first snow. Count on it."

Judith stood. "My young man!" Another quick hug and she shoved him toward the back door. "Be safe!" He gave a thumbs-up sign and was gone.

Judith faced the door, unarmed.

· ✳ ·

GRIZZLY LOOKED OVER HIS SHOULDER AT HIS BAND. HE HAD LONG considered himself to be descended from the likes of Blackbeard the Pirate or Attila the Hun. Now he stood tall, clothed in black leather. His beard was tied in knots and spilled down to his chest; his hair fell in dreadlocks. The scar over his left eye throbbed with excitement.

His band of misfits stood restlessly. Several weeks had passed since they last attacked anyone.

Grizzly relished the smell of fresh blood, the sight of death. Now, with a wicked gleam in his eye, he made a quick nod toward the village. A shout went up from the horde as they raced forward.

There was no real battle. The raiders worked in teams of six, each heavily armed. Each team took a house, busting in the door if locked, splitting up, and searching each room.

The villagers who had weapons made a feeble attempt at self-defense. Men who did not immediately surrender were cut down, disemboweled, and dragged into the street. Women and children were pulled out and bound—there would be further use for them. It took less than an hour.

The team of three men and three women found Judith standing alone and unarmed. One of the women put a knife to her throat.

"Go ahead, cut me down." Judith's green eyes blazed. "Then your boss will never know our secrets."

The woman hesitated. "Whatcha talkin' 'bout, bitch?" She lowered the knife.

"Oh, there's a reason our little town has been so successful." A wry smile crossed her lips, then disappeared. "Kill me, and your boss will never know about it. The same goes for the others here. Those that are alive."

"You'll be talking soon enough." The woman grabbed Judith's arm and flung her at the men. "Go on, fellers! Do what you want, you horny assholes. But keep her alive for Grizzly!"

* ✳ *

GRIZZLY STARED AT HIS TIN PLATE. FLIES BUZZED BACK AND FORTH OVER it. *Always the flies getting the last bits.* He came back to the task at hand. Orders were out to settle in for the night, secure the survivors properly, and start gathering all supplies. He considered his options. They would be staying for several weeks, at least, but winter was coming.

If he continued his march, livestock could be kept alive and brought along. Perhaps even some of the prisoners, depending on how cooperative they were, could make the journey. He left those details to his lieutenants.

He was only slightly bothered by the report that two boys had escaped. *Let them spread the word. Grizzly's on the march!*

His mind was churning. He sat at the kitchen table of his chosen house, where he would set up headquarters. A voice came from a radio across the table. This broadcast gave him pause. Many years had passed since he last heard this preacher. He fingered the tuning knob. Nothing, not even static up or down the dial. He found the original frequency number and shoved the receiver aside.

I'm a survivor. More'n that, I'm a leader, a boss. No. More like a general!

It was so long ago. How long? Thirty years? Maybe. He was no longer sure. Nobody was interested in counting years when you had no idea if you'd survive through the night. He did more than survive. He had built an entire militia, a horde of marauders. Their purpose? To prey upon the weak. *The suckers and losers!* He belched.

Grizzly stared at the radio. Pulling out the tattered map, he placed his finger on a spot northwest of Lake Erie. *We're about here.* He stabbed down at the map. *Figure they're about here.* His finger slid down and due east through Ohio.

"Bradshaw!" he yelled at the top of his voice.

Bill appeared immediately. "Yeah, boss."

"I've been listening to this radio." Grizzly's voice was rough. "Seems there's some sorta settlement down here." He pointed to the map. "A big one. An' I want it."

"Sure, boss." Bill was adept at handling the old bear. He was the one to nickname him, figuring it gave the other fellers something more to look up to. Grizzly did not mind.

"Get the others in here now." Grizzly nodded toward the door. "Tell our men I'm making plans to stay here this winter. I'll give out assignments as soon as you git their sorry asses in here. Got it?"

"Got it, boss." With that, Bill was out the door.

Grizzly stared a hole in the map. *Learn from your mistakes. With proper planning, I could overcome that town. Even set up a permanent place. Hell, who knows? Maybe I can build a real empire!* He laughed at the thought.

REBIRTH

"I used to believe in heaven and hell. But my studies and prayer life took me further. What if we are reincarnated after death—to live again as part of our self-evolution? Fascinating!"

— A BUTTERFLY IN FLIGHT: THE BIOGRAPHY OF
THOMAS SPEAKER BY JAMIE LIVINGSTON

Thomas Speaker completed his broadcast, switched off the microphone, and glanced around the office. He had chosen the renovated Victorian house because of its proximity to the quaint downtown area. The library addition to one side of the home, shaded by an ancient oak tree, was the icing on the cake. Upgrades at the time of the renovation included the installation of broadcast equipment.

"That's some tale, Muriel."

"That's not the worst of it, Pastor Speaker." Muriel Cummings's sad eyes welled up with tears as she remembered the horror from her past. "It's no tall tale, and I ain't lyin'. Ol' Samuel just plain went crazy. We were afraid it was some kinda disease or somethin'."

"So tell me, there were more of you. Why didn't you jail this

Samuel, at least for his own good?" Speaker thought a moment. "Then too, if he committed murder ..."

Muriel looked horrified. "Why, Pastor. You know we wouldn't. We couldn't. Where would we be in God's eyes if we had? Besides, to be completely honest, ol' Sam never actually killed anyone. He would wait for someone to die before he would eat them. When we caught him with Mr. Johnson we thought we had put a stop to it. But then there were the graves. At first, we thought maybe wild animals were digging them up, Until one night, we caught Samuel at it. He had hacked off a leg from ol' Pete Petersen, just freshly buried, and was carrying it back to his church. The rest of us got together and decided it would only be a matter of time before he'd start 'helping' a sick or dying person, if you know what I mean.

"Then, too, there was a meat shortage. A person can't live on veggies alone. What if we started to act like Samuel? So we decided it was high time to move on, to come and find you. Samuel wanted no part of it. He said he had a calling. So we just up and left him on his own."

"Ah, yes. I understand it better now." The pastor stood and clapped his hands together. "I had to ask. You see, I try to be honest and upfront about our village. We welcome everyone, but we've had our share of characters through here. Some fit in; others don't. I think you'll like it here."

Muriel beamed. "Oh, that would be so wonderful!" She reached over to hug him. A knock at the door interrupted her. Then another, more incessant pounding.

Speaker reached for the handle as the door burst open and a young girl rushed in.

"Pastor Speaker." Gasping, she tried to catch her breath. "It's time."

"Fantastic!" Thomas jumped up. "Now, Joanie, calm down. I'm sure we'll have plenty of time. Let me get my things."

Joanie was beside herself. "Hurry, Pastor! The midwife said to tell you the baby's head is crowning."

"Wh-what? Oh, my heavens!" Speaker pulled a small black satchel down from his bureau. He thought for a moment and turned to the girl. "Joanie, please take Ms. Cummings over to our Greeters Building to join her friends. Then hurry back to Doc and Maggie's. We may need your help there." He raced toward the door.

Pausing, he quickly turned back. "My apologies, Muriel. Joanie here will tell our elders to help you and your friends get settled in. I'll catch back up with you later this evening. My friends are having a baby!" With that, he rushed off.

*　*　*

SHELDON "DOC" LIVINGSTON WAS ONE OF THE FEW PEOPLE THOMAS Speaker would ever call a friend.

"I demand too much of a friend," he tried to explain to Doc at one point early on. "Are you sure you want to be mine?"

"Can't be too hard," Doc quipped. "After all, what's not to like?"

They met as volunteers for the stem-cell clinical trials. Speaker took an instant liking to the man.

"They call me Doc because I have degrees in both electrical and mechanical engineering," he explained, smiling broadly. "That, and I can fix almost anything, given the proper tools, of course. And materials. You gotta have the right materials."

Speaker liked that about him—the casual flippant remark whenever Doc explained anything.

The first few weeks of the stem-cell trials consisted of a battery of tests, both physical and psychological. At that time, the volunteers were allowed to mingle and get to know each other. Their friendship grew as they shared their life experiences. Thomas often felt that their lives paralleled each other.

Doc, too, was at the bottom of his own particular barrel. His job as an upper-level manager for a defense contractor got cut as government funding dried up. Then word came from the war front. His wife, the love of his life, was missing in action. She was a helicopter pilot in the U.S. Army. She wanted to be all that she could be.

"She was a strong-willed woman," Doc confided one day at lunch. "The Army was her life, and there was nothing anyone could do to stop her from doing what she wanted to do. I guess I played second fiddle to that. Still ..." He shrugged and squeezed his nose. "But that was all right. That was all right." He took a ragged breath.

Taking a bite of his sandwich, he wisecracked, "So what's your sorry-ass story?"

Thomas filled him in on his tribulations—divorce, death of his best friend, decline into addiction. "I doubt I'll pass the shrink test."

"Shrink test?" Doc came alert. "What's that?"

"Sorry." Thomas stirred creamer into his coffee. "Make that my 'psychological profile,' if you will." He made air quotes with his fingers.

"I doubt you need to worry about that." Doc sipped at his beverage. "They're looking for cannon fodder, test rabbits, monkeys in cages sort of thing. If the trial goes bad, you're 'discarded.'" It was his turn to make air quotes. "I met a gal the other day. She was heavy into drugs. If *she* passes, *you* have no worries."

*　＊　*

THOMAS NOW HURRIED DOWN THE HILL, SHAKING HIS HEAD TO CLEAR his thoughts. *They both won the stem-cell lottery, for sure, along with that gal Maggie, now Mrs. Livingston.* He smiled as he passed the once-abandoned lots now flourishing with gardens. Well-tended homes, with flowers and shrubs surrounding them like pretty skirts, filled in between the green areas. *Life everywhere! And now this extraordinary baby. It will be a first for us. Both parents being part of the experiment. Now a baby from the two of them. What can possibly go wrong? We're going to make it.*

He waved at Gail Conner as he passed by her home. Posted on her front porch in her rocking chair, she kept a watchful eye on the neighborhood.

"What's the hurry, Pastor?" She craned her neck to follow him.

"No time," he shouted over his shoulder. "The baby's coming!" *Well, the whole town will know now.*

Sure enough, Gail the Gossip lived up to her name. She rose from the chair and began yelling at the top of her voice. "Hoorah! Hoorah! Baby's on the way!" Then, jumping from the porch, she ran to the backyard and repeated the chant. "Hoorah! Hoorah! Baby's on the way!"

From a distance, another voice picked up on the message. "Hoorah! Hoorah! Baby's on the way!" Then another. And another. By the time Thomas reached Doc and Maggie's front porch, it seemed like the whole town was singing the news. "Hoorah! Hoorah! Baby's on the way!"

As he bounded up the steps of the porch, Thomas met two interns, Andy and his wife, Alicia. The midwife had selected them for training when they showed an aptitude for the medical arts.

"Sorry, sir." Andy stepped in front of him. "The midwife says no one comes in. Not even you."

"Don't count on it." Thomas pushed him aside. Then, entering the house, he called out, "My apologies."

Andy looked at Alicia helplessly. She shrugged and shook her head. "Men!"

The house was also an old Victorian style, with a sitting room/den to the right, behind French doors. The room, now converted into a birthing room, emitted the cry of a baby. Thomas hurried to the doorway and peeked inside.

Doc sat next to Maggie in the bed, his arm around her shoulder. The baby nuzzled her mother's breast, making a cooing sound.

"It's a girl!" Doc beamed.

Thomas was all smiles too. "And a beautiful baby she is. Look at that golden hair, sister. Oh, my!"

"She is wonderful," Maggie gushed. "And so easy to bring into this world. I hardly felt a thing when she pushed through."

"It's true," Grace, the midwife, chimed in. "I've never assisted at an easier birth. It's remarkable." Then, turning to Thomas, she asked, "Do you think it's because of the stem cells?"

"Possibly." Thomas pondered the question. "I'd say probably. It is a first for all of us. Without proper medical facilities and staff …"

"Not to worry, Thomas." The midwife patted his shoulder. "I'm well aware of those needs. Still, with the trained EMTs and those willing to learn, we're not doing too badly."

"Oh!" Maggie cried out. They all turned to her.

"I think she's sucked me dry." Maggie turned pale as she pulled the baby from her breast. The midwife hurried over.

"Well, I'll be!" Grace gently picked up the child and placed her on her shoulder, patting her back.

The girl let out a belch and smiled. The onlookers laughed in relief.

"She does have an appetite, too." Maggie's color returned. "I feel so drained. And I'm famished, too. If baby's gonna eat, then momma's gotta eat."

Doc jumped up. "Of course, dear. I'll rustle up a sandwich and a glass of water. Be right back." Racing out the door, he bumped into the interns. "It's a girl!" Doc grabbed Andy by the shoulders and shook him. "A very, very healthy little girl!" He ran on to the kitchen.

The interns hugged each other and headed out of the house with the good news. A small crowd of people had gathered about the porch and sent up a cheer with the report.

Thomas, reassured that the mother and child were doing well, followed the interns to address the group. He spoke up as the cheering died down.

"Thank you all for coming on such short notice." He beamed. "Now, you all know that this is not our first newborn." Thomas looked around and spotted Muriel Cummings and several of the newcomers among the onlookers. "This baby is special to us because she is the first to be born of parents who were both a part of the stem-cell research several decades ago. We don't know if the ability to heal was passed on to her genetically. Unfortunately, we don't have the scientific equipment to help figure that out."

He paused. *What if the child does have that ability? Or maybe some other? How will we handle it? Can we accept her?*

"Well, momma and baby are doing just fine. And we're all going to have to be patient and let the babe grow a bit to find out the answer to that. Now, unless someone has a question, I ask that you all go back to your business and let these folks rest in peace."

"Do they have a name chosen?" someone yelled from the back of the crowd.

Thomas laughed, spotting a young man craning his neck. "We know all about the naming pool. By the way, I have dibs on 'Laura.' Doc and Maggie will let us know as soon as they've had a chance to think about it. And I promise, no undue influence from me."

With that, he shooed them away and went back inside.

Maggie was cuddling the baby in one arm and devouring the remnants of a sandwich. Doc sat next to them. The midwife was off to the side, cleaning things up.

"Still deciding." Maggie spoke through a mouthful. "I was famished. Between my repair work going on in here"—she nodded to her abdomen— "and the little one's appetite, I've never felt so hungry."

"Take your time. Take your time," Thomas said soothingly, pulling up a seat.

Doc spoke up. "Well, I was leaning toward Robert or James if she was a boy. It would be in honor of my dad, Robert, or Maggie's dad and brother, James Hendrix."

"But now we have this beautiful little girl," Maggie spoke up. The baby had awoken, and she was staring into the girl's sparkling blue eyes.

"Jamie!" Maggie blurted and looked around incredulously.

The others stared at her. "I don't know where that came from. I was looking deeper and deeper into those remarkable eyes, and the name just came to me. It's like she was introducing herself."

"Well, Jamie it is, then." Doc beamed. "She's still named after your dad, the old farmer." He gave Maggie a huge hug.

Grace coughed slightly. She was accustomed to this sort of post-birth discussion, but now she needed to interrupt. "I had an idea. It may answer the other big question." She held up a scalpel. "I'll just make a slight cut on her palm, see how it heals."

Maggie and Doc looked at each other, then turned to Thomas. Thomas nodded back to them, deferring the decision to the parents. The two quickly gave their consent.

The midwife gently held Jamie's hand and ran the blade's edge over the child's palm. The babe flinched automatically, then cooed and smiled. As they all stared, a thin red line appeared, and a drop of blood formed at one end. Soon the skin returned to normal; only the bead of blood remained.

Grace had a microscope slide prepared and waiting. She used it to scoop up the droplet, hoping to study it later.

Thomas let his breath out. "Well, I guess that answers that."

Maggie and Doc stared in wonder.

"Oh, by the way," the midwife said. "I had 'Jamie' in the naming pool."

RIVER CROSSING

"I remember reading of an experiment where the researchers placed some rats in a limited environment with plenty of food, ideal living conditions. The rats soon multiplied beyond the capacity of their environment to sustain them, and they turned on each other. Maybe that's what happened to us."

— *A BUTTERFLY IN FLIGHT: THE BIOGRAPHY OF THOMAS SPEAKER* BY JAMIE LIVINGSTON

Christian and Thomas Cat headed east out of Auburn, Nebraska, leaving Samuel the Cannibal behind. Staying close to Highway 136, they found it relatively easy to cross the Missouri River using the old steel trestle bridge connecting to the once Great State of Missouri. The partially fallen bridge was long past its value for wheeled traffic. However, storm debris flowing down the river had piled up against it, maintaining its usefulness for foot traffic.

The going was undemanding, and the days passed swiftly. One morning Thomas went off to consult with a deer. Christian began dressing, keeping a watchful eye on his friend.

"So, any news?" Christian fastened his pants as the cat trotted up.

"Not really. It's just sad," Thomas shook his head.

Christian hunched down. "What is?"

Thomas nodded toward the deer, who was now nibbling at some brush. "That young fellow over there. He didn't know what a human was. I had to point to you and tell him that's what they looked like."

"How can that be? Where I come from, there were more people than anything. Except for bugs, maybe."

Thomas snickered. "Exactly! Sometimes, I think maybe that's what went wrong when you get down to the nitty-gritty."

"I don't get it." Christian sat next to his friend and gazed across the meadow. Several other deer joined the young buck.

Thomas sat back on his haunches, shaking his head. "There were just too many people. They were everywhere. And everywhere they went, they messed it up. Pollution. Fouled waters. Mountains decapitated. Giant holes dug into our Mother Earth. The list goes on and on."

Christian grabbed a long stalk of grass to chew. "Mama said that Mother Earth was huge, that all folks should be able to live quite nicely on her."

"She was right. Scientists kept coming up with better ways to feed people. Engineers invented new housing for them. There was enough for everyone to have everything they ever needed to be comfortable. The keyword is 'should.' They *should* have been happy. But, sadly, they were not."

Christian thought a moment. "Whenever Mama had a big problem she didn't understand, she would read her Good Book. She always found answers there." He spoke wistfully, remembering times spent sitting in Mama's lap, listening to the words she read.

"Yes." Thomas half-closed his eyes. "She was right to look there. Every country, every people, every religion had their good books to consult. Really, when you got down to the basics, they all said the same thing. The simplest of answers was there. Love. Love God. Love each other."

A big grin spread across Christian's face. "Love one another. That's what Mama would always pray."

Thomas stood and stretched. "Well, it's too late for that. Time to get moving."

Shouldering his backpack, Christian picked up his walking stick and counted the notches in it. There was one for each day of travel. His lips moved silently.

"Sixteen," he announced. "How close are we, anyway?"

"My friend James had an old map. As best as I can remember it, and figuring we cover about six or seven miles a day, I would say we're almost to the Mississippi River. It's good we were able to stay on this one road."

Christian set the pace as they made their way east. The daylight dimmed as dark clouds formed in the northwest, threatening a late summer storm. They could see the remains of buildings ahead to the east. An old highway marker, bending over on its post, confirmed they were still on Route 136.

The sun continued its descent and clouds grew ominous as they approached a truck stop. The aluminum roof over the pumps had collapsed long ago, but the building, made of cinder block, was still intact. They decided to shelter there.

Christian picked his way through the broken door, Thomas following. They found the interior to be mostly dry. Piles of debris littered the floor. They continued to the rear.

Christian kicked at an old magazine lying on the floor. Curiosity got the better of him, and he picked it up. Turning a few pages, he looked at Thomas, surprised.

"It's a map book!"

Thomas leaped to a nearby counter. "Let me see."

Christian sat the book down and carefully turned a few rotting pages.

The cat stared at the magazine. "This is more than lucky. It's an atlas. It's got maps of all the nearby states. We'll be able to find our way quickly now. If only we knew where we are exactly."

They continued to rummage around in the dim light. Christian held up a ragged envelope. "Will this do?" He could barely make out the address. "Al … Alex … Alexandria. Alexandria, Missouri." He beamed, placing the document on the counter.

Thomas peered intently at the envelope. "Fantastic!" He looked at Christian wide-eyed. "We're right at the Mississippi River. That's the last major hurdle. From there, we head due east and north. Pack the map, my boy. We'll head out at dawn."

Night settled in rapidly, and the two made do in a back corner of the building. Sleep did not come readily. The wild boat ride dream returned to both.

Outside, the wind picked up and rattled portions of the downed roof. Rain began falling, softly at first, then became a steady downpour.

Christian tossed and turned, suddenly awakening. Thomas was gone. The man jumped up, struggled to see through the dark, fighting down his panic. Lightning flashed and lit the area as rain fell in sheets, flooding the old parking area. The cat stood in the doorway looking out. Another bolt of lightning cast his shadow towards Christian.

"Thomas!"

The cat turned and tried to smile, then patted back to his friend.

"It's okay, Chris. Just a dream."

Christian picked his friend up, holding him close. "But it was so real."

"Still only a dream. Let's settle down." Thomas began to purr.

*　*　*

MORNING DAWNED. THE COMPANIONS AWOKE TO THE TWITTERING OF a bird and sunshine pouring through the shattered windows. They hurried to the doorway.

To Thomas's relief, the water had drained from the parking lot. Anxious to go, they agreed to hold off their meal until they crossed the river.

The bank of the Mississippi was closer than they thought, perhaps a hundred yards across an old farm field, now evolving into a woodland. The river lived up to its nickname. The brown water rushed past them.

Christian looked to Thomas. "Now what?"

Thomas nodded toward the north. "Let's see what's up that way. There may still be a bridge we'll be able to cross on."

Christian grunted his approval, and they set off. Soon they came to a dead end. Another river was in front of them, feeding into the Mississippi. They consulted the map.

"Well, at least we know exactly where we are," Christian quipped.

"Yes. That must be the Des Moines River. It flows into the Mississippi right here." Thomas touched a spot on the map.

Christian looked around and pointed to a utility pole sticking out of the riverbank. "Look there! That might be of some help."

A heavy cable arched out from the pole and over the great river, connecting to another post on the other side. A heavy-duty snap ring hooked onto it and dangled another line to the bottom of the pole. They got closer and found an aluminum fishing boat secured to the other end.

The crossing rope hung about four feet from the rushing water's surface. Christian jumped into the boat and grabbed it. "Ah-ha! Like this." He made a motion of pulling along the cable, hand over fist. The snap ring guaranteed that the vessel would not be swept away in the current.

"Excellent." Thomas jumped in as Christian tugged at each rope with all his might. They held. He nodded his approval as Thomas moved to the front.

Christian eased the craft into the water and held the cable tight as he began pulling them along. The current, refreshed by the night's rain, quickly caught the boat and tried to push it down-stream. Thomas paced at the bow of the craft.

Looking ahead, they could see the opposite shore where the other pole stood firmly anchored. Downriver, all was clear as the muddy water churned its way south. Upriver, the golden dome of the trees on Mud Island shimmered in the morning light. Autumn had magically colored them red, yellow, and orange. Save for the rushing water, all was peaceful.

Christian spotted it first and hollered. "Up there!" He nodded toward the island.

Thomas sat up on his hind legs. A large log, pulled from the shore, was charging toward them.

Thomas turned to his friend. "Hold tight. Hold on for dear life. It's going to hit us. Hold on! We can make it!"

The current drove the log along, crashing it into the side of their small boat. Christian held desperately to the rope and stepped to the edge. The pressure from the trunk forced the craft to twist upward and flip its passengers out.

"No!" shouted Christian, catching sight of Thomas in the water. "No!"

He let go of the rope and plunged into the river. When he came up, the log was between him and Thomas. The cat was struggling to keep his head above water. Suddenly, he disappeared.

"No!" Christian bellowed as the river pulled him under again. Flailing his arms, Christian resurfaced. The log was just within reach. He grabbed for it and pulled himself up.

Looking downriver, he saw no sign of Thomas. "No," he sobbed. "Mr. Thomas, no."

MAMA RUTH

"We were able to contact and keep in touch with other outposts through shortwave radio. Sadly, we lost contact with some. So we were very excited to hear about the people from New Orleans attempting a visit."

— A BUTTERFLY IN FLIGHT: THE BIOGRAPHY OF
THOMAS SPEAKER BY JAMIE LIVINGSTON

Christian clung desperately to the log as the flood carried it downstream. Any movement threatened to roll it over, and he couldn't swim. *Mama was so afraid of water. Said she nearly drowned once. That's why she never learned to swim.* Now he too was fearful of what could happen if he lost his handhold.

"Mr. Thomas!" he yelled, barely raising his head. "Please don't be gone." He craned his neck to search both banks. Nothing. No sign of the cat. "Oh, Mr. Thomas, please don't be gone." A sob tore from his chest. He laid his head on the tree, thoughts racing.

Dear Lord, he prayed silently, *please protect my friend. Help him find his way. If you should take him, though, please send him back to me. He's my only friend—my only real friend.*

Christian continued the journey down the river as the day

wore on. Every attempt to paddle for the shore risked him capsizing, so he clung on and allowed the current to carry him. Day turned into night, and the river widened out, calming down. Christian looked from side to side. A full moon reflected in the water. And stars. Lots and lots of stars. *So pretty. So peaceful.* He felt himself drifting off to sleep, cradled in the current, rocking gently back and forth. His eyes grew heavy.

Suddenly there was a jolt, and the log stopped, paused, and swung around. Peering into the darkness, Christian made out the form of a large boulder rearing up in the middle of the river. Moonlight glistened off it as he floated away.

"That's not a good place for that," he said. "A boat could hit it. A boat could hit me if I'm not careful. What am I talking about? There are no boats. There are no people. The animals all say so." He laid his head on the wet wood. The current flowed smoothly, calmly. Christian slipped in and out of sleep.

* ✳ *

"HALLOOOO!" A SHOUT CUT THROUGH THE EARLY MORNING MIST. Christian blinked. Daybreak had arrived while he dozed. He looked across the river, his face close to the timber. There was nothing but water and the bank beyond. It must have been a dream.

Hew-ew-ew-ew! A loud whistle pierced the morning stillness. Christian lurched to see the other side. The log rolled, spilling him over. He came up out of the water, grabbing desperately for his perch. Clinging tightly, he looked around. *What on earth! Is that a boat?*

He had never seen anything like it before. It looked like a large box with a big wheel on the back of it. Smoke was coming out of two chimneys on top, and people were gathering around the sides on three levels.

Hew-ew-ew-ew! The steam whistle blew again. Voices came from the boat.

"It's a man, Mama Ruth!" shouted one.

"It sure is and lookit. He's alive!" another confirmed. More people gathered on the decks looking across at Christian.

Christian raised an arm and waved. "Hey! Here I am!"

"Well, glory be and praise the Lord," a woman's voice cut the others off. "Let's get busy now. Get the skiff lowered and go pick him up. Captain, please hurry. We don't want to lose him."

Crewmen jumped to order and lowered a small boat over the side. Two of them clambered aboard, one taking the oars. As they set off toward Christian, the other hastily tied a rope into a lasso.

Christian hung onto the tree with one arm and tried to paddle toward the men with the other. The current ran slower in this part of the river, and the small boat quickly caught up to him.

"Where in tarnation did you come from?" one exclaimed as they hauled him aboard.

"That way." Christian pointed upriver, panting for breath. "It … it's a long story."

"I'll bet it is," the crewman replied. "Well, doncha worry none now. Mama Ruth will take good care of you."

"Who?" Christian looked at the man and calmed a bit. He liked the sound of that name, Mama.

They began rowing back to the large ship as Christian looked on in amazement.

"Is that a boat? How's it run? What's that big wheel on the back?"

"Now, big fella," the older crewman soothed, "you'll get all the answers you need and more. Once we getcha on board." He smiled. "I'm sure we have a lotta questions fer you, too."

"But what is that?" Chris jabbed a finger at the boat. "I've never seen anything like that."

"Why, that's the *Delta Belle,* finest stern-wheeler on the Mississippi," the older crewman said proudly.

"The *only* stern-wheeler on the Mississippi," his mate quipped. "It's a steamship. An' that wheel is a big paddle. It pushes the boat. You'll see."

At the side of the ship, other hands reached down and helped Christian aboard. He swayed as he got his footing back, and one of the crew held out a hand to steady him.

Remembering his manners, Chris nodded to the crewmen. "Thanks. I've been in the water all day and all night." He shivered in the early morning chill.

"Well, what have we here?" A man in a dark suit and brimmed Captain's hat approached. He smiled as he extended a hand. "Captain Cornelius Curry, at your service."

Christian clasped it in both of his hands and shook it vigorously. "Christian, Christian Chance. Thank you for saving me."

"Now, now, that's what we're about here on the *Delta Belle*, Mama Ruth's flagship. Sailor!" he addressed one of the crew. "Get a blanket for this poor fellow before he catches a cold."

"Sir!" came the curt reply, and one of the men made a snappy salute and hurried off.

They wrapped a heavy blanket around Christian, and someone placed a cup of hot tea in his hands. He smiled his thanks.

"Now then," began the captain. "You say you've been in the river all night?"

He nodded vigorously. "Yes, sir. And all day yesterday, too. We were trying to cross over in a fishing boat when that log knocked into us and spilled us out."

"We?" The captain looked sharply at Christian.

"Yes." A tear came to his eye, and his voice caught. "My friend Mr. Thomas. I saw him trying to swim. It was all I could do to hold on to the log. I got dunked and … and … and he disappeared." Christian sobbed.

"Perhaps he made it to shore." The husky voice of a woman came from behind Christian.

He turned to see a tall, brown-skinned lady dressed in slacks and a colorful blouse. A silk scarf covered her head. A tender smile spoke of her goodwill.

She turned to Cornelius. "Captain, can we go up the river a bit more and search? If we sound the whistle, perhaps his friend will hear and come to the riverbank."

"Why, certainly, ma'am. We'll get underway as soon as we have a full head of steam."

Mama turned to Christian. She placed her hands on his shoulders and looked deeply into his eyes. "Now you, sir." She spoke with authority. "First, you get a hot shower and dry clothes. Something to eat, too, maybe? Yes."

"But … Mr. Thomas is out there." Christian looked at the river. "He's out there somewhere. I hope."

"Now, don't you worry, son." She squeezed his arm. "These sailors are very sharp-eyed. And we'll go slowly. If your friend is there, then we'll find him. Now off you go." She gave him a gentle shove toward a crewman.

"Oh." Christian turned. "There's a big rock in the middle of the river, too. I hit it last night."

"So noted," called Mama. "We'll keep a lookout for it too. And we don't travel at night. We'll be safe."

Christian thought of his friend. *Mr. Thomas is so small. I hope they'll be able to see him.*

The mate ushered Christian toward the bow and invited him to enter the first room. A large bed and storage closet stood to the side, and a small bathroom with a shower, commode, and sink filled the room's rear. Several antique photographs of sternwheelers decorated the walls.

The crewman pulled items out of the closet. "Here's a towel and washcloth. Fresh clothes in here, too." He smiled. "Shower etiquette says you only use what you need. So wet down. Turn off the water and soap up. Turn the water back on and rinse. About the time you finish is when the hot water gets there. Sorry!" He laughed.

"It's better than a cold farm pond, that's for sure. Thank you so much."

"I'll check on you in about fifteen minutes. The captain and Mama are anxious to talk with you."

Christian showered, dried, and dressed within the allotted time, so he stepped out onto the deck.

A squeal and voices from up forward caught his attention, and he peered up the side of the boat. What would have been the most forward room had its walls down, and stored wood piled to the ceiling. There were also several large cages—the chattering issued from these.

Christian went to investigate. To his surprise, he found pigs in the cages. Each animal was about a yard long and well-fattened.

"Hello, gentlemen," Christian greeted them.

The pigs looked directly at him and snapped to attention. *"Morituri te salutant,"* the lead pig proclaimed.

"What? Say that again." Christian crouched down to get closer.

"Morituri te salutant!" The pig spoke slowly, emphasizing each syllable.

"I'm sorry, but I don't understand."

"Understand what, mate?" The crewman came up behind Christian.

Startled, Christian jumped. "Oh, the pig. He said something, but I don't understand the words."

"You talk to pigs, do you?" The crewman laughed. "That's a good one. Wait'll my mates here this."

"It's true!" Christian stood his ground.

"Well, you can tell the captain and Mama Ruth. They're waiting for you to join them for breakfast. The cook made eggs and *ham.*"

With a laugh, the sailor escorted Christian to Mama Ruth's stateroom on the top deck. Dark wood paneling covered the walls, and sconces hung on either side of the surrounding windows for nighttime illumination. A double-size mattress and spring set placed in a frame and covered with a brightly colored quilt sat at the far end. Just inside the door sat a cabaret table and four chairs. A personal writing secretary filled the opposite wall. A tree limb, fastened to the floor next to this desk, bowed out, forming an upside-down "L." An African gray parrot was perched there, enjoying a treat from Mama Ruth's hand. The captain was there also, looking over a map.

"Uh-oh, visitors," squawked the parrot.

"Now, LinLin," Mama admonished. "Please meet Christian Chance. He's the man from the water. Be nice." She nodded toward the bird. "Christian, this is LinLin. She's my famil— my close friend."

Christian held out his hand. "Pleased to meet you, Ms. LinLin."

LinLin grasped his finger with a claw. "Ditto, kiddo," she said, releasing his finger.

Christian was flabbergasted. "She talks! And you both understand her? And she understands you? Both of you?"

"She has over a thousand-word vocabulary." Mama petted the parrot.

"She talks to me, too," the crewman chirped up.

The captain looked at him sternly, and he snapped to attention.

"Sorry, sir, ma'am." He saluted. "It's just that, well, this feller says he can talk to the pigs and I—"

"What's that? You can talk to the pigs?" The captain stared at Christian.

"More like *with* them, sir. 'Cept for I can't understand their language. It's not English."

"Oh, I see." The captain chuckled. "What exactly did they say?"

Christian squinted, trying to remember. *"Mor ... morituri te ... te salutant."* He grinned.

"That's Latin," gasped Mama.

"What's Latin?" Christian was curious.

"The pigs speak Latin!" The captain peered suspiciously at Christian.

"It's an ancient language, Christian," Mama explained. "Many of our modern tongues are based on it."

"Now, wait a minute." Captain Cornelius spoke up. "Pigs speaking Latin? What did they say again?"

"*Morituri te salutant,*" Christian repeated.

"Those who are about to die salute you," Mama translated. "The story is that gladiators would say that to the emperor just before they would do battle."

"You're not going to kill them, are you?" Christian looked from one to the other.

"They are food," the crewman pointed out. "And you say they're ready to die, anyway."

"No. Captain! Mama Ruth? You can't do that. Mr. Thomas told me all about how we're connected. How we're the same."

"Oh, so you've been listening to Pastor Speaker also?" Mama looked surprised.

"No, well, yes. My mama always listened to him, and then we heard him the other day at Samuel's place. But my friend Mr. Thomas told me all about the other stuff. He's my best friend, and he's lost. The poor cat."

"Wait a minute." The captain turned on Christian, looking him in the eye. "Your friend Mr. Thomas is a cat?"

"Yes, sir. He's taught me so much on our journey. He's very smart."

"First, there's talking pigs. Now we have talking cats? Preposterous!" The captain began to pace.

LinLin flew over to Mama's shoulder. "He talks to cats. He talks to cats," she squawked as the room turned to chaos.

Christian stared into LinLin's eyes. They widened as the parrot perceived the truth.

"He understands, Mama. He knows, Mama. Look for the sign. Look for the sign."

Mama raised her voice. "Everybody be quiet. Please!"

The room grew still.

"Now, Chris, please tell us the truth. Your friend is truly a cat?"

"Yes, ma'am. A black one. With a star on his ear, like this." He undid the top button of his shirt and showed the birthmark to Mama.

LinLin flapped over to his shoulder and landed lightly. Leaning down, she peered intently at the mark, first with one eye, then the other.

"That's the mark," she announced.

Mama crossed her arms and cradled her chin in her hand. "So I see. This changes things. Captain, please bring the boat about. I'm afraid we are not going to find this Mr. Thomas."

"But Mama!" Christian protested.

She held up her hand for silence. "Please understand, Chris, we've been traveling upriver for over an hour. We weren't even looking for a cat. Besides, the riverbanks are overgrown. It would be nearly impossible to see a cat onshore."

"It's true," Christian admitted sadly. "I don't even know if there are other people out there. 'Cept for that crazy Samuel. The other animals told us."

"Oh, now you talk to *all* the animals," the captain scoffed.

"Captain, please!" Mama insisted. "Bring us about. Have the men keep an eye on the banks. Maybe they will spot this cat as we return. And sound the whistle. He may hear it and try to show himself."

"Yes, ma'am." The captain saluted and left with the crewman.

The room grew quiet. LinLin hopped to Mama's shoulder.

Mama reached over and pulled Christian's shirt open. "Let me see your mark."

"It's the mark," LinLin confirmed.

Mama undid the top button of her blouse and pulled it open. A star-shaped birthmark seemed to pulse over her heart.

"It seems we share a gift."

BREWING DISSENSION

"We need to know evil so we can define good. But what of the evildoer? We have numerous tales of good triumphing over evil, of wicked people redeemed by good acts. But what of the genuinely demonic person? Is there any hope for them?"

— A BUTTERFLY IN FLIGHT: THE BIOGRAPHY OF THOMAS SPEAKER BY JAMIE LIVINGSTON

Grizzly looked up from his table as Bill Bradshaw, his chief lieutenant, shoved a woman into the room. She looked dirty and disheveled, used but not used up.

"Here she is, boss." The lieutenant threw her across the room. "She's a fighter."

The woman glared at Grizzly. She wore a long gray skirt and an old flannel shirt. Dirt and grass stains testified to how she spent the last few hours.

Grizzly stood and walked to her, motioning Bradshaw to leave. The door shut behind him.

"My name is John Darby." He tried to sound kind, caring even. It didn't work. His voice was a growl.

"I know who you are." She didn't try to hide her contempt.

"The Grizzly. Your reputation precedes you." She scanned him up and down. "I must say, it doesn't look like you can live up to that reputation. Ha!"

Grizzly covered the distance between them in two quick steps. A sharp slap to the face sent her sprawling.

She rubbed her jaw. "So that's where your boys learned that." She gazed at his waist, calculating. "You teach them anything about how to treat a lady?"

Grizzly grabbed her hair and heaved the woman up. She quickly turned on him, bringing her knee up to his groin. It hit something substantial. Grizzly laughed and tossed her aside.

"One old trick for another." He undid his jacket, revealing a blacksmith's apron. A long knife sheath hung in the middle of it, empty for now. The heavy leather cover proved to be adequate protection.

Still, he kept his distance. His eyes grew narrow as he appraised this hellion. Did she look to be in her forties? *Maybe. But her eyes have a look of what, wisdom?* Something stirred in him. He knew he had to have her. *What's this? Why her? Ain't nobody else going to have her.*

Crossing to the table, he picked up his Bowie knife. Another quick step, and he held the tip under her chin. "What's your name?" He wanted his voice to be kinder-sounding. *Why?* It came out as a snarl instead.

"Judith. My mother named me for the Old Testament character." She did not attempt to avoid the knife's point. A drop of blood began oozing from the cut and stopped.

"Never heard of her." He lowered the blade, shoving it into the sheath.

"I'm not surprised. Can you read at all?"

Grizzly raised his hand, ready to slap her. She stared defiantly. *Those eyes!* His hand turned into a fist as he tried to hide the fact that he felt helpless.

"I don't take crap from anyone." His chin jutted out as he scrutinized her. "You don't think I'm smart? I've survived more an' thirty years in what's left of the world. I got an army. I'm their leader, nobody else. It takes brains to do what I've done."

"You got squat, and you know it." Judith's finger stabbed at him, poked his chest. "You survived? Ha! A slow-witted squirrel can survive nowadays. You got an army? That's just a band of thugs you've got. A real army has a purpose. They don't go rampaging around the countryside. They have a reason for taking a town. What's your purpose, *John?* Do you have one? Or are you just an old bear?"

He snatched her wrist and twisted it, forcing her to bend. Judith brought her left hand up and under the apron, grabbing him.

"I don't take crap from anyone either!" She squeezed harder. "Let go before I make it so you don't ever need these again."

"I'll break your arm!" Grizzly twisted her wrist tighter only to feel her grip tighten.

"If you let go, I'll let go."

Easing his grip, Grizzly pulled Judith upright. *What's this, now? What's she want? To live? Doesn't everyone? No, this one wants more.*

He guided her to the table and forced her to sit on a chair. He straddled another one, elbows on the table, glaring.

"So you're a smart gal, eh? You know enough about survival. That's plain to see. What do you want from me?"

"Oh, I'm about a lot more than just survival, John. By the way, I think 'Grizzly' is a stupid nickname. Pretty childish, if you ask me."

"Nobody asked you. It serves a purpose, having a name like that. You're right. These boys aren't too well-educated. The nickname helps keep 'em in line, gives 'em somethin' to look up to—to respect." He let out a huff. "Again, what do you want from me?"

"How old do you think I am, John?" Her eyes penetrated his, looking deep into his soul.

He looked away. "I'd guess early forties. No more than forty-five."

"I'm forty-two. Plus another thirty-three since the world fell apart."

"How can that be? You ain't seventy-seven."

"That's seventy-five. I see math isn't your strong point." She stood and paced. "I was part of an experiment—a test subject. It all happened during the wars. I was one of the lucky ones, I suppose. I survived the trial; now, I don't age."

Grizzly stood slowly, almost painfully, and stretched to his full six-foot-six height. "I know what you want. That's simple. It don't take a fancy education to figure it out. You're no different than anyone else. You want to live. And I've got the smarts and the power to make that happen. I know women like you."

"Ha! You don't know me at all." Judith faced him. "Yes, I want to survive. So did that rabbit you had for dinner. So does every living creature. I've endured a very long time, and I intend to keep on doing so. But I want more, you see? I'm like you. I want power. I want to control life, not just live it."

Grizzly studied her and saw fire smoldering in her eyes. *This one's a real hellcat. You* are *like me. Well, well! What do we do with this?*

"Bradshaw!" He pushed past Judith and stomped over to the doorway. "Git in here."

The house Grizzly had taken for his own was huge. The first-floor master bedroom and bath were now his living quarters. Bill appeared in the doorway leading out to a corridor and beyond to the kitchen and great room.

"What's up, boss?"

Grizzly glared like a madman. "Git this one settled upstairs. Give this witch the room with a bath and make sure she uses it. She'll need clean clothes, too."

Bill looked back and forth at the two, bewildered. "But, boss! I was settling in there."

"You take the other one. Make sure she can't open the

windows. And put a lock on the door. With a guard! It seems this Judith thinks she's smarter than all of us. Well, I got plans for her." He leaned against the table and took a deep breath.

"OK. Right away, boss." Bill grabbed Judith's shoulder to lead her away. She shot a glance at Grizzly, a haunting smile on her lips. Then it was gone.

The room empty, Grizzly breathed in and held it, shuffling slowly to the bathroom. He got to the sink and flipped the spigot. Cold water ran out. He dropped his pants and quickly grabbed a cloth, soaking it. A ragged breath testified to the soothing effects the compress had on his aching balls. *That bitch has quite the grip!*

⋅ ✳ ⋅

JUDITH SHOWERED QUICKLY, ANNOYED THAT BILL WAS JUST OUTSIDE the door. She wrapped a tattered towel around her and stepped into the bedroom.

"I found these down in the other bedroom." Bill held out a pair of slacks and a shirt. "These look like they'll fit ya."

"Yeah, maybe." Looking around the room, she tried not to show interest. The battered dresser and bed were familiar items. A small solar light illuminated a homemade child's toy—a push truck. It triggered her memory. *Ben! My boy. Where is he now?*

"I put the other clothes in the closet. Grizzly wants to see you as soon as you dress."

"Thanks. These will do fine." *Of course, they'll fit. They're mine! My clothes. My house. That bastard's in my room … our room.*

Judith choked back a sob, turned it into a cough as she returned to the bathroom.

"We'll be sealing the windows while you're gone. Ol' Grizzly thinks you're something else. Ha, I bet he does. I can't wait to see what he does to you."

"And I'll enjoy watching what he does to you if anything happens to me," she shouted through the door. Dressed, Judith strolled back into the room. "Besides, you men have got all you want from us, right? Maybe if you treated us better, you would be treated better in kind." There was a twinkle in her eye, and a catlike smile crossed her lips briefly.

"What do you mean?"

"We're all remnants of what was. We all want to live—to see the next day. It looks like your gang is going to be settling in here for the winter. Why not make the most of it?"

"It'll be like any other winter, I suppose."

"Will it? Why not make it better? Hot meals instead of cold rations. Maybe a bedmate rather than a whore? It's all in your attitude." The smile appeared again.

Bill considered this. "Nah. Grizzly says we're moving on in the spring. We got a fight to pick in Ohio. We're building an army."

"You call that bunch of sluts and dickheads an army?" She laughed in his face. "Maybe you never saw real, trained soldiers. So where are you going to get this army? You killed all the men here. People hear about you, and they get out of the way. You're going to have to work with what you got. Maybe Grizzly isn't smart enough to have figured that out. But you? I think you play along with him only to save your own butt. Maybe you would rather things be different?"

Bill sat on the edge of the bed. "So, whatcha sayin'? You believe I should be in charge?"

"No! Grizzly would have his butcher knife in your gut if he ever knew you wanted that. But *if* that's what you want—"

"Wait. I never said that." He jumped up.

"All I'm saying is that you can live comfortably here. But that's not what you want, is it? None of your gang wants to settle down? That's hard to believe." Judith strode to the bed. "If you're going to build an army, you'll need to convince our women to join you. Turn them into fighters like you." She touched his shoulder. "How old are you, Bill? Forty-five, maybe?"

"Fifty-two. Why does that matter?"

"None of us is getting any younger. Perhaps what we want

changes the older we get." She sat him back down. "What do you dream about, Bill?"

"I don't dream about nuthin'. I always figured a man like me, like any of us, never had any future. So no, I don't dream."

"I think you should start. You and Grizzly have made your own rules all these years. It might be time to make some new ones." She patted his knee. "You've got the power. You can change yourself."

Bill looked deep into her eyes. "I wouldn't know where to start or even how to. I will tell you this. There's one thing I've learned from the boss and that's never to trust a bitch." He looked away.

Judith stood. "I have a friend. Well, maybe, if she survived. Her name is Sarah. About my height, long red hair. If you find her, tell her I sent you. She'll help you. But for now, Grizzly awaits."

She headed toward the door.

NEW FRIENDS

"Sometimes, when I meditate, I feel this overwhelming connection to everyone and everything. I can't explain it, but when I take an enhanced journey with psilocybin, I can actually see and feel this golden thread connecting me to … everything."

— *A BUTTERFLY IN FLIGHT: THE BIOGRAPHY OF THOMAS SPEAKER* BY JAMIE LIVINGSTON

Thomas awoke on the riverbank and tried to stand, but his legs gave way under him. *A little wobbly-legged, are we?* He pushed back up and shook the fogginess from his brain. Sniffing the air, he noted the remnants of a fish close by. He tightened, then relaxed, working the stiffness from his muscles, and went to the carcass. Flies buzzed at his approach. He sniffed at the dead creature and winced, the aroma triggering his memory.

Was it yesterday that he and Chris tried to cross the water? The memory of spilling out of the tiny boat was fresh. *Well, I hope it was only a day ago.* The rushing flood had propelled him down the river. *How far? There's no way of telling.* He had struggled to keep his head above the foam. Debris caught up with him and floated on. He tried to snag onto a limb to no avail.

Exhausted, he felt himself sink, then rise. Once. Twice. He took in a deep breath as he submerged again, too tired to do anything about it.

Without warning, he had felt himself rise. Something was under him, keeping him afloat. He dug in his claws.

"Easy there, fellow!" a voice had bubbled up from below. "I'll get you to shore."

With that, they had moved quickly. Thomas tried to make out what it was he was on. All of a sudden, he rose into the air and flew toward the shore. Gathering his wits, he managed to land on all fours and turned around, catching sight of a giant fish. It jumped and flipped its tail before crashing back into the torrent.

"Thank you!" Thomas had yelled.

"No problem. I've been watching you. Sorry, but at first I thought you were food," the fish said. "Oh, here." A swift kick of its tail sent a smaller bluegill out of the river, landing next to Thomas. "I imagine you're hungry."

Thomas stepped on the smaller flopping fish. "That I am. How can I thank you enough?"

"I sense you understand the way life is—that all life is inter-connected. Then you know that when you receive a favor, you must pass it on, not pass it back. You will likely have many oppor-tunities to do so." With that and another flip of his tail, Thomas's savior had disappeared.

Now he turned his attention to the remainder of his meal. Shadow patterns dappled the ground around him, telling the time as about midday. *Where is Chris? Is he alive? Should I go downriver?* The thoughts tumbled through his mind.

"Hew-ew-ew-ew!"

A shriek cut through his thoughts. Thomas jumped. The sound came from the river. He ran to a nearby tree. Making his way along a low-hanging branch, he peered out. A strange boat was about fifty yards away, making a broad turn in the river, preparing to head back down.

"Hew-ew-ew-ew!" the whistle shrieked again.

Thomas strained to see. There were men aboard. Some were looking through binoculars, searching the riverbank.

"Hey! Over here!" he yelled, knowing no one would hear him. *I wonder if they found Chris. Were they able to save him? I can't feel him!* A sneeze shook his body. "Ah! Now a cold. No wonder I can't pick up on Chris."

The boat slowly moved downriver and out of sight. There were so many questions, and Thomas had too few answers. He jumped from the tree with a sigh. *What to do now? Try to go down-river? I would never catch up. Trust that they saved Chris, that's all I can do.*

With that, he made up his mind to continue east. The river-bank was heavily overgrown. Thomas picked his way slowly up the bank and found the remnants of a highway heading due north. He chose his way cautiously along the side of the road. Coming to a small town, he dodged between buildings until he was confident the place was abandoned.

He remembered the map he had shared with Chris. *This way should lead to Highway 136 and go back east.* Sure enough, the road intersected the main highway cutting to the east and west and passed through a retail district. Thomas hurried from building to building, past dilapidated homes and out of town.

The sun grew lower in the western sky. Sensing an oncoming chilly night, Thomas headed toward a small stand of trees for shelter. As he neared the thicket, the distinct sound of arguing voices rolled out. Thomas crouched low, approaching cautiously.

"Jusssst leave me alone, you young whippersssnapper," one voice whistled.

"Oh, come on, Gramps, I was only funning with you. I don't mean you any harm." This one sounded youthful, almost mirthful.

Thomas crept through the underbrush and into a small clear-ing. A young fox was looking up into a large maple tree. "Please come down, Pops. I won't eat you. I promise."

Thomas followed the fox's gaze and detected movement

among the branches. About a dozen feet up, he made out a groundhog perched on a side branch, shaking his paw at the fox.

"You're jusst a punk!" he hissed, glaring at the fox.

Thomas called out to the fox. "What's going on here?"

The fox looked over. "Oh, the old man thinks I want to eat him or something. I was just funning with him." He sprang back, surprised. "Hey, a cat! I haven't seen a cat around here in, like, ever. Pops, there's a cat down here."

"What'sss that you sssay?" The groundhog squinted down at them. "A cat? Well, I'll be." He began backing down the tree.

The fox trotted toward Thomas, who took a pace back, hissing a warning.

"Whoa! Easy, friend cat. I won't harm you. Just like I'm not going to hurt him." The fox looked back over his shoulder as the groundhog jumped the final two feet to earth.

"What'sss thisss, now?" He waddled up to the fox and Thomas. "Ssso, it isss a cat. Pleasssed to meet you, missster." He nodded. "And you"—he punched the fox on the shoulder—"you need to ssstop ssscaring the bejeesusss out of me."

The fox winced. "Ow! You don't have to hit so hard."

"Now, just hold on." Thomas stepped between them. "What's going on here? What's with you two?"

"My apologiesss, sssir. Thisss youngling here keepsss harasssssing me." He shot a nasty look toward the fox. "My name isss Garsssseya, by the way."

"And I'm Reynard." The fox rose on his hind legs. "Like the great warrior fox. That's me."

"Reynard wasss no great warrior." Garcia poked at him. "He wasss jussst a trickssster. Like you."

"Now, now." Thomas held up a paw. "Calm down. My name is Thomas and—"

"Thomas!" Reynard cut in. "Like in 'Tomcat'? That's funny."

"Hoo! It sssure isss!" Garcia rolled back with laughter.

"Okay, okay, have your fun. But show a little respect, please." Thomas held his head up with pride.

"Of coursse, of coursse." Garcia waved him off. "Ssso, what bringsss you to these partsss?"

"I'm on a quest of sorts." Thomas relaxed.

"A quest?" Reynard jumped up. "That's just the thing for me. Where are we going? When do we leave? I'm a warrior, you know. I'll be great on any quest you want to take."

"Now, now. Not so fast, youngster." Thomas scowled from one to the other. "This is a dangerous journey. We can't just go running off. I've lost two comrades so far. I'm not going to take anyone else on only to lose them."

Garcia yawned. "Well, count me out. It'sss almossst hibernation time for me. If sssomebody quitsss bothering me." He looked pointedly at Reynard.

"I'm sorry, Pops, er, Mr. Garcia." Reynard lowered his head. "It's just that ever since those animals took Mother and my littermates, I've been alone. What I know is what I learned on my own. And what you taught me. I guess I just want to belong with someone or … or something."

"Tell me what happened to your family." Thomas tilted his head, curious. *There's something about these two. What is it?*

"It was the last sun cycle." Reynard lowered his head. "We were just weaned and learning to play and chase butterflies—that sort of thing. One day two strange animals came across our hill. They carried sticks to beat us, but I managed to run off and hide. Mother tried to fight them. Now I'm alone." Tears welled up at the memory.

"Animals? On two legs? It sounds like humans. Tell me more." Thomas paced.

"I don't know what you call them." Reynard shuddered. "But they were tall. They swung the sticks hard. They stood on their hind legs all the time."

"Yesss. Humansss!" Garcia hissed. "You can't trussst a one of them. Look what they did to me." He stood on his hind legs to show a star-shaped brand on his chest. "It burned my fur and flesssh when they gave me that. And they did other thingsss when I ssslept."

"What sort of things?" Thomas asked.

"I don't know. I wasss in a place—in a cage. They fed me well, but sssometimes they would take me out. I sssaw sharp pointed thingsss. They poked me with them, and I ssslept. I woke up, and I wasss … changed."

Thomas looked him up and down. "What do you mean, changed?"

"How old do you think I am, Thomasss?" Garcia's eyes looked tired.

"I honestly have no idea," Thomas admitted.

"We groundhogsss can live, at bessst, about sssix sssun cyclesss. I don't know the name of numbers after that, but I have already counted sssix normal lifetimesss. They did sssomething to me to make me thisss way. I go to hibernate, and I wake up feeling like a youngling."

Thomas sniffed at the groundhog. "You were a 'scientific experiment'—a test subject of sorts. What they tested is anybody's guess. It sounds like you rejuvenate during your hibernation. Maybe they were looking for a way to stay young and use it on themselves."

They all fell silent for a minute, lost in their thoughts.

Thomas spoke first. "Garcia, it seems you have an unexpected gift. One the humans gave you. Perhaps you can help me on my quest."

Reynard jumped up. "Hey! What about me?"

"Ah, yes." Thomas eyed the fox. "Have you ever looked in a pond of water?"

The fox grew wary. "Sure, every time I get a drink. Why do you ask?"

"Did you ever notice the white marking in your left ear? The one that looks like mine?" Thomas turned his head and showed the star mark to his new friends.

"Sure, but I never paid attention to it." The fox craned his neck, trying to get a view of the mark. "Now that you mention it, it does look like Mr. Garcia's too."

Thomas looked from one to the other. "Maybe you have the gift also. If so, then yes, you can join my quest."

Garcia pushed Reynard aside. "Well, you two can go on a-quesssting all you want. *I* need to get sssome sssleep."

Thomas thought of Christian. *Is he even alive? I sense that he is, and he's okay.* He made his decision and squared his shoulders. "So it looks like we need to plan on staying around here for the winter, what with you hibernating and all, Garcia."

"That wasss my plan all along. I wasss digging my burrow when thiss wise guy busshwhacked me. I told you he ssscared the bejeesusss out of me."

"Well, if you've got one started, maybe Reynard can help you finish." Thomas looked around. "If you make it big enough, we can all survive the winter here."

"We're going to have to make it twice the sssize I'm usssed to, cause I don't want to be around that fidgety young 'un all winter."

"I'm sure we can accommodate." Thomas placed a reassuring paw on Garcia's shoulder.

BEN AND BRANDON

"I often wonder why it is I meet certain people. It almost feels as if it was our destiny, as if someone guided us to each other. Is that God's hand shoving us along?"

— *A BUTTERFLY IN FLIGHT: THE BIOGRAPHY OF THOMAS SPEAKER* BY JAMIE LIVINGSTON

B en met up with Brandon at the cow barn, as planned. After a quick handshake and shoulder bump, they nodded in agreement and set off down the road at a trot. Prodded by shouts from the village behind them, they picked up their pace.

"We'll take a break when we get to the outpost," Ben huffed. He took another deep breath. "Mom says to pick up whoever is on watch there, take them with us."

Brandon kept pace with him. "Right. But we can't stay long. Those raiders may send a party chasing us if they know we're gone."

The cousins covered the two miles to the outpost in fifteen minutes, a record time for both. The station was a simple, one-room shack, with a single window in each wall allowing full view of the surrounding area. Inside, a battered oak table and chairs sat to the left. A small, pot-bellied stove filled a corner. It sat cold to the touch. The chalkboard hanging on the wall opposite the doorway held a simple message written in a rough cursive. *I went back to stand with my father. Aliyah.*

"Aliyah was on watch?" Brandon caught his breath.

Ben shook his head. "Oh, man, no! She's gonna get hurt bad. A girl can't stand up to those barbarians."

Brandon dropped his pack and sat down. "Don't bet on that. Yeah, she's only eighteen, but since her mom died ... well, I wouldn't want to face her blade."

"Ha! You wouldn't get past her slingshot." Ben set his pack on the table and rummaged through it. He found the Y-shaped piece of hickory and pulled back on the rubber band. It sounded a satisfying twang when released. He tucked it in his belt, over the left hip.

Brandon untied the crossbow fastened to his backpack. "Best to go armed from here on." He secured the quiver so that it was in easy reach when he shouldered the pack.

Ben followed suit, and without another word, they set off.

Both boys had accompanied scouting parties since they were six years old. The adults used these trips to pass on the necessary skills to survive in any weather. This time was different. They were on their own, unsupervised. Still, they walked with a confidence that belied their age.

Several days into their journey, they crossed into what was once the great state of Ohio and turned south. Untouched by nuclear war, the region still suffered the effects of civil unrest. The abandoned small towns and villages held the ghosts of a crumbling civilization. There were no other people to encounter. Or so they thought.

The sun was setting on the eighth day as the duo walked into a small farming village. Although they had braved most nights camping in the woods, the sky now turned cloudy, threatening rain this night.

A large brick building stood near the center of town. A weathered placard hung beside the door while windows on either side of the entrance allowed them a look inside. There were tastefully decorated rooms behind the glass.

"What's it say?" Brandon sidled up to Ben, who squinted, trying to make out the lettering.

"Dunno. It's pretty beat up. Something Mill B&B is all I can tell." Ben looked at it from different angles, then shrugged.

Brandon laughed. "B&B? Ben and Brandon, of course. Well, I'd say that's a sign for us to go in."

Just then, the door flew open. The cousins jumped back as a man stepped into the doorway. His skin was black, a darker black than they had ever seen before. White whiskers peppered his cheeks and chin. His eyes were clouded, nearly white.

"Fee, fie, foe, fum. Who is this that has come?" the man bellowed.

Ben spoke up. "T-two weary travelers, sir. W-we mean no harm. We had no idea anyone lived here. We thought the house was empty."

"You sound like white boys, that I can tell." He sniffed, first at Ben, then at Brandon. "Proves me right, from what I smell. Whatchu boys doing around here, anyways?"

"Grandpa, what's going on?" A middle-aged woman appeared behind the man. She was tastefully dressed; carefully applied makeup softened her face. "Oh, I see we have visitors."

"Strangers!" the old man barked. "Like in stranger danger. Call the rangers!"

The lady patted his shoulder. "Now, Grandpa, these two young men appear to be tired from their travels."

Ben shook his head vigorously. "Yes, ma'am. My name is Ben, and this is my cousin, Brandon. We've come from Michigan.

"You walked all that way on your own?" She shook her head. "My name is Lilly, and this is my grandpa, Otis, Otis Johnson."

"Pleased to meet you," the boys said together.

"I imagine you have some tales to tell," Lilly continued. "We do take in boarders now and again. If you want to stay the night, you may. But since money's no good anymore, we expect you to help with some chores."

Brandon shifted his backpack. "That's fine by us. We're used to work."

"We were going to offer," Ben chimed in.

"Well, come on in. I'm about ready to make dinner, and I need some firewood chopped. It's out back here." She pointed down the hall to a door. "If one of you wants to do that, the other can help clean some vegetables. Grandpa, you come along, too. Why don't you find your guitar and play us a tune or two? And for heaven's sake, take those contacts out. You're going to hurt your eyes."

It took little time for the boys to complete their chores. The wood was aged and easily split. Lilly cut up some cooked meat, placed it in the simmering water, added some herbs, and waited for the boys to clean and cut the veggies.

"It's squirrel stew tonight," she announced. "Beggars can't be choosers, I always say."

"We've been eating fish, mainly." Brandon made a face.

"And apples. Lots of apples." Ben groaned, remembering what too many would do to his innards.

Lilly smiled. "Well, it's going to be a while before dinner is ready. Let's go see what Grandpa's up to. You can tell us about your journey and such, I suspect."

She led them to the dining room. Otis was there, tuning an old acoustic guitar. He looked up as they entered and smiled, eyes twinkling.

Brandon stared. "Hey, what's happened to your eyes? Oh, I'm sorry, that was rude of me."

The old man laughed. "It's okay, son." He dug into his shirt pocket and pulled out a small box. "They're contacts. They're caps I put over my eyes to make it look like I have cataracts. I used them all the time when I was younger and playing the clubs. They called me Blind Otis Johnson back then." He let out a loud whoop. "It got me some nice tips."

"Grandpa is a bluesman," Lilly boasted.

"Yeah, I used to play all the clubs over in Toledo." He picked at the strings on the guitar. "These days seems the blues is the most appropriate thing to sing." His fingers flew across the strings as he stomped his foot.

Mama Nature done cried like a baby that night.
Bombs in the bays as the warplanes took flight.
Nuclear destruction, you will not survive.
It makes me wonder, do I want to be alive?

It all broke apart, not long after that.
No magic got pulled from the old magic hat.
Greed corrupts, no matter how much good strives.
It makes me wonder, do I want to be alive?

"Now, Grandpa!" Lilly reached over and grabbed his arm, ending his playing. "That song is so depressing. We have guests. Play something more pleasant."

Otis's shoulders sagged. "I'm sorry, dear. But the blues is about depressing things. It's what makes them the blues." He straightened up. "You are right, though. We have guests, so here's something a bit happier."

He began slowly, picking out a smooth tune. The words rolled off his tongue, singing about his special girl and how he had so much honey, the bees envied him.

The boys sat misty-eyed. The song ended, and Otis looked their way, concerned. "I hit a bad note, didn't I?"

Ben took a deep breath. "Oh, no, sir! It's just that my girl is my mom. And the song describes her perfectly."

"Yeah." Brandon sniffed. "Me too."

They sat quietly for a long moment. Lilly broke the silence.

"So why don't you tell us about yourselves? You say you came from Michigan. We don't get out much around here. Tell us what's going on."

Between them, the boys were able to tell their tale of the attack on their village and the approaching danger.

Ben summed it up. "We don't know when they'll come this way—"

"But they will come," Brandon finished. "You're the first folks we've come across. We have to warn you and anyone else around."

Ben nodded in agreement. "Our elders told us to get to Thomas Speaker and warn him. Maybe he can get an army together. Maybe he can stop these raiders."

Otis stroked his white stubble. "I see. Well, we've been listening to Pastor Thomas all of these years. He persuaded us to leave the city and move out this way when the troubles hit. He helped us survive all of it. But our neighbors—they're spread out for miles and miles all around us. It's going to take time to warn them."

"Please, sir, whatever it takes." Ben pounded his fist into his hand. "These people are ruthless. It's just a matter of time before they come raiding. You should all pack up and follow us."

"Yes, we'll need to decide that." Lilly rose. "Time enough tomorrow to worry about that. For now, dinner's ready. Go wash up."

PONDERINGS

"Memories? Of course! I have nearly a century's worth. I try not to remember the bad times, but there they are."

— A BUTTERFLY IN FLIGHT: THE BIOGRAPHY OF THOMAS SPEAKER BY JAMIE LIVINGSTON

Thomas Speaker sat alone on the park bench, looking out over Smitty's Pond. The town leaders named the pond after John Smith, one of the town's founders and owner of the property. Of course, its original name was Smith's Pond. It changed somewhere in the 1960s when the great-great-grandson of John, John Smith IV, renamed the family business Smitty's Auto Repair.

Funny how you think of the strangest things when you can't concentrate on the one thing that matters. The pastor sighed and fumbled in the pocket of his old cardigan. He rubbed the bowl of the briar pipe like a talisman. When the stem-cell effect took hold, his nicotine cravings ceased. *I stopped using tobacco over thirty years ago. Still, this old thing does come in handy. Thirty years! That was after things settled down. It was after the Forever War finally and forever ended. It was after the collapse of civilization, and after humankind went crazy, and … and …*

And yet, here we are. This is my hometown. He pulled the pipe from his pocket and stared at it. A gift from a long-ago admirer, it still held its sheen. *First anniversary present of my new mission. Before the collapse.*

His memory skipped back like a flat rock across the pond. Each time it struck the surface, he touched on a particular moment. A brief memory came and went. Each strike sent out ripples just as the moments of his life rolled out to affect others.

Thomas's mind reeled with the images. His wife, the divorce, his best friend's death, drinking, drugs and despair, the clinical trial, meeting Doc and feeling, the real deep-down soul-searching feeling of his call to ministry, the war, annihilation, calling his flock together, rebuilding this town and now, here.

"Am I disturbing you, Thomas?"

"Wh-what? Oh, no!" He recognized the woman standing in front of him. "Not at all, Eleanor, not at all. Please have a seat."

"Such formality, *Pastor* Thomas?" The woman kidded.

"Hmm? What? No! My apologies, Ellie. I got lost in my thoughts, I'm afraid."

She sat down next to him, tucking a gray strand behind her ear. "No apologies needed, silly. I just came to find Josh over there." She tilted her chin to point across the pond, where a young boy was fishing.

"I think you may have bluegill for dinner." Thomas gave a slight laugh and shoved his hands into his pocket. "So, what else is up?"

Eleanor Davis had a sad smile. It seemed older than her forty-plus years. She was only ten when she came to the village with her parents. As the girl grew, she showed a particular interest in books and organizational structures. Formal education stopped long before the final blows to civilization, but she picked up everything she could from the adults around her. With her nose always in a book, it was no wonder that the young lady founded the town's library at the age of sixteen.

"Well, you do have several books overdue. I wouldn't mention it, but we've got a hold on one for one of the new folks, Muriel Cummings."

"Really? Those folks are settling in fast."

"They sure are. This new group has been here, what, a little more than a week? They picked out the homes they want to rehab. In fact, two couples decided to take on one of the nearby farms. It appears they know a lot about organic methods. They're so excited."

Thomas turned to her. "Did you explain to them the rehabilitation rules, especially the farms, with winter coming on and all?"

"Of course. This isn't my first rodeo!"

"Ah, sorry. I keep forgetting you've been head of the town council before. How many times?"

"I'm beginning my third term. Sometimes I think it should be longer than a three-year term. Although I admit that John Rigby brought some good ideas during his last term."

"You two keep flipping back and forth in those duties." Thomas pulled out his pipe and pointed the stem at her. "I agree. I sometimes think we need some new blood to take over. You know, bring some fresh ideas into the mix. Still, you're both doing what's right for all of us, in my opinion. The two of you are so … simpatico." He waved the pipe. "It's like when one thinks of something, the other is already doing something about it. Two peas in a pod, as they say."

Ellie laughed. "Are you trying to marry me off?"

"What? Me? No! I'm just an old geezer looking out for his kids and grandkids now." Thomas leaned back. "Besides, if you two decide to marry—and I'm not suggesting that you do, mind you—but if you do, remember you don't have to take his last name."

Ellie looked at the pastor sternly. "And what's wrong with Eleanor Rigby?"

"Nothing! Nothing!" Thomas held up his hands in surrender. "It just reminded me of an old song. That's all." He smiled at the memory of good times long past.

"So, what's this talk about being an old geezer?" Ellie

frowned. "You don't look any older than the day I met you, and that was thirty years ago. Snap out of it! 'Old' is a relative term, especially for people like you—and Doc and Maggie."

"Hmph. I've used that excuse myself. What you don't understand, what you can't imagine, is that, while our bodies aren't aging, neither are our minds."

"What do you mean?" Ellie's brow furrowed with concern.

"Old people are supposed to forget. I can't. I mean, I can put things out of my mind, like how many times you were head of the town council, but it comes on in full detail when the memory is triggered.

"Before you got here today, I was sitting and thinking about my past. Every thought, every memory, is crystal clear. Like it happened moments ago. And it can make a mess up here." Thomas jabbed a finger at his temple.

"Can it be that bad?"

"You tell me." He clasped his hands around the pipe and leaned forward, elbows on knees. "Now that you're here, I remember you coming to town with your parents and eight other folks. They said you made your way up from Kentucky. You were a sorry-looking lot, I must say. And now I remember that winter two years later when your folks died of pneumonia. And then you were marrying Josh Davis. You did that right after you opened the library. And that reminds me of that marauding band and how Josh died fighting them. Josh Jr. wasn't even born yet. I could go on."

"No, no. I … I see what you mean. You're right. We do allow ourselves to forget, especially the bad times." She dabbed an old handkerchief at her eyes.

"I'm sorry, Ellie. I didn't mean to bring back all those bad memories." Thomas allowed her to compose herself. "What's on the agenda for the town meeting tomorrow?"

"Do you always change the subject when the conversation gets … difficult?"

"Why, yes, I do. It's a defense mechanism. I don't like

confrontation. However, I won't shy away from it either. If there's a need."

The image of Josh Davis leaped to mind. They stood side by side, fighting the marauders. Thomas could again feel his knife plunge into one of them. He was pushing the man away when the arrow struck Josh in the chest—a mortal wound to his heart. Thomas knelt, tried to stop the bleeding. He couldn't.

He shook off the memory. "What's on the calendar, then?"

Ellie perked up, pleased to show her expertise. She handled the position of Town Council Chairperson efficiently. "Well, Item No. 1, the census, is now at 2,642 with the new arrivals. There will be reports on how they are settling in. Most have declared their fields of expertise and settled on committee assignments, which reminds me—Muriel wants to borrow that book on comparative economic systems you have checked out."

"The Gregory/Stewart book? Certainly. It's some heavy reading, though. How interesting." He tapped the pipe stem against his front teeth.

"She says she's interested in capitalism." Ellie looked doubtful

"Hoo! That will cause some spirited debate." The pastor brandished his pipe. "How about I bring it to the meeting? You can let the paperwork catch up later."

Ellie laughed. "That's one of the things I love about our town. We don't let paperwork get in the way of getting things done. Anyway, also on the agenda is a report from the Utilities Committee. I understand they have some good news."

"What about? It's not easy keeping up with all the progress we're making."

"One of the salvage teams found some sort of siren or something like that. They're very excited."

The pastor clapped his hands and jumped up. "Then so am I. Can't wait to hear more."

"Thomas, don't you dare go over to Doc and Maggie's this evening. Between their work and that child of theirs, it's a wonder they have time to breathe. Doc will fill us all in tomorrow. Why don't you join us for supper?"

"We should see if Josh caught enough for all of us first."

Ellie stood and shouted, "Joshua, the sun's setting. Time to get home!"

The boy waved from across the pond and pulled in his line. He wrapped it around the old fiberglass pole and picked up a five-gallon plastic bucket next to him.

Thomas waved back and smiled. "That boy gets taller every time I see him. And the last time I saw him was yesterday."

"Now he's not growing that fast. Not like Doc and Maggie's little girl."

It was true. The whole town was talking about how unusual little Jamie's growth was. Born ten days earlier, she was already rolling around when placed on the floor. She would even try to crawl.

"I swear she'll be walking by springtime." Ellie smiled.

Thomas lowered his head in thought. "It has to be their genes. We all know they're the first two from the stem-cell experiments who survived and had a child—their first. We lab rats are in our nineties now." The pastor looked across the pond and shook his head. "We weren't even sure a baby could be conceived, let alone if the genetic change would transfer. Maybe this growth is part of it. If only we had one of the researchers here."

Ellie looked at the ground, kicking at a rock. "Josh's daddy was a researcher and a 'lab rat,' as you call yourselves. He could have helped. We don't know what, if anything, passed onto Josh Jr. He didn't get the rapid healing properties like you all carry. He's got a skinned elbow to prove it."

"Sh-sure do!" Josh came up, struggling with the bucket. "H-h-hello, P-pa-pastor."

"Hey, Josh. Let me give you a hand with that." Thomas reached down for the bucket. "Goodness! How many you got in here?"

"S-s-six or s-s-seven b-bl-bluegill. I saw you t-tal-talking w-wi-with Mom and th-th-thought we c-co-could ask you to dinner."

Ellie gave Josh a quick hug. "He's already been asked. It's sweet of you to think of that."

"Well, I can't refuse such a kind invitation." Thomas peered in the bucket. "These are some nice-size bluegill. How about I help clean them?"

"I-I-I was h-ho-hoping y-y-you would offer."

Thomas picked up the bucket and reached out to Josh. There was a slight tingle when they touched. Laughing, they walked down the pathway.

DELAYS

"Some folks call me a prophet as if I can foretell the future. In reality, the best I can do is apply what I know to any situation. It's not hard to predict the future when you understand human nature."

— A BUTTERFLY IN FLIGHT: THE BIOGRAPHY OF
THOMAS SPEAKER BY JAMIE LIVINGSTON

Christian stood near the rear of the stern-wheeler. Peering intently at the shoreline, he mumbled a prayer. "Please keep my friend safe, God. Please."

Is he alive? Is he out there in those woods? Did he keep going down-river? Or did he drown?

"Hew-ew-ew-ew-ew!"

He glanced up to see the steam released from the large brass whistle poking out of the pilot's cabin. Turning back, he caught his breath. *What was that? Something in the tree. Thomas? A bird?*

The ship heaved into a wide arc, turning around in mid-river. Christian ran to the other side, trying to keep his eye on the spot in the trees. *Was it there? Or there? No. Where are you, Thomas?* He leaned against the railing, straining to see … what? Anything!

"Hew-ew-ew-ew-ew!" The whistle sounded again.

"Ah, there you are, Christian." Mama Ruth approached. She stood with him quietly for a moment. "You miss your friend." It was a dry statement of fact. "I, too, have lost friends. Many friends." The quiet grew uncomfortable. "I have instructed the captain to sound the whistle every fifteen minutes. We are moving slow enough. Maybe your friend will hear it and come out."

"I thought I saw him. Over there in the branches. But it could have been a bird." He stared dejectedly into the muddy water.

"If he's out there, the crew will see him. You are the only person we've seen since leaving Cairo, Illinois. I don't believe this area is very populated."

"Mr. Thomas says there's a village way west of here—about a week's journey—but that's all." Christian slammed his fist on the rail. "Where'd everyone go? There used to be lots of people."

Mama reached out a comforting hand. "The war. And afterward, too. People turned on each other. It's a sad testimony for humankind."

She brightened a bit. "But for now, at least, we're heading back down the river, returning to Cairo. There's a small settlement there where we left two of our crew on our way up the river. They are setting up a ham radio, restoring communications with the rest of the world." Mama turned to look downriver. "We'll be there in about a week."

"Why does it take so long? Your boat is fast."

"Well, not that fast. I understand your impatience, but the river is long, over three hundred miles back to Cairo. And we can't go too quickly. There are logs and other boulders like the one you mentioned and bridges partially down. We have to navigate around them. It makes traveling at night impossible."

"I see." Disappointment crept into his voice.

"Take heart, Chris. You have much to learn about the boat. You can help the crew with some of the chores." She gave him a quick hug. "We usually make landfall about an hour before sunset and send out teams to search for food and firewood. Other crewmen will fish the river, clean the decks, or handle kitchen duties. You can have your choice of jobs. You'll see. The time will pass quickly."

Christian stared out across the river. "My mama always said to make the best of a bad situation. I'll be glad to help."

Mama Ruth smiled. "Very good. But first, I must speak with you privately. Please come back to my stateroom."

*　＊　*

LinLin, the parrot, squawked at them as they entered. "Welcome back, amigo."

Chris smiled, remembering being called a caballero. "Why, thank you! It's good to see you again. Can I come in?"

The bird tsk-d. "You *may* if you *can.*"

"Now, LinLin, we've discussed this." Mama lowered her chin and glared. "Just because you have a decent education doesn't mean you have to correct everyone all of the time."

"My apologies, Mama. But you know I take language skills quite seriously."

"And you know that is our little secret. We can't afford to have the entire crew know how well you speak. Someone will want to start a carnival show and make you the main attraction. They will want to take you away." She raised the back of her hand to her forehead for dramatic effect. "I will be so desolate without you."

"All right. All right. I know sarcasm when I hear it."

Christian looked back and forth between the two. "I don't understand. Why can't LinLin talk with the crew?"

"While I do not ban her from talking"—Mama glared at the bird—"we have to be careful. There is still a lot of superstition and misunderstanding in the world. I'm not certain how people who don't have the gift would handle learning that all beings are sentient."

"Se-sentient? What does that mean?"

"It means they are conscious or aware of themselves and

others. Most people think of animals as being stupid. So they try to control them, own them, enslave them. It would be a far better world if we all understood how each of us fits into it."

"That's what Mr. Thomas told me, too. He didn't call animals se ... sentient. He just said they were more aware of life forces than humans realize. I don't think he liked humans, but he said people were okay." Christian smiled at the memory.

"He seems to be an exceptional cat." She paused a moment. "And you are an exceptional man." Mama sat down at the breakfast table and motioned for Chris to do the same. "Did Mr. Thomas ever say if he knew of other hu— er, people who could talk with him?"

"Oh, yes. He had a friend named James, but he passed on when they had an accident and their truck fell into a big hole." Chris scratched his head. "That's another thing he tried to explain. This James 'passed on.' He didn't die. At least that's what Mr. Thomas said. That's why we were heading east to find Pastor Thomas. My friend Mr. Thomas said he was on a mission and that Pastor Thomas would understand and help him explain everything to other people. I was gonna help."

"Ah, yes." Mama nodded her approval. "He understood that one's spirit moves on when their body perishes. Perhaps your friend was hoping to find his other friend, this James? This friend would be born into another body, yes? That's the way the spirit behaves. Some people are aware of their past lives. Most are not. I had to learn this outside of medical school."

LinLin flew from her perch and landed on the table. "Mama Ruth is a medical doctor," she declared. "And a voodoo queen. Not to mention she is self-taught in the world's religions and can speak four languages—English, French, Spanish, and Creole. Plus, she—"

"Now, LinLin!" Mama scowled. "There is no need to boast. Besides, I am *not* a voodoo queen." She looked at Christian. "As part of my medical apprenticeship, I spent time in Haiti. I learned about the Vodou cult and their beliefs, just as I learned about

Muslims, Hindus, Christians, Jews, and Buddhists. I studied them all at one time or another."

"So why does LinLin call you a voodoo queen?"

Mama pointed to the parrot. "That is all her doing. She thought that if people believed I was Vodou, they would steer clear of me, be afraid. It is her way of protecting me from the ugly humans, no?"

"It's worked so far, yes." LinLin curtsied. "In Haiti, no one messes with a voodoo queen. Even the truly evil steer clear of them."

Mama shook her head. "Yes, but such tall tales you tell. Like that one about me riding a tsunami into New Orleans. It's amazing people believed that one!"

LinLin bobbed up and down, chuckling. "A voodoo queen would have such powers. I think that made your reputation. You're welcome."

Christian was intrigued by his hosts. "So where do you come from, LinLin?"

"I was born in Africa, of course, and was captured at an early age and sold into slavery."

"There you go being overly dramatic." Mama shook her finger at the bird. "You were not 'sold into slavery.' A very respectable Chinese businessman acquired you. So they tell me."

"Call it what you want. I was taken out of my nest and forced to live where I did not want to go. What is slavery? He thought I was property. So much so that he gave me to you as payment for services."

"You make a valid point. I'm sorry." She turned to Christian. "I treated the man for an illness he wished to keep secret. I had a private practice at the time and could get the medication he needed. He could not risk leaving a money trail, so he told his wife that LinLin got out of her cage and flew away.

"As for you—" She turned to the parrot. "You are free to leave whenever you want. You know that."

"Yes, yes! You've told me that before. But why leave now? Things are just getting interesting." LinLin looked at Christian.

"They sure are," Chris and Mama said as one, then laughed together. Falling silent, they enjoyed the moment of synchronicity.

Mama stood and retrieved a small hand-carved box from her desk. Sitting back down, she took out a deck of cards wrapped in a black cloth. Spreading the fabric out on the table, she deftly spread the cards in front of Christian.

"Do you know anything about Tarot, Chris?" She looked deeply into his eyes.

"Never heard of it. Is it some kind of card game? My mama would play cards sometimes, but hers weren't as pretty as yours."

"While we use a unique deck of cards, it is not a game. Some people call it fortune-telling, but it is not that, either. I like to think of it as a way to understand the world around me. It is a method to tune in to the spirit of the universe and understand our place in it. May I show you?"

Christian eagerly nodded as Mama picked up the cards and shuffled through the deck. LinLin hopped on the table. "May I help?"

"Of course. I was about to ask you." Mama held out the pack of cards, and LinLin grasped them momentarily. Then she flew to Mama's shoulder.

The doctor held the cards in front of her, prayerlike. "Now, Chris, it's critical that you open your mind. Try not to think of anything except the one question you wish to have answered. Here." She handed the deck over. "Shuffle the cards like I did and think of your question."

"Okay." Chris took the oversize cards and shuffled them clumsily. Closing his eyes, he thought a moment. "I guess what I really want to know—what I really need to know is if Mr. Thomas is okay."

LinLin nodded. "Your friend? It is good that you think of him."

A single card fell from the deck.

Chris glanced around. "Oops, sorry." He went to scoop it up.

"Wait!" LinLin hopped down and inspected the card. A picture of a gray-haired man stared from it. A wand, a cup, a sword, and a medallion floated in front of him.

"That man looks awesome." Chris picked up the card. "Magician," he read. "What does he do?"

LinLin reached out to Chris, touching his finger. "The card is your Significator. It represents you. From what I have learned about you, I would say that you are in touch. Am I right, Mama?"

"I believe so!" She took the other cards from Chris. "You see, Chris, the Significator tells us about you. In this case, the Magician represents someone who has the skills needed to handle a particular task. However, you must have the willpower to do so. You must be confident."

"What task? What am I supposed to do?" Chris fidgeted in his chair.

"The cards will advise us. But only that. When the reading is complete, you will have an answer to your question. But you will have other questions. As I lay out the cards, we'll see if they can lead us to an answer."

"I need to know about Mr. Thomas. Is he alive? Where is he? Can the cards help find him?"

"Whoa, whoa!" Mama held up her hand. "One question, please. We'll see what the cards say about that and go from there. Let's try, 'Please tell us of our friend Thomas the cat.'"

"That sounds good. Anything. Anything! Just please tell me about Mr. Thomas."

Mama stopped shuffling and laid the first card on the cloth. "We have different patterns to place the cards. This pattern is called the Cross of Truth. It is good for general questions and helps to direct us to more information. This first card tells us about you, your feelings about the question."

The card showed seven golden goblets.

"The Seven of Cups means you are facing many choices." Mama touched a finger to the card. "Perhaps it is overwhelming?

Several paths are opening to you. You must remain practical in your decision. Remember the Magician. You have the skills you need to do this."

Chris nodded. "But what choices do I have?"

"Shh. Let the cards play out."

Mama pulled another card. It showed eight swords surrounding a blindfolded girl. She gently placed it above the first.

"This represents your desires, what you wish to happen. The Eight of Swords shows that fear is binding you. You cannot see the answer, although it is there for you." She placed another card on the table. "This next card will tell us what helpful matters are available to aid you."

The card showed eight wands floating in the air. Mama placed it to the right of the second card. "This is very encouraging. It points to a quick answer following some good news. Perhaps some travel is involved."

"Of course, some travel is involved." Chris jumped up. "We're traveling right now. If Mr. Thomas is alive, then he'll be traveling also. Don't tell me something I already know."

"Patience, Chris. Remember, the cards told us you were feeling overwhelmed. I believe this card is telling us more. Your question was about your friend, Mr. Thomas. This card tells us he has had setbacks also, but he is to receive some good news; perhaps he will be traveling. Chris, if he is receiving good news and planning to travel, then he is —"

"Alive! I forgot the question was about him and not me. Is he alive? That's wonderful news. I'm sorry, Mama Ruth. I ... I ..."

"It happens. Now calm yourself. This next card will tell us of the challenges he faces."

Chris sat back down as Mama placed a card to the left of the second one. It showed two wands stuck in the ground. A traveler came to a fork in the road.

"Ah. It appears your friend is doing fine. He has reached a

point where he will have to decide which path to take. However, he may have picked up a partner or two. Interesting."

"A partner? Does that mean me? Will I see him again?"

"Remember, Chris—this is about the present situation. So no, the partnership is not you and him. The most likely scenario is he may have met someone along the way who will be helpful to him."

"Oh." Chris hung his head. "I wonder who they can be."

Mama smiled cheerily. "Don't be so glum. Nowadays, everyone needs a friend. Maybe you'll get to meet them. Here." She placed a final card above the second one, forming a cross. "This tells us of the outcome to your question."

The card displayed a golden wheel against the sky. Planets were in the background, and some sort of machine was in the foreground. "Wheel of Fortune" was written at the bottom.

"This is favorable." Mama placed her hands firmly on the table. "The Wheel of Fortune tells us a new, better cycle is ahead for your friend. I don't think you need to worry about him, Chris."

Her guest stared at the cards. "It's funny how the pattern looks like my birthmark. The star."

"I hadn't noticed before, but you are right. That is curious."

"You were right about one thing, Mama." Chris reached out and touched the cards. "I have a whole lot of other questions."

There was a knock at the door. LinLin flapped to her regular perch and began to preen.

"Yes?" Mama called out.

"Excuse me for bothering you, ma'am." The captain sounded agitated. "The radioman just received a message from Cairo. It appears the Ohio River is blocked."

CAIRO

"Before the end came, I think most folks had no sense of mission. Like they lost a sense of purpose in this life. I only found mine when I received the stem cell treatment. Now my belief is we must engender that in the next generation."

— *A BUTTERFLY IN FLIGHT: THE BIOGRAPHY OF THOMAS SPEAKER* BY JAMIE LIVINGSTON

The journey back down the Mississippi proved painstakingly slow. Several days passed with the *Delta Belle* anchored to the shoreline as late autumn rains pummeled ship and crew. Mama Ruth was right when she told Christian there would be plenty to do on board. The steam engine's appetite for wood was enormous, for it now provided heat for the living quarters as well as power to the huge paddle wheel. When the rains let up, most of the crew spent two entire days foraging fuel, then cutting, splitting, and stacking it.

"With any luck, that might last us a week," a young crewman moaned, stacking a final piece on deck. "Then we git to do it all again."

Christian looked at his hands, now dirty and scratched, the

callouses thickening. "Still, it beats kitchen duty." He smiled back at the lad.

"And what's wrong with kitchen duty?" A surly voice growled from behind.

Christian swung around. A woman stood with her hands on her hips; a stained apron hung from her neck, covering a pair of overalls and tattered shirt. She clinched a corncob pipe between stained teeth. A tattered bandanna covered her short-cropped graying hair.

"I asked you a question, buddy. Are you some kinda chauvinist or sumpthin? Do you think kitchen work is just for women?"

"N-n-no, ma'am!" Christian took a step back. "I did plenty of cooking and cleaning for Mama. And I took pretty good care of myself af-after she passed." He choked on the memory.

"Ah, don't git all defensive." The woman tapped her pipe on the rail. A small ember dropped to the river. "I'm just trying to recruit you to my kitchen. I'm the cook, so they call me 'Cookie.' Git it?" She squinted at Christian and shrugged. "Guess you can do the same."

"She's also a little touched," the crewman whispered to Christian. "So we actually call her Kookie."

Christian stifled a laugh. "Pleased to meet you, er, Cookie. My name is Christian. Everybody calls me Chris."

"Chris, eh?" Cookie looked him over. "I've been watchin' ya. Where'd you go to school, Chris? When you were a kid."

"Excuse me?"

"I'm curious. Where'd you go to grade school? Somewhere in Nebraska, maybe?"

"Why, yes, ma'am." Chris's eyes bugged out. "It was Johnson County Elementary School, Tecumseh, Nebraska. They called it that because Tecumseh was in Johnson County, Nebraska."

"You were in the 'special' class, weren't ya?"

"Mama says we're all special in God's eyes." Christian threw back his shoulders, ready for a fight.

"I'm sure she did. Do you remember Ms. Perlmutter? Maybe it was fifth grade." Cookie dug into a pocket of her overalls.

"How on earth do you know Ms. Perlmutter?" Chris raised his hand to his mouth. "Were you in her class too? She tried to teach us music. That was just before all the troubles began."

"I remember." Cookie took her hand out, clutching a small object. "I wasn't in your class, but I went to that school when you did. I was a year ahead of you. Here, this is yours."

She opened her hand as she extended it to Chris. A shiny chrome case, engraved with the word "BluesBand," gleamed in the sunlight.

"My harmonica!" Chris snatched the instrument up. "This was a birthday gift from Mama. How did you get it? Ms. Perlmutter took it from me. I remember. She said I couldn't play it while the other kids were studying. She put it in her desk drawer."

"Yep, and I took it from there when you all went to lunch. I heard you playing it and liked the sound. So I took it. I was nasty like that, back in the day."

It was Chris's turn to look Cookie up and down, staring. His eyes widened as he recognized her.

"Meany! Meany Mary! Why did you take my harmonica? It was a gift from Mama."

"No reason. I was just like that. If I saw something I liked, I'd take it. The school shrink said I was a kleptomaniac. That's all behind me now."

Chris eyed her suspiciously.

"What have you been doing with it all these years?" His hand clamped down on the instrument as he held it close.

"I learned to play it. The crew thinks I'm pretty good. Maybe I can teach you."

"We'll see." Chris placed it deep inside a pocket. "You should never have taken my Mama's gift." He shoved his way past her.

* ✳ ·

Captain Cornelius traced his finger along the map as Mama Ruth watched, her frustration growing.

The captain explained. "The problem is that the Ohio River was navigable only because of the lock and dam system. That's how the tugs and barges were able to get past the falls and other low points."

"We are currently here." Mama pointed to a spot on the Mississippi, just above the confluence with the Ohio. "And the report from Cairo said the river is blocked where?"

"Just here, ma'am, at Smithland, Kentucky."

"That isn't very far upriver. What happened?"

"According to Cairo's scouts, debris mainly. With no one maintaining the system, flooding poured trees and all sorts of human junk into the lock. Even cars. The first blockage, whenever it occurred, caused more flooding over the years. Things got worse from there. They claim it will take months to clear this one lock. There's no heavy equipment operational anymore, just draft horses." The captain pounded the table.

"And there are other places that would be blocked like this? We can only assume it's just as bad or worse the farther upriver we would go." Mama sat down and held her head.

"Exactly. Cairo is sending another party to explore further. No matter what, we'll need to know what things are like ahead. For future planning, if nothing else."

She shook her head. "Yes, the future. Who knows what the future holds?"

"Aren't you a fortune-teller?" The captain winked.

"Ah! The Tarot. I guess the superstitious among the crew think it's for predicting the future. If only it could! No, it can only advise of likely challenges on our path. We must make our own decision about how to handle it. For instance, my reading this morning indicated that I achieved a goal but I now had to choose between two paths to continue. It appears it was quite accurate."

"I always thought you could read whatever you wanted to into those things," the captain teased.

"Certainly you can. But that would ignore the advice it provides for the individual. A reading may advise you that there is a choice of paths ahead. Only you can say what the two paths are. That's why it's such an individual thing." Mama stood.

The captain began to pace. "The people of Cairo have offered to put us up for the winter. Our two paths. Should we stay, or should we go?"

"You said Cairo now has a dry dock. *Delta Belle* could use some repairs. Perhaps we can get those done."

The captain shuddered. "You know I hate being beached. Still, it would give the crew a chance to mingle, maybe let off some of their own steam. It would be good for morale."

"I agree with that. So long as no one decides to jump ship." Mama caught herself. After she said it, the idea took on a note of reality. "Well, let's hope Cairo isn't *that* attractive."

"Oh, I doubt it, ma'am. This crew loves their jobs, life on the river, and working for you."

"Okay, okay. We'll let the crew in on our plans after we anchor for the night. Now I have more work to do."

"Day's nearly done. Best prepare our speeches." The captain nodded and left.

* ✻ *

MARY WATCHED CHRIS DRY THE LAST OF THE PANS AS SHE FILLED HER pipe. "So, Chris, can I ask you sumpthin? It might be kinda personal." She picked up a twig from the kindling pile, opened the stove door, and held it in the embers till it flared up.

"Sure. If it's too personal, I'll tell you to butt out." He smiled. Now that he knew a little more about this plainspoken woman, his initial dislike faded.

Mary put the flame to her pipe and puffed till it lit. "I mean no offense, but back in school, you were … different. Like you were touched in the head or sumpthin." Her brow creased. "Know what I mean?"

"Oh, that!" Chris put the towel down and stuffed his hands in his pockets. "Mama called them my fuzzy-headed days. I had a hard time understanding a lot of stuff back then. I guess that's why I was in those 'special' classes." He shuffled his feet and looked around for a seat. There was none.

"Just before the troubles, Mama heard of some medical experiments that promised a lot of stuff to a lot of people, so she signed me up. I don't remember a lot about it, though." Chris stared at the floor. "I woke up one day and the cobwebs were gone from my head and I could think clearer. Things changed after that. They weren't so simple anymore."

Mary puffed out a ring of smoke. "Ain't that sumpthin! Sounds like a miracle to me. I mean, the way you were back then compared to now." She took a step closer and tapped her pipestem on his chest. "I think you're a better man for it."

Chris's face turned red. "Th-thanks. But Mr. Thomas had something to do with that, too."

"Your cat friend? How so?" Mary stepped back.

Chris glanced around, searching for the words. "It-it's hard to explain. When he lay on my chest, there was a warm feeling, like my heart got bigger. I—I felt connected, if that makes any sense."

Mary considered this when a crew member poked her head inside the galley's door. "Sorry to break this up, Cookie, but the captain's called a special meeting."

*　*　*

THE NEWS GOT A MIXED REACTION FROM THE CREW. ALTHOUGH ALL were disappointed they would not be sailing up the Ohio River, some wanted to head home immediately.

"My kids are growing up without me," complained one of the engine crew.

"Mine, too," another agreed. There were other rumblings.

"I understand that concern." Captain Cornelius held up his hands for silence. "We've all been gone from our families for a long time. If we were going straight up the Ohio River, we'd be gone a lot longer. We all understood that from the start."

"Yeah, that's true." The engineman crossed his arms. "But now that journey's been cut short. Why shouldn't we head home? The engine is purring along like a contented cat. I'll attest to that." The crew's grumblings grew louder as others joined in agreement.

TWEEEET! The captain's whistle cut off all argument. He held it between his lips, looking around the room. With a short grunt, he let it drop and dangle on its lanyard.

"I will have no more commotion like that! Hear me out. Mr. Scott, I know the engine is in great shape. You and your crew do a first-rate job of maintaining it. Nevertheless, this will give us a chance to shut it down and give it a proper inspection." He scanned the room. "I do have some concerns about the hull. We took a few hits on rocks and other debris. Being in drydock will allow us to make sure we're not an accident waiting to happen." Several of the crew nodded in agreement.

The captain continued. "Now the crew we left behind to set up Cairo's radio report there is plenty of housing for each of you, and the townspeople are very excited to meet new folks. I think we'll have a warm welcome there."

He shifted his tone from stern leader to gentle father. "So here's the plan. We'll make the confluence of the rivers in two days. We then head up the Ohio to the drydock area. It used to be a railroad siding, but they're converting it into a shipyard. How about that? It seems there's progress everywhere."

Seeing the crew's interest, the captain explained. "On another front, Mama Ruth has talked with Thomas Speaker. He says they've just welcomed a group of migrants. And here's some excellent news: President Bancroft's expedition also made it to Speaker's town. They're establishing ties to the east, beyond the Appalachian mountains. For our part, the trip isn't a waste. We've learned there aren't many survivors upriver, at least along the banks where we'd expect them. That opens up a lot of land for settlement.

"This is just the beginning." He beamed with confidence. "Our explorations will allow other expeditions, maybe even pioneers, to come back this way. There's a bright future ahead for all of us!"

The crew's disappointment turned to excitement. The captain finished to a round of applause and cheers.

"Nice save," Mama Ruth whispered in the captain's ear.

"I meant every word of it, ma'am. It's a rare crew. The way they all work together is like no other I've commanded. I would never give up one man or woman of them." He grew misty-eyed.

"It's your doing, Captain." Mama patted him on the shoulder. "You are a respected leader. The crew loves you, too."

"I think it's more than that, ma'am." Cornelius dabbed at his eye, wiping away the tear. "It's like they're on a mission, and each is doing his and her level best to make certain the mission succeeds."

"Life *is* a mission, Captain." Mama's smile seemed to brighten the room. "We each have the challenge to learn our place in the universe. We forgot that somewhere along the line. Now we are beginning to realize it again."

EMISSARIES FROM THE NORTH

"I continue to be amazed at how resilient our children are. As parents, we fuss and worry over them even into adulthood. But when push comes to shove, they always have what it takes to overcome any obstacle. They show this at an early age."

— A BUTTERFLY IN FLIGHT: THE BIOGRAPHY OF THOMAS SPEAKER BY JAMIE LIVINGSTON

"Here, Jimmy." Doc Livingston handed two wads of cotton to his helper. "Put these in your ears, and we'll give it a trial run." As the lad jammed the plugs into his ears, Doc followed suit and stepped back. They were in the clock tower of the courthouse and the village's highest point. Others removed the nine-foot clock faces long ago, as they had fallen into disrepair. The openings, usually shuttered against the elements, now opened onto the chill November afternoon.

Doc patted the large rectangular horn of his latest project and stepped off the lazy Susan where it was mounted. With a thumbs-up, he leaned into the push bar and began turning the contraption in circles. Jimmy grabbed the horn's hand crank and began turning it as rapidly as he could. A low moan issued forth as the antique air raid siren came to life. The pitch increased to a howl with each turn of the crank. Doc continued to walk the siren through three circles before he stopped, signaling Jimmy to do also.

The two shared a handshake. Jimmy couldn't stop smiling. "That was great, Mr. Livingston. Can I be an operator?"

"That's going to be up to the Safety Committee to decide, son. But I'll give you my recommendation." Doc cuffed him on the shoulder. "I think that will come in handy this tornado season."

"Helloooo up there!" The shout came from the street.

Doc peered over the side and waved. "Hey, Earl. Whatcha got there?" Standing with the watchman was a white-haired man, a much younger woman, and two young boys.

Earl cupped his hands to his mouth. "These youngsters say they're from Michigan. They've got some big news, too."

*　＊　*

WORD OF THE NEW ARRIVALS SPREAD QUICKLY, FOLLOWED BY RUMORS of the news they shared—a marauding band's vicious attack on their village leaving all the men dead, and one could well imagine what happened to the women. A raucous crowd had packed the council chambers by the time Eleanor Davis gavelled the emergency meeting to order.

"People, please!" Ellie banged the gavel for the umpteenth time. "I said QUIET!" She stood and stared from person to person. "Now, I know this is troubling news—"

"Troubling?" Someone shouted from the back. "There's a whole army coming our way."

"If you can believe those boys. What if they're lying?" A man pointed to the boys.

Another chimed in. "We're pretty much defenseless. We did away with the militia years ago."

"Well, it has been so peaceful all those years."

"Yeah, but now look at us. We are totally unprepared for something like this."

Ellie hammered on the table again as Otis Johnson stood, a tall, imposing figure.

He turned to Ellie. "May I say something, ma'am?" His voice was raspy, like gravel in a bass drum.

Ellie placed the gavel down as the room grew quiet. "Folks, this is Otis Johnson. He and his granddaughter, Lilly, brought Ben and Brandon here." She looked around the room, saw that she had their attention. "We've heard the boys' report about the attack on their village. It's a miracle they were able to escape and bring us their warning. Now let's hear the rest of the story."

"Thank you, ma'am." He smiled at the chairwoman and turned to the audience. "We come from a small town west of Toledo and run a hotel of sorts there." He shook his head. "No, we don't get many guests these days. As you can well imagine." A patter of laughter came from the crowd as they warmed to him.

He motioned to Ben and Brandon. "The boys here showed up on our doorstep about two weeks ago. I admit that at first, I didn't believe them, figured it was a tall tale by a couple of runaways." He allowed a quick laugh and glanced at the boys. "But we adults can see through children's lies. These boys aren't lying. *And* they are no longer children."

Otis paused a moment, thinking. "Best I can figure is that our town is about halfway between here and the boys' village. There's only a couple of dozen of us living there and another dozen or so farmsteads around us." He spread his hands. "We are completely at the mercy of whoever may want to harm us. So, in a way, I guess we're here to ask for your help. And to offer ours."

A murmur went through the crowd. It seemed odd that someone from outside of their town could offer them help. Most were refugees seeking shelter. Ellie banged the gavel.

Otis continued. "Ben and Brandon wanted to hurry here with their warning, but I wanted to know more about them. You see, I thought that it's remarkable they traveled as far as they did alone.

I've found them to be quite exceptional." He nodded toward the boys. "Show them your note, Ben."

The youngster stepped up to Ellie, pulling a tattered sheet from his pocket. "It's a code. My mom and I made it up just before we left—when the attack was beginning."

Ellie read from it. "'Days equals boys; fair weather equals good condition; foul weather equals injured.' I don't understand." Her brow creased.

"It was Mom's idea. We didn't have much time, and she was so worried about us." Ben drummed his fingers on the table. "She thought that since we can listen to the pastor's radio show, maybe you can let her know we're okay. I thought you could talk about the weather, you know, say 'We've had two days of fair weather.' That way, she'd know we're both safe." He choked back a tear.

The pastor, sitting two chairs down, reached over. "May I see that?" After studying it, he regarded Otis. "This gives me ideas."

Otis's eyes shone. "Exactly! We met with our neighbors before coming here and have scouts heading toward Ben and Brandon's village. It's interesting. Seems that no one followed the boys, so I believe this army is going to hunker down for the winter."

John Rigby spoke up. "All well and good. That will give us time to rebuild the militia. But it's going to be tough communicating back and forth." He looked down the table. "Doc, can we set up a ham radio in Otis's town?"

Doc tilted his chair onto its back legs. "We've got the equipment for it and something more." Bringing the chair upright, he leaned forward, elbows on the table. "Sandy and her crew in electronics have been able to recondition several CB radios. They're short-range, but we can string them out between here and there— set up watch-posts along the way. We only have three units so far, but it's a start."

Ellie looked up and down the table. "I like what I'm hearing. It'll be good having eyes and ears out for this horde. Then it comes down to our own defense." She stared at the table a moment, remembering her deceased husband, then looked around the room. "Everyone here over twenty years old can remember being in the militia. But can you honestly say you've all retained your fighting skills? Is there anyone here that has *any* military background?"

"I may be of help." A senior man stood up. His blue eyes flashed from under heavy silver brows. The close-cropped hair spoke of a man with military training. "Sergeant Bartholomew Hopkins, Third Division, Second Corps, Civilian Emergency Response Team, at your service." He clicked his heels and gave a snappy salute.

The town leaders all sat up. "I … I had no idea." Ellie eyed the man. "Didn't you come in with Muriel Cummings's group?"

The sergeant saluted again. "Yes, ma'am. By the way—" He laughed. "Please call me Bart. It's been a long time since I served our country, but the training never leaves you." He looked over the audience. "Those of you who served in the town's militia, this is a new call to duty. As for the new generation, we need your skills also. Together we'll build the finest fighting force in existence, and those marauders can be damned."

Cheers and applause filled the council chambers. Ellie allowed it to continue for several minutes. *Now that's the sort of speech we needed just now!*

CHANGES

"No matter how hard the lesson, it seems we tend to go back to our old ways. It's disheartening. Will we never progress?"

— *A BUTTERFLY IN FLIGHT: THE BIOGRAPHY OF THOMAS SPEAKER* BY JAMIE LIVINGSTON

A cold wind blew fallen leaves past the group as Eleanor Davis pulled the Town Hall's door shut. Assuring the deadbolt had slid into place, she turned to the group.

Doc Livingston tried a half-hearted smile. "Well, that got ugly. Who's this new gal, Muriel, and why does she think we need laws anyway?" His wife, Maggie, shot a warning glance his way. He ignored it. "I mean, we've gotten by all these years without a written code. Why now? Especially with everything else happening."

Ellie held up the key. "That's the point, Doc. A year ago, we never thought of locking up our houses or businesses. Now, because of a couple of vandals, we lock up."

Doc huffed. "I told you back then the public shaming wasn't enough punishment. Those boys needed a good ass-whooping."

Ellie stuffed the key in her pocket. "I'm sure they got it when they got home. Still, I believe Murial is correct in suggesting we finally have a set of written laws." She wrapped her woolen scarf around her neck. "What do you think, Pastor?"

Thomas was staring up the stone façade of the old courthouse. "Clear skies tonight. And look. I think our star satellite may be getting closer." He shrugged. "It's going to be a cold one. Maybe an early winter, too."

Maggie chucked him on the arm. "Thomas! Don't avoid the subject."

The pastor looked at each of his friends. "Sorry. You know I've always tried to stay neutral on political matters, especially with the day-to-day operations of the town." He thought a moment. "Since you asked, I believe you are all correct. The town's population is nearly three thousand, and we have new people joining us weekly, not to mention the young people, a whole new generation." He looked at Doc and Maggie. "I think you two can appreciate that. So, yes, it is time to codify our rules, our standards. Perhaps even a constitution to lay out where we want our civilization to go."

The pastor shuddered as the wind caught him in the face. "As to the other matter, Doc is correct regarding the more pressing issues. Those boys who got here from Michigan last week, er, Ben and Brandon, we need to heed their warning of this marauding band. They sound worse than all the others we fought put together."

Ellie stomped her feet and shivered. "How about we take this over to my office? I'll put some tea on."

Thomas pulled up his coat, clutching it at the throat. "Thank you, but no. I still have work to do back home, and these two"— he nodded toward Doc and Maggie—"have a young one to get back to."

"But I was hoping —"

"Hoping I would have all the answers?" The pastor laughed. "I don't, but you do. There's a lot of expertise in our village. And Muriel brought more. The older military man, eh, Sergeant Bart

Hopkins, he'll be able to help plan our defense. Trust in their expertise." He gave Ellie a reassuring hug. "I'm off. Take care, my friends!"

* * *

Doc and Maggie rounded the corner onto their street. Maggie gasped. Their house, the third one down the block, was ablaze in light.

"What on earth?" She broke into a run. Doc followed quickly behind her.

"Rebecca knows better than to burn all the lights at once," Doc fumed.

As they bounded up the three porch steps, the front door flew open. The babysitter, a girl of fourteen years, stood in the doorway, arms crossed in front of her. Her scowl spoke volumes.

"Becky, what's wrong? Where's Jamie?" Maggie looked frantically from the girl to the house.

Rebecca jerked her head toward the door. "She's in her room. She's possessed, I tell you. My parents thought so, but I know so. Possessed by the devil!"

"Oh, for heaven's sake." Maggie pushed past the girl, rushing into the house.

Doc stooped to the girl's level. "What on earth are you talking about? What do you mean by that? The devil doesn't possess our daughter."

Rebecca stared ahead as if in a trance. "It's just as my mother thought. Your child is possessed. Her eyes see into your soul. She knows things."

"For pity's sake! Our daughter is only three months old. How can she *know* things?"

Becky grabbed Doc's arm. "Her eyes, Mr. Livingston, her *eyes!* I can tell she sees into my soul. Take me home, please. Take me home now!" She tugged at him, pulling him toward the steps.

"Just hang on a minute. We'll get to the bottom of this first."

Maggie stepped back on the porch, cradling the infant. "Jamie's fine. No harm done. See? She's all smiles." Jamie cooed and began chattering, holding tightly to Maggie's sweater. "But Doc, she's unbelievable!" Maggie held their daughter up. "She was standing up in the crib. Now listen to her."

Doc bent over his family, holding out a finger to touch his daughter. "Incredible. She shouldn't have reached this stage of development yet. It must be a new genetic makeup from the stem cells. We'll need to watch this closely."

"Pa. Pa!" Jamie grasped Doc's finger. "Pa. Pa! Papa! Papa!"

Letting go of her father, she reached out to Maggie. "Mum! Mum! Mum!"

"What? My heavens! She's talking!" Maggie bounced the child on her hip. "She's actually *talking!*"

Rebecca hauled on Doc's arm. "It's the devil inside her. Take me home now, please!" Tears rolled down her cheeks as she pleaded.

"Ba grl." Jamie looked at the babysitter. "Ba grl. Ba grl!"

Doc looked from Maggie to Jamie and back again, his mouth agape.

"Mr. Livingston, please!" Rebecca's wail pierced the night. Lights came on at the neighboring house.

Maggie nodded for Doc to go as she looked nervously toward the neighbors. "Honey, take Becky home. I'll take Jamie in and calm things down."

Doc caught her concern. "Yes, of course, dear. Okay, Becky, let's get you home. It's been a long night."

"Never again, Mr. Livingston. I'll never babysit that child of yours again. The devil's inside her!"

"Everything okay, Doc?" Earl Piper stood at the edge of his porch, backlit by the house light.

"Yes, yes," Doc waved to them. "Becky got a little spooked, is all. I'm getting her home now."

Earl returned the wave. "All right. Give us a yell if you need anything."

"Will do. Sorry for the commotion." Doc put his hands in his pockets. Rebecca wrapped herself in her arms.

Earl's wife, Betty, stepped out, an afghan pulled around her shoulders. "What's going on?"

Earl shrugged. "That girl is afraid of her own shadow. She always seemed peculiar to me."

"Now, Earl. Don't be so judgmental. I'll make us some chamomile tea." Betty patted Earl's shoulder and smiled as he opened the door for her.

Doc strolled beside Rebecca. The girl stomped her feet as if she was squishing bugs.

"Becky, you said the devil possesses Jamie. What did you mean by that?" Doc was apprehensive. He had no idea where this conversation would go. *The girl's parents are a little odd, what with keeping to themselves and all. They don't participate in many community activities. Still, they never actually did anything wrong.*

"That's what Mother and Father say. Remember? They watched her last week while I did my studies. You folks had some town business to attend to."

"I remember. Your folks were a big help on such short notice. I hope we didn't interfere with your studies."

"No. Father had me read some of the ancient Bible scriptures. There was a part about the devil possessing men, and I had to ask what that meant. He said the devil was pure evil and sometimes he gets into people. That's when he looked into Jamie's eyes. He said, 'See! See how her eyes shine? That's the devil's work. I believe this child may be possessed.' I think he's right, too. No baby I've ever known can move around like she does at her age. And now she talks. She called me a bad girl. You heard it!" Becky began to cry.

"Where does your father get such ideas? I haven't heard such talk since, well, since the end times."

"Father said that Grandpa told him about those times, how terrible they were. There was a big war between God and the Devil. Grandpa expected to get whisked away to heaven, but that never happened." The girl grew quiet, remembering. "Maybe that's why Grandpa was so sad all of the time. He said he was left behind. I guess he meant God left him behind."

"I think maybe your grandpa and now your father misunderstood that story in the Scriptures. There is a story about the end times, but it's an allegory. It uses fictional characters and events to teach a lesson. Lots of folks read it literally, however, and take it as fact. It's a good story to tell if you want to scare people into behaving correctly." Doc took a deep breath, relieved that he could explain the matter.

Rebecca snorted. "Well, *we* take it very seriously, Mr. Livingston. How else do you explain Jamie?"

"That has more to do with genetics than it does with the devil. That's certain." Doc grasped for an explanation the girl would accept. "No, we don't understand it all either. You see, some genes get passed on from the father, and the mother passes on others. They mix, and with any luck, the good ones dominate. Maggie and I had a, um, *procedure* when we were younger. It mixed up our genes, made us able to heal quickly. Somehow these got passed on to Jamie. Whatever is happening to her is caused by that. At least, that's what we think."

Rebecca stopped suddenly. "So you don't know?" Her brow furrowed.

"We can't know. Not for certain. We aren't able to test for it. There's no equipment, and nobody here has the expertise. It's the best we can do."

"Then it's just as possible that my father *is* right." Rebecca got wide-eyed. "After all, Pastor Speaker talks about our godstuff all the time. What if Jamie has devil-stuff? Grandpa said there will always be evil in the world. Why not in Jamie?"

"Because she's *my daughter*. That's why. No parent ever expects their child to be evil." Doc threw up his hands.

"Father says that it's the devil inside her that's evil. He needs cast out; then Jamie will be fine." Rebecca set her chin firmly, her mind made up.

Doc stared at the heavens and shook his head. "I give up. Look, we're at your house. It's been a long night. You get along now and try to get a good rest."

Becky brightened. "Okay, Mr. Livingston. Maybe you should talk to Pastor Speaker. He may know how to cast out that devil." She skipped up the porch steps and into the house.

Doc stared after her. *Oh, I'll talk with Thomas. It's unbelievable what kind of thinking survived. Why do we humans have such a terrible time evolving?*

BATTLE PREPARATIONS

"I once knew a woman who argued with everyone. Because I prefer to discuss matters, to work things out, I could not get along with her. One day, she pointed out that her reason for being argumentative was to show she cared deeply about the subject— deeply enough to fight for it."

— A BUTTERFLY IN FLIGHT: THE BIOGRAPHY OF THOMAS SPEAKER BY JAMIE LIVINGSTON

Sergeant Bartholomew Hopkins gazed about the place. The building was named Country Lanes and Billiards when first constructed sometime in the 1980s. It sat empty during the troubles until Thomas Speaker asked the town council to revive it some ten years after he located to the town.

Electricity was unavailable, so the drop ceiling was removed and large skylights were inserted into the roof. They removed the mechanical pin setters, reverting to human power. It proved a popular activity for the townsfolk, a positive sign of things returning to normal.

But now, the building would serve as an indoor training ground. Bart sat in the town council's meeting some three weeks earlier and volunteered to raise a defense force. The threat was real—a scouting mission returned to confirm the story of the two young boys from Michigan—an army of some two hundred marauders overtook their village, killing the males and holding the women and girls. It appeared they were settling in for the winter. It was safe to assume they learned of Speaker's village and were likely making plans also.

The sergeant scrutinized his fifty recruits. *Oh hell, what was I thinking? I figured I left the army behind thirty years ago, but no. Dammit! I bet half of these kids aren't even that old.*

He thought of his old drill sergeant, Jesús Gonzalez. *What would Jesús do?* "All right. I want ten lines, five people each. MOVE!" The recruits jostled each other as they followed the command.

"You young men and women are the first of four classes. We believe you are the best of all the volunteers and will make up the core of our fighting force." Remembering his old sergeant, he began strutting in front of the ranks. "You have been chosen because of your intelligence and physical strength. My job is to turn you into an elite, combat-ready unit, trained in the use of all weapons."

With a click of his heels, he wheeled around and began the walk back down the line. "Your job, ladies and gentlemen, is to learn what I teach you and take that knowledge home. You each are assigned two other volunteers whom you will train at home. In this way, we will triple our force and be more than ready when this *Grizzly* attacks.

"Now, I know most of you have no experience with weapons. We will meet for two hours, six days a week, for the next four weeks." Bart looked from one to another, staring at each till they looked away.

"First rule. We will treat each other with respect and refer to each other with the terms 'Sir' or 'Ma'am.' Am I understood?"

Several recruits responded. "Sure." "Yeah." "Whatever."

The sergeant turned on them. "Am I UNDERSTOOD?"

"Yes, sir!" One of the women shouted back. Others soon joined.

"Good." Bart put his face in front of the nearest male. "When I look at you, I expect you to look at me."

The man glanced at the sergeant; his gaze wavered.

"In the eyes!" Bart shouted. "Is *that* understood?"

"Yes, sir!"

"We set the lanes up for archery and spear practice, but we'll also use them in simulated hand-to-hand combat. Now get your weapons and line up, one group to a lane."

* * *

THE PASTOR PAUSED IN HIS DAILY BROADCAST, SEARCHING FOR THE words. "Well, I guess where I'm going with this is to suggest that because of this duality—this difference between positive and negative, yin and yang, that sort of thing—maybe we'll never get along. Perhaps humanity is destined to forever battle with itself." He strummed his fingers on the desk. *Good God of us all, give me the words to talk this Grizzly fellow out of his plans.*

"I remember a song. It was about two lovers breaking up. The guy says there are no good guys, no bad guys. They just disagree." Speaker looked out the window. "We're rebuilding human civilization. I suppose we won't ever see eye to eye on a lot of things. But that's why we make rules, laws, agreements on how we can get along." *Careful. Don't hint that we know his plans.*

The pastor pressed his lips together. "We've had some disagreements amongst ourselves recently. It created some terrible feelings between parties. I hope that we're getting past the animosity stage and can agree to disagree. Remember, God's command is to love your neighbor. That means we work things out." *Does that sound too lame?* He looked toward Alice B. She held up a record, an unasked question in her expression. Speaker nodded.

"Well, I think you all can pick up on what I'm trying to say here." A slight smile crossed his lips. "I think I'll turn it over to Alice now. Whatcha got there, dear?"

"It's one you picked out, Pastor. The one by Dave Mason you felt would be fitting."

"Ah, yes! Not the best segue, but it will do."

* * *

THE DAY RUSHED BY FOR SERGEANT BART. THE WORD WAS OUT ABOUT his training methods so that when the fourth group arrived, he had little preliminary lecturing to do. Now dusk was darkening the assembly hall as he completed his instructions for the following day.

Without warning, the exit doors burst open, and a group of kids pushed in. They carried an array of wooden shields and weapons. Some wore outlandish makeup and costumes. The boys from Michigan led the group as they formed into columns and marched up to the sergeant.

Bart looked on in amazement as the group came to a halt in front of him. Several of his recruits sniggered as they elbowed each other. The sergeant turned on them. "QUIET! You will show respect at all times. Understood?"

"Yes, sir!" The troop was in unison as they returned to attention.

Bart turned back to the children. "What have we here?" He stood with hands on his hips.

Ben stepped forward and saluted. "If I may, sir, I present to you the Children Crusaders. We wish to help defend our town."

The sergeant scanned the group, counting thirteen. "Um-hmm. And how do you propose to do that?"

"If we may, sir." Ben motioned to Brandon, who stepped forward, carrying a three-foot-wide, round wooden shield. Bart nodded, and Brandon trotted to the end of the nearest alley.

Ben stepped away from the sargeant and took his place,

nodding toward his cousin. "On my mark." Brandon returned the salute, raised his shield, and stood ready to charge.

"Now!"

Brandon gave a whoop and rushed forward, shield raised, while Ben stood, calmly waiting.

A quick motion and Ben had his slingshot in his left hand, pulling a flat rock from its pouch with the right. A moment later, the stone held tightly in the pocket, Brandon pulled the rubber bands taut and waited.

"Aaaaargh!" Brandon's shout bounced off the walls as he ran the distance. Ten feet separated the two when Ben let go of his shot. A loud *thunk* brought Brandon to a stop.

Bart grabbed Ben by the shoulder. "That's a dangerous game you two are playing."

The boy pulled away. "That's our point, sir. It's not a game."

Brandon crossed the remaining distance and held out the shield, showing the projectile embedded into the leading edge. "If I'm the enemy charging at you, I'll have to drop my guard to see where I'm going."

"And *that's* when I fire." Ben holstered his weapon. "Right between the eyes."

"Impressive, indeed." Bart tried to pull the stone out and failed. Rolling his thumb over the edge, he gave a low whistle. The two-inch oval had a sharp edge to it, increasing its lethality.

The other crusaders jostled around them. One of the costumed boys stumbled, bumping into Bart. He saluted. "Sorry, sir."

"What have we here, anyway?" The sergeant looked the kid up and down, saw three others dressed in similar costumes. They each had their faces painted in black and white garish designs. Six-inch platform boots boosted them to a man's height, while body armor fashioned from old fiberglass car parts hung over their shoulders.

The boy held out his rectangular shield. "We're shield bearers, sir. If nothing else, we figure we can shield the archers as they fire."

Bart shook his head, then nodded approval. "Very impressive, kids. It's something to consider. Of course, we'll have to run this by the town council—and your parents."

"Karl!" A recruit broke ranks and pushed to the front. "Is that you, Karl?"

The sergeant turned on him. "Explain yourself, recruit."

"This is my little brother, sir." He turned to a costumed youngster. "What the hell are you doing dressed like that, Karl?"

The boy held his head up. "It's Kabuki makeup—like from Japanese theater. I first saw it on one of Alice B's records. The band was called Kabuki Is Some Shit, and they dressed like this."

The sergeant parted the two. "All right, all right, you two." He squinted at the boys in makeup. "Is there any chance the band just used the first letters of their name?"

"Yes, sir. They did, but how would you know?"

Bart chuckled. "Because Kabuki *is* some shit."

Karl stuck his tongue out at his brother.

WOMEN'S WORK

"In a good relationship, the woman will have a positive effect on the man. It's not that she's taming him. It's more like she calms him, allows him to see the brighter side of life."

— A BUTTERFLY IN FLIGHT: THE BIOGRAPHY OF
THOMAS SPEAKER BY JAMIE LIVINGSTON

"Oh, c'mon. It'll be fun!" Judith plunked down on Grizzly's lap, pouting. Her work over the past two months was paying off, or so she thought. She was proud of herself for cleaning him up. He no longer caused her to gag when he got close. *Still, you can take the man out of the asylum, but you can't take the asylum out of the man.* Now she twirled a finger in his beard. "We've been doing it for years. The Solstice Celebration helps chase the winter blues."

Grizzly tried to shove her away. "I ain't never heard of it. Besides, what's there to celebrate?"

"Solstice, of course." Judith persisted, squirming in her seat. "The days will get longer. Spring is coming. Winter may still be ahead, but it will pass."

"Do you think your future is so bright, then? You women

learn quick enough, I'll admit. You know what's right for you, how to git along. Most of you, anyway. 'Cept for that young black bitch."

Judith swung a leg off, ready to stand. "Aliyah. You really shouldn't have given her to that sadist. She's more than that. She enjoys abusing the girl."

Grizzly pulled her leg back around. "Your gal needed to be taught a lesson. She killed two of my men. Doris will tame her."

Judith placed her hand under his shirt, a slight smile crossing her lips. "You have your ways. Still, you attract more bees with honey. I told you before. We're survivors in this world. Like you and your gang are. We've mourned our men, accepted our fate. Time to get on with life."

"They ain't no gang!" Grizzly rose, dumping Judith on the floor. "They're my troops. My army!" He raised his hand to strike.

Judith scurried back, avoiding the expected blow. "Okay, okay. No harm meant." She stood and squared her shoulders. "Besides, I think we women are proving ourselves just as good as your other fighters."

Grizzly nodded. "You're comin' along. I've watched you practicing with the blade. Pretty good, for a gal."

She let the insult pass. "So what I was thinking—maybe you can use Solstice to reward your troops. Maybe *we* can use it like a graduation party. It's only a month away." She stepped closer, her hand again on his chest. "Do you think we'll be ready to … graduate?" She leaned in to nuzzle his neck.

Grizzly cocked his head away. "What've you got in mind?"

Judith stepped back. "We've always used Solstice as a holiday. We eat far too much. Drink too much. This time, we make a big deal of it. Maybe give out awards like best spear-chucker or whatever. You know, welcome the new soldiers. It'll give us all something to celebrate. Announce our plans for the coming year. That sort of thing."

Grizzly strode to the table, grabbing the edge, trying to control his irritability. "I don't need no ceremony to build my army. I am

Grizzly! My troops obey me. We take what we want and never show mercy."

Judith stepped up to him, placing her hand on his shoulder. "You don't need a ceremony. But the women do. They need to know they're accepted, and on your terms."

"Women!" Grizzly turned to her, looking into those green eyes. There was no smile on her lips, no deceit. He nodded his understanding. The slight smile returned to Judith's lips.

* ✷ *

JUDITH ASSEMBLED A GROUP OF SIX OTHER WOMEN. THEY WERE allowed to meet twice a week. Grizzly had insisted on once but Judith pointed out that the Solstice was rapidly approaching and there was much planning to do. They compromised. By the third meeting, the men assigned to watch over them grew bored. The promise of food and wine lured them out of the room, and they occupied themselves with a card game and loud talk.

Aliyah was among Judith's choices. It allowed her some respite from the merciless Doris. Besides, the teen had a talent for fashioning weapons from the innocuous.

"Take this wire." The girl held up a thin, four-foot length of yellow-clad copper. "It's light enough to sew into your clothing as a decorative touch. You can even strip the insulation and use the copper for a bracelet, or weave it into your belt." She wrapped it around her thin waist. "The important thing is that you can use it like this." Aliyah grabbed an end in either hand and looped the wire.

"Hold this." She handed a dried ear of corn to the nearest person. "Imagine that is his neck." One quick move, and the wire flicked around the corn. A sharp tug on the strand sliced the cob in half. Her partner picked up the pieces and held them high. "Let your anger make you strong!" Aliyah announced.

"Ooh, I like that." Sarah stepped forward. "Here's something I saw in a movie once. It was about a female spy." She climbed onto the table, sitting on her haunches. "Let's say you got your man in bed. Maybe you're just playing around." The women giggled, embarrassed. Sarah looked at each of them. "Or maybe he's just horny. Again!" Nervous laughter rippled through her audience. "So you're on top. He reaches up to grab you. You go all mushy on him. 'Oh, baby, unhh.' You pull his head to your breast ..."

The women looked on in silence as Sarah went through the motion, using her left hand, pretending to bury his face in her bosom. Moaning, she reached behind her head and pulled out a hairpin, her long red curls falling around her shoulders. A flick of the wrist brought the pin around to the back of the imagined head, and she held it tightly between thumb and forefinger. "Now, let him down easy. The point is aimed right below the skull where there's a soft spot." The women each felt the back of their neck, noting the spot.

"Now push!"

They cringed, imagining the head forced back on the point.

Sarah jumped down. "Now this is important. There should only be a small drop of blood. Get it cleaned up. You don't want evidence. Play it right and they'll think the dude had a heart attack." She smiled and pinned her hair back. The group murmured. Some shook their heads in distaste, others in approval.

"Okay, okay." Judith waved for silence. "Keep it down." She tilted her head, listening for activity from the men. The laughter coming from next door assured her. "We don't have a lot of time. Angel, what have you got for us?"

The apothecary dug into her apron pockets. The apron was an affectation from a bygone era, making her look like a pioneer. Still, it served a purpose. She held out a half dozen packets.

"I'm not sure how potent these still are. They're from last season, and you know I like to use fresh ingredients." She unfolded one envelope, pouring the crushed leaves into her palm.

"This is azalea; it can really mess with your stomach." She held her hand out.

"You have such beautiful flowers around your house in the spring." Aliyah smiled. "So this is why you grow them?"

"I do like fresh plants for their, er, medicinal qualities." Angel returned the smile. "And fresh is always better. We'll have to wait till spring for lily-of-the-valley, though." She poured the contents back into the packet. "And foxglove. Those berries can give you a heart attack. I have some dried here." She produced another envelope. "I suppose we can test them."

"Excellent." Judith took the packet. "Look, we only have an hour. And we still need to plan the dinner. Sarah, will you work with Angel? Inventory what all she has. Put a plan together to try this stuff out. We don't want to draw too much attention until we know how it all works. Then we'll share it with the rest of the town." The women all whispered their agreement.

One woman spoke up. "We may have to fake being sick, too."

"Good point." Sarah stood next to Angel. "We'll come up with instructions on what to expect from each drug. You can act accordingly."

"One other thing." Angel held out a handful of seeds. "I've been able to keep my castor plant going in the solarium. We have a bumper crop this year."

Judith inspected one of the beans. It reminded her of a pinto bean. "I know you use these for your medicines, Angel, so how will they help here?"

The apothecary smiled. "Ricin. Small amounts make an excellent laxative. Eight beans will kill you."

* ✳ *

BILL THREW THE CLIPBOARD DOWN. "IT ALL SEEMS ON THE UP-AND-up, boss. It's going to be one helluva barbeque. Sarah's tried some of the recipes on me. Herbed chicken! Who would have thought?"

Grizzly looked over the notes and grunted. "Are we going to have enough wood for the pig roast? If not, get a detail out there."

"Sure thing, boss. Anything else?"

Grizzly slammed his fist down. "Damn right, there's something else. I don't like it." He flung the notes aside. "They're up to something. I can tell. Never trust a woman. That's the only good advice my ol' man ever gave me."

Bill retrieved the clipboard, keeping a wary eye on Grizzly. "But boss. We never had it so good. Decent food, a warm house, and the, um, companionship—"

"You horny bastard!" Grizzly turned on his lieutenant. "You're lucky you got paired with someone just as horny as you." His finger jabbed at the air. "Keep it in your pants, for Chrissakes. It'll be the death of you."

"Well, at least I'll go with a smile on my face." Bill poked the bear's arm. "Admit it; life's been good to us so far."

Grizzly swung himself onto a chair, nodding at Bill. "So far, yeah. I got a feeling something's up." He pulled out a pocket knife and began whittling his fingernails. "Talk about food. Judith's been making fancy dishes, too. Last night it was pork chops with mushroom gravy. We never had anything like that in lockup." He kicked his feet up on the table. "And now, my dreams. I see weird shit in my dreams."

Bill pulled up a chair and slumped down. "Me too. Nearly every night. They may be weird, but it's in a fun way. You know what I mean?"

"That's because you think and dream with your dick." Grizzly stuck his tongue between his teeth. "And that's why I don't like it. Something's up. Those bitches are making it too nice."

*　✳　*

"Okay, quiet, please!" Judith held up a hand, shushing the other women. "I think we have everything set for the celebration. It's two more days till Solstice. The men are butchering the animals tomorrow, we've got the fire pits set up, and drinks are ready." She looked around the room. "I think we should stop experimenting with the herbs now, then spike the applejack the men will be drinking."

Angel stood up. "Excuse me. I have to disagree." The apothecary stepped forward. "It seems the drugs are only good enough to make people sick, not kill them. At least in the doses we've been using."

"Tell that to Barbara." Millie spoke up, her voice cracking. Their efforts to keep the truth from Grizzly's men led them to make themselves ill. Barbara had overdosed.

Angel turned to the others. "That was very unfortunate indeed. And it's why we should stop the experiments altogether. What if any of the children get into the stuff?" She looked directly at each of the women till they averted their eyes, even Judith.

"You've made a good point, Angel." Judith's voice was barely audible. "I was hoping we could kill most of them off and make it look like some disease was sweeping through town. We need a Plan B."

Millie took the floor. "Well, first, there's no need to kill them all off. They're not all evil or even bad, for that matter. Take my Howie—"

"Please!" Aliyah shook her head. "Your Howie is weak. He's not even a fighter."

"That's my point. Most of these men joined Grizzly to save their own necks. I don't think they want to be a part of his army."

"It's a mixed bag at best." Sarah nodded. "From what Bill tells me, there's maybe two dozen of the original crew—the escapees. They're the savage ones. But I think some of the others are just like them. We need to sort them out. That is, if we want to spare any of them."

Judith allowed a few minutes for the committee members to talk among themselves, picking up on the snippets of concern, feeling the hostility. She held up her hand for silence.

"I get it. You ladies are all right. I don't believe we should kill them all off. So here's what I'm thinking." She sat down and leaned into the group as they gathered around. "We continue to learn from them—how they fight, what their pure hearts tell us. Grizzly's still planning to attack Speaker's town in the spring. By then, we'll have the skills to turn on them. And we'll know who we need to eliminate."

"Why not just kill the old bear?" Aliyah slid a finger across her throat.

Sarah shook her head and shuddered. "Because Bill will just step in. He can be as bad as Grizzly. We need to sort 'em out and take 'em out—all at the same time." She looked from one to the other. They all muttered their approval.

"The only thing ..." Aliyah leaned in, determination in her voice. "I know one woman who will also die." She rubbed her newest bruise. "I am certain of it."

*　*　*

GRIZZLY TOSSED THE COVERS AND JUMPED FROM THE BED. HE BARELY made it to the bathroom before he felt his bowels let loose. Beads of sweat popped from his brow as he clasped his stomach. Another wave of nausea overtook him, and he groaned.

Some bug had swept through the village a week before the Solstice celebration. The bouts of diarrhea and vomiting lasted a day or two, then cleared up in time for all to enjoy the graduation ceremonies. All appeared normal.

After the celebration, the men especially felt the aftereffects of overindulgence. The women had tried new recipes, and the men overate. Chicken, beef, and pork each had a special herb flavoring. And the drink flowed like water.

Now, spring approached, and they needed to make plans for their march south. Grizzly clenched his teeth and let out a low moan as another wave of nausea hit. *It's been going on for two days. God, is there no mercy?* "As if He might care." More brown soup splattered in the toilet bowl as he clutched his gut.

*　*　*

"Are you okay?" Judith pushed the bathroom door open a crack and looked in. "Oh, my. You poor thing!" She grimaced at the odor.

"Git out!" Grizzly reached to push at the door. His hand fell limply to his side. "I'm not used to those fancy dishes you've been making lately. There was something different about the taters tonight."

"We have to stretch what we have. Spring is here, and the winter vegetables are nearly gone." Judith talked through the door. "I mixed turnips in with the potatoes." She didn't dare mention the daffodil bulbs and their effect.

"Well, don't use any more of those." Grizzly rolled off the toilet. "One or the other must be rotten." He got his face to the rim in time to vomit.

Judith leaned back on the wall outside of his view, stifling a laugh. The plan was working. None of Grizzly's men suspected a thing. The apothecary explained that the bouts of illness throughout the winter were commonplace for the town. Still, the women, too, had to endure some sickness. *What won't we do for our men!*

The sound of the toilet flushing interrupted her thoughts. She checked on her charge. "Are you going to be okay?' Her voice sweet, caring. *These guys trust us. They're so clueless.*

Grizzly sat on the floor next to the toilet, breathing heavily. "That's the worst of it. I ain't got anything else to heave or shit out." He hoisted himself up, waving Judith's helping hand away.

"I'll get you some water."

"No!" The bear grabbed her shoulder and spun her around, grabbing her by the throat. "I don't know what's going on here. Maybe it is some 'normal' disease. Maybe it isn't." He pressed his thumb deeper. "It doesn't really matter anymore." Judith gasped for air. "I'm tired of this hellhole you call a town. I'm tired of all the fancy crap you've been feeding us. I ain't letting my men go soft." His grip loosened. "We got a town to conquer. Speaker's town."

Judith's voice cracked as she struggled to breathe. "But why? Nobody ever means you any harm. We were willing to give you food and send you on your way. You *had* to kill all our men? Now you want to raid another town, kill more people? Why?"

Grizzly pushed her aside and walked into the bedroom. "'Cause that's the way we bees."

STEVE'S VACATION

"Why am I here? What is my purpose? Do I even have a purpose? If not, how do I find one? If I depend on God to tell me, how do I know it is Him who speaks to me? These are the questions that keep me up at night."

— A BUTTERFLY IN FLIGHT: THE BIOGRAPHY OF THOMAS SPEAKER BY JAMIE LIVINGSTON

"Careful there, Thomas, it's slippery!" The fox took a tentative step forward. The previous night's mix of rain and snow iced over, making for hazardous walking. Winter was proving to be a challenge for the pair.

Thomas dug his claws in and bounded up to the fox. "I guess Garcia's pretty lucky, being able to sleep through this."

Reynard yipped in agreement. "Mother taught us how to make the most of it." He plunked himself down, facing back down their hillside. "Like this." Pulling up his front paws, he began sliding, spinning slowly around. "Wheeeee! C'mon, it's fun! You've got to try it."

"Kids!" Thomas harrumphed. "I suppose I can humor him."

Sitting down, he placed his front paws on either side to steady himself. He pushed off and gained momentum.

"Hey! This isn't so bad, after a—Whoa!" Snow covering a rock had created a ramp. The cat ran squarely over it, sending him flying into the air. Tumbling around, he quickly recovered and stretched out all four legs. His claws failed to dig in as he landed, and he continued sliding down the hill, coming to rest in front of Reynard.

"Cool move, Thomas. Could you teach me how to do that? It looks like fun."

"Hmph! Fun, you say?" Thomas licked at a paw.

"Hey, fellers!" A shout came from the edge of the woods. The friends froze, looking to see who was calling.

"Hi, fellers. That looks like fun. Can I play with you?" A tall, fur-covered creature stepped out from the sheltering trees and waved.

Reynard gulped and backed away. "Human! Very bad, very bad."

"Hold on." Thomas sniffed the air. "I don't think so. Hmm." He took another deep whiff. "No, not human. But what?"

The animal strolled across the field, hands dangling below his knees and a big smile showing beneath his beard. Reaching the pair, he crouched down to be on their level and extended his hand, palm side up.

"Hi! My name's Steve. What's yours?"

Thomas and Reynard each sniffed at the proffered fingers. Reynard backed off. Thomas studied Steve's face, recognition dawning on him. "Are … are you a Squatch?"

Steve let go of a belly laugh. "Right you are, little feller. I'm Steve of the Sasquatch tribe. We live up near Canada, a bit north-west of here." He pointed in the general direction. "I'm on vacation. How about you fellers?"

The cat relaxed. "My name is Thomas. The shy guy"—he indicated the fox—"is Reynard, my traveling companion. He thought you were a human. He doesn't like humans."

Steve regarded Reynard. "I don't blame you there, fella. Hoo, the stories I could tell." He sat down cross-legged, arms in his lap. "But it seems they're mostly gone now. The world's a lot safer place. That's why I'm on vacation."

Thomas and Reynard relaxed as the conversation continued, each sharing their story. The sun nearly reached its midpoint when a rumbling came from Steve's stomach.

"Whoowee! You fellers are so fascinating, I plumb forgot about eating. Y'all want to come fishing with me?"

Reynard stood up. "Can't. The pond's frozen over."

"No problem, lil' feller." Steve patted the fox's head. "I found a big stick in the woods. I'll poke a hole through the ice and taa dah! Breakfast, or is it brunch, is served."

Thomas jumped up. "You are a godsend. The hunting hasn't been too good lately. Fresh fish sounds wonderful."

"Well, come on then. I'll fetch that tree branch. I nearly forgot my daddy's advice—always to carry a big stick. That and walk softly in the woods." Steve headed across the field, Thomas and Reynard following.

* ✳ *

STEVE THE SQUATCH PROVED VERY HELPFUL IN THE DAYS AND WEEKS that followed. Besides fishing, he also taught Thomas and Reynard how to find nutritious lichens, berries, and nuts. In return, the pair rewarded their guest with an occasional field mouse or ground mole.

One morning the trio found a fallen deer on their pond. Steve first approached it and confirmed the creature was dead. It had stepped into their fishing hole and broke a leg. The freezing weather did the rest. After mourning the sacrificed life, Steve prepared their campfire and spitted the hindquarters of their meal.

Within minutes, the meat sizzled over the flames. Steve added a few sticks to the fire as fat dripped down, hissing when it hit the hot coals. "Thomas, we've been talking about a lot of stuff lately. Do you think we all have a purpose in life?" He turned the spit over. "I mean, okay, take this deer. Its purpose was to feed us. That's simple—"

"Not quite so simple as that." Thomas paused in cleaning himself. "But yes, everyone has a purpose. I believe that one's purpose can change, however."

"How do you mean?"

"The deer, for instance." Thomas padded over to where Reynard was gnawing a bone. "At one time, her reason for living was to grow and raise babies. Now she is fulfilling a different need—that of feeding us." Reynard stopped chewing, turning his attention to Thomas.

Steve sat back on his haunches. "But she couldn't have known that was her purpose, could she?"

"Ah! Philosophy." Thomas swiped at the air. "We could go on and on. Does God guide our lives? How can we know that? I don't hear voices. God's not talking to me. Or is he? Do you hear voices?" He chuckled. "See what I mean?"

Steve placed his chin in his hand. "So tell me this then. You keep saying how terrible humans are, right? Yet you say your purpose is to meet up with this Thomas Speaker guy. A human!"

Thomas stretched out in front of the fire. "Speaker is other than human. He is people."

Reynard stood up. "Now I'm confused. Aren't people humans, too?"

Thomas sat up. "Sorry. By my definition, humans are, well, humans. They don't feel their connection to the universe. They think everything is about them. The only time they think of other humans is when they're trying to use them." He shook his head. "People, they get the connection, at least to some degree. So far, I've met two people who speak to animals and understand what animals said to them. I feel Thomas Speaker is like that also. Except he has not awoken to the fact."

Thomas looked from one to the other of his friends. "Speaker is a very influential person. If I can awaken him, think about how the world will change. All creatures, great and small, communicating with each other. Imagine."

Steve stood up. "Well, good luck with that. Humans talking with the rest of us. Yeah, imagine that." He pulled the spit from the fire. "Anyway, it's dinnertime."

WHAT DREAMS FORETELL

"I read about the process of 'letting go' in my spiritual practice—
to become detached from earthly things. Eventually, one is to be in
this world without being of it. I'm not sure I want to go there."

— *A BUTTERFLY IN FLIGHT: THE BIOGRAPHY OF
THOMAS SPEAKER* BY JAMIE LIVINGSTON

Pastor Thomas Speaker closed his office door, leaving the
blaring music behind. Alice B. was exploring the music
archives, preparing for her next show.

Crossing the foyer, he greeted Maggie Livingston. "What is
that?" she winced.

"What, that?" Thomas nodded toward the office door. "Bebop.
Charlie Parker, to be more accurate."

"She's not going to use that on her show, is she? The town will
be up in arms." Maggie's face spoke volumes. For years, the
townspeople's only access to music was a limited supply of CD
recordings. However, they adapted, performing versions of
remembered songs on acoustic instruments. Those with the talent
even wrote original tunes, forming duos and bands as needed.

Still, the compositions all tended toward a quieter, retrospective genre.

The discovery of a complete library of vinyl recordings piqued the interest of Alice B., the pastor's broadcast assistant. The teen quickly convinced the pastor to allow her to follow up his noon-time broadcast with a selection of recordings—to finish out the hour if time permitted. Within weeks, the town council gave the OK to have a separate evening program. *Alice B.'s Honey Kitchen* was born. "I'll be serving up some of the sweetest sounds around —sweeter than Tupelo honey," she gushed every evening at six o'clock.

The closed office door muffled Parker's rapid-fire sax work. "I really don't think we're ready for that sort of thing." Maggie scrunched her shoulders. "I don't believe we should be censoring it, however." She allowed Thomas to guide her to one of the two wingback chairs in the foyer. He sat in the other.

"Well, you *can* simply turn off your radio." He wasn't going to argue that point—he'd fought against censorship ever since he took the name Thomas Speaker. "Alice is young. She needs to explore everything before she takes wing. It gives her a chance to discover what *her* life is about and not try to live up to others' expectations."

"Ha! Says the man without children." Maggie shook her head. "Having a child will quickly change your perspective. They need guidance as they grow."

Thomas frowned. "It must be difficult figuring what limits you need to set up. And I foresee those limits changing as the child grows, too." He leaned closer, trying to shut out the music.

Maggie smiled. "It's going to be an exciting journey, that's for sure."

"So how's our girl doing?"

"You mean since you last saw her?"

"It seems like only yesterday."

"It was only yesterday." Maggie chuckled as she shook her head. "I swear, your mind seems to be elsewhere these days."

"Yes." Thomas leaned forward, elbows on knees, cupping his hands under his chin. "There's a lot happening lately—those boys from Michigan warning about the marauders, how we're going to defend ourselves, little Jamie—"

"Okay, okay, stop right there." Maggie laid her hand on his shoulder. A feather weighed more than that touch. Still, it brought comfort. The pastor reached up and held on loosely. "One thing at a time."

Maggie's fingers tightened. "First, Ben and Brandon are amazing. Their arrival gives us plenty of time to prepare for an attack. Remember, the town council is in charge of the militia, and Sergeant Bart has their training under control. We've got outposts up into Michigan, and they're all equipped to wire a warning when the time comes. We'll be ready."

Thomas nodded. "We've got a great team of people. I understand they have several plans drawn up, depending on which direction these vigilantes come at us."

Maggie gave his hand a quick squeeze. "Precisely. We think they'll be in a hurry, so we look for them to stay on the roads for speed. If they come down Route 9, it will force them to stay on the road through the swampy area just north of town. That'll bog 'em down and give us an advantage."

"Yes," the pastor acknowledged. "I can envision it. They come over the hill, stop, and see the swamp. He gets angry. They have no choice but to bunch up on the road—easy targets. Mark my words."

"Okay, then. Let's change the subject." She dropped her hand.

"Your young 'un. Is she still talking to the dog?"

Maggie shook her head. "It's more like *with* the dog, not *to* the dog. I swear, Jamie sits there yammering away while Doggie grunts and growls—like dog-speak or something." She laughed. "They both get so excited. Jamie will bounce and swing her arms, and Doggie turns in circles. I wish I knew what's going on."

Thomas leaned on an elbow, resting his chin in his hand. "Hmmm. I've listened to her. Besides the usual 'mama, papa,' she seems to be saying real words. It's hard to understand her, though."

"She's too young to have the muscle control to form the words, is all. I've got to tell you, Thomas, it's a little scary. What have we created? Sometimes, I wish I never got the treatment."

"It saved your life. And you met Doc—and me, for that matter."

Maggie pushed herself farther into the chair. "Yeah, I was messed up back then. That's why they chose me for the experiment—they wanted to see how the treatment handled drug addiction. I was a great candidate."

"You were a kid. You got mixed up with the wrong crowd—although, under the circumstances, I don't see how you could have avoided it, being a draft dodger and all. The important thing is that the treatment worked on you—destroyed the effects of the drugs and the desire to use them."

She let out a sob, sagging into the chair. "I know. I know. But what about Jamie? She heals just like we do, but there's something else going on. Is that a genetic thing with the stem cells too?" She pulled out a handkerchief, dried the tears. "I mean, look at Ellie's boy, Josh. Ellie had the treatment. Josh's dad didn't, and now Josh seems pretty average. Just like the other boys and girls."

"Yes, the mystery of life. It is not predetermined. Look at yourself. The treatment didn't stop you from maturing, but it did halt the aging process once you matured, just like Doc and me. How long will it last?" He shook his head and laughed. "Sometimes, I think I stick around only to see what happens next."

The music grew louder as Alice B. stepped out of the office, holding a record. A lone trumpet sounded a melancholy tune. Miles Davis. Thomas couldn't help being distracted. Music did that.

Alice strode forward. "Sorry to interrupt you folks. Pastor, there's something wrong with this album. There's no breaks on this side, you know, like they put between songs." She handed it over gingerly.

Thomas tilted it, allowing the light to hit at an angle while he inspected it. He grinned. "It's okay. See? Check out the label. There's only one song on that side. And it's a whopper."

"Really? They could do that?"

"Sure. They did it all the time for classical pieces. I believe this particular one was one of the first for rock and roll." Thomas handed the disc back.

"Fascinating. I liked the band's name. Can you imagine an iron butterfly? Not in *my* craziest dreams." She turned to go back, shaking her head.

"Speaking of dreams ..." Maggie wiped the tears and memories away with a quick swipe of the handkerchief. "The nurse says she's concerned you might be using too much of this." She pulled a small packet from her handbag.

The pastor opened the pouch and took a slight sniff. "Yes, 'shrooms! There's no reason to get excited. I'll talk with her. She'll understand. I think I've reached a plateau anyway."

Maggie bit at a fingernail, a nervous habit when she was upset. "Well, *I* don't understand. Why do psychedelics in the first place? Aren't you afraid of addiction?"

"No. It's not the same as opioids." He tucked the packet into his shirt pocket. "The stem-cell infusion takes care of repairing our physical bodies. Opioids damage areas of the brain and the stem cells fix it. That's why the treatment healed you. Mushrooms activate parts of the brain, releasing natural chemicals that the body recognizes as its own. That's why the stem cells do not affect the effects." He paused and smiled. "Affects the effects. Say that fast ten times."

Maggie smiled, picking up on the mood. "Still, why do it at all?"

"For inspiration, mainly. I get ideas for my sermons while on these journeys."

"Uh-huh." Maggie's concern showed on her face. "We've all noticed your teaching has become more spiritual. I just figured it came from your prayer and meditation practice, not drugs."

"Ah!" Thomas leaned forward, making a pyramid with his fingers together, touching his lips. "First, they all work. I get into the same space either way. It's where I feel at one with everything —people, animals, plants, trees—the universe. Psychedelics get me there faster, is all." He spread his hands open. "It's as if a golden umbilical cord stretches out from me to every other being. I feel everyone; I feel connected to everything through these thin strands of gold. It's marvelous. I believe the experience is universal love touching me."

Maggie brushed the idea aside with a wave of her hand. "Thomas. Look at me. You can't expect everyone to trip out and be all-loving and wonderful. Poof! Just like that." She snapped her fingers.

"No, of course not. That's what evolution is for, and reincarnation. We're all on the same spiritual journey. But we each have separate paths. The goal is the same. Sometimes it takes multiple physical lives to realize that simple truth. The truth that we're all on this journey together."

Maggie shook her head. "Back in the day, I was too young to understand what was going on, but I always wondered why we were at war. It seemed like we were *always at war*. Now I understand. We stopped believing in the spiritual altogether."

The faint sound of an organ droned from Thomas's office. It was the solo portion of the album Alice showed him. The two friends sat quietly.

Thomas finally spoke. "Yes. Now that I have realized that, it has become my mission to teach it. My past sermons covered just about everything we need for our physical survival. Now it's time for the next step."

Maggie stood and placed a hand on Speaker's head. "That's a big task you've taken on. I think I can speak for Doc when I say we wish you well on this journey. We would all benefit from it." She dropped her hand. "As for me, I better check on my two." She slung the handbag over her shoulder and turned toward the door.

Thomas stood and gave her a peck on the cheek. "Thank you. Both of you. I appreciate your support."

"Of course, silly." Maggie stared into his eyes. "We all love you. You know that."

Thomas smiled and showed her out. He paused at the door a moment before shutting it. The music from his office ceased, then a new piece began. It was Beethoven's Fifth. *Jazz to psychedelia. Now classical? I wonder what's next?*

Thomas made his way to the living room and sat on the over-stuffed couch against the wall. He slipped the packet from his pocket and stared at it a moment, then dumped the contents on his tongue. Lying back, he folded his hands over his navel.

Minutes passed. The preacher's eyes shifted under their lids, rolling. The familiar golden umbilical stretched out, seeking others, touching. His breathing calmed as the cord spiraled out into the universe. Suddenly, it detached itself from his body and began floating away. Thomas snatched at it and missed it. His dream-self reached out again, but the lifeline drifted away.

CROSSROADS

"You always have a choice, and it's not always an either/or matter. Your path has many forks in it. Consider them before choosing."

— *A BUTTERFLY IN FLIGHT: THE BIOGRAPHY OF THOMAS SPEAKER* BY JAMIE LIVINGSTON

The weeks went by swiftly for the crew of the *Delta Belle*. Christian Chance pondered this. *Time sure does rush by these days. Even when I'm not having fun.* He laughed to himself. That was a joke he shared with his mother. She would look at him and say something about how much he had grown. She always followed it up with the comment, "My, time sure does rush by nowadays." Christian was in his early teens when she last said it. She had caught him in an irritable mood. "Yeah, it sure does," he snapped. "Even when I'm not having fun." It made them both laugh as she hugged him close.

Those days back then were troublesome. They had taken to hiding in the old warehouse. At night they would scavenge the town, looking for food. Each day seemed the same, hiding away, avoiding any other people. As the food became scarce, so did the people. They took to hunting—rats and pigeons were easy prey and plentiful. They survived, and those days flew by.

Now there was much to do. With the ship in drydock and repairs nearly complete, the crew worked with Cairo's citizens on various projects. Chris liked the hard work. He would get home after a grueling day and barely eat before he fell fast asleep, seldom even dreaming.

The people of Cairo rebuilt their town using houseboats. Except for the old town center, protected by a series of dikes, they gave up the idea of fighting the annual floods long ago, preferring a floating city to none at all.

Massive concrete slabs, recycled from fallen highway bridges, were floated in and dumped to act as anchor/piers. As the flood-waters rose, the boats bobbed, connected by a series of moorings. During these gray winter months, they settled next to these anchoring slabs transformed to docks between the homes.

And life with Mama Ruth and the *Delta Belle* crew wasn't so terrible as Chris fell into a daily routine. He forgave Cookie—Meany Mary, as Chris called her jokingly—for stealing his harmonica (because Mama told him that's what the Good Book said was the right thing to do). She gave him lessons, strumming along on an old guitar. He got pretty good at it, too. As the weeks passed, he took her into his confidence, as she also did with him.

But Christian was awake now; his dreams had turned to his old friend, Mr. Thomas. *How is he? Where is he?* He closed his eyes and tried to force himself to sleep.

"Argh!" Chris sat up and threw the blankets off. "I hate it when my brain skips around like that." He swung his legs out. The cold of the houseboat's floor seeped through his woolen socks. Bundling the blanket around his shoulders, he stepped to the window.

Chris shivered as he stared out the window and down the line of homes, his breath fogging the pane. Wiping it clear, he continued watching, mesmerized by the diamond sparkles of frost glistening on the railing outside.

He noticed a light in the window across the way. It was Mary's place. He could see her shadow moving and wondered if there might be something wrong. She appeared at the window, concentrating on the task at hand, which was filling her teapot. Looking up, she saw Chris at his window. With a smile, she held up the pot and motioned for him to come over. Chris felt the grin spread across his face and held up a finger, asking her to give him a minute, then grabbed his coat. As he made for the door, a thought occurred to him. With a long sigh, he sat down and pulled his boots on. *I know, Mama. Lest I catch my death of cold.* It was a pleasant memory, where Mama was watching out for him.

Standing, he checked his pockets. *Wait. Where is it?* Panicked, he dug deep into each pocket again, looking around the room. A glint of moonlight on chrome caught his eye. With a quick sigh of relief, he retrieved his harmonica and went out the door.

Chris picked his way slowly across the frosted deck, his shoelaces dragging along. He paused just a foot from Mary's door. The moon was halfway to the western edge of the sky, indicating it was about 2 a.m. His gaze caught the north star, blazing brightly, following it along to others and picking out familiar patterns among the tiny lights. The guiding star Mr. Thomas had pointed out was not visible at this hour.

"Well, don't just stand there. Come on in." Mary held the door open.

Chris nodded in appreciation and took a step forward. A loose shoestring got caught under his other foot, causing him to lurch forward.

"Woof!" Mary broke his fall but was unable to hold him up. They tumbled back inside, falling to the floor.

"You smell like flowers." Chris lifted his head from its resting place at Mary's neck.

"It's called perfume." She allowed him another deep breath before gently nudging him off. "Mama Ruth made it."

"It smells like springtime." Chris leaned closer, attempting to take another whiff.

"Well, spring is coming, you know." She raised her chin, allowing the full aroma to fill the space between them.

"That's right!" Chris pushed away and got to his feet.

Accepting his offered hand, Mary bounced up and faced him.

"And spring means changes are coming." She gently patted his chest and, with a wink, turned to close the door. "How about some tea?"

"Sure. I like sassyfras tea, you know. With some honey, if you have any."

"Oh, I have enough honey for you, honey." Mary giggled.

Christian liked her laugh. It reminded him of a silver bell ornament he would hang on the Christmas tree when he was a child. Now he laughed with her.

"I'm afraid I don't have any sassafras root, though. But Mama Ruth gave me a different herb blend just for you if you'd like to try it. It has damiana, yohimbe, oat straw, and some other things. I never heard of those things before, but she says it's tasty."

"If Mama Ruth made it, I'll try it. Besides, what could happen?" Chris settled on the old couch against the far wall and close to the wood burner while Mary pulled two cups from the shelf and poured the tea. "I brought my harmonica if you'd like to practice some." He held out the tiny instrument. "But let's play something happy."

She handed his cup over and sat next to him, cradling her mug in both hands. "Maybe later. First, I'd like to talk about your plans now that it's nearly spring. Mama and the captain will be taking the *Belle* back down the river and home in a week or two. They say they can't go very much farther up the Ohio. Besides, she's concerned about the folks back home." She took a sip, eyeing Chris through the rising steam. "She told me you were making ... other plans."

"That's right," he sipped his tea and swirled it over his tongue.

"Emmm. That's tasty." He smacked his lips and sampled some more.

"Mama's been reading her cards for me. I know my friend Mr. Thomas is okay. I can *feel* it. I need to find him. A couple of the townsfolk said they would come with me, soon as the weather breaks." He touched the star-shaped birthmark, rubbing it with his index finger. "We've got to be together. Even the cards say so."

Mary reached over and placed her finger over his. Her touch was warm.

She put her mug down and turned toward him. Taking his hand in both of hers, she placed it in her lap. "I understand all that, Chris. I've been talking with Mama Ruth, too." Her eyes met his. She saw the silent question. "She says she could have a couple of the crew go with you also. Maybe even a cook."

Chris stopped drinking his tea and slowly put his cup aside.

"You mean you want to come along with me?" He couldn't hide the nervousness in his voice. "It could be dangerous. I mean. I mean …"

She tossed his hand back at him. "You don't think I can take care of myself? I didn't get the name *Meany* Mary for nothing. I can use a knife for more than slicing vegetables, you know."

"No. Wait! That's not what I meant."

She glowered at him. "Precisely. What did you mean? Come on. Spit it out."

Chris stared in horror. The horror immediately gave way to shock, and the shock gave way to amazement. It happened in seconds.

"I never realized you had green eyes."

"They go with the red hair—minus the gray. It has something to do with being Irish." She reached behind her head and undid the knot in her now-long hair. It cascaded to her shoulders.

Chris clasped his hands around hers. "Your eyes light up when you get mad. I care about you. I don't want you to get hurt. Not on my account."

Mary turned to lean against him. "There are lots of ways to hurt a woman, Chris. Don't you worry. I can take care of myself."

Chris put his arm around her, pulling her in. The faint aroma of flowers drifted up as he stared at her. "I guess we better talk with the captain and Mama Ruth then."

Mary wiggled in the embrace. "We can do that tomorrow." She placed a light kiss on his cheek. "Drink your tea, dear."

SPRING AWAKENS

"I don't believe that people just pop into our lives. They are there for a purpose. We may not always understand that purpose initially, but it reveals itself."

> — *A BUTTERFLY IN FLIGHT: THE BIOGRAPHY OF THOMAS SPEAKER* BY JAMIE LIVINGSTON

A drop of water hit the cat's nose, waking him. He shook off the sleep and stretched. Reynard still slept soundly by his side, and a low snore confirmed Garcia slumbered farther down in the den. The groundhog maintained his state of dormancy save for a brief day about six weeks earlier when he poked his nose out of the burrow and confirmed winter weather was there to stay.

Another splash of water landed on Thomas's head. Then another. He held guard duty the night before, sleeping just inside the entrance to their den. It was a task shared with the fox, who now opened one eye.

"What's going on?" Reynard barely turned his head.

"I'm not sure." Thomas stood. "Something's different. I don't think it's dangerous, but something is obviously different. I'll check it out." Another drop of water plopped on the floor.

Thomas peered out from the entrance. The sun was rising in the east, sending out brilliant beams of light. The cat heard a soft rustling above and looked up. A snowbank had formed over the entrance months earlier. Thomas noted a water drop was accumulating on the underside. He peered closer. The drift quivered, and a large clump broke away, smashing into his face.

"Har!" Reynard had come up behind him. "Now that was funny. I don't care who you are." He bent down and licked the snow away.

"Glad you enjoyed it." Thomas grimaced and backed away. The fox stepped forward just as another chunk fell from the snowpack, catching him squarely atop the head.

"Ha!" Thomas tried to restrain his laughter, failed, and gave in to it. "You're right. That *is* funny."

"Whatsss all the commotion going on up here?" Yawning, Garcia waddled up from his burrow.

"Iss thiss youngsssster behaving himsssself, Thomasss?" The old gopher's whistle bounced off the walls.

"Look out!" Thomas leaped at his friends, pushing them back down the entrance. Remnants of the snowdrift crashed down, blocking their exit.

"Oh, great." Reynard pawed at the ground. "We're trapped! Who knows how deep this is? We'll never get out. We're all gonna die!"

"Jussst hold on, sssonny!" Garcia shouldered past his friends and snuffled at the packed snow.

"Shucksss! This is jussst sssspring melt." He grabbed a handful. "Ssee? All sssslushy. It meansss sssspring iss here. Spring is here?" His eyes gleamed with a new youthfulness as he turned and dug furiously at the blockage. "Woo hoo!"

Reynard joined in, and the trio was soon basking in the morning light.

Thomas appraised his friend. "Garcia, you surprise me."

"Why's that, sonny?" The groundhog sat back and began grooming himself.

Thomas walked a circle around him, eyeing the youngish-looking hog up and down. Reynard trotted over.

Thomas sat down, looking quizzically at his friend. "You seem downright … what? Downright youthful. Look at your coat. It shines in the sunlight. And your voice. All of a sudden, you don't drag out your *S*'s like you used to."

Reynard stepped closer and sniffed at him. "You even smell new!"

"Ha!" Garcia jumped up and assumed a kung fu pose. Then he took a step forward. "Ha!" He paused. "Ha! Ha! Ha!" His front paws shot out like he was punching an opponent.

"I told you. The humans did something to me. Poked me with needles and gave me this." He pointed to the star shape on his chest. The scar now glowed a bright red.

"Ah! I remember. They called it Accelerated Rejuvenation or something like that. All I know is that when I wake up in the spring, I feel like a kid again. It's great!" He jumped up and came down on all fours. He looked from side to side, lowered his head, and made a beeline toward Thomas.

Thomas leapt out of the way as he narrowly missed being bowled over.

"Whoa! Okay, okay. You made your point." Thomas strode over to Garcia. "I don't know. It's not natural."

Garcia poked at Thomas. "Who cares? Come on. Wanna fight?"

"No, I don't want to fight. I think maybe the humans gave you some of their traits."

"I'll fight you!" Reynard pawed at Garcia. "Come on, old man. I'm a warrior, you know."

"Enough!" Thomas commanded. "This is ridiculous. Garcia, it's incredible that you got some sort of fountain-of-youth treatment. Maybe it's a good thing for you."

Garcia reared back. "Maybe? Maybe? Look at me. I'm a vigorous young hog. Maybe the humans should have tried this on themselves. If they did, they could live long enough to wise up." He sat down and began grooming again.

Thomas shook his head. "I'm not getting into a philosophical debate about humans again. Besides, it may be too late for them."

Garcia paused and looked up. "What do you mean? I thought you were on a quest to find some."

Reynard came closer and looked at the two.

"Maybe you should tell him about Steve." There was a note of sadness in his voice. His eyes reflected it.

Garcia leaned forward. "Steve? Who's Steve? One of your human friends?"

Thomas shook his head. "Not quite. Or maybe more than human."

"He's from the Squatch clan," Reynard piped up. "Big, tall guy. Lots of fur. I found him while we were hunting."

Garcia sat upright. "Wait! You met a Sasquatch? Here? Don't be ridiculous. They're just an old humans' tale. They aren't real. Besides, even if they were real, what is one doing way down here? They *live* in the northwest." He laughed at the thought. "Rather, that's where they're supposed to call home. Hmmph."

The fox frowned. "It's a good thing I found him. We were starving, and here comes Steve, strolling across the field. At first, I thought he was a human and got scared."

"Can't trust humans, that's for certain," Garcia agreed. "I thought you were insane wanting to go find them, Thomas."

Garcia stood and poked at Reynard. "But now, wait a minute. *You* met a real Squatch?"

The fox nodded.

"Unbelievable. So what's a Squatch—this *Steve*—doing so far from his territory?"

"Taking a vacation." Thomas was matter-of-fact. "He said winter is their vacation time, and now that there are so few humans, the Squatch get to travel pretty far. We got lucky, I must say."

"Steve caught fish for us every day," Reynard blurted. "For

some reason, there aren't any mice around." He glanced at Thomas. "Anyway, we had a good time with Steve. Too bad you slept through it."

"Yeah, too bad." Garcia shook his head. The three fell silent, pondering the events.

Garcia broke the silence. "So, what's this about it being too late for humans?"

"They're an evil plague!" Reynard howled. "They killed my family. Steve knows all about them, too."

Thomas reached out to the fox. "We talked a lot with Steve. The Squatch sees the demise of humans as a good thing."

"Squatches call humans 'Nofurs,'" Reynard explained. "That's because humans have no fur. Get it? Nofurs. Except there are some he calls Fuzzleface. I guess some of them are okay. They wanted to be friends with the Squatch. But most Nofurs just wanted to kill Squatch and any other creature they came around."

"I believe Fuzzlefaces may be explorers or scientists," Thomas went on. "Not all of them wanted to harm other creatures. But Steve was pretty cautious about them, too. Humans! They are the only living thing that can admire how beautiful something is and then want to destroy it."

Reynard spoke quietly. "Steve told us of his friend, a big buck with a giant set of antlers. Steve said that he hid high in a tree one time, perched over some hunters. They talked about a beautiful deer they saw the day before and how they were anxious to kill it just to get its head and antlers. Steve never saw his friend again."

"I believe that." Garcia found a patch of emerging grass and began nibbling a stalk. "As a matter of fact, the lab they had me in was in a big building along with a place they called the Natural History Museum. I escaped my cage once and skedaddled down a hall. I turned a corner, and there was a whole forest in front of me. At least, I thought it was a forest. It turned out to be a big room. There were deer and rabbits, birds and squirrels, and other creatures. All of them dead. Dead! But the humans fixed them up so that they looked alive, and they put them in this big room. Imagine that!"

Thomas paced. "There's no explaining humans. Besides, Steve claims there are very few of them left between here and his home. It's a positive thing for the Squatch, though. They're making babies and taking back the forests."

"I agree with Garcia, Mr. Thomas," Reynard spoke up. "If humans are so bad, and we know they are, why are you looking for them? Shouldn't we stay away and keep to ourselves?"

"That's just the thing. I keep telling you they aren't *all* bad. Oh, I've seen my share of really nasty ones. But the good ones have so much potential. I've even met a couple who understand what I say. We can *talk* to humans. Think of it. Can you imagine a world where we can all live in peace? Now, with the Squatch coming back, it's even more urgent that I reach them. My friend Chris is out there. I can feel his spirit. James Robert, too. He died, but his soul is still with us. That's why I have to find them. We can build a better world. That is, if they want to. We must convince them."

Garcia snatched more grass and bit down, grinding away at it. "Hmmph. I don't believe it. Not a word of it." He swallowed hard. "First, you want me to believe you spent the winter with a Sasquatch. Now you want me to trust there are *good* humans. Well, hmmph to that."

Thomas stopped pacing and looked first at one, then the other of his friends, searching for something in their eyes. An idea struck him.

"Reynard." He puffed out his chest and said sternly, "You claim to be a warrior. Well, this is a battle that we must win. You have been called to duty, young man. Can you not feel it in your heart, in your soul?"

Reynard stood at attention. "Yes. Yes, I can. I'll go with you, Mr. Thomas. Lead the way."

"And you, Garcia?"

"Hmmph. I'm happy just where I am—thank you."

"OK, Gramps." Reynard padded over to the old rodent and

sniffed. Then he winked at Thomas. "Hey! You don't smell so moldy anymore."

"What do you mean, 'moldy'? And stop calling me Gramps. I told you that I'm a vigorous, young hog."

"Yeah, sure," Rey taunted. "If you're so lively, why aren't you out chasing girl groundhogs?"

"What? Girls? I just woke up, you pup." He took a swipe at the fox. "I need to get some food in me. Then we can talk about girls." He pulled up some more grass and chomped down.

"Mr. Thomas, where'd you say we're going, anyway?" The sly fellow winked again.

Thomas caught his drift. "Ohio. Southeast Ohio, to be specific."

"Oh! O-hi-o!" Rey drew the word out. "I hear they have some wild women there."

Garcia was unimpressed. "Hmmph, wild women. You should go to Kansas City if you want to meet some crazy women. Now those were the days, my friend." A big grin crossed his face.

"Still." Thomas picked up on the fox's line. "Ohio has some fantastic farmland. And where there's farmland, there's good eating."

"Fields full of good food," Reynard broke in.

Thomas continued. "And good food means other critters, which means other groundhogs. And that means—"

"Females," Garcia finished. "Okay. You got me. Let's go check out the, er—farmland in Ohio."

THE HEROES' HIGHWAY

"War! Does anything good ever come from it? One might argue that our medical miracles resulted from the need to repair our trooper's bodies. No need to worry about their souls. They had God on their side."

— A BUTTERFLY IN FLIGHT: THE BIOGRAPHY OF THOMAS SPEAKER BY JAMIE LIVINGSTON

Christian opened his eyes. Mary lay asleep, facing him across the tent floor. The pre-dawn glow filtered through the tent wall, giving a halo effect to her tousled red tresses. He smiled.

Rolling quietly onto his back, he looked at the tent's ceiling, staring at the stains. Patterns became images, and those images became memories. He assembled this troupe a week ago, back in Cairo. Mary helped with the selection process, as there were plenty of volunteers to join them on their journey to Speaker's town. She chose Ralph, an old geezer who had worked in the engine room of the *Delta Belle*. Chris picked two older teenage boys from Cairo whom he had worked alongside. Their willingness to take on any project impressed him. Chris and Mary both decided to allow a young family to come along—early thirties parents and their young daughter. Chris couldn't think of a good reason to allow them along. Nor could he or Mary come up with a good excuse not to allow them. It just felt right.

Chris blinked twice. One particular stain looked like a sitting cat. *Mr. Thomas!* He touched the warm mark on his chest. *I know he's safe, and we're getting closer. I feel it, too.*

He pitched over onto his side and looked at Mary. A slight smile graced her lips. Those lips! His eyes grew wide, remembering the night in her houseboat. They were sitting together, his arm around her shoulder. What were they talking about? *It's all fuzzy.* She laughed at something as she reached up and tickled his ear. He pulled back a bit, but her finger slid over his jaw and guided his mouth to hers. *I saw stars! Mama never kissed me like that!* Then her hand slipped down, caressed his chest, and dropped farther to his pants. A strange feeling overwhelmed him, something he never felt before. *I exploded! The hot liquid just burst out. Why? What?*

He had jumped up in a panic, covering the wet spot on his pants. Mary called after him as he rushed out the door. Embarrassment drove him back to his houseboat, where he lay till morning.

It took days before he could speak with Mary again, avoiding her by rising early and volunteering for expedition jobs beyond Cairo. She finally caught up with him after dinner in the communal hall.

"Chris, we need to talk about this." She pulled on his arm until he faced her. There was no need to play dumb. Not with Mary.

"My mama told me about this. That one day I would meet a girl. One that I would fancy a lot." He shifted on his feet. "She said I would know the girl was special by the way she kissed me." He looked into her green eyes. "Th-the way you kissed me, Mary."

Mary tilted her head, stared into Chris's eyes, and nodded. "Your mama was a very smart lady. I—I didn't mean to upset you,

Chris." A smile tugged at her lips. "I guess I felt that you were special, too. I just wanted to show you how I felt."

His eyes widened. "But Mary. You made me explode. And it felt wonderful. Now, that's all I think about." He grabbed her shoulders, holding her tightly. "Mama told me that when I feel that way about my special girl, then I should marry her."

"I'll bet she also told you that you should wait until you were married to do … other things with your girl?"

"That's right." He let go of her shoulders and stepped back. "She told me I would want to do wonderful things with her. And that it would be special because my girl would want to do them too. But those things should wait until we're married."

She cocked her head to one side, the slight smile returning. "So are you asking me to marry you, Chris?"

"I suppose I am, Mary." He cupped her hand in his and looked away, imagining. "If you want to, that is."

Her eyes sparkled as the smile widened. She took a deep breath. "That works for me! Now what?"

Chris bounced up and down. "We have to tell Mama Ruth. And LinLin. Maybe we can have Pastor Speaker marry us."

Mary pulled her hands free. "Well, the captain of the *Belle* could, also. That way, we could do it soon."

"But I want my friends to be with us. Mr. Thomas is heading to the pastor's town. I can feel it. I want him to be there."

Mary's smile faded. "In that case, we better start planning our trip."

Christian heaved back over, smiling at those memories. He felt below his waist. *I hope we get to Pastor Speaker's soon.*

"Rise and shine, lovebirds!" There was a slap at the tent flap as Ralph's voice boomed from outside. Christian sat bolt upright, pulling his hands out from the covers.

Mary rolled over and pulled the covers over her head. "What? Morning already?"

"Already? It's been morning for nearly a quarter of an hour!" The old man was moving to the next tent to rouse the teens.

"I am *not* a morning person," Mary grumbled as she crawled from her sleeping bag and looked over at Christian. "Morning, honey. Sleep well?"

"Like a log." Chris stood up and crouched under the low ceiling. He held out his hand to help Mary get up. "I had nice dreams."

She looked him up and down, noting the bulge below his waist. "I bet you did." She gave him a peck on the cheek as he pulled her to her feet.

Outside, the young couple was tending the campfire. The man spoke. "Morning, Ralph! Looks like another glorious day ahead."

"And a good day to you too, Bob," Ralph exclaimed. "And, you, too, Miz Kelly. Where's your young 'un?"

Kelly pointed into the nearby trees. "Izzy's over there, gathering a little more wood."

Ralph appraised the boiling teapot. "Let's not go overboard and make it too big. I'm hoping to get a quick start and get some distance on us today." He spotted the boys, Terry and Isaiah, wiping the sleep from their eyes. "All right, I hope you boys slept well. We'll break camp as soon as breakfast is over."

For his part, Christian didn't mind the old fellow taking control of the general duties. He preferred being a helper. Besides, Mary had the instinct of a leader. They decided before the group set out that Mary would be in command. Ralph was her lieutenant. As for Chris, they trusted his intuition to set the direction of travel.

Izzy came out of the wood with an armful of dead branches. She said her good mornings and bent over the fire.

Chris and Mary stood for a moment, taking it all in. He gave her a quick hug. "Now I know why we chose Bob and Kelly," Chris whispered in her ear.

"Why's that, dear?" She cocked her head, listening.

"Because they're a family, and I don't know a thing about being a family. All I remember is being with my mama. Now there's you and me. When we're married, we'll be making a family, too. They can teach us."

"Oh, sweetie!" There was a lilt to Mary's voice as she giggled. "I think that you and me, we'll do just fine."

Breakfast went quickly. Ralph pulled out a tattered map and consulted with Chris and Mary as the others broke camp.

"I've been trying to map our journey, Chris, Mary …" Their guide looked from one to the other. "I figure we've got at least another month ahead of us at our current pace."

"A whole month?" Chris looked at Mary as they both spoke.

"It's not like we can just jump in the car and drive wherever we want. Maybe back in the day but not anymore." He crumpled the sheet, then smoothed it out again. "Hmph. Those days are long gone. Here. Look." Ralph pointed to the map.

The three put their heads together, studying the faint lines. Ralph's dirty finger indicated a spot toward the bottom. "Here's Cairo." He traced a line over about an inch. "Here we are." His finger moved across the page. "Here's where we think we're going."

Chris poked at the map. "But we've been hiking nearly a week now."

Mary placed her hand over Chris's. "It's been a little rough going so far. For one thing, it's the rainy season, and this two-lane road has gotten overgrown, slowing us down. What if we cut over to this one, I-64? Maybe we can pick up our pace on it?"

"I was thinking the same thing." Ralph let go of the map, allowing Christian to hold it. "Back during the troubles, the inter-states weren't a safe place to travel—too many desperate people on them. We may still come across someone—friend or foe—who knows? Maybe we can make some time cutting across Kentucky. Then we follow Route 52 up the Ohio River again." Ralph furrowed his brow, looking at Chris.

Mary smiled at Ralph. "Sounds like a plan. Let's make it happen." Turning to Chris, she noticed his frown. "What is it, sweetie?"

Chris sandwiched the tattered paper between his hands, eyes closed. "Mr. Thomas—he's … here." He scratched at a place a finger length up the map from their location. "I feel him!"

· * ·

THE DAYS PASSED QUICKLY AS THE TRAVELERS FELL INTO A ROUTINE. Terry and Isaiah assumed the role of big brothers for Izzy, much to her parents' relief. The young teen grew bored quickly as they walked along, so the boys taught her some traveling games.

Soon enough, they hiked up a slight incline and accessed the highway. The four lanes stretched straight ahead, undulating through the hills. A wide median separated the two ribbons. Brown-painted signs marched down either side for as far as the eye could see.

Izzy skipped up to the first one. "Staff Sgt. Maurice Brown Memorial Section," she shouted to the others and hopped to the next. "Cpl. Margaret Dundee Memorial Section." Izzy clapped her hands and laughed. The boys ran up to join her.

"Major John Grimes Memorial Section," Terry announced.

"This one says 'PFC Howard Johnson.'" Isaiah joined in as the children danced from sign to sign.

"What on earth is this about?" Mary stepped onto the highway, Chris by her side.

Ralph pulled up beside them. "I've heard about this. It must be the Highway of Heroes."

"Why is it called that?" Chris stared down the way. The signs were evenly spaced and stretched as far as he could see. Some sections toppled together like falling dominoes.

"Oh, back during the Forever Wars"—Ralph spat on the ground—"they used to name entire roads or highways after some war hero. But with the war going on and on, they ran out of roads and highways. Then they started renaming streets." He hawked up some phlegm and spat again. "Hell, it got so bad somebody finally got the bright idea of having a fundraiser. A person could contribute a thousand dollars to the war effort and permanently memorialize their son or daughter. So here it is, the Highway of Heroes." He spat again. "Maga!"

Mary shook her head. "Wasted. So many lives wasted."

Izzy jumped and waved, shouting at her parents. "Mommy, Daddy! I found one with Daddy's name on it!"

Bob and Kelly ran to where Izzy stood, pointing up at the fading white lettering. The others followed quickly. "Capt. Robert A. Rutherford," Izzy read.

"Who?" Kelly looked at her husband.

"My dad." Bob spoke softly. "I remember Mom talking about this. I was too young to remember much about him, of course. He was a chopper pilot. Mom said he died trying to rescue the crew of another helicopter that went down somewhere in the Middle East." He touched the aluminum sign, invoking the memory. "I hardly knew him. Mom got a medal with a ribbon on it and a citation from the Army. It praised his efforts. Then they asked her for the thousand-dollar donation for this sign. They wouldn't even send his body back home until she paid them. Imagine that." Bob looked at his friends. "What sort of society would ransom the bodies of its troops?"

Christian stepped up and wrapped his arms around the young man. "I'm sorry, Bob. I think we learned a lesson, though. We were supposed to be the good guys. Maybe we weren't after all."

THE MISSIONARY'S POSITION

"I've been called a false prophet. It's funny because I never aspired to be a prophet, let alone a false one. What is false about my emphasizing a path of love for one another?"

— A BUTTERFLY IN FLIGHT: THE BIOGRAPHY OF THOMAS SPEAKER BY JAMIE LIVINGSTON

Interstate 64 proved to be a wise choice. It was relatively clear, save for the exits, now clogged with the rusting hulks of cars and trucks long abandoned. Christian and Mary soon led their party into southeastern Ohio. Spring burst forth in a riot of sound and color as nature reawakened. A new sense of urgency gripped the party as they neared Speaker's town.

The company reached the top of a rise and stopped in its tracks. A line of men crested the next hill, approaching them. These were the first people they came across in their entire journey.

Christian's group stood in hushed surprise. Mary finally broke the silence. "What? Who on earth?"

A tall man dressed in a long white robe led the group. Twelve others followed, each dressed in a tattered barber's shirt and leading an overburdened donkey. The man walked backward, gesticulating wildly as he talked. The next in line caught sight of Christian's party and pointed.

The tall man turned and clapped his hands together. "Travelers!" He strode up the hill, leaving his followers to catch up. Reaching the group, he put out his hand. "Howdy, strangers. My name is Saul. Some people call me Utah Saul, though I don't know why." The man stood six inches higher than anyone else.

"Maybe because you tall, Saul," Terry remarked, jabbing an elbow at Isaiah.

Saul looked around and over everyone's heads. "What, er … Well, yes, I suppose I am." He placed a finger on his chin. "It's a joke, then. I get it!" He turned to his followers, now gathering around him. "Say, are you making *fun* of me? I can't believe it. I am *SAUL*. Your leader." He held out his hands, pleading. "There's no making fun of your *leader*. Not when you're on a mission." Some of the men stifled a snigger. They all lowered their heads. "I said there's no making fun of your *leader!*" He went from man to man, shaking their shoulders.

Christian stepped forward. "Maybe we should just let you pass."

"No, no, no!" Saul turned to him. "We have an urgent calling from God. I am to establish a new order of monks and bring God's word to the people. These are my disciples." He stretched out his arm, presenting the men and donkeys. "We are on our way to Damascus!"

"Damascus? Where's that?" Christian eyed the animals. "And why do the donkeys carry such big loads?"

Saul swaggered up to Chris, fire in his eyes. "It's in Alabama, of course. I had a dream. God told me I would find a receptive audience there. And look. Here." He hurried back and opened a saddlebag. "God has showered us with so many blessings!" He pulled out a pack of paper money and waved it in the air.

Ralph began laughing. "Blessings? Maga! That's nothing but old government greenbacks. Completely worthless!"

"No, no, no. Look!" Saul strode up to him, holding out the cash. "It's *God's* Greenbacks. Says so right here." He pointed to an inscription on one of the notes. "In God We Trust" scrolled across the bottom, with different numbers printed in the corners of each bill.

Ralph snatched the wad of money from Saul. "There is no more government. This is just worthless paper." He crumpled the bills and threw them to the ground.

"Sacrilege!" One of the disciples cried out and raced up to gather the bills, returning them to safekeeping.

Saul turned back to Christian's group. "It's how we measure God's blessings. The more greenbacks you have, the more you are blessed by God. That's my gospel and what I preach."

He reached into his robe pocket and produced a pitch pipe and a carved stick. "Here, I wrote a hymn about it." He turned to his men. "Gentlemen, assume your positions." The twelve split into three groups. Each quartet jostled into a lineup, shoulder to shoulder.

Saul held up the instrument. "Now, as I have taught you. There are three stanzas. Each group will sing one of them. All join in for the chorus." He blew a single note. The twelve harmonized to the sound with a collective "Hmmm."

Saul smiled broadly. "Very good! You begin, Quartet One." He pointed to the first group, raised his hand, and paused.

The four men took a step forward, hummed the tone again, and began:

> *Prosperity is what we preach*
> *It's how God shows his favor.*
> *Money in our pocket, we beseech.*
> *Now that's our kind of savior!*

"Now, all together on the chorus." Saul slashed the air, and the other quartets joined in:

> *God's love is colored gold and green.*
> *It's how he gives his blessings.*
> *You may think that it's obscene,*
> *But that's what we're professing.*

"Excellent!" Saul's face glowed, ecstatic. "Now, Quartet Two." The baton slashed out.

> *Faith, hope, and love are nice to know.*
> *But leave us much appalled*
> *Those virtues only bring us woe.*
> *Our answer is, "Call Saul!"*

"Again, chorus!" Beads of sweat began dripping down Saul's face. He paid no attention to it as the twelve sang:

> *God's love is colored gold and green.*
> *It's how he gives his blessings.*
> *You may think that it's obscene,*
> *But that's what we're professing.*

"And now you, Quar—"

"Wait, wait, wait." Ralph stepped forward and marched to the first donkey. "You're not talking about this stuff, are you?" He pulled out a bundle of hundred-dollar bills. "In God We Trust" seemed to glow. "This stuff is barely worth the paper used to print it. Greenbacks, that's what they are. Worthless, government greenbacks."

"*God's* greenbacks." Saul held his head high.

Ralph stuffed the wad back in the saddlebag. "I know what we called them. That was then. This is now. That worthless paper has nothing to do with God's graces, for heaven's sake." He spat on the ground.

"It's what we believe. Am I right, gentlemen?" Saul stared at each of his disciples and received vigorous nods in return. "Besides, who's to say I'm wrong?"

"Pastor Speaker, that's who." Christian moved closer. "I've listened to his teachings, and he says money is what caused all of our troubles in the first place."

Saul tut-tutted. "Oh, him. He has his beliefs; we have ours. Forget that 'blessings in the afterlife' crap. We have God's favor now. In this life. He shows it with these greenbacks." He waved at the twelve donkeys standing patiently with their burdens.

Christian stood his ground. "Don't you understand? Life isn't about what *you* can get. It's about what *you* can share—how we all connect."

Mary stepped forward. "Lookit. We're going to get nowhere arguing about religion. I suppose you'll do just fine with your beliefs, just as long as you don't harm anyone with them."

"Agreed." Saul crossed his arms in front of his chest. "Although *I AM* right."

Mary let out a long breath. "Yeah, yeah, whatever. Listen. We're heading to Speaker's town. Any idea how far away it is?"

Saul sniffed and jutted his nose toward the north. "If you must. Stay on this road. He's two days' journey away."

"Thank you. That's very helpful." Mary proffered her hand.

Saul ignored the friendly gesture. "Oh, there are several farmsteads along the way. I'm sure they'll put you up for the night in exchange for some chores. They certainly don't know the value of a greenback!"

Mary lowered her hand. "Thanks for that. That's good to know." She turned to her group. "C'mon, guys, time to hit the road."

As they hiked past Saul, Terry turned and elbowed Isaiah. "Good luck in Damascus!" Terry waved as he passed along the pleasantry. Isaiah sniggered.

FEEL FLOW

"This ability to self-heal is truly a blessing. Those of us who were the successful recipients have, I believe, been a benefit to humanity."

— A BUTTERFLY IN FLIGHT: THE BIOGRAPHY OF
THOMAS SPEAKER BY JAMIE LIVINGSTON

It was all Thomas could do to keep pace with the rejuvenated Garcia. The three friends had been on the road for two weeks now, and the steady pace was wearing on him.

Reynard nipped at Garcia's heels as they barreled down the hill. Thomas huffed after them. "Darn you, kids! It's hard enough to keep up with you. I can hardly see you. Stay out of the tall brush."

Reynard laughed. "What's the matter, old man? Are you out of shape?"

Garcia stopped and put his paw out. "Rey, a little respect for your elders. I've told you before; we elders hold knowledge. If you want to learn from us, you're going to show some respect, darn it."

Reynard skidded to a stop in front of Garcia. "Ah, take it easy, Gramps. Besides, you sure aren't acting your age, either."

"I can't help it. This happens every year. When I come out of my sleep, I'm … I'm fixed. But in a *good* way. You know what I mean?" Garcia turned as Reynard walked behind him, sniffing.

"Oh, I know what you mean, for sure. Man, you've got some big ones."

"Get your nose out of there!" Garcia swiped at the fox, missed, and tried again.

Thomas caught up to them, panting from the run downhill.

The cat separated his two friends. "It's simple biology. That and young creatures, especially guys, have two things on their minds at springtime."

Garcia smiled as he munched on a dandelion. "Food, for one."

"And girls." Reynard began skipping around. "When I meet a girl fox, I'm gonna … I'm gonna … Hmm. I don't know what I'm gonna do."

Garcia got in the fox's face, poking at his chest. "Here's what you're going to do. Over the years, I've learned you should be respectful and gentlemanly. You kids think all you have to do is strut around and act tough and the girls will swoon over you. Ha! You catch more flies with honey, if you catch my drift."

"I have no idea what you're talking about." Rey's shoulders sagged as he sat down.

Thomas craned his neck to look beyond the two. "It is complicated. It's not easy controlling your urges, but that's what you have to do. But I think Garcia may have a chance to demonstrate what he means."

The two turned and looked up the next hill. A female groundhog had emerged from her burrow, kicking debris out of the entrance. She hadn't noticed them.

Garcia's eyes grew big as he stood on his hind legs, trying to get a better look. His nose twitched, and a visible shudder shook his body. He stared at the lady, mesmerized.

Rey jumped up and waved a paw in front of Garcia's face.

"What's going on, Gramps? Why are you acting so weird?"

The groundhog shook his head vigorously and regained his composure.

"Hmph. Yes. Well … this *is* a lovely day, indeed. Step aside, sonny!" He elbowed past Reynard. "This is how you do it with respect and charm." He proceeded up the hill and began singing. "Hey, there. Pretty girl with the stars in her eyes."

"Whoa! Gramps has some chops. Listen to him sing." Rey sat down with ears perked.

"He sure knows how to turn it on." Thomas smiled. "Watch and learn, son. Watch and learn."

"What? Who?" Rey looked around.

"Now, you stay here and observe. I think you can learn a thing or three from that old groundhog. You're going to need to know this stuff soon yourself."

"Wait, where are you going?"

"I need to go back up the hill here. I believe we may have gotten turned around a bit." With that, Thomas headed back the way they came.

At the top of the hill, he stood up, sniffing at the air. The road they traveled stretched down, crossing through a swampy area. Thomas felt an inkling that they were close to their goal. His dreams over the past week had gotten more and more confusing. His thoughts of Christian co-mingled with images of Thomas Speaker. Sometimes they were apart. Other times together. Chris was well. He was positive about that. But where exactly was he?

How is it possible I can feel him so close? He was heading down the Mississippi when we got separated. Ah, my friend, what's become of you?

Reynard came loping up the slope. "Hey, Mr. Thomas, guess what? Garcia's got a girlfriend."

"What? I knew the guy was smooth, but this seems so sudden."

"I think it was the song." Reynard winked. "Boy, I've learned a thing or three, that's for sure."

"Hey there, my friends." Garcia hailed them as he strolled up the hill, the female by his side. I would like you to meet my new, er, friend. Yes, my new friend."

The girl tee-heed and gave a slight bow. "Pleased to meet you. My name is Charlotte. Garcia's told me all about you two. You're quite the adventurers. Oh, my! Is it true you came all the way from the big river? What's it like there? Are there lots of other animals? How about humans? There are humans near here."

"Now, now, dear." Garcia turned to his friends. Hiding his words from Charlotte, he whispered, "She's a bit talkative."

"That she is." Thomas laughed. "But Charlotte, did you say there are humans near here?"

"Yes, indeed. Lots of them. Well, when you get to their town, there are lots of them. There are just a few here and there around these parts. They grow the best vegetables. And berries. Let me tell you about the raspberries they have. That's why I came here. I simply love raspberries, don't you?" She sniggered and took Garcia by the paw.

Garcia blushed. "Yes, I do. But it's not raspberry season yet, is it? If it is, then this truly is my lucky day. Why I remember one year—"

"Hmm, hmm." Thomas began to pace. "Look, lovebirds, keep it to yourselves. Please!"

"Yeah. You two are a couple of chatterboxes." Reynard almost rolled with laughter.

"Me? Us? No, no, no." Garcia held his paws up in protest.

Charlotte's laughter was infectious. "Oh, sweetie, it's okay! Besides, I think we should invite your friends to dinner. It will be dinnertime soon. I found some nice dandelion and coltsfoot. I could make a salad."

"Thanks, but no, madam." Thomas made a face. Reynard suppressed a gag.

"They're not vegetarians, dear. Besides, I think you got Thomas interested in meeting the humans. Am I right?" Garcia winked at his friends and nodded for them to go.

"Right, right." Thomas turned to look down the hill. "How far away are they, Charlotte? The humans, I mean."

"There's a farm down this hill and up over the next." Charlotte pointed. "Just follow the road about a half-mile beyond that to get to their village. You'll find a lot of humans. As for me, farm living is the life for me."

"Now, now, my dear. You do go on. I so love to talk with you, but please don't take offense. I think my friends are in a bit of a hurry. Am I right?" Garcia looked eagerly at his friends.

Reynard jumped up. "It's more than a mission. It's our calling. Am I right, Mr. Thomas?"

"That you are." Thomas turned to Charlotte. "I've found a human who can talk with animals. Then I lost him. I think he may be trying to find me, too. I dream about him and believe he is with those other humans in the town. Can you see why it's important that I find him?"

"To be completely honest, no." Charlotte sniffed. "The only thing humans are good for is growing veggies. Then they won't share them. What's the point of talking with them?"

"They're not all like that. I've met a few good ones. They have a prophet who is working to change their attitude. I hope to help him." Thomas listened to himself, hearing how weak his argument was becoming. "Anyway, I have to try. It's my calling."

"I hope you don't mind me staying behind, Mr. Thomas." Garcia waved a paw, shooing them away.

"Not at all, my friend. I've enjoyed getting to know you. We'll meet again. I'm certain of it." Thomas gazed down the hill.

"Oh, goody!" Charlotte jumped up and grabbed Garcia's paw. "Come with me. I spotted a nice patch of clover not far from the burrow. I think you'll enjoy it." She tugged at him, and they made their way back down the hill.

"What now, boss?" Reynard stood expectantly.

Thomas nodded to the south. "I know Thomas Speaker is in the town ahead. I get a sense that I'll find my friend Christian there also. Let's go find out."

PLEASED TO MEET YOU

"Perhaps we're at the next stage of human evolution. We can only guess what will happen next."

— A BUTTERFLY IN FLIGHT: THE BIOGRAPHY OF
THOMAS SPEAKER BY JAMIE LIVINGSTON

T he early spring sun hung high in the sky as Pastor Speaker stepped onto his porch. A smile crossed his lips as he remembered his latest broadcast. *Mustn't get smug about it, that's for sure.* The most recent scouting reports indicated Grizzly would be marching soon. A coded message left by one of the village's women confirmed that Speaker's town was their target. *Our militia is ready. Bart's done a helluva job whipping them into shape.*

Messages smuggled out of the Michigan community showed that the pastor's broadcasts were getting through to the dissenters in Grizzly's ranks. Illness was taking its toll there, weakening his original force, and the women were ready to revolt.

"Hey, Pastor!" Joanie, the young Greeter, waved as she approached, followed by a small group of strangers.

Thomas returned the wave. "Hey, Joanie. What have we here? New visitors?"

"No, sir. They say they plan to stay on. These are the folks from Mama Ruth's *Delta Belle.*"

"Of course, of course!" The pastor stepped down, hand outstretched. "We've been expecting you. I take it you had no problems on your journey, eh?"

Chris raced forward. "Pastor Speaker? Pastor Thomas Speaker? *The* Pastor Thomas Speaker?" He grabbed Thomas's outstretched hand and shook it. "I listen to your show *all* the time, sir. It's really you! Hi. My name is Chris, er, Christian. Christian Chance." He looked over his shoulder. "Mary, it's really him!"

Thomas reached out his left hand, stopping the handshaking. "Yes, yes. Mama told me about you. I'm pleased to meet you."

Mary ambled up and extended her hand in greeting. "Pleased to meet you, pastor. You'll have to forgive my boyfriend. He's been anxious to meet you for months now."

The pastor grasped her hand with both of his, hoping to avoid a repeat of Chris's greeting. "And I, him, for that matter. The word from Mama Ruth is he's quite an interesting fellow."

"Oh, that he is, that he is." Mary smiled and freed her hand.

Thomas waved at the rest of the group. "Well, come on in. Welcome, welcome." He turned toward the Greeter. "Joanie, please run to the Greeters Building and get some snacks for our guests. Ask for help if you need it. We're going to need to get these folks settled."

As Joanie ran off, Thomas shooed Chris's company up the steps. "Alice B. will be ending her broadcast soon, but come into the parlor here to the right. Make yourself comfortable."

Chris stepped up to the pastor. "I have a friend, Mr. Thomas. Has he gotten here yet? He told me to meet him here. He's a—"

Mary tugged at his hand. "Now, Chris. There'll be time enough for that. Besides, I'm sure if Mr. Thomas were here, he'd be asking about you."

Thomas frowned. "No, no, we haven't had any other arrivals for several weeks now. But I'll let folks know to keep an eye out for more travelers."

Mary smiled. "Thank you, sir." She tugged at Chris's hand, getting his attention. She mouthed the words "Not now" and pulled him up the steps.

*　✳　*

THOMAS AND REYNARD LOOKED DOWN THE HILL TO A SMALL farmstead. The fox sat up and sniffed at the air.

"Chickens! I smell chickens!" Rey licked his lips. "Eggs, too! Lots of chickens and eggs."

"I bet you do! But you must remember your promise. We don't want to get off on the wrong foot with these folks."

"Oh, for pity's sake! Please! Just one. That's all. Just oooone!" Rey flopped down in front of Thomas. "It's not natural! Fox and hens go together like, like—"

"Cats and mice. I get it." The cat held out his paw. "I'm hungry, too, but we can't let that get in the way of our mission. We're so close. I can feel it! There's something in the air."

Rey sniffed at the breeze. "I don't *smell* anything."

"It's not an aroma. It's a feeling." A door slammed in the distance.

"What was that?" Rey looked around. "What was that noise?"

"Easy. Easy. That's just the humans settling in for the night. They hide everything behind big wooden slabs so no one can get at them."

"Why would they do that?" Reynard paced back and forth nervously. "I thought you said they were friendly. Friends wouldn't shut out friends. I'll bet they even eat chickens! Ha! How about that? A true friend would share their chickens."

Thomas shook his head. "It's complicated. C'mon. We've got to get to town."

Rey slinked behind his friend. "Stupid humans! No wonder no one likes them. It's just plain selfish. That's what it is. Everyone shares. That's how Mom raised me. Take what you need; share the rest. It's part of the golden rule."

Thomas looked back over his shoulder. "The humans had a saying. 'He who has the gold makes the rules.' They used to horde everything they could—gold, silver, money, even food, for that matter. Why some would also have collections of books and pictures and keep them all to themselves. They called it 'wealth.'"

"Wealth? What does that mean?" Reynard stopped.

"Wealth is, that is, well …" Thomas paused and scratched his head. "Wealth is riches. It's something you hold dear."

"Like friends? Or family, maybe? Those are the things I hold close."

"It's something like that except wealth—riches—are just things. They have no spirit, no godstuff, no soul."

"Well, it sounds like they have a pretty messed-up value system to me." Reynard resumed walking. "Tell me again why you want to meet up with these humans."

"Because we can change things. We *can* make a difference. My friend, Christian, understands us when we talk to him. He *knows* our words. He'll help translate to the other humans. This Speaker —Thomas, pastor, whatever they want to call him—he has an open heart. I can tell from his preaching. He wants to make the world a better place. He'll listen to us." He picked up speed.

Reynard began trotting to keep up. "I don't know anything about that. But I do know that foxes eat chickens and cats eat mice. If you can change that, then you can change anything."

*　＊　*

THE PASTOR SAT IN HIS OFFICE, FIDDLING WITH A MEERSCHAUM PIPE. Its white bowl mellowed to a golden tan many years earlier. Now he avoided using it. His latest experience using 'shrooms left him unwilling to indulge in any psychoactive. The golden thread—his tie to the universe—was cut, and the loneliness left him empty. He set the pipe aside and clasped his hands.

"So how can I help you two this evening?" A wan smile appeared briefly. He tossed it aside, forcing himself to focus.

Christian looked to him and then Mary. "Well, sir, there's two things, actually. We wanted to talk to you about getting married." He fidgeted—they'd just arrived earlier in the afternoon and were barely settled in the town's hotel. Now he wondered if this was the proper time.

Thomas patted the top of his desk. "I see." It was his turn to fidget. "Normally, I would counsel you about your decision—in several meetings—over several weeks."

Chris leaned forward, clasping his hands. "I thought you might say that. But we've been together for months and months now, and … and …"

The pastor stood. "I thought you wanted to wait until your friend, er, Mr. Thomas arrived."

"We did. I mean, we do." Chris wrung his hands. "That's to say, I—I mean—"

A loud screech came from outside. Thomas and Mary jumped as Chris looked up, startled. Another shriek followed a dog's bark.

Speaker turned toward an open window. "What the … a dog must have treed a cat!"

Christian jumped up. "Wait! I heard my name. Someone's calling me!"

"Christian! Hey, Christian!" It sounded like a screeching cat to Thomas.

A series of dog barks followed. "Do you see him? Is he there?"

"Give me a minute. I can't tell for certain." The cat inched along a limb that reached out toward the house, nearly touching the window. The branch bowed under his weight. "He's here! I can see him. Chris is here! Christian! Hey, Christian!"

"Confounded cats!" The pastor stood and reached up to slide the window closed.

"Wait! No!" Thomas the cat jumped from the limb toward the window. Falling short, he reached out and caught the sill. "Christian!" He tried to claw his way up.

"I'll help!" Reynard leaped under the cat and tried to push him up with his head. "Can you reach it?"

Speaker gasped, sliding the window closed. "What the devil? A cat's trying to get in! And it looks like a fox is helping!"

Chris and Mary rushed to the window.

Chris pulled the pastor back. "Excuse me, sir. I know that voice."

Mr. Thomas heaved himself up on the sill. "Christian! Hey, it's me. Remember me?" He pawed at the window.

"Well, glory be!" Tears welled up. "It is him. It's my friend Mr. Thomas." Chris shoved the window open, and the cat leaped into his arms.

"Hey, buddy, it's great to see you!" Mr. Thomas snuggled into Chris's arms and purred.

"It's been a long time, that's for sure." Chris hugged his friend.

Outside, Reynard continued to yip for attention. The cat squirmed in Chris's arms, leaped out and onto the desk. He looked up at his old friend. "Chris, that's my buddy Rey outside. Can you let him in?"

"Of course!" Chris stuck his head out the window. "Hey, Mr. Rey!" He waved a greeting. "I'm Chris, er, Christian."

"Well, hey yourself, Mr. Chris Christian. I've heard a lot about you." The young fox jumped at the window. "By the way, you can call me Rey."

"Okay, Rey." Chris waved again. "Come around to the front. I'll let you in."

"Gotcha. This is so exciting." Reynard scampered off.

The pastor and Mary stood, mouths agape. Mary found the words. "Chris, honey, are you really talking with that cat? A-and the fox?" She looked sidelong to the pastor. "Preacher, you gotta understand. All along our journey, Chris would go off and 'talk' with the animals. I mean, *I* never thought he *actually* talked with them. I figured his voice affected them, calmed them down some-how, that's all. I don't know what to think."

"This is fascinating." The pastor bent down toward the cat. "I was speaking with Jamie's parents about how she seems to talk with their dog. I wonder—"

Chris leaned in. "Pastor, I was about to tell you about Mr. Thomas here. He talks with me, too. And he was hoping you could talk with him."

Thomas held out his paw. "Pleased to meet you, Pastor. We have a lot to talk about."

Reynard let out a yelp from the front porch. "Hey guys, let me in, please!"

"I forgot." Chris excused himself and went to the door.

Thomas Speaker reached out to Thomas Cat, extending his forefinger. A spark leaped from the cat's paw. Speaker yanked his hand away. He felt a tingling sensation climb his arm, cross his chest to his heart, where it paused, then jumped to his spine, up, and into his brain.

The pastor grasped his hand, staring at the finger. He staggered, and Mary reached out to steady him.

"Are you okay, Pastor?" She grasped his shoulders. A tingling sensation climbed up her arm and across to her heart. She shook her head, trying to clear it.

Speaker stared at her. "I—I feel str-strange."

Thomas stood on all fours. "Yes, but can you understand me now?" He looked from one to the other.

Mary pointed at him. "You … I … can … I know what you're saying!"

"Yes!" the pastor exclaimed. "Fascinating. But how?"

Chris and Reynard walked into the office, sharing a joke. Chris looked at his friends. "So, what did we miss?"

Mr. Thomas looked serene. "We've traded godstuff."

SWEET MUSIC

"All music affects me. It helps me connect to a higher plane. Perhaps it's a vibrational wave type of thing—coordinating my brainwaves to something else."

— A BUTTERFLY IN FLIGHT: THE BIOGRAPHY OF
THOMAS SPEAKER BY JAMIE LIVINGSTON

A small group of townsfolk gathered in the community building. Rays of gold from the setting sun pierced the windows, illuminating the joyful group. Christian Chance shifted from one foot to the other, wondering what to do next. Mary Chance beamed with excitement, nodding thanks to the well-wishers as the pastor turned them to face the guests.

"I present to you Mr. and Mrs. Christian Chance!" Thomas encircled them in his arms. "It's okay, Chris, you may kiss the bride."

"Again?" Chris's face turned a deep red. "If I have another kiss like the last one, my head might explode." He stared wide-eyed at Mary.

"Oh, you big, wonderful man!" She wrapped her hands around his neck, pulling his head down to her level. "It's okay, baby. I'll hold it together." She placed her lips on his as Chris flailed the air.

"Gosh!" He looked at the group as they smiled and applauded.

"A toast!" someone demanded as another handed two glasses of hard cider to the couple.

"That reminds me." The pastor spoke up. "I have just the thing. It's a message from Mama Ruth." He reached into the inside breast pocket of his jacket and pulled out a crumpled piece of paper. "This came in earlier today, and I quote, 'Dear Christian and Mary, may your lives be forever blessed with peace and joy.' And then there is this from your friend LinLin. 'May you be fruitful and abundant and know the joys of many hatchlings.'"

The members of Chris and Mary's crew tittered as Thomas Speaker looked about and shrugged. "I thought it was an odd wish, but I like the sentiment."

"You'd have to know LinLin," Ralph shouted, laughing.

The others chimed in as they raised their glasses. Mary gave Chris another peck on the cheek, causing him to blush again. As if on cue, the music coming from the radio switched to an old folk tune. A trio sang of gathering together in love and receiving God's blessings. The crowd grew quiet.

Suddenly, Chris snatched Mary up in his arms and swayed in time to the tune. She gave him a quick hug as he led her in stepping to the right, heels together, and then right foot back. Slide the left foot over and heels together again, and then the right foot forward. It was a simple, slow dance. It allowed him to hold her close, to smell the faint scent of springtime flowers. His head whirled.

*　*　*

ALICE B. TURNED THE VOLUME DOWN, FLIPPED THE SWITCH TO GO live, and spoke into the microphone. "Well, a marvelous greeting to all of you listeners, and welcome to Alice B.'s Kitchen, where the music is as sweet as Tupelo honey!" She paused, turned the volume back up, and allowed the tune to fill the air. Seconds passed before she turned it back down. Needles in meters bounced along, showing the sound level. "I hope that I have a rather memorable show for you this evening."

The music shifted to sound effects—birds chirping, a babbling stream. "Spring has sprung! Our thoughts are turning to more pleasant things." Alice flipped a new record around and dropped it on the second turntable, cueing up the third track. "Things like fresh flowers, tilling the soil, and warm spring days. Let's start with that. Welcome spring!" She placed the needle down, bumped the turntable into action, and then deftly faded from the intro music to the new song. A chorus sang of hippies strolling in a park, birds everywhere chirping their happiness, and flowers braided into young lovers' hair.

Alice looked around Pastor Speaker's office. The broadcasting area had grown from a single microphone and now encompassed a full one-half of the space. The pastor had pushed his desk to one side to accommodate two turntables, a mixing board, a second mic for interviews, and a single speaker hanging on the wall. Stacks of vinyl records sat on the floor and any flat space that could be found. She picked up the next one from the nearest pile and cued it up on the first turntable, ready for the other song to end. This was her heaven.

The young DJ flipped the mic switch as the loving hippies faded away. "This evening's show is dedicated to two special people. They arrived the other day—came all the way from Nebraska to join our community." She sent the turntable spinning, suspended the needle above the chosen track. "Here's to Christian and Mary as we celebrate their marriage today. Like the song says, 'All you need is love.'" The needle floated down, and a trumpet fanfare blared from the speaker. Alice grabbed the next record.

*　＊　*

REYNARD FOUND HIS TRAVELING MATE THOMAS SITTING AGAINST THE wall watching the festivities. "So, Mr. Thomas, I thought everything would change once we met up with your friend. You know, like, we'd be talking with all the humans and stuff."

Thomas looked down. "Yes, I admit I was hoping for some kind of miracle like that. Nothing has happened when I've tried touching others. When I first met James Hendrix, we had no problem understanding each other. Same with Chris, except when I slept on his chest, I felt a … a warmth. He says he felt it too."

He sat back down. "That spark between the pastor and me—I never felt something like that, ever. Then Mary touched both of us. It was amazing! Maybe the human needs something—I don't know, maybe an open heart?"

Rey sat down. "Maybe it's that godstuff you talk about. Who knows where it will take us?"

"P-pa-pardon me." A boy looked down at the two friends. "M-ma-may I j-join you?" He reached out a hand, palm up, to allow them to smell. "M-m-my n-na-name is J-Josh. Josh Davis."

Reynard stood and approached the boy, sniffing his fingers. He looked at Thomas. "He checks out. I smell chicken." His tail began to wag.

Thomas sauntered over and took in short whiffs, analyzing the boy. "You're right, Rey, it's chicken. And I think this human is okay, too."

Josh crouched down and extended both hands, palms down. "D-do you like s-scr-scritches? Everyone likes s-scr-scritches!" The pair allowed him to scratch behind their ears.

The cat began to purr. "Okay, you got me. Do the other ear, will you?" He moved his head to allow the play of the boy's fingers. Thomas felt the warmth grow.

"M-Mo-Mom says you c-can talk to P-Pa-Pastor an-and he talks to you." Josh began stroking Rey's back. "W-we-well you d-don't always need w-wo-words to talk."

* ✳ *

ALICE REALIZED THERE WAS A BETTER SONG TO FOLLOW UP THE current one and began flipping through albums. A tap at the office door startled her. "Sorry," Sergeant Bart, the head of the town militia, whispered as he slipped in. "We've come up with the weather report for you."

"I didn't realize it was that late." Alice set up the newfound record, ready to segue from the current music choice. "How's the reception going?"

The sergeant sat down and handed her the script. "They love your choice in music. You even got the happy couple dancing—several folks got all teary-eyed. Amazing what a song can do."

"It can soothe your soul." Alice took the paper, mouthing the words as she read. "This isn't completely truthful." She frowned, looking at Bart.

The sergeant sighed. "It doesn't have to be. It just has to be believable. We're trying to get Grizzly to come into town where we want him—where we can best defend against him. If he's listening—and he probably is—we're hoping he'll take the dry route."

"Gotcha. So rain coming in from the west and leaving in the east." Alice smiled. "So things are drying out just north of us. That's a weird weather pattern, don't you think?"

Bart chuckled. "Hey, it's Ohio. If you don't like the weather, stick around. It'll change tomorrow." It was an ancient joke that nobody laughed at any longer. It was mainly true.

"He'll come out of Michigan. He should stick to the major highways for speed. We hope to force him to take the road passing through the swamps north of town, which will cause his army to bunch up as they come off the hillside—easier targets for our archers. We're not soldiers. We're not even fighters. We need any break we can get."

Alice thought of several of her friends—young girls and boys her age and younger who volunteered to be a part of the militia. They told of practicing for battle ... and of being frightened. Primitive fighting was savage, ferocious hand-to-hand combat. "What about the women? Do you think Grizzly would bring them along?"

Bart took a deep breath. "The scouts report he will. We need to figure something out about that."

"Wait and see, I guess." Alice got ready to flip on her mic. "Why is war the only answer?"

*　*　*

JUDITH WATCHED AS GRIZZLY FLIPPED OFF THE RADIO AND STARED at it.

"So, whatcha thinking?" She busied herself cleaning up after their meal, keeping a wary eye on this madman.

"Stupid farmers!" Grizzly's smirk warped into a smile, showing the pointed fangs he affected. An accident chipped one canine tooth. He liked the look and had the other filed to match. Now he laughed aloud. "Stupid, stupid farmers! They just gave the weather report! To me!"

Judith sat, played dumb. "Well, the weather is critical to a farmer. I mean, it's hard work plowing and planting. You need the weather to cooperate."

"I suppose they do." He pulled the tattered map from his coat pocket. "Well, so do I."

He kicked aside a chair and spread the map on the table. "Knowing the weather helps me plan our attack. I've got more 'an two hundred fighters to move three hundred miles, and I've got to do it quickly. Spring makes the men restless."

"You mean horny!" Judith stepped behind him, touched his shoulder. "Your men seem to be adapting to village life. Give 'em a chance, and they'll fit right in—maybe rebuild what we had."

Grizzly slammed his fist down. "I don't build, I take!" He glared at her. The glare turned into a squint. "Are you telling me my men are going soft? What about you women? You've been training too. You're a part of the army now."

Judith stepped back. "We *women* do what we need to survive.

Yeah, some of your men are growing comfortable. Your 'volunteer' recruits you picked up along the way, they've had a taste of their old lives. I wanted to make sure you haven't gotten simple."

Grizzly stepped up to her, grabbing her throat. "Doncha ever think I'm stupid! I know my men. When we march, the prissy ones will stay behind, hold down the fort, as they say." His grip tightened. "A good general has a fallback plan, and they're it." He heaved her away.

Judith stumbled, fell to one knee, head down. "Soon. Soon," she muttered.

"What's that, woman?" Grizzly shot a glance at her.

Judith rubbed at her throat as the bruise faded. "I said, 'Soon, soon.'" She stood and squared her shoulders. "Soon, we'll be there. Then we'll get this damn battle over. We'll take over Speaker's damn town! Then what?"

"Eh! You women think you're fit enough to be in the army. Ha! You just want an easy life." He eyed her. "I know what you're about. You'll get it soon enough. Now tell Bradshaw to come here."

Judith bowed her head and turned away. *You have no clue! Do you think all of your men are loyal? Or that women are not fit for the army? You're in for a little surprise, you bastard!*

She made her way across the yards and to Sarah's house. As she approached, the front door flung open, and Bill rushed out. He brushed past her without acknowledgment while Sarah stood in the doorway, pinning her hair up. She allowed a wicked smile at the sight of her sister.

"Your boss wants you!" Judith called after Bill. He waved her off with his middle finger. Shrugging, she turned back to Sarah. "What's that about? I thought I'd be seeing a smile on his face."

"The horny bastard! He thinks he can have me anytime he likes. Well, not today, not today." She allowed Judith in and escorted her to the kitchen. A kettle steamed on the woodstove.

The sisters were bound by more than birth. The trials of living brought them a friendship of trust that only a few people are allowed. They worked silently together, preparing the tea.

Judith sat down and embraced her cup. The steam arose, engulfing her face. "Grizzly's making his war plans, plotting the route now. It looks like we'll be heading out in a few days."

"Should some of his men get, er, 'sick' again?" Sarah let her hair down and set the pearl-tipped hairpin aside. "We managed to take out five of his best this winter."

"No! He's too suspicious. Besides, the apothecary barely convinced him it was a seasonal disease—that we were immune to it and his men weren't." Judith sat the cup down. "There's been some coded notes in Speaker's broadcasts. They know we're coming. And I don't think that bastard Grizzly has a clue. Ha!"

"Thank God the boys are safe!" Sarah sipped at the tea. "It's good to know our messages are getting through."

"The pastor's people are likely to be on it. I'm betting they'll have scouts out all through Ohio. For now, we play along, keep them comfortable and off guard. Maybe we can manage a couple of 'accidents' along the way."

Sarah combed her fingers through her long red tresses, twisted the hair around and behind her head. "Well, maybe his favorite lieutenant can have a heart attack tonight." She slid the pin into place, holding her hair up.

Judith looked out over the cup brim and arched her eyebrows. "Maybe?"

* ✳ *

Josh felt the warmth stream from Thomas as the cat purred. The petting grew more intense until Thomas pulled back and stared at the boy.

"Whoa! What was that?" They spoke together, blinking.

Josh sat back and crossed his legs. "I—I feel strange. It's different, like ... I don't know."

Reynard stepped up and nuzzled the boy's hand. "What did you say?"

Josh stared at the fox. "I said, I feel different. It's like I'm—"

"Not tongue-tied?" Thomas approached the pair. "You're not stuttering anymore, and—"

"I can understand you!" The boy looked from one to the other. "I can understand both of you!"

"I'm sorry to interrupt." Maggie Livingston plopped down on the floor, Jamie squirming in her arms. "But it seems my young 'un wants to meet you, Mr. Thomas."

The girl bounced in her mother's lap. "Tom. Tom. Tom!" She reached out, grasping at the air. "Cat. Cat Cat!" Her little hands opened and closed as she squirmed.

Thomas took a cautious step forward, then another. "What? Who have we here?" He paused and stared in amazement. "James, is that you?"

GRIZZLY'S RAID

"You cannot reason with a madman, no matter how condescending you are. Don't let your desire for peace blind you to the need for security."

— A BUTTERFLY IN FLIGHT: THE BIOGRAPHY OF THOMAS SPEAKER BY JAMIE LIVINGSTON

Grizzly stood atop the hill surveying the route ahead. Mist rose from the swamp that bordered either side of the road below. *A trap!* He cursed and yanked on the length of rope wrapped around his fist. Judith, hands bound and tied to the opposite end, lurched forward.

"What do you know about this?" Grizzly clasped her by the throat, creating another bruise.

"I'd say property values are pretty low," Judith croaked. Her voice was barely audible through newly swollen lips.

"You did this! You led us here!" Grizzly's words spattered on her face. Judith didn't flinch.

She attempted a grin. "You heard the weather reports. You followed the map, made your choices. Here we are."

"Argh!" He threw her to the ground, knowing there was some

truth in what she said. Still, he wondered. The past three weeks were a nightmare. He and Bradshaw laid out plans for their march on Speaker's town, and preparations got underway. Two days passed as he assembled the army—now enhanced by the townswomen into a well-trained force of over two hundred soldiers—checked weapons, and packed up.

Then disaster. He and Judith awoke to the pounding on their door. Still in a fog from the dinner drinks, he pulled on pants and staggered down the stairs, Judith following. Bill's redheaded bitch stood outside, a blanket wrapped around her naked body. He only made half-sense out of her sobbing babble. Bill. Heart attack. Dead.

The words sobered him. Grizzly wrapped his fist around Sarah's long tresses. "Show me!" He shoved her back out the door and grabbed a jacket. "Come on!" He clasped her shoulder and pushed her along. Judith, holding her robe closed, rushed to keep up as they hurried across the neighboring yards.

Grizzly shoved Sarah along and into Bill's house and up the stairs. Pushing her aside, he stood at the doorway. Bill lay in silent repose. *Is that a smile on his face? That sonofa—*

He felt Judith's hands on his shoulders, moving him aside. He watched as she stepped to the side of the bed, and leaned down, cheek next to Bill's face. Her frown spoke volumes as she slid her hand under the man's head.

The bear stared at the scene, his hands opening and closing helplessly as Judith turned to him and Sarah. The woman slunk down in a corner, blubbering.

Judith had Bill's jaw in her hands, opening the airway. "Snap out of it! CPR! NOW! Sarah, get the doc. NOW!"

Grizzly took a faltering step forward as Sarah picked herself up. She thought to grab clothes as she hurried out.

"You do know CPR, don't you?" Disdain dripped from Judith's words. Grizzly looked at her, bewildered.

"Like this!" She placed her palms on Bill's chest and pushed down, counting the thrusts. She paused, took a deep breath, and blew it into Bill's lolling mouth. "Will you help me?" She looked up at the useless man and began the compressions a second time.

Grizzly stood, dumbfounded. "I—I—I—"

"You're useless!" Judith forced another breath into Bill. The minutes rushed by as she continued her efforts.

For Grizzly, the nightmare played out in slow motion. *Dead! My friend is gone—the only one I had. If I ever had a friend. Bradshaw, you S.O.B.—*

"Move aside!" The apothecary was there, shoving him away, bending over Bill's lifeless body, shaking her head.

Their voices sounded slow and muffled to Grizzly as he watched dumbfounded.

"Noooo!" Sarah threw herself on Bill, held his head, kissed his lips, made sure the bundled sheet showed no sign of blood. She allowed Judith to ease her off.

The apothecary grasped Grizzly's arms, looked him in the eye. "I'm sorry for your loss." She led him out. "We'll take it from here."

*　＊　*

THEY CREMATED BRADSHAW'S BODY, AS THEY HAD DONE THE VICTIMS of the winter's disease. Judith felt the brunt of Grizzly's rage. She thought to change his plans—stop the raid on Speaker's town—only to receive the first of many beatings.

"Nobody tells me what to do!" The first blow knocked her down. "Especially a damn bitch!" The first kick bruised a rib. "I"— he glared at the mourners—"I am Grizzly!" The next boot, less violent as his anger waned, nearly cost her a kidney. She blacked out.

Grizzly's eyes burned as he scanned the crowd, his army, looking for anyone who might disagree. He snorted in satisfaction, motioned the apothecary over to tend to Judith, and tramped off. The funeral pyre's embers cooled.

Back at the house, the bear rummaged in a cupboard and

pulled out a cut-glass container. The handmade label read *Harry's Hot Damn M.F.er.* It was a concoction of moonshine and who knew what else. He spilled it into a mug and took a gulp. It burned. *Yeah, it burns just like Bill's fire cooked him. Hell. Maybe I'll rename it. Wild Bill's Fire. Yeah, sounds good. Maybe I'll start a bar.* He grunted. *Maybe I'll rename this whole damn town!* He took a swallow and gasped as the drink stung his throat.

Grizzly stared at the wall. *I never thought of him as a friend. You can't afford friends nowadays. Simple as that.* Another gulp emptied the mug. *That mother was always at my side, had my back. Always!* He poured the last of the bottle into the cup. The setting sun pierced the kitchen, catching the etched glass pattern. Grizzly held it up, watched the design shift as he turned it around. *Oh, what the hell!* He smashed it on the floor.

* ✻ *

THERE WERE STILL EIGHTEEN FORMER CONVICTS FROM GRIZZLY'S original horde. Not one was capable of replacing Bill. Grizzly was alone in his command, giving orders and doling out punishment when there was a need. *Bully and beat—that's how Daddy did it. That's how you keep control.*

They began their march south.

He picked scouts from out of the recruits taken in other raids and sent them out ahead. They never returned. Suspecting desertion, he sent two of his best to reconnoiter. An hour later, they came upon their bodies bristling with arrows. There was no sign of an enemy. Grizzly's suspicions grew.

Days passed, and his frustration mounted. Grizzly ordered women to lead the march and surround the caravan, acting as a shield and preventing an attack. Still, every other morning brought news of desertion. In frustration, the bear took his fury out on Judith, berating and beating her in front of the other women. The desertions stopped.

Now atop the hill, Grizzly pulled Judith onto her feet. She

stumbled into him and backed off. He yanked again and led her back down the slope, a plan forming.

· ✳ ·

Sergeant Bart stood atop the rise across the valley and stepped forward, followed by Ralph and Thomas Speaker. The town's militia stood in formation just down the hill behind them.

The pastor strained to see the activity opposite them. "What's your take, commander?"

Sergeant Bart lowered his binoculars and glanced over at Ralph, the ex-military man from the *Delta Belle.* Ralph nodded.

Bart scowled. "It's him, based on the description we have. He has a woman with him, but she's tied up. From the stories we have, she's likely Ben's mother."

"Now a prisoner, maybe. He's on to them." Ralph again peered through his binoculars, watching their enemy turn back. "My guess is he's making his plans on the run. He sees the trap. He's likely to surround his main group with the women, which means we have a problem." He dropped the glasses and looked at Speaker. "They can't go through the swamp, so they'll take the road as we hoped. But with civilians as shields—"

"We can't fire on them." Speaker shook his head and looked down.

Ralph pointed down the valley. "Once they cross the swamp, they'll probably spread out on either side of the road. The deserters say that the women, and even some of the men, don't want to fight. It's going to be hand-to-hand combat for sure. How do we sort them out?"

"Perhaps a flag of truce?" the preacher was hopeful.

"That didn't help Ben and Brandon's town." Ralph spat on the ground. "No easy choices. We'll just have to wade in and let God sort 'em out."

Thomas the cat rushed up from the rear, followed by Reynard. He scanned the opposite hillside, now deserted. An occasional shout drifted over, muted by the hill. "So, what's going on?"

The preacher glanced down. "Grizzly's preparing his attack. It isn't going to be pretty. What do you think, Commander?" He turned to Sergeant Bart and Ralph.

Bart gestured toward the far side. "We agree it's best to bring up all of our force, spread 'em out across the hill. Grizzly will bunch his troops to cross the road over the swamp. Once on this side, he'll likely spread his troops out also. We'll come down in a pincer movement on either side of the road, meet them at that choke point." He turned to Ralph. "Give the order."

Reynard stood on his hind legs, straining to take in the scene. "Hey, guys, wait a minute." He hurried over to the preacher. "I think I see Garcia and Charlotte's home over there. See that burrow?" Reynard pointed to the other hill. Fresh dirt was piled just below a hole in the hillside.

"Oh, Lord!" The preacher grabbed Bart's binoculars.

The cat didn't wait for Speaker's confirmation of what he knew. He turned to Reynard. "Now you *are* a warrior. We have to save our friends." They set off running down the hill, shouting, "Garcia! Charlotte, stay inside!"

Garcia poked his head out and spotted his friends. "Hey, fellas! What's going on?" He strolled out to greet them.

The pair made it over the road and past the swamp. "Go back! Hide!" they both shouted, running up the hillside.

Garcia caught up with them. "C'mon, fellers. What's going on here? And what about all those humans? Up to no good, I'd say." Garcia eyed the troops forming on the opposite hilltop.

"There's going to be a battle." Reynard jumped up. "The enemy's coming up from behind your hill. But we're ready for them. I'm a warrior, you know."

Garcia looked over his shoulder. "A battle, you say? The enemy's over there, behind *my* hill. Can't these humans ever get along? Wait! Behind my hill?" He turned and ran. "My Charlotte's there, in our home!"

Thomas and Reynard followed. At the entrance, Garcia paused. "What'll I do?"

"Hide!" The fox pushed his friend deep into his tunnel.

"You both will be safe in there." Thomas was at Reynard's side. "Go back as far as you can." Their friends' safety assured, the fox and cat retreated across the marshland.

They reached the group of humans as Ralph brought the militia forward, ordering them to spread out to either side of the road. Bart walked the line with him, shouting words of encouragement.

The cat looked to Speaker. "I think our friends will be safe now. Is something bothering you, Thomas?"

The pastor shuddered. "It's been too many years since we had to defend ourselves. I fear the worst. I let them grow complacent."

. * .

JUDITH STUMBLED FORWARD WITH EACH TUG OF THE ROPE. HER LEFT eye swelled half shut as her body fought off the latest injury. She shook her head, clearing the fog, trying to find an opening. There was the Bowie knife that dangled at Grizzly's waist, out of reach, but his latest weapon, a hatchet, swung at his hip. Could she grab it quickly enough? Raise it high, smash it into his skull? No, he paced too close to his men.

Another yank on the rope. Grizzly ordered the troops into formation—five abreast, with the women, their hands bound to their shields and weapons removed, forming the perimeter. The males shoved them along for protection, their blades ready to deal with any resistance.

Judith caught the eye of several of the shield bearers, tried to look stern, nodding her own encouragement. Her lips formed a single word. "Soon."

The troop moved forward, Grizzly striding back and forth in the lead and pulling Judith behind. The highway's pavement had succumbed to decades of neglect. Potholes and cracked pavement made it difficult to maintain the battle line. The bear ordered them to the side and level ground as they crested the hill.

They paused for a final assessment. Their enemy stood atop the opposite hill, waiting silently. Grizzly snarled his defiance, turned to his troops with a bellow. They returned the howl as he led them downhill.

Judith weaved back and forth, towed along by the madman as he crisscrossed the battle line. Grizzly strode forward, shouting encouragement as his men raged.

Judith spotted it. There was a hole ahead and only a step to the side. *An animal burrow?* She wasn't sure, but an idea quickly formed. Another pull at her bindings. This time she did not resist but staggered forward, crashing into Grizzly.

He lurched backward and to the side. His left foot came down, failing to touch the expected earth. It continued the plunge into the hole. He heaved over. A sound like a branch snapping broke through the din.

Judith was on him, flipping him to his back and sitting across his thighs.

"That's gonna hurt in the morning." Grizzly moaned, struggling to rise. "Stand me up. I'm gonna kill someone."

"You think that's going to hurt?" She fumbled at his waist and found the blade. "Try this!" She plunged the knife through the leather apron and into his chest, twisting it back and forth. Grizzly's eyes bugged out, startled.

"Die, you bastard!" she hissed, pulling the knife and rolling to one side. Revenge carried her forward as she snatched up the hatchet and hacked at the barbarian's neck. The spine gave way. Another swift motion and she grabbed the knife, jamming it into the base of his skull. Judith stood triumphant, brandishing the grisly trophy.

The army pulled up and stood transfixed. To one side, Aliyah dropped to all fours, kicked out, and felled Doris. Like a hellcat, the girl sprang up, holding her buckler high. "I am Aliyah, daughter of Daniel and Laila! Die, bitch!" She jammed the shield down on her tormentor's throat. Moving quickly, she grabbed her abuser's knife and turned to the woman next to her. She, too, had dropped her captor and now held her hands out for the bindings to be cut.

Similar acts played out along their battle line. Sarah jumped to the forefront, knocking troops aside. She wiggled free of her bindings, found a dropped spear, and dispatched the nearest barbarian.

Now armed, the women turned on their partners. Many of the newest recruits dropped their weapons and held their hands up in surrender. A village woman picked up her partner's bow and shoved it at him. "Harold, get a backbone! Join us!"

The man stared at her for a moment, saw the resolve in her eyes, and grabbed the weapon. With one quick motion, he notched an arrow and let loose in the direction of Grizzly's loyalists. One fell.

Those faithful to the bear found themselves bunched together, facing the women and defectors. Sneering at their fate, they sent up a war-whoop and attacked. Aliyah's swift blade took down two. She stepped on their bodies, snarling at the attackers. The women pushed back with their shields, forcing the troops into a cluster.

Judith took in the melee on the hillside. Grabbing Grizzly's spear, she jammed the blade into the ground, and slipped his head on the shaft. Adrenaline coursed through her blood as she strode up the hill, Two fell under her bloody blade before the renegades realized the attack from their rear.

A barrage of arrows felled the last of Grizzly's men. The women waded into their midst. No mercy was asked for and none was given as spear thrusts finished them off.

Judith found Sarah and exchanged a quick embrace. Sarah held Judith at arm's length. "You're our leader, sister. What now?"

Judith stepped back, a slight smile on her lips. She marched back to where Grizzly's spear displayed its trophy. Grasping the shaft with both hands, she freed it and turned to the villagers. "Victory!" She thrust the pike high. A cheer went up.

Judith's thoughts raced back over the past year—Grizzly's attack, the death of her husband, the ongoing beatings at his hands—and what about Ben? Where was her son? She suppressed her emotion and turned to face the opposite hillside, brandishing the bloody head.

A young boy called out from across the way. "That's my mom!"

A FAIR WIND

"We really are stardust. And all things must pass on. I like the idea of a funeral being a joyous celebration. Let the music play on."

— *A BUTTERFLY IN FLIGHT: THE BIOGRAPHY OF THOMAS SPEAKER* BY JAMIE LIVINGSTON

Mr. Thomas padded into the pastor's office and leaped onto his desk. "Is everything okay, Thomas?" The cat sat back on his haunches and licked at a paw.

"Hmm? Oh, my, yes. I just wanted a little break. The whole town is abuzz about the shooting star this morning. And now our morning star is gone."

The cat cocked his head. "Do you think it's some sort of omen?"

"No, no. Nothing like that. We figured our star was actually a satellite of some sort. Its orbit finally decayed so it fell out of the sky. That's all." Speaker rummaged through the top drawer, found the pouch, and set it on the desk.

Thomas eyed the small purse as the pastor pulled it open.

"Shouldn't that be shared, if you're going to use it at all?"

"It's not what you think. Here, check it out." He placed the open bag in front of Thomas to sniff.

"Hmm, it's faintly familiar. Wait, don't tell me." He inhaled and sneezed. "Why, it's—"

"Tobacco! Yes indeed. Those folks that arrived from Kentucky the other day brought it, so I figured I'd give it a try. Old habits die hard." Speaker fished out the aged briar pipe and filled it. "They were surprised we weren't growing our own. We're all very excited. The town council is drafting up a trade agreement for them to take back. Every week there's some new contact like that. Things can only get better."

Thomas backed up a pace as the pastor lit the pipe and began puffing. "It has been a remarkable month."

"Indeed it has! The threat of Grizzly is gone—forever. The Michigan folks are on their way back home." Speaker leaned back, tapping his chin with the pipestem. "That gives us nearly a dozen towns in our circle of friends. That's promising!"

"Hmm. Friends, you say? The cat cocked his head.

"Are you concerned about something?" Smoke swirled around the pastor's head.

Thomas edged to the other corner of the desk. "Well, yes. I wasn't going to bring it up now but—"

"No time like the present. C'mon. What is it?" Speaker pointed with the pipestem.

"When we first met, I felt a connection with you. I hoped you and I would link together. Like when I met James or Chris." He walked back to the other corner, tail twitching. "Both of them had the gift, but I had to have a physical touch with you, just like with Josh and the others, for you all to get it."

"I see. When Christian told me about how he was able to talk with animals, I was completely skeptical. Then you came in, and we touched. It was like … well, it was like when you bite into fresh fruit and the juice pours out. You know what I mean?" He leaned forward earnestly, brandishing the pipe.

Thomas sat down. "It's called 'awareness.' Your mind opens

up. You become capable of knowing and doing things you thought were impossible. It's kinda like learning a new language."

"So, what's your concern? That you may have to make physical contact to pass on the gift?"

Thomas's tail quivered. "Yes and no. I tried reaching out to Judith. We didn't connect, but there was something else. I felt something … cold."

"Hmm. I didn't get that feeling. But she does have the strangest smile. I'll give you that."

"Maybe I hoped for too much. I was looking forward to, er, 'spreading the gospel,' if you will."

"Ha!" The pastor nearly choked. "The Gospel of Thomas?"

"Sure! Why not? Only I wouldn't want it ignored like the biblical one."

"Nor be like the one old Saul was preaching." He sent another smoke ring floating.

"Chris told me about him. Quite the character." Thomas caught a whiff of smoke and coughed.

"I'm sorry. I didn't realize the smoke bothered you!" Speaker waved at the air, dissipating the cloud, and placed the pipe aside.

Thomas coughed. "It's okay. I lost my first life in a barn fire. I still get a little antsy when I get a whiff."

"That's another thing I don't understand." Speaker shoved his hands in his pockets and leaned back in the chair. "This rebirth, reincarnation, or whatever you want to call it. Do you believe that little Jamie is somehow also her uncle, her mom's brother? How can that be?"

"Ah, yes. That's a tough concept to grasp." Thomas settled in front of the pastor. "Each religion has a different explanation. When you die, your soul or godstuff leaves the physical body. Being energy, it seeks a new place to abide. Some religions hold that it goes directly to heaven or hell, where it will dwell for eternity. Others say it may still have work to do, so it must unite with another physical form. It must live a physical life again. It does this over and over until it reaches perfection, that is, till it unites with God, the One."

"Karma?" The pastor scratched his chin. "At least, that's how I understand Karma to be, the working out of one's issues until he or she reaches perfection."

"Not quite. Most people think of Karma as a reward and punishment system—you do good, it comes back to you; you do bad, ditto. But reincarnation is about attaining spiritual perfection through the physical body. The physical allows your godstuff to learn its spiritual lessons. Then it moves from one plane of existence to the next, improving as it goes."

"Fascinating!"

"Yes, I pray that my next life will be as a dolphin. Those guys really have it together!"

Speaker smiled at the thought. "Okay. But what if one is evil, then what?"

"Then the soul has to take a step back. I was fortunate to be at James Robert's passing and able to pray and help guide his godstuff to the next level. Of course, I had no idea he would find a newborn relative. Fascinating, indeed!"

The two grew silent, lost in their thoughts.

There was a rap on the doorframe, and Doc Livingston poked his head around the corner.

"Sorry to interrupt, guys, but Maggie is getting impatient. Can we start the ceremony?"

"Right, right, right!" The pastor jumped up and clapped his hands. "Come along, Mr. Thomas. The naming of godparents is an important custom for our community."

They crossed the foyer and into the dining room, where the table and chairs were moved to the sides, allowing the guests to gather. Maggie was seated on the floor, Jamie perched between her legs. Reynard peered at the picture book they shared.

"Ca, ca, ca." The infant bounced up and down and tore at the page.

"Car." Reynard placed a paw on the drawing. "Car. That's good. You're getting it."

"The nurse says she just needs time to develop her mouth muscles." Maggie looked around at the other guests. "Then she'll be talking our ears off."

Jamie caught sight of Mr. Thomas and pointed. "Tom, Tom, Tom! Cat, cat, cat!" She flipped the pages, slapping at a picture of a yellow truck. "Cuck, cuck, cuck!"

Thomas strolled over. "What's that, kiddo? Ah, yes, the truck. I remember." He looked at her intently. "Next time, watch where you're going."

Jamie giggled. "'Member . 'Member."

Maggie stood and picked her daughter up. "Let's get this started." She cradled Jamie as Doc joined her. "Chris, Mary, we appreciate you stepping up for us. Good godparents are essential."

Christian bowed his head. "I … I never had godparents before. I'm not sure what we have to do."

Mary nudged her husband. "It's okay, hon. We'll learn along the way."

"Yes, yes." The pastor rubbed his hands together. "And your first lesson starts now." He motioned them to gather in a circle, Doc, Maggie, and Jamie in the center with him. Chris and Mary stood on either side of the family while the other guests closed around them.

Speaker began. "The old civilization's religions have survived humankind's downfall. They did so because of their core values, that is, their essence of True Love. They all recognize our spiritual foundation: Our connection to God is through love."

"It was religions that led to wars," Ralph muttered to Sergeant Bart, getting a nod of agreement.

"Ahem!" The pastor glared at Ralph. "This is not the time nor place for a history lesson."

The old warrior looked away. "My apologies."

Speaker continued. "We are here to—"

Awooooo! The mournful sound of the tornado warning arose

outside. Reynard took up the howl. The guests looked at each other, confused.

"People! People!" Thomas Speaker raised his hands, signaling for silence. "No need to panic. A tornado may be forming. This is a precaution. Now let's get down to the basement. We'll be safe there. Doc, will you guide them? Quickly now. Quickly!"

Maggie took the lead, holding her child tightly, while Doc motioned the others along.

Satisfied all was going smoothly, the pastor crossed the hall to his office. Thomas followed.

"Where are you going? What on earth are you doing?" The cat looked nervously about the room.

"We might need to shelter for awhile. I figured I'd grab a book, maybe some poetry to calm folks."

Outside, the wind began to howl. Tree branches swayed and bent.

The cat backed toward the doorway. "Well get your fingers walking. I don't like the sound of that! It's déjà vu all over again!"

"What's that?" Speaker ran his hand across the book spines, instinctively snatching one as the wind turned into an ungodly howl.

Suddenly, the roof lifted. Speaker looked up to see the giant oak falling toward him.

Thomas leaped toward the man only to be caught by the whirlwind and carried upward.

"Noooo!" His voice faded as the wind dissipated.

"Oh, my God! Thomas!" Doc rushed into the room. He clambered over debris as he caught sight of the pastor's prone figure under the tree limb. "No! This can't happen. Not now!"

"Thomas!" Chris was right behind Doc. "Where's Mr. Thomas? My friend. Mr. Thomas, where are you?" He looked up through the remnants of the ceiling. The sky was clearing. "Gone? I can't *feel* him."

Maggie shoved into the room and made her way to Doc. He

was pulling at the tree limb, but it wouldn't budge. She knelt beside the pastor.

Thomas Speaker's eyes glazed over. Blood bubbled from the corner of his mouth. "Too much damage," he gasped. "Better use this." He managed to hold up the book he had instinctively retrieved.

Doc bent down and took it—*The Tibetan Book of the Dead.* He opened it at a dog-eared page. It was the verse they had discussed many times—the prayers of passing to the next life. Maggie joined him and knelt beside their friend. She wiped away the blood as Doc began.

Christian stumbled over to them and gingerly touched Doc and Maggie. He knelt. "I guess it's time to pray."

EPILOGUE

Time passes, and this old world spins around in perfect cadence with the celestial clock. The events that give life its meaning work at a different pace marked on the heart's calendar.

Christian and Mary lived a fruitful life, finding their calling in the operation of the village kitchen. The loss of Mr. Thomas left a hole in Christian's heart that even the birth of their son, Chris Jr., could not heal. Still, he faced his responsibilities, throwing himself into the dual tasks of raising his son and feeding the community.

As the years passed, he found that the healing properties granted by the stem-cell treatment were not as beneficial to him. He aged. He thought of it as a blessing as he kept pace with his wife's own mortality.

Christian took some solace in the marriage of their son to Jamie Livingston. But the loss of Mary to the seasonal flu plunged him back into the dark space, a place where even the birth of his granddaughter seemed trivial. The effort of living became a burden until …

· ✳ ·

"MOMMY, DADDY!" RACHEL RAN INTO THE KITCHEN. "MISTY'S having her kittens!"

Jamie grabbed a towel to dry her hands. "It's about time. I thought I'd give birth before she did." She patted her swollen abdomen.

"She's out on the back porch, Mommy. Hurry." The girl grabbed her mother's hand and rushed her along to the screened-in room.

"What's all the racket?" Junior stepped in from the garden.

"Misty's having her baby!" The girl hopped over to her dad and pulled him along. Their cat lay in a wicker basket with towels placed in it for her comfort. She panted as a small black head emerged from her body.

"Ohh, look. Look! It's so cute." The girl bounced up and down.

"Now, Rachel, calm down. Misty's been in labor all night. Patience." Jamie pulled up a chair to watch and rest. "It's just a kitten, you know."

"Oh, no, Mommy. This one's special. I can feel it. I can feel it!"

Junior bent down for a better look. "I don't know. Maybe." He petted Misty's head as a spasm racked her body. She mewed softly. "Easy now, little one. It's almost over."

Another spasm and the kitten was born. The mother began licking and cleaning it immediately.

"Looks like there's just one." Junior felt Misty's belly. "But he's a big un', that's for sure. Rachel, honey, you may be on to something." He turned to his wife. "You have the gift, dear. What does Misty say?"

Jamie leaned forward as the cat began to purr. "Yes. She says there's only one kit."

The cat meowed softly.

Jamie smiled, reaching down to stroke Misty's head. "Yes, well, of course, all kids are special to their mothers. But there *is* something different about this one."

There was a knock at the front door. Jamie rose to answer it.

"I'll get it, Mommy. You rest." Rachel jumped up and ran out just as there was another knock. She returned, towing Christian by the hand, excitedly telling of the new kitten.

"It's PopPop!"

"I had a funny feeling something special was going on here." Christian walked to the basket, steadied by his cane.

"Hello to you, too, Dad." Junior grinned.

The elder straightened up. "Oh, you know I don't mean to ignore you. And how's my favorite daughter-in-law?" He gave Jamie a quick peck on the cheek.

"We're fine, Dad. But Misty had a time of it. She was in labor all night."

"Poor girl. I hope it was worth it." Christian turned his attention back to the basket and peered inside. Misty had cleaned the kitten's face and head. It was sniffing as it burrowed toward her belly, seeking food.

"Would you look at this!" Christian reached into the basket and touched the kitten, stroking its head with his index finger. He felt a slight tingling. "Can it be?"

The black head turned toward the old man's voice, eyes still closed. He let out a soft meow. The white star marking on his left ear seemed to glow.

"Mr. Thomas, is that you?"

* ✴ *

ACKNOWLEDGMENTS

This is proving more difficult than I thought it would be. How do I say thank you to everyone who has influenced this novel? First, there are the musicians. Music plays such a significant part in my life, I've added a suggested playlist at the back of the book. Forgive me if I have not identified all of the artists I reference throughout the work. You may find others buried inside the text. Congratulations.

As for individuals, oh my! Let's try, at least. Thanks to my associates at the Palm Bay, Florida Writer's Group for the soft critiques, as well as my critique group buddies and comma Nazis: Melissa Jordan, Rita McCarthy, and Iris Culhane.

Of particular note are my beta readers, Simon Peck, Scott Balawander, Laura Foster, and Michael Scott. Without their insights and suggestions, the first draft (and second and third…) would have yielded an inferior first novel.

I've read that one's editor is an essential colleague. I am most fortunate to have Chris Kridler and Sky Diary Productions referred to me.

Finally, here's a big hug and kiss to my life partner, Cindy Norris, whose patience allowed me to be me. Her encouragement kept me focused throughout the process.

Music has a profound impact on my life. I have often found songs to match my mood and lyrics to match my thoughts. A single word, an expression, or the entire work, one way or another, it hits home. With that in mind, here are some of the songs that influenced this work. There are likely others hidden in the writing. Listening to these songs while reading the accompanying chapter will give you a clue as to my mindset at the time.

Title: Michael Stanley Band, "Winter"
Acknowledgments: The Beatles, "A Little Help From My Friends"; Ben E. King, "Stand By Me"
Chapter 1: Barry McGuire, "Eve of Destruction"
Chapter 2: Imagine Dragons, "Radioactive"
Chapter 3: R.E.M., "The End of the World as We Know It"; Crosby, Stills, & Nash, "Teach Your Children"
Chapter 4: The Who, "Won't Get Fooled Again"
Chapter 5: Nick Lowe, "(What's so Funny 'Bout) Peace, Love, and Understanding"; Arlo Guthrie, "Alice's Restaurant"
Chapter 6: Bob Dylan, "All Along the Watchtower"; Quiet Riot, "Bang Your Head"

Chapter 7: Poco, "Pickin' Up the Pieces"; Johnny Nash, "I Can See Clearly Now"

Chapter 8: Tom Rush, "Child's Song"

Chapter 9: Grateful Dead, "Touch of Grey"

Chapter 10: Heads Hands & Feet, "Safety in Numbers"

Chapter 11: George Harrison, "All Things Must Pass"; Chiddy Bang, "All Things Go"

Chapter 12: Breaking Benjamin, "Blow Me Away"

Chapter 13: The O'Jays, "I Love Music"; Stephen Stills, "Love the One You're With"

Chapter 14: Van Morrison, "Rough God Goes Riding"

Chapter 15: Bob Dylan, "With God on Our Side"; Flatt & Scruggs, "The Ballad of Jed Clampett"

Chapter 16: Neil Young, "After the Gold Rush"

Chapter 17: The Beatles, "The Fool on the Hill"; The Beatles, "Here Comes the Sun"; Bill Haley & the Comets, "Shake, Rattle, and Roll

Chapter 18: Wall of Voodoo, "Mexican Radio"

Chapter 19: Frank Zappa, "Centerville"

Chapter 20: America, "Sister Golden Hair"

Chapter 21: Youngbloods, "Get Together"

Chapter 22: Creedence Clearwater Revival, "Born on the Bayou"

Chapter 23: Marvin Gaye, "What's Going On"

Chapter 24: Elton John, "Friends"

Chapter 25: The Temptations, "My Girl"

Chapter 26: The Beatles, "Eleanor Rigby"

Chapter 27: Roxy Music, "The Space Between"

Chapter 28: The Clash, "Should I Stay or Should I Go"; Nitty Gritty Dirt Band, "Will the Circle be Unbroken"

Chapter 29: Phosphorescent, "New Birth in New England"

Chapter 30: The Staple Singers, "Got To Be Some Changes Made"; England Dan and John Ford Coley, "Love Is the Answer"

Chapter 31: Dave Mason, "We Just Disagree"

Chapter 32: Joe Walsh, "Life's Been Good"

Chapter 33: Cyndi Lauper, "True Colors"

Chapter 34: Charlie Parker, "Cherokee"; Van Morrison, "Tupelo Honey"; Iron Butterfly, "In A Gadda Da Vida"

Chapter 35: Cream, "Crossroads"; 38 Special, "Hold on Loosely"; lovelytheband, "Broken"

Chapter 36: Lou Rawls, "A Natural Man"; Fats Domino, "Kansas City"

Chapter 37: Tina Turner, "We Don't Need Another Hero"

Chapter 38: Danger Mouse & Daniele Luppi, "Black" (feat. Norah Jones)

Chapter 39: Manhattan Transfer, "Feel Flow"; Harry Connick, Jr., "Hey There"; Vic Mizzy, "Green Acres Theme"

Chapter 40: Rolling Stones, "Sympathy for the Devil"; U2, "I Still Haven't Found What I'm Looking For"

Chapter 41: Peter, Paul, and Mary, "Wedding Song"; Roxy Music, "Avalon"; The Cowsills, "The Rain, the Park and Other Things"; The Beatles, "All You Need Is Love"

Chapter 42: Sam Cook, "A Change Is Gonna Come"; The Traveling Wilburys, "End of the Line"

Chapter 43: Howard Jones, "Things Can Only Get Better"; Genesis, "Invisible Touch"; Leonard Cohen, "Hey, That's No Way to Say Goodbye"

Epilogue: Gregory Alan Isakov, "Time Will Tell"; Neil Young, "Comes a Time"

ABOUT THE AUTHOR

T.W. Lofgren's career began as a photographer, passing through a period in construction trades and as a claims adjuster for a major company. His creative writing developed from a challenge set down by his daughter—to explore a talent first discovered in a college creative writing course. His writing style blends satire, reality, and fantasy to make a poignant commentary on today's critical issues.

His short stories were published in several anthologies, and his novella, *Dodging Butterflies—The Autobiography of Thomas Speaker,* gained recognition for participation in the *Writer's Digest* self-published book awards.

An active member of The Space Coast Writers' Guild and Palm Bay Writers Group, Mr. Lofgren currently lives in south-central Florida, where he struggles to keep his garden thriving.

Find him at twlofgren.com.

 facebook.com/T.W.Lofgren42